CITATION

LIBRARY SYSTEM RESET

K.T. HANNA

Jenn
For being there no matter what
You are amazing

PREVIOUSLY IN THE LIBRARY

After being isekaid into the Library of Everywhere, Quinn and Lynx (the Library manifestation) begin the arduous task of restoring the Library.

Milaro the grandfatherly king of the elves, and his grandchild Malakai remain an integral part of the hunt for overdue books. They keep her safe, teach her combat and mind walking, and encourage her to her full potential.

The books retrieved from the wrecked Dabilian homeworld allow Quinn and her team to truly begin rebuilding the Library. As more branches open up, more power is needed, and the team must focus on solving the puzzle that is Ashiron (the tenth pillar) before it blows up the entire universe.

Quinn's training ramps up, and her cosmicisodracus abilities evolve as she grows into her role as Librarian. But even so, she can tell there's still something dangerous lurking in the Library.

The holes in the memories of Lynx and the Library aren't filling in as quickly as they'd like. At times it almost seems deliberate, as if the holes are coming from inside the house.

With the Culinary, Medical, and Combat branches up and running, the Library begins to feel like the great entity it should. And yet shadows lurk around every corner. Distant memories confuse not only enemies, but allies as well.

Golem cores are compromised, and the glitch in the Library System presents itself in multifaceted ways. Dravishk, the Library's brother, and his accomplices will do everything they can to complete the sabotage they started.

Trap after trap waits for Quinn, and the last one cost a dear friend her life. More determined than ever to save her Library, and thus her remaining friends and the universe, Quinn must push her mourning aside and analyze everyone's motives to figure out just who she can trust, and who is pulling the strings.

1

NONETHELESS

QUIET TENSION PERMEATED THE HOSPITAL FLOORS, UNDERCUT BY THE scent of lemon and bleach. The hospital wing was less busy now that half the injured Salosier had left it. Quinn's wounds took no time at all to heal, but the same couldn't be said of Drukala's dragon-fired face. Nor Geneva's wings. Apparently, the gossamer strands that made up the wings were difficult membranes to regrow.

Or something.

At least they'd pulled through.

Quinn's fingers wouldn't flex the way she wanted them to. In fact, her whole concentration was blown, especially when she tried to multitask. Maybe it was the compartmentalization issue.

In that she refused to retrieve emotions that threatened to tear her apart.

She'd realized, in the course of everything, that she didn't deal well with loss. The fact that her senses expanded in sensitivity with her last synchronization didn't help either. She was acutely aware of everyone and everything going on around her, approaching her. So she knew who it was, even before they gently brushed a hand against her shoulder.

With sheer willpower, Quinn steeled herself.

"Hey, Mal," she said instead of leaning into the touch like she wanted to. Just for that bit of tactile reassurance. Something about her nerves just then told her that if she leaned back, she'd end up curling up and hiding from the rest of the world.

"I'd ask what's going on in your head," he said softly, "but I'm pretty sure it's the same spiral you've been going through for the last few days."

Quinn wanted to shake her head, to deny it, but she couldn't. Pursing her lips, she sighed instead, knowing what he was about to say.

"It wasn't your fault."

Malakai's words ground into her like a corkscrew. He might have been right, but it didn't hurt any less.

"Yeah." She glanced down the hall toward Geneva and Drukala's doors and shook her head. "I know, but it doesn't make me feel any better."

"Never said it would. But right now, you're needed elsewhere . . . everywhere, really."

Quinn tried to smile in response because she knew Malakai wanted to cheer her up. But a part of her just couldn't. It felt dark around her, as if everything was distant. Like that was how she should keep everyone.

Malakai frowned as they made their way out into the main part of the Library. He hesitated, as if he wanted to say something, and then thought better of it before continuing. "Got your list, then?"

She nodded, bringing it up in her head to make sure she did. There was still so much to go over. "Check on Misha's progress, on Betty and Dottie's workplace cohesion, Milaro and Lynx's deep dive into memory, and we should probably look into the pillar. I've felt the damned ground rumbling every so often." The latter made her mad. She wasn't entirely sure how to process all this. Except that she had to.

So, she would.

Mal shot her an unreadable look and jostled her into her office instead of to any of the other destinations. He closed the door behind her and leant on it, the frown deeper now, so much that it accentuated the crease in his forehead.

She raised an eyebrow and crossed her arms defensively. Her fingers squeezed her inner arms. "What did I miss?" Because that had to be it, right? She'd obviously missed something on her list, and he wanted to tell her.

"Stop the whole woe-is-me, self-pity, and recrimination act," he said, and his voice sounded tight, painful even. He was angry, but she could tell it wasn't solely directed at her. His gaze bored into hers and then he sagged a bit. "You weren't the only one there."

He was right, and she knew it. But that somehow made it worse. Still . . . he did have a point. She nodded begrudgingly. "Perhaps. I mean, I know we were. It's just a lot harder—"

"Than you thought? That whole losing someone because we let our guard down for a split second? Of course it's hard, Quinn." He reached forward, and this time pulled her into a hug.

At first, Quinn just didn't let herself be pulled, and then her body defied her, melting. Hugs were definitely one of those things that worked wonders for the psyche. She wasn't sure how long they stood there, maybe a couple of minutes, before she muttered her thanks into his arm. He was a lot taller than her.

"Feel like we can push through with what we need to, now?" he asked quietly, his tone full of concern.

Quinn nodded. "For now. I mean we can always"—she waved a hand around, gesturing vaguely to everything—"we can always deal with all that after we've solved the whole sabotage angle, right?"

"Very right." Malakai smiled, and Quinn could see the shadows still there behind his mood, too.

Maybe it was selfish, but it felt better knowing she wasn't the only one in mourning.

It definitely made it easier for her to suck it up and soldier on as she so eloquently put it in her own head.

She cracked her neck from side to side, sparing a brief thought of where Aradie might be. The owl had been quite scarce since they'd returned, and Quinn had some trouble wondering if it was because of her. Likely not, but still, paranoia felt like a tangible thing right then. "We should . . ."

But a knock on the door pulled her up short, and Malakai spun to open the door. His expression changed to one of indifference. "Oh, it's you."

Milaro poked his head in the room, raising an eyebrow at how Quinn stood in the middle of the room with her arms crossed, a slight scowl on her face. "Oh, I see things are going well in here. Would you like me to try that entrance again?"

Despite her current mood, Quinn laughed. "No, come on in." She broke her stance and made her way over to her desk. It felt like she hadn't sat in her chair in forever when, in reality, it hadn't even been a week. So much had happened, so much of it bad.

"To what do I owe this pleasure?" she asked, forcing a smile onto her face.

Milaro looked at her, as if he could see right through her, and pursed his lips in thought. "You're not sleeping well enough, and you need to reinforce your shielding."

Quinn blinked at him, pushing through her shields, confused by his statement. Her scales practically rippled through the blue and gold as she inspected them and she opened her mouth to speak, only to be cut off.

"Not your physical shields." Milaro's impatience leaked out. "Your mind."

She paused, shocked.

Her routine! She hadn't been reinforcing anything. Since they got back, she'd just fallen into a sort of boneless routine. It'd been days since she'd gone through her usual exercises that included making sure her mental shielding was at its strongest. Slamming her walls into place, checking and double checking them to verify their strength, she sighed with relief, not finding anything untoward.

Granted, they'd been at full strength back during the fight with Drukala and Dro.

"Sorry," she murmured, her shoulders slumping.

Milaro narrowed his eyes as he approached. He reached out one elegant elven hand and rested it briefly on her forehead, frowning. "You don't have a fever. As far as I can tell, your vitals are fine. Would you like to talk?"

Quinn stared at him. He sounded so sweet and understanding and grandfatherly. And for the first time in a long while, the elf king actually seemed well rested. The worry she carried for him on an almost constant basis dulled a little in relief. She shook her head. "Not right now, but I want a rain check on that."

A strange buzz sounded in her head as the translator had difficulty with that phrase and Milaro eyed her quizzically. "A rain check?"

She dug deep to figure out just how to explain that to him. "Like . . . at another more suitable time."

"Ah." He watched her, his expression thoughtful. "Anytime. And always." His smile was gentle, full of understanding.

"Thanks." Out of the corner of her vision, she could still see Malakai leaning next to the door. It didn't matter that he'd witnessed a vulnerable moment. She'd been having a lot of those over the last little while and frankly . . . both Milaro and his grandson had become a type of family to her.

"Anyway. I didn't come in here to chastise you or demand you rebuild shields." Milaro's grin was contagious.

Quinn smiled back at him. "Fine, then. What dire news do you bring me this time? Who do I need to hunt down and fine now?"

Milaro laughed, that same comfortable sound that usually filled the room. It eased all the tension she'd been holding in her shoulders as she waited for him to answer.

"No fines this time." He winked at her. "Just thought you might like to see the progress Harish has made with Misha."

A pang of guilt shot through her, followed closely by something akin to hope. But she couldn't help the caution that held her back from jumping up and running to the room. If Misha had fully recovered, then Milaro would have phrased his statement differently. She pushed some of the errant curls out of her face and counted to three, hoping her tone would come out even. She was mostly successful. "What is it you're not telling me?"

Malakai shifted by the door, changing how he distributed his weight as if he was reacting to something prematurely. Milaro eyed her contemplatively for a few seconds before answering. "Misha isn't restored yet, but there has been significant progress."

Again, Quinn frowned. "It's more something I have to see for myself?"

Milaro's eyes crinkled to go along with his sad smile. All he did was nod.

Quinn pushed herself up from her chair and headed out toward the room Harish had Misha in. She ignored the patrons, or at least tried to. The Library teemed with people, and power thrummed through the soles of her feet. Or perhaps that was just her own power in sync with that of the Library.

We're always in sync now. The voice glossed through her mind, just a gentle nudge, like the Library was specifically responding to the emotional turmoil Quinn was experiencing.

Quinn sighed, but this time it freed some of her pent-up sadness. It seemed like, in the last week or so, she'd lost so much, perhaps too much. Her heart hammered in her chest as she approached the room. It wasn't as if she was scared, exactly, but her emotions ran raw, and she wasn't sure she could handle a negative outcome.

The door opened silently, slotting into the wall. Quinn hadn't remembered it being a pocket door, but it wasn't like the Library couldn't change on a whim.

Harish stood at the center console, reaching over screens and projections, maximizing and analyzing all the data in front of him. As the door swooshed closed behind them, he turned, a genuine smile spreading across his face.

Quinn had to bite her tongue to keep from gasping in surprise. She'd never really seen him smile before. Not like this, anyway.

"You're here! Come along," he said, motioning them over to the massive tub where she knew Misha's parts resided.

She watched it as they approached, noticing how it was larger than she recalled. "Has it expanded?"

"Yes. Yes." Harish flashed her an absentminded smile as he ushered them all toward the incubation pod. "Here."

He reached forward to something on the top of the pod, and with a brief murmur, activated its magic.

The lid became transparent, and this time Quinn couldn't contain her gasp. In the pale blue liquid with strings of purple lightning pulsating all through it was Misha.

They looked exactly like Quinn remembered before they'd had to tear their mind apart. Short, strong and somehow petite without being fragile. Gorgeous silver limbs and a face that looked like they were asleep.

"Will Misha be . . . okay?" There was hesitance in her voice because Quinn wasn't sure if she could take another loss. Not now.

Harish smiled, and it was filled with a sort of enigmatic kindness. "I believe I've recovered the majority of their personality and purged the old. There will be some gaps. But Misha is strong, and fought the influence. All the simulations and diagnostics show as full a recovery as I could have hoped. Give me a couple more days and you'll have them back."

The relief rushed through Quinn, took her breath away and she smiled. "Thank you."

Malakai reached over and squeezed her hand briefly, providing contact to ground her. Quinn wasn't sure when he got to know her so well, but she appreciated it nonetheless. Now, all she had to do was get through Jasper's memorial. That was . . . if she could convince the Library, Milaro, and Lynx that it was safe for her to leave.

2

———

WOUNDED ENOUGH

IT FELT LIKE A LIFETIME AGO THEY WERE LAST AT THE DESILISH HOME base the first time. When she met Jasper, who tried to kill her, or at least maim her, because of a book misunderstanding. The living area was still vibrant thanks to the domes that covered this planet. Its quaint little cottages beyond the swamp and fresh garden beds with all the herbs and flowers an alchemist could want.

Quinn wasn't certain they should be there. After all, if it wasn't for the Library and herself, Jasper would be bouncing around being her wonderful self, full of life and mischief and goals for her future.

Someone nudged her arm, causing her to look over, blinking away the tears.

Savinth's expression was tight. The much older human woman of the genome type 31785 stood next to Quinn. "You shouldn't beat yourself up so much about this. It's not something within your control."

Quinn blinked at her. The sentiment was nice, and while Quinn was fully aware that she hadn't personally killed her friend, she did know that she put Jasper in harm's way to begin with.

"And none of that, either." Savinth's voice was whisper soft and directed solely at the Librarian. "Don't go on about her only being because of you. Jasper loved being your assistant. Just use this as more incentive to bring them down and keep the Library safe. Yeah?"

Quinn nodded, because she knew if she spoke, her voice would crack.

She wasn't expecting the ceremony to be so . . . well, so magical. Nets of magic were woven around Jasper's body, held in stasis by levels of intricate gravity magic that Quinn definitely hadn't mastered yet. Malakai squeezed Quinn's shoulder, and she reached for the comfort she needed.

When Jasper's body began to dissipate, sparks shot up into the darkening sky of evening and cascaded from the highest point out through the domed areas. Some of them headed to the swamp, some of them settled in the trees and the gardens. A part of her in all elements of her home.

As the last one landed, Quinn felt her resolve strengthen. Not that she'd needed the extra motivation. They'd already done enough. Wounded enough. Killed enough.

Endangered enough.

Their own were expendable. Nothing was sacred. As long as they reached their goal of letting chaos magic run rampant.

Now, at least, they knew some of the faces, most of the motivations, and had foiled some of their plots.

Quinn felt an itch under her skin. Like it was waiting, egging her on. She watched Jasper's family as they mourned her, and the guilt twisted in her gut like a knife, a poignant reminder of what she . . . of what they all had to accomplish.

"Let's go back," she whispered to Malakai.

He nodded and walked at her elbow, almost like a shadow who saw everything. Savinth nodded as they left, and Quinn wasn't sure, but she swore she could hear her say something along the lines of: make them pay.

Quinn decided she liked that motto.

———

QUINN'S RESOLVE AS THEY STEP THROUGH THE DOOR AND BACK INTO the Library sharpened.

Especially since the magic permeating the area told her in no uncertain terms that the pillar was still a looming problem. She frowned as she stepped into her office, grateful again that she could transport directly to it. She didn't have the time for Betty to bombard her with questions needing answers. Nor did she have time to be waylaid by anyone else. And Aradie still wasn't around, which really began to grate on her nerves.

She muttered under her breath as she made her way to her desk, falling into the seat with a heavy sigh. "Pillar. Memories. Hospital . . . how do we link it all together?"

The memories are coming along quite nicely. The Library spoke into the room.

Quinn looked up with a frown, realizing that Malakai had somehow disappeared since they returned. That wasn't like him at all. At least not without telling her. She could track him through the Library, but felt like he'd probably had a reason. "Define how the memories are coming along well. Because frankly, you keep saying that, and right now, I'm having a hard time believing you mean it."

I mean it every time. It's just each time I think we're close, we discover that we are, in fact, not. The Library sounded irritated and slightly sulky.

Quinn sighed. They really hadn't had much time to talk since she'd come back. "Have you talked to your sister?" she asked softly instead of giving in to her frustrations and the lingering anger at Jasper's death.

Of course I have. The Library sounded offended at first, but then her tone became gentle. *I don't personally remember when I last saw her. I thought it had been tens of thousands of years. But . . . Milaro helped us compare memories, and it appears I saw her several hundred years ago and gave her that book to take care of.*

"She did mention that," Quinn said, her lips quirking into a smile. "How's the retrieval going?"

The Library hesitated, like perhaps it was reformulating exactly how to phrase the answer. *We've established that her memory is true, and where it should be in my head is just a blank space. Milaro thinks Korradine scrubbed it somehow. Instead of locking them away, or filtering them out, or replacing them with something vague, she actually entered the system for this and removed it. Sand blasted it away.*

Quinn cringed. "That sounds oddly painful and different from her usual modus operandi."

I don't feel pain the same way I did in my singular corporeal form, but I do believe it would have had some effect on me. The edges are frayed in a way consistent with pain and tearing.

She wished the Library didn't sound so clinical about it all.

Anyway. We're working on retrieving and establishing the course of events around that time. It's like a knot of information all wound around each other. Almost as if it was an attempt to obscure than to remove. Another pause by the Library before it barreled on ahead. *And even though I don't want to assume, I'm quite certain Korradine only found out about the conversation retroactively when she went to search for that specific book. The Parsneauvian book having been with Drukala might be the feather in our cap. Hopefully.*

Quinn mulled that over in her head. If Drukala took the book and hid it away with her in hibernation, immediately enacting all the safeties that cosmicisodracus had in place for when they were helpless hibernating, then Korradine wouldn't have been able to find it. She'd obviously expected to plot her way through, gradually remove all the books and magic and support she needed to, while carefully eliminating all traces of her machinations.

After which, she'd been prepared to blow the Library up.

Except both the Library and Lynx weren't as complacent as Korradine expected, and while they didn't stop her, they did acquire themselves a stay of execution. But Quinn knew she was missing something. She crunched her eyes up, trying to force her brain to do more thinking, to give her useful revelations.

The damned thing gave her literally no answer.

Just as she was about to speak to the Library again, the door opened. At first, she wanted to reprimand whoever entered without knocking, but it was Malakai, balancing a tray of something he'd obviously retrieved from the kitchens, while a gorgeous black owl with vivid green, purple, and red feathers darted in with a protesting hoot to sit on the back of her chair.

"I didn't go anywhere without you that you didn't know about," she said to Aradie's offended string of noises. "And you . . ." She paused as Malakai put the tray down, a grin on his face.

He cleared his throat. "M'lady is served."

Quinn rolled her eyes, even though she was secretly starving and ridiculously grateful. Her stomach protested quite loudly for her to stop thinking and start eating, and she glared down at it reproach-fully. Perhaps Malakai had just been paying more attention to her noisy body, or else he'd been with her all day anyway and knew she hadn't eaten yet. Either way, it gave her a fuzzy, warm feeling. It felt nice to have someone else care about you.

"Thanks," she said before digging into the pasta in front of her. Luckily, it also afforded her time to gather her thoughts. They needed to establish what took place that led to the Library asking Drukala to care for that book. Then she had to see what they could sort out for Ashiron. Not to mention checking in with Hal about anything from their prisoners. She was particularly interested in seeing if he'd gotten anything out of Kajaro. Then there was Misha, more Library branches, retrieving all the books, making the Library a safe space, boosting power levels to optimum and overflowing . . .

Quinn centered herself. One breath. Two breaths. She knew she could do this. Her mind was easily segmented now, allowing her to work on her shielding both mental and physical, and dissect the books she was absorbing while taking care of other tasks. It was still the best book she'd memorized. With Milaro's help, she'd taken it into her and evolved the information until it was a seamless part of herself. The ability to multitask and condense the time it took her to process and analyze things? Best gift Milaro could ever have given her.

She tried not to be aware of the way Malakai watched her from the door. The way the concern marred his otherwise perfect brow, or the slight hike to one of his eyebrows, as if he was permanently asking her what's up.

Worrying people wasn't her goal.

Yet, it seemed it was one she achieved effortlessly.

"Okay," she said as the food spread warmth throughout her body, making her wonder just how long she hadn't eaten for. The last few days were a blur, after all. "Do we have an ETA on your reconstruction of that memory?"

Malakai looked confused until the Library spoke.

It's a delicate process, but Milaro is helping me work through it. Maybe tomorrow . . . maybe late tomorrow. Or perhaps a few days?

"Vague, but I can work with that," Quinn mumbled. She knew now why the Library needed a manifestation and a Librarian. It wasn't just about the balance of power. After synchronizing more with it, she'd realized just how huge the tasks were that the Library undertook. From the filtration chamber operation. The way it filtered and distributed the mana and energy. The ley lines. The doors that opened to everywhere and anywhere. Not to mention the constant scanning for those with nefarious purpose.

Then there were the golems to monitor, the assistants to track, the borrowing and return of all the books to multitask. Also, the different branches and the species-specific room requests. She knew there was more she'd forgotten. But the reality was that the Library managed so much, all the time, never stopping, without fail.

It wasn't a god; it was just a very busy Library, who'd sacrificed its dragon form in order to become the thing that kept the universe safe from chaotic magic. From magic, that would devour all of them.

And it needed its Librarian and manifestation to take over the administrative and logistics. Which, it turned out, included trying to solve the rest of the bloody "who was conspiring against us" puzzle . . . and solve it.

Quinn grinned. "Yeah. I can work with that." She said it this time with more force.

Malakai raised his eyebrow fully. "Should I know what you mean?"

She shook her head as she pushed herself up from her chair. "No, but the Library . . . you have another sibling right?"

Yes. The tone was filled with hesitancy.

"Do you think you can contact them? Or are they hibernating?" Quinn had the glimmer of an idea forming that she didn't want to give words to yet.

Several seconds passed. *They appear to be coming out of hibernation.* The tone sounded like the Library was frowning.

Quinn suppressed a sigh. Being frustrated wasn't going to help anyone. "Well, that's the two you knew were hibernating, then. How long until they're coherent enough to talk?"

Not long. Maybe a day or five.

Excellent. That made the next few days nice and busy. Quinn nodded. "Then I'm off to the hospital wing to check on Geneva and see if good old auntie Drukala has any ideas."

3

NOT JUST A PRETTY FACE

The hospital wing was just as sterile as ever. Although at least they'd begun to add a bit of color to the walls and the beds. Nothing too outrageous, of course, but it didn't have that lingering sense of death Quinn associated with the human hospitals she'd grown up around.

The sensation made her pause. She'd deliberately described them as human and wasn't exactly sure how she felt about that. She slotted it away so she could overanalyze it later.

She walked through the halls with Malakai trailing behind her, Aradie perched on her shoulder. He finally jogged a few steps to catch up.

Just before they reached the door she wanted, Malakai put a hand on her wrist, making her pause. "You've gone into super serious mode. Are you okay?"

Quinn watched him for a few seconds, rapidly cataloguing her massive to-do list, before finally nodding. "I am. Just trying to stay on task." She wasn't sure she could explain the urgency she felt to sort all of this out. Or the trepidation that kept gnawing at her gut like there was still something huge she was missing.

Malakai nodded and removed his hand. "I just wanted to check.

Sometimes I feel like you don't know when to reach out, that you don't understand that not everything is up to you."

She cocked her head to one side, studying him. "You're right, you know? Sometimes I feel like it *is* just me, but that's only because before I came here, I didn't have anyone but me. I'm getting better, and trust me, if I figure something out that I can ask for help with, you'll be the first to know." She tried to give him a reassuring smile but wasn't sure she was successful. Just about to put her hand on the door handle, she turned back to him. "Wait. Can you use your magic again?"

He chuckled and waved a hand up and down his torso as if he was showing something off. "As of yesterday. All cleared."

"Perfect. That means I'll be safe for a while again." She grinned and opened the door, feeling less off kilter now, as if things were right with her current world. That, and she had been tightly wound. His ability to use magic and audacity in pointing out that she could ask for help truly helped.

The room was dark and warm, and if Quinn hadn't known better, she'd have thought they were back in Halschius. It took several seconds for her eyes to adjust completely. Even with dragon vision, the difference between the white and bright hall and the dim and rumbling room was shocking.

There was a shifting in the room. The floor over nearest the far wall rippled.

Squinting, Quinn approached, taking careful steps toward it. Unable to suppress the gasp completely when she identified the ripple, Quinn stopped moving and waited.

There, just along the wall, was a long, sleek dragon. Except she was only about ten feet long, and much smaller than Quinn would have expected. Her elegant lines reflected the red glow of the lava that appeared to permeate the room, and her flanks rose and fell gently.

Drukala was about twenty percent of the size she'd been when she'd leant down and asked Quinn why she smelled like her sibling. There was a melancholy air to her breathing and huffing that made Quinn's heart ache, and she yearned to reach out and scratch her eyebrow ridges. Idly, she wondered just what made her think of doing that. Maybe some cosmicisodracus knowledge was innate.

"I know you're there." Drukala's voice was soft and breathed warmth through the room.

The room, which, now Quinn really gave it some thought, was quite massive. Not cavern like massive, but probably around twenty by thirty feet. Technically, no room in the hospital should have been like that. But sometimes the Library, physics, and its dimensional manipulation capabilities didn't make any sense whatsoever.

"How are you feeling?" Quinn asked, keeping her voice low as well. While what she really wanted to ask was why Drukala had reverted to dragon form, and not taken the full form either . . . so many questions.

"Has anyone ever told you"—Drukala opened one moon-like eye lazily . . . on the left-hand side of her face where she hadn't been burned and studied Quinn—"that you think far too loudly?"

Quinn had the good grace to blush. "Actually, yes."

"Color me not surprised." The dragon shifted ever so slightly, causing the air around them to sizzle, and the ground to move ever so slightly. "I'm in dragon form because I heal faster and more thoroughly this way. It'll keep the scarring to a minimum."

Quinn nodded. It made sense. "I sort of wanted to ask you your interpretation of everything that happened. You know, with the book?"

Drukala sighed, causing a brief spark of fire to light around her. It was gone as soon as it arrived, just a fraction of a second of molten light, plunging them back into semi darkness. "I only remember my conversation with Drev. The Library summoned me, which is, by the way, not something it can do often. Or again, perhaps? It certainly didn't summon me this time while I was hibernating, and I almost feel like right now would have been more import."

Quinn cleared her throat to interrupt. "I know. It kept saying that it couldn't reach you, so the Library just kept prodding, hoping you'd realize you were needed."

"Well . . . I did, sort of. Made me half awake, not in a deep slumber, so that when you arrived smelling deliciously like one of us and yet not quite, it was all I needed to awaken fully." They fell silent for a few seconds before Drukala spoke again. "It seemed highly important that I take the book. Take it and keep it away from anyone who wasn't me. That's precisely what Drev said. Probably should have asked more questions, but it seemed so urgent, and I didn't. Since I was due for hibernation and also didn't exactly have anything else to do, I figured the 'don't look at me' spells and the concealment of most of my potential lairs would help keep it and me safe. And I mean, I was right, right?"

"What else did you talk about?"

Drukala huffed out a breath of air again and blinked that eye ever so slowly. "Hmm. Do not return it to anyone but the Library, or a new Librarian. I did wonder just why Drev specified a new Librarian. I figured something had happened to Kor, but I wasn't about to ask. I've never been much into the politics of the entire universe. All too sticky for me."

"What changed?" Malakai practically spat out the question. It seemed irritation got the best of him.

"Why . . . they tried to hurt Drev. There's politics with rampant meetings and boring agendas, and then there's dangerous politics. Drev sacrificed its body . . . its corporeal dragon form, and all of its personal power in order to create a solution to chaos magic's devouring rampage. There is no way I would ever let anyone undo that, belittle it, disregard it, or disrespect it." Dru didn't need to be a dragon to have heat behind those words.

Quinn could tell their sincerity from where she stood. "Does anything else come to mind? Any sort of clues or giveaways?"

Drukala shifted again and her shrug was almost liquid in movement. "Lynx wasn't . . . right." She paused. "It was as if he was somewhere else. His attention span was sporadic and almost staccato. Just when it came to interactions with me, which I found odd, because we'd usually gotten on so damned well. The hum of the Library was different too. Like an occasional sputtering." Her eyes were both closed now, as if she was trying to recall the exact sensations she'd gone through. "But that's about it. After all, it was a long time ago, and I was in one of my moods since my sibling made demands of me."

Quinn chuckled. "You don't like people telling you what to do?"

"Nope." The *p* in the word made a popping sound.

"Then what changed your mind enough to help hide the books, to help back then?" Quinn's eyes were adjusting again, and Drukala's breathtaking details were starting to become visible. The ridges down her spines were almost like gemstone rocks.

"Because, despite everything, Drev has never, not even once, asked me for something before. Not since the initial conception of the Library." Dru sounded so contemplative. "And now . . . well, I'm not overly fond of anyone trying to disfigure me, or kill me, or whatever my blasted sister was trying to do. Spite is my greatest motivator. I'm nothing like Drev. So just tell me what I need to do to help."

Quinn decided she adored her auntie and grinned openly for the first time since Jasper passed. "We still have one more book to locate. Do you think the Library might have given it to your other sibling? The only one we haven't been able to track yet?"

"Dri . . ." It sounded like Drukala was about to say the whole name but barely stopped herself. She pursed up her dragon lips in deep thought and took quite a bit to eek around to an answer. "You know, he's never been very fond of our oldest brother. I don't know what he thinks about the whole fiasco, nor do I know if he got a book from Drev like I did, but I am fairly certain that if he knew what was going on, he'd be pissed. You don't know how much work went into making the Library, how much we poured all of our power into this. The filtration system? Wouldn't even exist without Dri, sooooo." She shrugged.

A wave of relief rushed through Quinn. At least it sounded like there were two dragons, at least not against them if not on their side completely. She could work with that. Since the Library no longer technically counted as a dragon. "Do you have any way of contacting him?"

"Nothing that Drev won't have already tried." She sounded

genuinely sorry, but then she hesitated before continuing. "So, you're my niece?"

Quinn balked a bit. "Yeah, I guess so. You'd have to ask Milaro how that precisely works."

"Are there more of you?" The curiosity in Dru's voice was practically alive.

Quinn shook her head. "Nope. Just me. And from what I understand, I don't believe they could make another." How strange it sounded to talk about herself having been made, like an object or machine.

"Shame. If we could just pop out another one of you, then we'd have even more power on our side."

This time, Quinn laughed. "They didn't pop me out fully formed. I had to grow into this."

One of Drukala's very gemstone ridged eyebrows raised ever so slightly.

"I lived in a human world until, like, six months ago."

The surprise that dropped Dru's mouth open was worth it. "I'm guessing that's a very long story you'll tell me later?"

"Got it in one."

There was a moment's silence between them while Quinn tried to apply what she'd learned to all the other facts they had. Apparently two of the five original cosmicisodracus ended up with buyer's remorse after creating the Library. But they'd had hundreds of millions, if not billions, of years to figure their crap out, so why was it only coming to head now? Not that she thought Drevicia would know, but the Library did seem to be fairly knowledgeable about things, and might have picked up some stuff unknowingly.

"Say, can you think of anything like ten thousand years ago"— which sounded absurd in Quinn's head—"that might have happened to trigger this strange turn of 'let's allow chaos magic to run free again'?"

Drukala actually appeared to be pondering the question. Not just for a few seconds, either. Like she was giving it serious thought. "Not really," she started and then it was like a lightbulb moment for her, where her eyes flashed an outstanding pearl before settling back into the moon like appearance. "That's around when Korradine became Librarian, right? You should probably go and ask the Unusceros the same question . . . if you can find them, that is."

Quinn blinked as she quickly leafed through everything she knew. Korradine's species weren't extinct. There didn't appear to be many of them, but . . . Quinn had no idea why the idea hadn't occurred to any of them before this.

"Thanks," she said, surprised by her own sincerity.

Drukala preened a little. "I'm not just a pretty face."

Quinn smiled and nodded, and got ready to figure out how to contact the Unusceros. "Thank you so much again, but I know you need your rest. I'll stop bugging you."

All Drukala did in return was whuff some smoke out of a nostril before closing her eye again.

They left the room and Malakai nudged her. "I have no idea why we didn't think of that."

"Staring us in the face. Couldn't see the forest for the trees." Quinn tapped her nose. "Outside perspective and all. Always helps."

Malakai chuckled. "Yeah. I think sometimes it just takes someone else to see what's right under our noses."

Quinn flashed him a somewhat confused smile, but she wasn't digging any deeper on anything else until they got the Library out of danger. Even if she knew he was hinting at things.

Right then, she felt good about the direction they were headed. They had so many leads, so many options to find out exactly how to diffuse the whole damned situation. How to get revenge, and how to make the bastards pay for everything they'd done, and everyone they'd hurt.

And as if to punctuate it. Her stomach growled. She groaned while Malakai laughed.

He took her shoulders and gently steered her toward the culinary branch.

$$4$$

GUT FEELING

The best thing about the culinary branch was Cook.

They had this strange calming effect on Quinn. No matter what was going on, how bad it might turn out, or how much she might wish she could ignore it, here—in the kitchens with food that sprinkled nostalgia everywhere—was where the Librarian most felt at home.

Malakai was off checking out the other stoves in use. Most people experimenting with magical food loved having guinea pigs who were eager to sample their experiments. Generally, just a basic antidote would do if the food somehow caused a bad reaction. Cook had plenty of those on hand.

Mostly though, Malakai's wandering gave her severely necessary alone time with her favorite golem.

She didn't even need to ask for comfort food, nor did she need to espouse a preference.

Cook always seemed to know her needs. They read her moods like an open book and arranged a specific set of food for her every time. If she hadn't already believed in magic, this would do it.

This time they'd made her crumpets with butter, and it was divine. The perfect texture, toasted just right, with the butter bleeding through the bottom. She savored the bite, closing her eyes, remembering how she'd loved them when her grandmother made them as a special treat when she was five.

When she opened her eyes again, Cook was sitting across from her, their expression somehow tender.

"Did I get the consistency correct?"

Quinn smiled and let out a breath of a laugh. "Yeah. It's perfect."

"Excellent." Cook paused, cocking their head to one side briefly, as if studying her. "Can you tell me then what it is that is bothering you?"

That was just it though, wasn't it? Quinn wasn't entirely sure what bothered her. No matter how much thought she gave it, which way she turned things, she just couldn't put her finger on why things felt wrong. Quinn ran her fingers through a loose curl that had, yet again, escaped her bun. It'd been messier than usual this morning.

"I'm really not sure what's bothering me," she admitted. And it was a much harder thing to admit to herself, or out loud, than she'd imagined.

"Elaborate?" Cook's enquiry sounded genuine, interested even. Their helpers were bustling about through the culinary branch too, so it wasn't like Cook had to assist patrons.

She studied her fingernails for a moment, activated a shield she'd modified into a privacy one, and then answered. "There's one of those gut feelings plaguing me like no one's business. I can't seem to separate it enough from myself to figure out exactly what's bothering me."

"Sound it out."

Quinn blinked at Cook, unsure how they could know just the right words to say on such a consistent basis. She gathered her thoughts and started. "The Library's brother wants, for some reason, to let chaotic magic reign unchecked. Everyone so far, and I'm including Sarila, Kajaro, Tenejo, and any of their other helpers—they all seem to think releasing chaotic magic means only the strong will survive, despite all the evidence to the contrary that absolutely no one will survive." She watched Cook, perhaps half expectantly, but they just stared at her, waiting.

"Now we've learned that not only do massive factions of several species out there believe the same thing, but not all the cosmicisodracus siblings seem to think making the Library as a filtration system was a good idea anymore." She was warming up to it a little more now. "Not only that, but this has to have been in the works for at least ten thousand years, if not more because Korradine was placed here that long ago and in all sincerity appears to have begun laying traps and sabotage around the place from very early on. Subtly at first . . . but more blatant and reckless after a while."

"Quinn," Cook interrupted her, a soft sense of curiosity in their gaze. "You are giving me information. Have you not yet found the question?"

She stared at him, as if it only just hit her. That was just it, wasn't it?

They had a series of events, of instances. History spattered here and there. A vague sort of thinly veiled motive—that was reason enough to preserve the Library all by itself. But, as a whole, she had no idea what their motivation was. It seemed so flimsy, so damned convenient.

"Thanks," she said, eating the last bite of her crumpet and wiping away the drip of butter that threatened to leave her chin. There was something deeper, some motivation that ran far under everything she'd assumed. And she wasn't going to find the answer by devouring food.

Quinn pushed herself up, a wide grin on her face. "I might have more questions than I started with, but now I feel like I have direction. Thanks."

She reached forward and gave them one of those sidearm hugs they usually shared.

Cook smiled. Even though Quinn was never quite sure how she knew what expression they were giving her at any given time, it was clear they were currently feeling quite accomplished. "Always. And when you find that question, come back and I will do my best to help you find those answers you seek. In the meantime, I shall add crumpets to your regular rotation."

Quinn grinned. "But with more butter."

"More butter?" Cook raised an eyebrow, for once taken by surprise.

"Definitely drown it in butter."

"Very well." Cook moved back over to their cooking station, and Quinn felt like her body was vibrating with excitement.

But it wasn't just excitement—it was a direction, a way to hopefully stop chasing tails and just find exactly what it was they needed to head toward.

"You seem to be in a good mood?" Malakai said as he plopped down next to her with a plate that rather looked like the intestines of a small animal, and Quinn had no desire to know what it actually was.

"I *am* in a good mood. But you should probably eat up and come join me in my office." She grinned at him.

He eyed his food mournfully. "But if I want to eat it, I have to stay around here so they can tend to me if I have an . . . adverse reaction, I believe, were the words."

Quinn laughed. "Fine, I guess I'd prefer to keep you around, but . . ." Her fingers twitched with eagerness at making her lists to figure out exactly what it was she needed to link together. The compulsion to figure this out made her skin itch like a bug had crawled underneath it. She hadn't had this feeling in a long time. Not since she'd been convinced in high school that she alone could establish the whereabouts of the lost Library of Alexandria . . .

She blinked, her eyes narrowed, and she focused her thoughts toward the Library. *You're not the Library of Alexandria, are you?*

What? No. There was laughter in the Library's response. *I was never open to Earth myself. Although . . .*

Although what?

There are many myths and rumors in your world. I cannot guarantee that someone didn't visit at some stage speak of me and influence your history. However, I highly doubt it, given the energy levels on Earth.

Highly doubt it? Quinn knew her tone held a distinct edge that wasn't the nicest. She wasn't happy with herself for it.

Sincerely. If it came from here, it was neither mine nor any of my Librarian's doings, not past, present, or future. I'm just saying I'm not the only means of dimensional and distance travel. Even if I do make it easier for everyone.

Quinn frowned. The Library did sound sincere. *Thanks.*

There're more questions aren't there? it asked simply.

Yeah, but it can wait until I'm in my office, once I drag Malakai from his food.

"Quinn?" Malakai frowned up at her as he poked her finger. "You doing okay?"

She blinked down at where he still sat, polishing off the last of his food. "Sorry. Miles away. That any good?" She gestured at his plate.

He contemplated his answer, his expression passing through several moods before he just shrugged. "Not horrible. Very different, and I do not appear to have any side effects."

"Yeah? They come on that quick?"

Malakai nodded. "They said pretty much immediately. I think I'm good."

"Excellent. Let's go."

Five minutes later, Quinn sat at her desk, a beautiful feather from Aradie transformed into a quill.

She noted down the creation of the five original cosmicisodracus by chaos magic. The creation of the worlds. The knowledge of what chaos magic did once it needed to devour its own creations to survive. *Weren't the cosmicisodracus the first beings created by chaos magic?* she asked the Library.

Yes. We were.

She frowned, adding it to another sheet of paper where she drew a set of columns with a line dividing the page. In the top columns she wrote what she knew, going into detail about Korradine and her infiltration and the bomb. Right down to the names of all the books that seemed to be missing from the restricted section, especially the five dangerous dimensional ones. Then she made sure to pencil in the use each book had been put to, where it was located, just like the devouring tree they'd found and the resulting Esposian backlash. Not to mention the botched retrieval from Kajaro, or the almost too easy retrieval from Drukala.

The memories were the major problem, though. Quinn couldn't fill those in. She frowned and reached out to the Library again. *Do you think it's possible for Harish to get me data on the dates and worst instances of your memory loss . . . or missing data processes?*

Definitely possible. Misha doesn't require constant monitoring, and I daresay he'll enjoy a task that means something in the bigger picture while he's idling away.

Quinn nodded and decided to send a note through the system. She often forgot about some of the system's perks. It made communication so much easier. Because, after all, each of these things was one piece of the puzzle. Just a lot larger, with more similar pieces than she'd realized.

Her correlation diagram began to get crowded, but she wasn't done with it yet. There was still something she was missing.

In the next column, she began writing down the different species they knew were definitely against them. All of them. From the Aracnios to the sedimentites, the Esposians and more. She frowned as she realized that many of those listed were pieces of the puzzle in locations where she knew for a fact they matched up with the timeline.

Had she found a link? Perhaps not *the* link, but it was definitely one. "Shit."

"That actually sounds like a *good* shit . . . is it?" Malakai asked, and Quinn couldn't help smiling.

"It's a not bad shit." But she started to laugh, and then sobered, because while it was sort of an answer, it wasn't definitive and just gave rise to more questions. "I need more detailed notes on what planets and species were created first."

"Do I want to know?"

"It's a gut feeling about influence."

"Color me intrigued." Mal raised an eyebrow.

"I have to double check." She frowned and got back to her lists.

She continued, continuing to make notes of the different species who were against them, of Sarila and the Balisor incident. Of the ritual net Jasper created so they could trace the books.

Trace.

Quinn stopped suddenly. "Is it possible to track a tracing spell back to its point of origin?" she asked.

Malakai looked up and shrugged, but the Library answered for both of them to hear. *Technically. If someone is looking for a tracker, or has triggered or expected one.*

Quinn blanched. She didn't like those implications. And she knew the ritual room was still set up downstairs.

5

ADDING TO THE LIST

There'd been so much change in the Library over the last several weeks. From new branches opening, to new supervisors and delegations. It extended through to the problems they'd encountered and sought to fix, like requiring new staff or fixing the filtration system, identifying and retrieving restricted section books, and boosting the Library's power levels.

All of this meant more foot traffic passing through the Library on a very consistent basis. Just regular patrons, but also allies, visitors, and all the new staff.

Quinn's gut twisted. She felt, knew . . . there was something she'd not thought to reason, though. She wasn't sure what it was, but only knew that focusing on tracking had given her a jolt.

She closed her eyes and pushed her senses through her connection with the entire Library—to every nook and cranny. From where energy pulsed evenly through the check-in desk, to the way ambient magic trickled consistently from all the visitors, all of it whispered power if one listened close enough. The filtration chamber, the core, the culinary, alchemical, and combat branches—all of them sent a steady hum right through the body of the Library, reinvigorating it and bringing it back to life.

Except there was one small blip on that radar. One tiny thing that seemed like a black mark.

And she should have known. On some level, anyway.

Where Jasper had left the ritual circle in place for future location spells, was a hum that clanged ever so slightly wrong.

"What happens if a tracker spell is set and left in place and then the caster dies?" she asked, very softly.

Malakai blinked at her and opened his mouth as if to reply, when the Library answered instead.

A tracking spell requires a medium to attach to. There was a pause, and then the air around Quinn warped briefly until she stood precisely at the entrance arch of the tracking chamber down next to the mana lake.

Quinn's stomach roiled, and she had to fight down the urge to retch. They'd talk about that whole warping her places without telling her first later, when her intestines weren't trying desperately to escape through her throat.

Runes and magic were alive all around her. They glowed, ever so faintly, as if they were feeding off something when nothing was supposed to be feeding it because they weren't currently trying to find anything at all. And that was just it.

"Why is it glowing?" The thing was, though, that Quinn had a hunch why it was glowing without actually having found the knowledge somewhere to back up her very specific gut feeling.

She just knew.

This is an active summoning circle. It was left dormant to be triggered to a specific location that would bring it fully online again.

"I know this." Quinn had to grind out the words, because she just needed someone to confirm that what she feared was actually true, and since the Library was the only one in this chamber, she'd have to wait on it.

Let me process. The Library snapped this time. As if this was all just a bit too much to process. And Quinn couldn't blame it. Because right then it really felt overwhelming.

The silence droned on and finally the Library spoke again. *It's being fed from an outside force now and is trying to track the Library.*

Quinn didn't have time to allow herself a reaction. Instead of shrugging and accepting her fate, she tried to remember just what it was Jasper had done when she created the thing. And the supplies she'd created it with . . .

She looked around, walking over to the box of supplies. Frowning, she crouched down, rifling through. Finally, she found one of the strange, chalk-like permanent markers. The only thing she could think of. Reaching over, Quinn drew a long, distinct line through one of the runes.

The light sustaining the glow puttered and extinguished.

Quinn sighed with relief.

That was one way to do it.

"You didn't help," she shot back at the Library.

I'm not criticizing, I just would have liked to keep the circle intact.

"I'm sure that one rune can be reworked," Quinn said absently. There were so many questions running around in her head that she could barely form coherent thought. She could hardly figure out what questions to ask. Or maybe it was easier to convince herself of that because she was scared to. "Did they . . . was her death deliberate, then?"

The Library didn't say anything immediately. Perhaps it didn't know, or didn't have enough data to draw a sample conclusion on. Something probably very science-y or universally mysterious.

Suddenly, Lynx was next to her. "Felt the power fade, and only just realized it shouldn't even have been powered up in that manner."

The Library must have needed all its concentration for something, which meant Lynx was Quinn's next best option.

"When did it start? Did they get to this before she died?" Quinn had to know, even though she was fairly sure she already did.

There was a slight hesitation before Lynx responded. "No. I don't think it's been going for long. I'd have to double check, but a day or so."

"How?" Quinn needed to know how they'd ever managed to do it, but even though she was playing at not knowing, she really did. It didn't take a genius to understand what had happened.

"A type of bound blood magic." Lynx offered no comfort with his answer at all.

Not that she'd really expected it.

"So they killed her, took her blood, and connected into the wards that way?" She needed to be clear. Jasper had actually been a friend. She'd helped delegate some of the more onerous tasks when Quinn first got overwhelmed. She'd had a fantastic sense of humor. This was very personal.

"I'd think that likely. Having her blood and randomly figuring out that it opens a tracking ritual circle inside the Library . . . seems a little too coincidental to me." Lynx didn't crack a smile.

Quinn liked to think Jasper got under everyone's skin. Like an itch no one could make go away, but that let you heave a sigh of relief when scratched. "How would they have known we launched a tracker for those books?"

Lynx shrugged. "There are any number of different combinations of affinities. Using several together, as you're aware, is not unheard of, but frankly . . . they would have had to. Hmm." His eyes flickered, bleeding through multiple purple variants before settling finally on his usual again.

"One of the most common ways to seek something is to know the name of it. In that case, it's now difficult to assume they may have put a trace on the names of the books. So if anyone was looking specifically for those books, whoever had set the alarm on them would be notified of the activity." Lynx refused to meet her eyes.

"They knew we were coming?" Quinn asked, her heart in her throat.

But Lynx just grimaced. "Not precisely. They knew the book was getting tracked, but not necessarily where it was. Because the trace they set up would only have triggered based on the name. Probably took some nifty combination spell work to figure out where the trace came from, and then to narrow it down when they were fighting us."

"I should have kept her shielded. I thought I had." Quinn couldn't believe it. She'd not reinforced Jasper's shielding before they left, because she'd been protected in the corner the whole time. But if the enemy had known to look for her magical signature, then they'd planned to kill her all along?

Was that it? She shook her head. Surely that couldn't have been it.

"I can practically read your mind." Lynx's tone was soft, commiserating.

"Yeah." Quinn fought with the anger she needed to push down. It wasn't going to help her solve anything. Especially since she realized now, she probably shouldn't have tried to stop the glowing before she understood if they could have reverse traced where the new trace was coming from. And that was just a nightmare of words.

She pinched the bridge of her nose.

"She would have been the first one to tell you to breathe." Lynx had moved closer. "You can't change what happened."

Quinn wanted to snap back that; of course she bloody couldn't. But there was a part of her that knew he was right. "I know. But I can find them and make them pay."

"Truth."

"Can we still reverse engineer the trace?" Quinn was pretty sure she already knew that answer.

"No. Not as such." Lynx started and then grinned somewhat evilly. "But we can trace the connection through the wards to find who was feeding power into the specific location of the tracking ritual."

"You could have just led with that." Quinn sighed, finally straightening and wishing she hadn't stayed in that uncomfortable crouched position for so long.

"Then I wouldn't have been answering the questions you needed to know, and you wouldn't have been able to work through your justifiable grief in small incremental ways."

Quinn just stared at the manifestation. And then she couldn't help but chuckle softly. "Thanks for that. Still . . . we can do this from my office, right?"

"Now that you've interrupted the ritual circle, yes."

Quinn frowned. "What was that sort of warping me directly down from my office and into this chamber thing all about?" She glanced over at Lynx, who seemed to look everywhere but directly at the Librarian.

"That's not exactly easy to explain," he said.

"Try me. Bet you I can follow."

Lynx laughed. "True. Probably. You're more attuned to the Library now, more connected. The magic is deep and attached. You can't quite just teleport everywhere. But . . . you can push through. Sort of fold the space and step through it." He took a second, as if he was trying to figure out if he'd explained it in the right way. "Yeah, that's it. You're just splitting the distance between two places within the Library and stepping through. If you like? It will take some of your own power, though."

"But I didn't do this. The Library sent me here."

"Because it knew you needed to get here now, so it used your own core attachment to send you here."

Quinn watched him skeptically but then nodded. "I guess. So, how do I get back?"

"A few more times and you should be able to manage it yourself. It's not as easy as you probably think, but I'll get the Library to warp you back upstairs."

Before he could say anything else, Quinn stood right back in her office, panting ever so slightly.

"See?" Lynx said. "Told you it cost your own energy. Even if the Library did move you, it made sure you paid for that move."

Yet another thing to add to her list. Beg the Library to teach her how to warp, because that would really come in handy.

Malakai looked up, a delicate eyebrow raised as if to ask *what the hell* in the nicest possible way. He hadn't budged from the couch and the book was still open on his lap. "Do I want to know?"

Quinn shook her head. "New magic trick. I'll share it with you when I can do it without killing myself."

"Fun, fun." He paused then, giving her a really good look and frowning. "Are you going to tell me why you ported out of here looking worried and came back looking like someone just . . . well, killed one of your friends?" It sounded harsh, but the compassion in his tone made it okay.

She waited several seconds before trying to articulate how she felt. "They knew about the tracking spell on the books. Not necessarily that we knew where it was, but that we had tried to track it in the first place. That we were looking for them in particular?"

"Could you tell what sort of spell it was?" Malakai asked gently.

She shook her head.

"Then it was probably put in place as an alert by Korradine in her time here."

"Ah," Quinn sighed, suddenly very tired. "That sort of makes sense, too. But anyway. When they found us, they were already aware of Jasper. I don't think killing her was an accident."

Malakai was quiet for a moment. So much that Quinn thought he wasn't going to say anything else.

But then he finally responded, and there was so much anger and heat in his voice. "I guess we add that to the list."

"What, of more things to do and figure out?" Quinn asked, suddenly feeling worn out.

"No." Malakai had to wrestle himself back in control. It was obvious he was angry. "Adding it to the list of what these jackasses have to pay for."

6

NOT TECHNICALLY

THE DAY DRAGGED ON, AND IT WAS LATE AT NIGHT BEFORE QUINN found herself sequestered in the restricted section. It wasn't that she needed restricted tomes specifically, but she did want some blessed peace and quiet. Right now, her office seemed to have become a gathering place. Not that anyone had ill intentions. But a steady flow of visitors popping in and asking questions they didn't actually need her to address grew old after a while.

She knew they were all just checking on her.

She knew they were all just worried about her.

It didn't make things feel any better.

Irias, the Balisor Salosier they'd saved from the life-sucking vines, was still healing, not to mention that Nishpa hadn't fully recovered yet either. Then there was Drukala. The only saving grace about the hospital was that many of the Balisors they'd rescued those weeks ago had recovered enough to be released. Not back to their home yet, no. Narilin's family were helping the Balisors, or what was left of them, fumigate their domain. Or something like that. At least, that's how it sounded to Quinn.

She wasn't entirely sure what it entailed. But after Sarila's demise and her obvious betrayal, after killing her own husband and admitting to helping with the slaughter of the Balisors—well, it seemed like helping with the cleanup was treated almost as penance by Jenishu Salosier, Narilin's family.

Quinn sighed and pulled the closest reference tome to her. Enough mulling over the current situation and what she was waiting on. She needed to figure out precisely how to combine affinities.

The tome was thick and dusty. *Mjikj's Musings on Affinity Combination Permutations.*

She had a definite feeling this was going to be dry reading. Informative, surely, but dry. Still, it was necessary.

Sinking into the pages, she delved deep. Mixing affinities was best done when the types were related to one another. Earth and water were basic elemental affinities that fed off each other well because they were complimentary. It made perfect sense. She knew she'd already utilized some of her abilities in that way. Then there were things like gravity and magnetic poles. Those two also worked together in a much more advanced way—one that made her fingers itch to practice.

Fire and air, mental acuity and mental fortification. And all of those had their little sub-affinities underneath them. Creating, destroying, unmaking, manipulating, growth, expansion, conjuration . . . there were so many little variations to all of them. Each of them had the potential to work with other affinities and sub-affinities.

Even if someone chose to use the same abilities as someone else, it didn't necessarily mean the outcome would be the same. It had to do with direction and intention, with motivation and perception. All in all, combining affinities, as far as Quinn could tell, was supposed to take the caster weeks if not months to master, and depending on the complexity, it could even take years.

Except in Quinn's case, she'd been casting things that combined multiple elements for a while now without fully realizing what she'd done.

Which led her to realize that perhaps her cosmicisodracus heritage contributed to that. An instinctual knowledge of what she was doing, of the universe and how magic fit into it. Or at least how to manipulate the affinities at her fingertips to most easily obtain the goal she aimed for.

It sounded logical, but it really wasn't. Not when she should be understanding how it worked before it could work.

Then again—perhaps that was also on an instinctual level too.

"I thought you might be hungry," Lynx said, his tone soft so as not to startle her while she was working.

Quinn hadn't precisely seen him pop into existence, but her connection to the Library now reached such a level that she just sensed his presence.

It extended to vaguely, in one of those compartments in her mind, letting her know exactly who was coming and going from her Library. In another area, she was fully aware of which staff members were present when, not to mention the fines ticking over, the overdue books being returned, and each and every species-specific room that was requested and maintained.

In her own mind, all of these things were there, separated out, marked, yet would only come to the fore if there was an alert and she needed to give it specific attention. Quinn couldn't believe just how much the Library dealt with on a daily level not to mention the filtration and distribution of mana and energy throughout the universe, if Quinn already had the urge to be overwhelmed when she didn't have nearly as much on her plate.

She turned her attention to Lynx, grateful that he'd waited for her to have her total sidetracked thoughts take place before she responded to his kindness for bringing her food. "Thanks. I *am* hungry."

He pushed a plate with a sandwich on it toward her, his eyes knowing. "Cook says it's a BLT? Said they think you like them this way—with the avocado and egg."

Quinn blinked and thanked her lucky stars that Cook was always this thoughtful. She hadn't had one of these in what seemed like an age. Her grandmother made them when she was a kid. "Yeah, these are basically the only sandwich I really like. Never been the biggest fan of them otherwise. But this? It's heavenly."

She could practically feel herself drooling over it. Idly, she cast a transparent shield protection over the book so she could eat her sandwich and not lose reading time while she ate. She was all about multitasking. At least for today.

"What are you reading?" Lynx sidled up to her.

She eyed him curiously. It wasn't like him to stick around unless he had something to say. Or at least, he usually didn't. "I'm really okay, you know?"

He frowned at her. "I find that difficult to believe. You get very attached to people. And it's okay to be attached to people. It's also fine to want to and need to grieve for them."

Quinn nodded, chewing very slowly on her first bite of sandwich. She knew, on an instinctual level, that it tasted good, because it was Cook and this was what they did. But with the subject Lynx just brought up, she wasn't entirely sure it wasn't just made out of cardboard. His words struck deep enough that she barely tasted a thing. And yet . . .

"We all grieve differently. Right now mine is fueled by spite and revenge. In order to achieve those things, I need to understand certain elements of my abilities before I can confidently use them. Thus, I am channeling my rage and grief into preparing to exact my revenge."

She watched Lynx as he took in her words, slowly nodding along with them. Frankly, she thought she'd reasoned that out very well.

"That makes very logical sense," Lynx said, his eyes flickering ever so briefly. Another tome, thinner than the first one and smaller, almost diary sized, landed on the table too. "There we go. That one should help too."

Quinn studied the spine. *Meram's Guide to Affinity Collaboration— Working Past the Blocks.* She grinned up at him around her sandwich. "Thanks."

"You know. Sometimes you just need rest too, Quinn. We're waiting for so much right now. You could afford to actually get some decent sleep for once." He sounded like he was desperately trying not to boss her around. As if he'd specifically phrased it in a nondemanding way.

Quinn narrowed her eyes as she looked at him. "Okay, what gives? Spill it."

He sighed. "We're just a little worried. You've been expending huge amounts of energy over numerous incidents lately, and we just all think you could do with a good night's sleep."

Concern.

It was a rather novel thing.

Not that no one had ever shown her concern in her past. Her family had, and even her foster mum had been pretty good about it. And then there was Hallee, in her own little way. But the concern of her Library and her new friends. That felt different. It felt oddly like family. Nice and warm. So instead of begging off or downplaying it, she chose to smile instead. "Fine. I have a few more pages to read through here. And then I'll get an understanding of the one you just brought me. After that, I promise I'll rest."

Aradie hooted as if she was saying she'd hold her to that, and Lynx looked relieved.

"Excellent. Then I guess I'll leave you to it." He paused and stared back at her. "I'll check on you, though. Make sure you're doing what you say. You'll sleep, right? Not just rest?"

Quinn laughed. "Fine. I'll promise to sleep as much as I can manage."

Lynx nodded and popped out of view.

She watched the empty space for the last couple of bites of her BLT and then returned to her books. He really needn't have done that . . . she could already feel the fatigue setting in. She'd be useless with taking in any new information in no time flat.

Lynx had got her a book. He didn't usually do that. There was a part of her that found it encouraging. He'd been adjusting slowly to whatever revelations his memories gave him, or at least his personality had been stabilizing. Perhaps this was just something returning that he used to do. It meant a lot that he'd paid attention to what she was researching and provided another book she could use.

Meram's Guide to Affinity Collaboration—Working Past the Blocks.

This book was definitely older than the previous one. The

language, even with her automatic interpreter, appeared to be archaic. It was handwritten in loopy script as opposed to the affinity driven script that most of the other books in the Library were created with. It made Quinn wonder if perhaps this book had been a part of some ancient civilization's collection.

Affinity Collaboration was advanced level affinity magic. Which made perfect sense. They probably wouldn't even want anyone to know affinities could be combined until they'd hit a certain level of control and depth. She could just imagine new young magic users getting all excited and obliterating themselves accidentally if they tried to combine and experiment with too much magic.

Many of the chapters as she skimmed them had already been covered in the book she'd just gone through. But there was one chapter about halfway through that gave a better overview of what blocks entailed. These were affinities that seemed to be in complete opposition to each other.

Affinity blocks, at least at first, appeared to be specific combinations of affinities that created roadblocks for each other unless very specifically worked around. An odd feeling of dread rippled under her skin, making it itch like something was trying to get through to the other side. It was as if her blood didn't agree with the information she read.

Interesting enough.

Perhaps what she needed was some of the books on cosmicisodracus history and their abilities. *Do we have studies done on the magical abilities of you and your siblings?*

Not technically, no.

Technically?

It was like the Library let out a long-suffering sigh. *There are notes on how our magic works, but it's all more in a sort of diary entry manner. You're very welcome to look through them if you want to. It is your heritage as well. And I did give you access to the space.*

Her skin rippled ever so slightly again sensing the truth of the words. *Is it just your contributions?*

No. There should be journals there from all of us. We were once very eager to understand ourselves, but that time has long since passed. As have most other things that started out with us. The Library sounded sort of sad. It made Quinn want to hug it. She settled for patting the window sill instead.

Forgetting all about her promise to Lynx, she snapped the book shut and stood up. "Well, then. Looks like I have some more reading to do."

7

DECREPIT

Quinn certainly wasn't expecting the Library to stop her. But as she tried to open the hidden doorway she usually used in the restricted vault to get to Drev's personal vault, it wouldn't budge. She frowned and tried again. *Okay . . . why won't the door open?*

There was a pause, as if the Library was asking her if she was serious. But then, after a very soft sigh that rippled through the room, it spoke. *Because you promised Lynx you'd sleep.*

And before Quinn could get any farther, the Library interjected even more. *I can't notice every minuscule detail all the time. That's just not possible for me. As more of my functions come back online, as the power levels grow, I need Lynx to act for me in many capacities. If you tell him something—actually. Whenever you've told him something, I've always known. It might be a blip, it might be like a notification . . . but you can't tell him one thing and then do another.*

Quinn wasn't entirely sure how she felt about that. Apart from guilty. Aradie perching over on the bench, basically laughing like an owl shouldn't be able to laugh, didn't help matters one bit.

Quinn had to admit the Library had a point, and now she'd had a moment to calm down and be rational instead of excitable. She was feeling that fatigue right through to her bones.

"Fine," she said begrudgingly. "You're right."

Did you get that, Aradie? the Library asked. *I wouldn't want to miss being able to replay that moment over and again.*

That's not nice! Quinn shot back mind to mind again. Except it was quite amusing a comment. She ended up grinning.

Aradie swooped to her shoulder, nipping at her ear with a definite chortle.

"Yeah, yeah," Quinn grumbled, suddenly yawning.

Maybe her body was trying to tell her something too. She gathered the few books she wanted to absorb before bed and began walking out. They were pretty hefty in her arms, but she'd had them suggested from both the Library and Milaro, so she felt like that killed two birds with one stone.

Not going to fight me more? The Library sounded oddly surprised by its victory.

Quinn shrugged as she walked through the Library, the books starting to weigh heavy in her hands. *No. When you've got a point, you've got a point. But you need to remind me first thing to go and check that tomorrow, okay?*

Done. I just know once you get started, you'll be at it at least twenty odd hours, and I think you should do that on a full night's sleep.

Definitely not wrong there. Quinn stopped and frowned. She'd spent ages earlier examining the warp ability the Library had imparted. What on earth was she doing walking when she could just warp now?

It was a disconcerting sensation, like a tug through her central core that somehow snapped her equilibrium and presence into the desired spot in the Library. She could feel the power it took being fed from not only the filtration chamber but right up through the entire Library.

And through herself.

The next thing she knew, she stood outside her quarters. Books in hand, she barely recalled what they were as she mechanically absorbed them, trusting that her brain would process things while she slept. After all, it always did.

She was asleep before her head hit the pillow

Voices tugged at her consciousness, but Quinn was tired. In a bone-weary sort of way. Her legs felt like lead, her brain like mush, as if something wasn't firing right. Had she got the flu?

It wasn't only that, though. Her entire being felt like it weighed a ton, as if she were bloated and weighed down with water. The pain that spread through her wasn't sharp or jarring. Instead, it was this ache of bones in positions they shouldn't be in, locked in place for too many hours on end.

It was just how she imagined growing old would feel.

Decrepit.

Aged.

Too much of a life lived, so all that remained was to seek and yearn for death.

Something wavered in her. Like a candle in the distance, flickering in place. Quinn focused on the flame, sure it was trying to tell her something. Trying to tell her more than that she was old and out of date now, aimed for the trash pile.

Because she wasn't, was she? In her twenties. That's where she thought she was.

And technically, she wasn't even human anymore. Not that she'd ever been. But her mind hadn't quite grasped the concept, and her memories were based on the first portion of the life she'd lived.

The life in which she'd fully believed she was human.

Belief went a long way.

But in this? No, in this it couldn't replace the memory. Those, for Quinn at least, were core things hidden behind a multitude of protections. Ones she'd built with Milaro's help and reinforced by both herself and the Library. So these thoughts, wherever this intrusion came from, it wasn't her own mind, or that of anyone she'd given permission to enter it.

Which meant that somehow, someone else was attempting to breach her mind protections.

That didn't sit well with Quinn, but she didn't think she'd given herself away yet. All those thoughts, those memories that weren't quite right, they lingered there in her mind, shuffling through like a remote-controlled deck of cards.

She made sure to separate her logical thoughts from the experience, to allow herself to analyze the situation. Logic dictated that she watch closely, try to glean who was doing this and what memories they were trying to replace or impose on her.

Their motives could be one or more of a few possibilities. They might want to know what it was she knew. That one was simple enough. Perhaps they sought to figure out why none of the attacks so far had killed her and spared most of her friends, too.

Then there was also determining exactly what affinities she had and how she might be able to combat them.

Quinn, however had a niggling in the back of her mind. She got the feeling that perhaps Dro who killed Jasper, had got a whiff of Quinn's scent and was trying to determine her origin. She could only hope that the smell of her other sister was mixed in with Quinn's and thus caused confusion.

She wasn't sure why, but Quinn was fairly sure they didn't want Dro and Drav to know Quinn was a cosmicisodracus yet. As long as they didn't get any actual proof, things should be fine.

Which was how she came to the conclusion that this right here, this was another one of those weird dreams. Except this time Kajaro was nowhere to be seen. In fact, no one was anywhere to be seen.

She was alone, in a strange, dark cloudy area. As if it was a massive cavern with nothing but indigo and black clouds. They swirled around her now, moving closer, gathering near her, yet never managed to touch her.

Quinn wondered if that had to do with her mental shielding, dragon scales, or something else.

What she did know was that the air filled with frustration. A guttural growl sparked the surrounding air as if agitated it couldn't quite reach her. As if she was on the tip of its tongue.

She closed her eyes within the space and breathed. There were a couple of options open to her since obviously nothing bad was happening to her body in the outside world, as otherwise she would have felt the tug of Aradie's panic settling into her from out there.

Perhaps she could gain some information, or at least verification of who was trying to break through her defenses right now. And then, when she woke, she'd check with Milaro about how this was even possible.

Although . . . there was something she thought she should know, should remember, hovering in the back of her mind about that. Something she'd absorbed.

She let her consciousness divide, allowing herself to traverse this strange, cloudy dreamscape cautiously. It wouldn't do to be too bold. While this appeared to be close to something of her own making, it still reeked like a trap. She'd fallen into far too many of those for her to be comfortable with any of this.

If she concentrated. Truly knuckled down and focused on the space, she could still hear those whispers, even as she camouflaged herself to blend in with the clouds that permeated the entire area.

Snatches of conversation began to filter back to her. All of which she took with a grain of salt. But all of which she made sure to commit to her memory so she could share it with Milaro later.

Shouldn't have gotten that book.

But this was a surprise.

The book was more important that whatever this is. It was the key. We're missing it.

I can get it.

You lost it in the first place. You were supposed to find Drukala.

*I did find her. I just didn't—*The voice was obviously pouting as it was cut off.

Silence. That voice hesitated for a second. *I've lost the trace.*

Does that mean she's woken up? The more feminine voice sounded worried. *That shouldn't be possible. I tracked it through the Library connection.*

Perhaps she's better trained than we thought . . . there's something off about that human.

I'm beginning to think she's not one.

I'm certain she's not one. The male voice, the one Quinn was fairly sure was Dravishk, held so much animosity it almost made Quinn gasp. *But I still don't know what she is. Regardless. We'll always be able to track the Librarians.*

Quinn made sure to reinforce her shielding even more. The fog grew thicker, as if it was gathering around not only to obscure but also protect her. She shuddered. This was enough. She had one piece of information, but her danger sense was starting to tingle. She needed to get the hell awake.

A strangled cry almost broke her concentration as she tried to reach through to Aradie.

This isn't subconscious. She's doing this on purpose. He sounded angry this time.

Quinn wasn't about to sit around and figure out if he could, in fact, reach her in her dreams. She pushed her thoughts out to Aradie, with a sharp twist, and all of a sudden the bird was pecking her.

It only took a couple of pecks to pull her out of the mist.

Quinn sat up gasping, her head swimming with a fog that momentarily still seemed to obscure her vision. The lights in the sconces lent a blurry halo over her room for several seconds before her eyes readjusted.

She regulated her breathing, pulling Aradie in close to stroke her feathers, and looked around to double check that nothing had somehow made its way back through her dreamscape with her. Not that she thought it possible, but she still wasn't sure of everything magic could do.

"Thank you," she whispered to the owl. While she hadn't been in immediate danger when woken, Quinn was fairly certain she was about to be.

Aradie gave her a weak glare and then cocked her head to one side as if to ask what happened.

Quinn shook her head, taking a moment to analyze and reinforce her shielding. Once her breathing returned to normal, she got up and took a shower and then centered herself, sorting through the conversation she'd managed to decipher. The thing was . . . there were other whisperings she'd missed.

While she'd been able to recognize the mumblings, the words escaped her originally.

Had she gotten so used to it that she'd finally been able to decipher what they were saying? Was it a glitch? A trap? A fluke?

And . . . if she'd managed to decipher some of it, did that mean she'd be able to decode more from the other memories if she went back and examined them?

A little confidence returned she realized it was technically early morning . . . sort of. In her usual Library time. But this couldn't wait. She took the time to notify the Library, Lynx, Malakai, and Milaro, and got ready to meet them in her office.

All in all, she'd really tried to sleep. It wasn't her fault it hadn't been restful.

8

TRACK THE LIBRARIANS

Always be able to track the Librarians.

The sentence rang in her ears as she devoured the coffee and donut Cook sent to her while she waited. It wouldn't be long before the others arrived, but it was plenty of time for her thoughts to run rampant. Quinn couldn't keep the frown from her face as she paced the length of her office and back.

Always be able to track the Librarians.

Despite her excitement that she'd managed to control the dream they'd attempted to wrest from her and get some measure of information from them, Quinn couldn't help but feel blindsided by that statement. Dravishk seemed so sure, absolutely positive, in fact. Which meant he'd tracked Librarians before.

A queasiness settled in her stomach, making her wonder just how the Librarian before Korradine died. Obviously, they had ways of contacting a Librarian through their dreams. Or perhaps it was something else that made this possible. One of the Librarian-specific affinities, perhaps. But was there more to it?

Surely not every Librarian had shields like Quinn's? After all, hers were well reinforced with her cosmicisodracus heritage. It lent her strength for everything. But considering the Librarians needed specific combinations of affinities and Quinn had every single affinity . . . it meant she had access to more skills than any other Librarian before.

She frowned, engrossed in her thoughts, and was still pacing when Lynx, Malakai, and Milaro popped into the room.

We're all present and accounted for. The Library sounded like it did when it was busy multitasking. Sort of distant and preoccupied. And yet somehow still there.

Before she could say anything, Lynx spoke up. "You look exhausted. You were supposed to go to sleep."

A worm of guilt tried to wind itself into Quinn's brain, but she wasn't having it right then. "I didn't exactly get a choice."

She was proud of herself for not snapping, yet at the same time, she actually felt irritated that she hadn't had a choice. For once, she'd actually agreed to go to sleep earlier than usual and done so. So much for her pro-activeness.

Milaro frowned, understanding immediately. "If it's Kajaro, you need to tell Hal straight away. He shouldn't be breaching any of the wards they're keeping him under. That's nigh impossible."

Malakai responded instead of Quinn, his voice an all-out drawl of boredom and sarcasm. The perfect marriage. "Just like it's supposed to be impossible that someone fries the brains of the prisoner before Hal can prevent it."

Quinn could've hugged him.

Milaro winced. "Valid point you're making, yet I can't help think things would be easier . . ." He shook his head. "Never mind. Carry on, Quinn."

She nodded, sort of grateful for the interaction as she reached up and petted Aradie's perfectly soft feathers. "Not Kajaro. It's the Library's brother. The Drav one."

There was a weight to the surrounding atmosphere. As if the Library was weighing the new information. Then a sigh permeated the room like a regretful breeze. *I wish I could say I'm surprised.*

Unsure of how to respond to that, Quinn relayed exactly what happened in her vision, dream, sub conscious invasion. After relaying what she heard, there was an uncomfortable silence in the room. To cover that, she continued. "They did say more, but it took a while for my translation ability to fire off. There could be more in there . . ."

Milaro looked up at her sharply, a thousand questions hidden in his gaze and she knew she'd caught his attention. Nothing like a bit of a mind puzzle to bring out Milaro's competitive streak. "What makes you think that?"

She wasn't completely surprised by the question, but really had to ponder it. "It took me a while to orient myself. I wasn't sure if it was a dream, if there were really people in my dreamscape or what-ever we call it, or if I could remain hidden. I spent time strength-ening my wards and making sure they wouldn't get through them where they might do harm to me. While I could hear people talking, I couldn't understand what they were saying without concentrating on it."

Malakai crossed his arms and leant against the closest wall. It gave Quinn a sense of relief to see him doing something so typically mundane while she waited for Milaro to process the information.

Lynx wasn't completely there, either. His eyes flickered, darting here and there, obviously tracking down something she wasn't sure of.

It only took a moment for Milaro to speak back up, but it seemed like such a long time. "And you're sure you managed to get all your wards and protections in place, right?"

Quinn nods again. "Yes."

"Hmm." He paused, stepping closer hesitantly. "What is it you want to do, Quinn? I feel like you have an idea and are just waiting for me to process all of this before you tell me. So, out with it."

She took a deep breath. "I'm wondering if you could help me with retrieving what they said. It could be bickering, but it could be enlightening. Maybe give us a piece of the puzzle we're missing?"

He nodded, frowning. "That sounds like an excellent idea, all things considered." He walked over to her desk and patted her chair. "Make yourself comfortable. I have to pop back and grab a couple of things. I'll sit opposite you. Whatever you need to do to relax, get in a meditative state. Let's do it. We'll dig in and see what we can't pull out of that fabulous brain of yours, yes?"

Quinn didn't expect the wave of relief that rushed through her after hearing that. "Okay."

Milaro, upon her acquiescence, immediately popped out of view.

Quinn pouted. "You think I'd be used to that by now." Maybe someday she'd be able to do more than warp.

Malakai was suddenly in front of her with a steaming hot drink that Quinn recognized as hot chocolate. She looked up at him, an eyebrow raised. It wasn't that she didn't like hot chocolate, but she felt like it was more of an evening or nighttime drink.

Malakai shrugged. "Cook insisted it would help you relax more than the coffee you've been drinking to keep you awake."

She'd already drunk half of it before Milaro got back. Sitting with her legs crossed, and her mind halfway to zoning out, Quinn gave Lynx, still searching for whatever he was looking for, a glance before taking a deep breath. "Ready when you are."

Milaro perched on a chair on the other side of the desk and extended his hands to gently hold hers. "Close your eyes and breathe. I want you to count to ten in your head with slow and even breaths, and I need to have you completely calm at this stage. There is no danger near you. We won't let any harm come to you. You are safe in this space. Do you understand?"

Not that she could see it, but while he spoke, a strange sort of mist began to envelop her mind. She was calm and easy within its embrace, able to pinpoint each thought she had with startling clarity. It felt like her mind was open and free and able to comprehend anything.

"I understand," she said and realized she more than did that.

Next thing she knew, they were standing in her memories.

Show me.

Milaro's words were no longer spoken but a part of her mind, shown to her in a way she'd not perceived before. She frowned. It was definitely him, and she was in her chair even if it felt so far away, surrounded by people and manifestations that would protect her. Breathing steadily, she drew him in, letting his presence become not quite a part of her memory self, but close enough to breathe the same dream air.

The words were garbled at first, and Milaro reached through, guiding the memory to the glimpses he needed to see in order to help her understand. While he utilized her mind, she found herself drifting.

Not from the recollection, but back to what they'd been saying. She didn't understand why they'd chosen this avenue of contact. Had she been meant to consume something that made her more susceptible to take over or something? Were there reasons she didn't understand about how they approached the Librarians? Or had they only used this approach with her because they'd not met her in person? Well . . . technically, anyway.

Or had the whole thing actually been inadvertent?

The muttered, mumbled, indecipherable conversations began to take a wisp of shape. Not completely done yet, but almost there.

So close she could practically taste what it was they were saying.

Quinn? Focus.

She struggled to pull herself back from her thoughts, wrenching the bulk of her attention back to the sound of the voices just beyond her comprehension. But that was just it. The words were less garbled now. Clearer.

Why did you let her wake up? There was some static overlaid with the words, as if it was bad reception, but there nonetheless.

I didn't let her. Those wards on her hibernation chamber aren't what I expected from her. Drukala never seemed so . . .

You shouldn't have underestimated her, Dro, you should know better than that.

Then a snarl, as if Dro was telling him precisely what she thought of that.

Several more seconds passed and the voices behind the static started up again.

This tracking thing is easier than expected. You're cleverer than I gave you credit for.

Quinn could practically feel Dravishk preening.

You shouldn't ever underestimate me.

Did you always know . . . that you'd undermine the Library like this?

For several seconds there was silence and then Dravishk sighed. There was an air of melancholy about the expression, as if he didn't want to go into it. *No. Not initially.*

Then how . . .

Originally, I didn't believe this would work. The shifting, the pocket dimension, the filtration . . . it was a shot in the dark, but I had to give Drevicia something to focus on. For it to feel like something had been attempted. I never expected it to work.

So you built a backdoor just in case?

Well, I wasn't going to let Drev die, was I? Diminishing Drev's power was a far better goal. The whole endeavor was supposed to fail and chaos would retain its natural order.

The static faded slightly, but was still there, almost as punctuation for the rest of it.

Wait. So you've been preparing to take it down since the start.

Another pause.

I never intended it to work, but it twisted, and it caught, and then it was this solid thing. Undoing it has proved more of a challenge than I ever imagined.

But you're almost there, right?

Drav gave a bit of a laugh before the answer. *Somewhat. There are several of my avenues that the blasted new Librarian has cut off, but I still have some tricks up my sleeve.*

I should have known.

Dravishk growled. *She really shouldn't have gotten that book.*

They were back where the conversation started for Quinn originally. Milaro extricated himself and Quinn had to pull herself out of the quasi trance she was in, too. So much of what she'd just witnessed was too much. But at the same time, it was far too convenient.

She'd already taken so much of the bait laid out for her and people had died. She refused to be responsible for that again. When she opened her eyes, she was scowling and had the satisfaction of seeing Milaro momentarily confused.

"What?" she asked.

"I expected you to be sad, or worried?" he half asked back.

She shook her head. "Oh, I'm both of those things. But I'm also done with this crap. We can't trust that to be true, but we also can't ignore what they told us. Because even if I'm skeptical, it sounds far too much like the truth."

The Library's voice had a hitch to it when it spoke. *It sounds far too much like exactly something Drav would do. I was always surprised he agreed in the first place.*

Quinn sighed, hating that the Library felt so slighted. "Okay, so that part is likely true, but we operate from here on in on the presumption that anything we glean could be a lie, could be a trap, or simply designed to lead us the wrong way."

"That's the smartest thing I've ever heard you say." Malakai drawled.

Quinn used Gravitas to throw a couch cushion at him, hitting him right in the face.

"Hey!"

"Sorry? I can't hear you over the sound of how awesome I am." She grinned, clinging to that brief delusion of normalcy. Quinn had a feeling she'd need it as they began to figure out the rest of the puzzle.

9

LINE OF SCARRING

The thing was—Quinn was tired.

Not necessarily sleepy-tired, but just sort of bone-weary exhaustion tired. She hadn't stopped since coming to the Library over six months ago now. That was such a long time to be on a constant move. Her bluffing wasn't the best—telling Mal she was awesome was a way to bluff herself to confidence.

As it stood, Quinn definitely didn't feel any measure of awesome.

Aradie perched on her shoulder, refusing to go to any of her regular haunts. Perhaps she sensed Quinn's disquiet.

She'd sent all the others off on errands to figure out their next steps. Well, sort of, anyway.

Milaro had ducked back home to grab reference materials and some implements he said they needed to go over her mental shielding and wards with. Malakai said he had to go home and get some training tools. Not that she quite understood, but perhaps he'd just wanted a reason to duck home with his grandfather.

Lynx and the Library were scouring the system for more information and clues to the backdoors.

And while Aradie had refused to leave, Quinn couldn't complain, considering she really didn't want to be alone.

With the office blessedly empty, Quinn found herself with far too much static in her brain. Like she couldn't quite wrap her head around the information Milaro helped her pull out of her head. Information that would have been good to know before she went and got Jasper killed.

She paused, centered herself, and took a few deep breaths.

That sort of thinking wasn't getting her anywhere. Now wasn't the time to dwell, but instead, she needed to focus on shutting down this ridiculously far-reaching thread of a scheme that never seemed to run out. Surely, they had to be getting close to the end. Or at least to finding an end.

The cosmicisodracus had banded together in order to create the Library. But apparently not all of them thought it was a good idea and had been determined, from the beginning, to see it fail. Which it didn't, much to her uncle's chagrin. But since the collapse that he'd planned hadn't come to fruition, Dravishk had to find alternate methods to execute it.

Quinn crossed her legs, sitting down to meditate. Surely there were several ways for her to map out the magic in her system. She thought as much at her internal console, prompting it to show her anything that might even partially relate to what she wanted to achieve.

She frowned as rows and rows of information flashed past her face until suddenly, there was a view of a body, probably her body, with internal pathways.

All along, where a scan would usually show blood vessels and nerve endings if it were back on Earth, it seemed to show something much more encompassing. It glowed blue like magic, with strong yellow undercurrents emphasizing the mana through energy. Which did a lot more to explain how both were interwoven and yet separate in her body.

Looking at it felt like a revelation. Her body had multiple power pools, big lakes of mana and energy that overlapped, sometimes superimposed over the rest of her, while the pathways made their way all around the interior of her body. She was fully aware that her body and the system only allowed this view because she'd devoured one of the vault books on cosmicisodracus physiology.

No wonder it was kept where only the Library and she could see it. It'd be so dangerous to see this much power potential in any way.

Hell, Quinn was slightly afraid of what it might mean, anyway.

That's certainly one way to gauge your power. The Library's voice pulled her out of her contemplations.

I'm more of a visual person. Just telling me what it means to be what I am isn't going to get me anywhere. This, however? Seeing how it works and flows together? I get the magnitude now. Yep, she was definitely a visual representation sort of person. Quinn stretched, feeling the muscle soreness acutely enough to wince.

It didn't escape the Library's notice. *Did you hurt something? In the dream?*

Quinn started to shake her head, but then gave it some real thought. *Not as such. Just . . . I was stiff and sore afterward.*

Hmm was the only comment the Library gave.

Quinn didn't press. If it had an answer, she'd get it as soon as it was certain.

You're still overtired. As long as you don't make a habit out of it, you should head over to the alchemical branch and grab an energizing potion. They can't be used indefinitely or too frequently. You'll either build up an addiction if you take them too much, or an immunity. Neither of those are good options. But I think, right now, you need your wits as about you as we can get them.

Quinn raised an eyebrow at the space around her. Aradie nipped her ear. "Fine! I'll go get one," she said out loud even though she didn't want to get up and go get one at all.

She pushed herself up and made her way out of the office before stopping short and realizing she could just warp there.

Nope. Don't do it. Don't make it the only way you travel around the Library. Especially not when you're as overtired as you are.

Fine. Quinn was starting to despise the word.

A few steps in, Dottie trotted up next to her. "Hi!" She sounded just as bright and cheery as usual.

It gave Quinn pause. She guessed the bench and Jasper hadn't really had much interaction. It gave her a wave of melancholy to know that so few people in the Library would miss her. Even though she'd done so much to help Quinn in so little time. It made her wonder if she could get any friends from Earth to come for a visit? Probably not. But for some reason, she found herself missing Hallee, who she probably owed a text.

Life had just gotten a bit out of hand over the last couple of weeks.

"Hey, Dottie." But even Quinn's mood couldn't remain sour with the bench trotting around with her. There was just something overwhelmingly positive about her.

"It's good to see you back. Is there anything you need that I can help with?"

Quinn glanced down at her with a frown. "Why, is there somewhere you know I need to be right now?"

"Technically," Dottie began, and Quinn could have sworn she was grinning, "You should already know to head to the hospital wing. There are still a lot of people in there. Do you think everyone is going to be fine? That little Irias is still there, you know. Nishpa too. I'm getting rather worried."

Quinn smiled and cleared her throat, bringing Dottie to an end. "I think you've been hanging around Betty too much," she quipped.

Dottie sounded flustered when she replied. "What? Do you think so? Is that a bad thing?"

This time, Quinn laughed. "No, not inherently. You just have a lot to say."

"I haven't seen you in a while." Dottie's tone managed to sound offended.

"Sorry, got a lot of my mind."

"Of course you do." The bench obviously took pity on her. "You tell me what you were fetching and I'll make sure you get it, while you run on over to take a look at the hospital branch."

Quinn frowned slightly. While she did love that her supervisors were taking responsibility, there was still a part of her who didn't like relinquishing control. But the part of her brain that knew she had too much to do argued that she had subordinates for a reason. "Thanks, Dottie. I need an energizing potion from alchemical and medicinal."

"Consider it done! I'll bring it to you in the hospital."

Nodding, Quinn took off, with Aradie still firmly affixed to her shoulder. "You know," she mumbled at the bird, "you could fly yourself. You're no baby chick."

Aradie huffed and the Librarian could have sworn she was laughing.

"So glad you have a sense of humor," Quinn muttered.

Passing through the now-massive set of hydroponics and other terrariums that Farrow maintained, Quinn waved hi to the golem and her two support staff, suddenly realizing she didn't recognize them. It was about time Farrow hired other people to help out.

She stepped through to the entry corridor of the hospital. When they'd first added the section after the Balisor Salosier incident, they'd made the hallway long to fit enough beds along it and allow the nursing staff and healers to just keep the influx of injured coming.

Now, however, when she traversed it, she felt like she was walking along a corridor that led to another world.

Considering she could simply open doors to accomplish that, it felt sort of weird.

Just as she was about to push through the entrance doors, there was a pop, and Milaro and Malakai appeared directly in front of her, almost giving her heart failure from their unexpected arrival as well as the oddly loud noise it made.

"You can't keep popping up like that!" she said, grasping at her chest. Not that she was trying to be melodramatic, but she kind of felt like it warranted it.

"Sorry." Milaro, for once, sounded contrite. "Anyway, you and I need to work with Nishpa."

"But she's still injured." Quinn felt panic rise up in her as memories of the Sarila attack assaulted her.

Nishpa's supine form in Milaro's arms had seemed so small and insignificant. So fragile.

Milaro nodded. "Miles is a great doctor, you know. And we have some stellar healers."

Quinn still couldn't get the vision out of her head. So tiny in that huge bed with all of those magical instruments attached to her.

"Quinn?" Malakai moved forward, taking her hand gently and squeezing it.

"She's not ready to help. We need to find another mind healer." She wasn't going to put her in danger again. Not yet. Not when she was so weak. She squeezed Malakai's hand back desperately.

Milaro stepped forward this time. "Quinn. You realize she's been in here for almost two weeks. While not fully recovered, she's almost there."

Quinn blinked up at him, not quite understanding, and then it was like her brain and math had a party and caught up. There'd been time between her attack and their trip. The adventure itself had taken time to reach, followed by the fighting, and it had been a week since Jasper . . . well, anyway.

"Oh." It finally felt like she could breathe again.

That's where Dottie, wielding a nice fat energizing potion, found her. "Here you go, Librarian!"

That pure joy in the bench's voice always helped Quinn pull away from dark thoughts.

"Thanks. I appreciate it."

"Just half of that one," Milaro warned, his eyes narrowed. "That's a multiple-dose bottle. You don't want to be bouncing off the walls. Have you had one before?"

"No."

"Then a quarter. The last thing we need is you on an energy high." Milaro tried to sound stern, but the way his lip quirked up into a smile at the end, Quinn didn't buy it.

She downed a large swallow in one go, wishing the greater universe had heard of grape flavoring medicine.

Ten minutes later, they were about to enter Nishpa's rooms. With her touching the doorhandle, about to go in, Quinn paused as she heard arguing within.

"I don't want to eat this garbage. Get me decent food so you can finish assessing my wings and let me the hell out of here!"

Quinn cringed. She'd rarely seen Nishpa angry in their short acquaintance, but if Geneva's moods were anything to go by, she didn't envy whoever was taking the brunt of Nishpa's current ire.

Armed with her owl, her elves, and her talking bench, Quinn figured now was as good a time as any to ask the Furionas fae they'd almost got killed for help. They pushed through the door.

Nishpa's face was just as delicate and golden as Quinn remembered, but now there was a thick line of scarring down from one side of her face all the way down her neck and Quinn was quite certain it traveled under her clothes too. The Furionas was paler than Quinn remembered too, but her eyes held so much fire, it was refreshing to see her so alive.

"Ah. Librarian. About time." Nishpa smiled, and a row of very sharp teeth glinted in the light of the room. "Now, tell me how I can get some of Cook's food. I'm starving. Healing takes a lot of work."

10

HERSELF TO SPEAK

QUINN CHUCKLED AS FOOD APPEARED DIRECTLY IN FRONT OF THE Furionas fae. After all, Cook did take care of everyone in the Library —or at least Cook and their army of helpers did. It was refreshing to see the feisty mind healer up and about, or at least awake. She no longer looked fragile, but like solid gold strength, and she devoured several dishes Quinn couldn't even recognize.

Her own muscles still ached in a way she couldn't pinpoint. Like she'd gone camping and slept on the ground for a week, lying over a stone outline of her body. Except she very obviously hadn't done that. Her scales flared over her skin briefly as she rolled her neck to work out a crick. She could feel the magical energy prickling just underneath her skin. And after a brief pause, made sure to send all those sensations through to the Library. Hmm, wasn't an answer after all. Maybe the Library needed more input.

Malakai nudged her arm.

She raised an eyebrow at him.

"You're being awfully quiet."

She nodded.

He laughed.

Nishpa looked up at them, giving her belly a pat, finally done with her food. Quinn could have sworn she could see ten thousand thoughts flitting around in her mind. The fae then glanced over at Milaro, a thoughtful expression on her face. A gentle smile followed, even if her brow was still creased with worry.

"Sarila, then . . . I didn't see that coming." She sounded so sad.

"None of us did." Milaro spoke softly, as if making sure he didn't startle her.

Nishpa cleared her throat, and her expression changed, sort of like a mask had suddenly taken her melancholy face's place. "I've got some people looking into it. I should get out of here shortly."

"Looking into it?" Milaro frowned and Quinn felt like she was watching something she probably shouldn't. "You know, I said I'd take care of it."

"Of course, dear," Nishpa said absently, "I do have sprites and others who can feed information back to me. Then we'll have all the knowledge we can, and we'll be better for it."

Milaro raised an eyebrow but didn't comment. At least for now, anyway. Quinn was fairly sure that once they were on their own again, it would be a very different matter. He continued, clearing his throat. "I need you to do a scan of Quinn if you're up for it?"

Quinn stepped in, shaking her head. "No. That's not necessary. I'm fine."

He shot her a glare and repeated himself. "Nishpa is going to give you a scan. Neither I, nor you, nor the Library is specialized in mind healing. Nishpa is. A diagnostic check of your mind and its shielding is beneficial to all of us at this stage."

When he put it that way, he probably had a point. It didn't mean Quinn felt right putting Nishpa, who'd only just recovered, in that position.

"Come sit with me." Nishpa patted the bed next to her. It still dwarfed her tiny frame, but Quinn obliged and sat. "Works better with physical touch while I'm recovering my strength."

Quinn nodded and closed her eyes. She could feel the swell of magic wash over her, like a wave on the beach swooshing in and then petering back out. She wasn't entirely sure how long it lasted, but finally it settled, and she could feel a sort of zinging over and under her skin, all around her skull and body.

"Done," Nishpa said, and Quinn opened her eyes to see a thoughtful frown on the fae's face.

Quinn looked over at Milaro and he just shrugged, which wasn't at all helpful.

After several seconds, Nishpa finally spoke up. "There's no foreign matter in your brain—no subtle doors left in there for someone else to attack. No storage for anything untoward. There's nothing in there that would lead me to believe you might have been affected by or fallen prey to something. But I would caution you to keep pouring more strength into your wards."

"Thanks," Quinn said, immediately beginning her reinforcement refinement. The last thing she needed was some damned cosmicisodracus trying to take her over now that she was apparently made from their DNA. She wouldn't put it past some of them to use and throw her away.

"Do you think you'll be up to helping Dru later on?" Milaro asked Nishpa softly.

She shrugged, and from the sudden shadows underneath her eyes, Quinn could only guess that the spell she'd performed was strong enough it required more energy from her than she likely had right then. "I should be able to, but not yet. Right now, I have to sleep."

It wasn't that she practically fell into the bed. Because she was already in it. But she did suddenly seem much smaller in that big bed.

Quinn and Malakai left first, just as Nishpa offered her a smile and then fell straight asleep. They were already heading down the hall when Milaro made it out of the room to stop them. He stood there, panting a little, making Quinn quite certain his grandson could run rings around him. She stood and simply waited for him to speak while Malakai looked like he was anything but impressed.

"You can't leave without talking to Irias, at least." His tone was stern despite being ever so slightly out of breath.

Malakai spoke first. "And why would we talk to Irias? She was a puppet, used to bait us into almost being eaten by a root parasite. How do we know she's even really herself?"

Milaro paused for a bit, watching his grandchild. "Irias is the one who gave us the warning about Sarila. The thing is, she has to know more than that. Logically, am I correct?"

Quinn nodded and then shook her head instead. "No. Like, I get that she was the one who handed us Sarila. But how did she know?"

"That's what we need to find out," Milaro almost snapped but managed to count down and stop himself from overreacting. "Hence, we need to speak to her."

"Shouldn't talk like you know exactly what you're doing then, old man, should you?" Malakai asked, his grin mischievous.

Milaro left his response as a disdainfully raised eyebrow and beckoned for them to follow.

Quinn fell into step. It wasn't as if she or Mal had anything to do other than trying to figure out how this whole mess of alliances and cosmicisodracus crap fit together. Talking to the Balisor could do them some good. After all, they had no idea who exactly Sarila was working for, or who the person was that impersonated Irias to begin with. Was the poisoning of the forest floor even something that aligned with the whole destroy the Library group?

She was frustrated. While they were getting answers, it seemed for every one of them, they managed to turn around and have five new questions, a new enemy, and a bloody new affinity. Okay, so the latter only happened once, but it had happened.

Plus—had they actually managed to get a trace on the tracker after Jasper died?

"Keep those thoughts in mind," Milaro murmured to her. "I'll be asking you about them later. Don't forget to reinforce and keep your shields up for the duration of the visit."

This time, Quinn gave him a questioning glance.

"Balisors, especially this injured and immunocompromised bunch —don't react well to much directed mind magic."

Quinn nodded. Determined to keep that in mind. She pushed into the room, surprised that Irias's mother, Karella, wasn't there this time.

Instead, the gentle tree teenager sat, looking out of the window that wasn't an actual window, out at a projected image pretending to be on the exterior of the Library.

As they entered, Irias turned to watch their progress across the room. Her eyes shone this time. They weren't as dull as they had been, and Quinn heaved a sigh of relief at the fact.

"Greetings, Librarian," Irias said.

Quinn wondered if it was truly a Salosier thing—where they spoke in such proper tones even when the situation didn't call for it. "Hi."

Milaro remained standing next to the door. Quinn got the feeling he'd fallen short when he attempted to retrieve more information. Nishpa seemed to be almost family to him, but then he had been good friends with Escadril before Sarila murdered him. She could see why Milaro would be frustrated. She turned her attention back to Irias, trying to figure out how to best approach this.

"You have questions." Irias made the statement. It wasn't a question.

Quinn studied her. There were still shadows under her eyes, and her bark, while starting to look healthier, also happened to be peeling ever so slightly. Sort of like the papery bark of a birch tree. "Are you holding up okay in here? Is there anything we should be getting for you?"

Irias blinked slowly and shook her head. "The doctors have been treating me very well, and I appreciate the offer."

"Are you comfortable talking about what happened leading up to your abduction?" Quinn swallowed hard around the word. It felt off to say it. How did one talk about people who'd kidnapped and puppeted them? They'd literally used her image and life somehow to take over and infiltrate and infect an entire species line.

"It was a morphing trick," Irias offered up, and her face scrunched up as she obviously tried to think of how best to express the experience.

Quinn waited with all her abundance of patience.

Malakai stood to the side, offering silent but unhelpful support.

Irias finally seemed to settle on what she wanted to say and spoke up, a small frown appearing on her lips first. "There are rituals to help reinvigorate those of our species. It is a unique Balisor trait. It allows us to consume a small slice of our flesh and transform into that specific Salosier so that we might help medicinally. There are requirements that must be met in order for this to be possible. The first is that the person being morphed into is still alive."

She held out her arm, and it was only then that Quinn realized the left one was much thinner than the right. In a way that showed pieces had been peeled and hacked off and she was lucky to still have a limb at all. Quinn couldn't help but shudder.

Irias offered her a sad smile. "I can regrow my limb. We all can. It is no great loss, and I will be okay. But I am lucky. Had they not wanted to slot into our society as me, I would already be dead."

"You said there were multiple requirements?" Quinn asked, still trying to digest that there was a way to basically clone themselves into other people? She didn't understand, but it was just another notch in her to-do list.

"Ah. Yes." Irias pulled up a blanket to cover herself, shivering ever so slightly. "The second requirement is that there must be a minimum blood relation to make the binding possible. It is minuscule for many reasons. A sixty-fourth. That's it. However . . ." She shrugged and left it blank.

Quinn swallowed, her throat suddenly thick. "That means it was a relative?"

Irias shrugged. "Likely. A distant one. There could be, I guess, ways to deceive the magic, but ancestral magic is always powerful. And we do have many species we are otherwise completely compatible with. It wouldn't have to be a Balisor. All that's required of the spell is that the bloodline exists. I hope this helps. I am tired, but I have vague recollections of Sarila from when she took my pound of flesh. Nothing . . . nothing solid. I will write down what I remember after I sleep."

It wasn't difficult to see how tired Irias had gotten simply from conversing. Quinn cleared her throat. "Thank you so much for helping us. You should probably get some rest."

Irias smiled and reached out suddenly with her good arm to grasp onto Quinn's hand. "Thank you. For helping us," she said, her eyes locked on Quinn's as if everything was direly important.

"You're welcome," Quinn said because *anytime* sounded sort of flippant.

They left the room, and for the longest while, Quinn's conscience felt so heavy she couldn't bring herself to speak.

11

STRANGE MEDITATIVE STATE

THE BEST THING ABOUT DREVICIA SHARING THE COSMICISODRACUS vault with Quinn was the history. Inside the vault, with its starry expanse of a ceiling and carefully crafted books, Quinn felt like she'd found a sanctuary. A whole portion of the floor had transformed into something akin to a bean bag section, where she could drop in and just go boneless with stacks of books surrounding her.

And there were so many she'd need multiple lifetimes to get to them. Good thing she was mostly dragon.

These weren't the type of books in the rest of the Library. Their knowledge had been gathered from even before the Library began. Quinn could feel it. An essence of sorts lingered around every single letter in them, all painstakingly handwritten and handstitched. The leather felt like it had been made from dragon scales that were tempered and softened. Given how large Drukala initially appeared to Quinn . . . she could see how that was possible.

Energy emanated gently from the pages and absorbing them took time. There was nothing instantaneous about it.

The level of power contained within these, the level of energy and magic, coated her protectively.

At least some of them did.

"Are they helping?" Drevicia's shadow was both more and less solid in this room than down in the Core. And it seemed hesitant, as if it wasn't sure how Quinn was taking spending time in the vault.

Quinn also didn't know how to answer that question. She didn't feel she'd found enough yet to answer anything. "These are much harder to process. The magic feels thick. Heavy, even."

Drevicia's shadow nodded in what Quinn liked to think was a thoughtful way. She continued to delve into the book of Drevicia's history with a sense of melancholy. The love of knowledge had always been there, an utter driving force with the presence of a thousand suns, with the motivation and determination to create something that would halt all the destruction.

Whatever the Library had lost by becoming what it was now, it had gained by fulfilling that almost childhood wish to corral the knowledge all into one place and share it out to the masses.

Which brought on the worst thing about the vault.

There was no real sense of the passage of time, and Quinn found herself easily lost in the subject matter she consumed in those pages. Comfortable, lulled into a safe place that she felt no one else could reach, Quinn spent her time devouring all the knowledge she could about the species she was proving to be a part of. If she was being honest, it was rather disconcerting.

And entirely confusing.

She worked her way through the accounts of Drevicia's process to become the Library.

The steps they'd taken as siblings to bring the Library online.

Quinn frowned and moved to grab one of the other journals. "Do your siblings know you have these?"

Drevicia hesitated. "They might assume I have them, or that they were lost to time. Technically, they're rather silly if they didn't think I'd have them. After all, they're just pieces of the puzzles that my siblings and I are. Why wouldn't I keep them if I happened to find them lying around?"

Quinn raised an eyebrow and didn't even have to say a word.

"Fine. Just because they left them here and didn't reclaim them.

They became mine." The Library paused and then asked belatedly. "Better?"

"I don't really care how you got them. Your accounts are the most coherent. Which is a good thing." Quinn paused, placing the current book she was using on top of her already-read-this-and-it-has-possible-connotations pile. It was the smallest pile she'd made so far. "You know . . . Drav said that he'd built in a trapdoor for him to get into your system. Do you think it means into this vault?"

There was a small gasp from the Library, which was odd since it didn't need to draw breath, anyway. "No. Not without my knowing."

"But . . ." Quinn paused, unsure exactly how to phrase this without coming off as a right horrible person. She figured if she was in for a penny . . . "But you've had so many memory issues, do you really think that if he got in, it was without your knowing at the time?"

The shadow just stood there, staring at her as if Quinn had grown a second head.

"Right, so that's a bit of a silly idea, then?"

The Library cleared its throat. "No, actually, it's just—as usual, I've managed to overlook something major, and it's not sitting well with me." Something rippled through the shadow, almost like a true glitch of static.

Quinn frowned and tried to console Drevicia. "You really are too hard on yourself. Right now we have multiple people, including yourself, Lynx, and Harish, working on getting your memories retrieved. It's an important thing for all of us. But it also means you should give yourself grace, because someone took your memories from you and you should be angry and get even, not be upset at your lack of vigilance or something inane like that."

This time the Library laughed. "Thanks. I think."

"You're most welcome. Now, explain to me what sort of relationship you have with your siblings?" Quinn waited, expectantly.

For a few actual moments, there was silence. "You see. It's not like we were created and raised as a family. We weren't like planets, but technically chaos energy is our parent. Sort of an experiment of sorts.

We popped into being one day, marveled at the universe, and then realized the massive sun was going to explode everywhere."

The Library gave Quinn a nudge, as if making a joke.

"Anyway, I was probably closest to Dru and Driv, which makes sense as to why Drav and Dro are currently working together."

"Enlighten me?" Quinn practically drawled.

"Oh, yes. I'm not entirely sure. You know I work well with water and most elements, but each of us has a particularly strong elemental affinity for something. And it was that combination that made it work. It's so hard for me to realize that all this time my brother was planning to undo all of this." The Library gestured around at the entirety of the magical Library. "Don't get me wrong, I spent years setting up the wards around this place and making sure no one could get to this little dimension unless they were specifically calling for the Library. It took hundreds of thousands of years to get all of this right."

Quinn processed that information as well as shifting back into research mode. "Well, I guess there's nothing for it, right?"

The Library looked at her quizzically, as if it wasn't too sure what was going on in her brain. "What do you mean by that?"

"Well, we can retrieve a lot of memories, and some of them will no doubt let us know exactly what happened, yeah?" She tried to sound encouraging.

A sense of melancholy emanated from the Library. "That's just it, Quinn. I don't understand how my brother did this and how I can access all this information while having glaring holes about things I know I should love. I'm terribly sorry, but I don't know what happened, and I don't even know what to look for right now."

And within the blink of an eye, Quinn was force warped out of her comfy bean bag chair and unceremoniously appeared in her office chair with one of Drevicia's books still clutched in her hand.

Quinn scowled and tried to reach out to the Library, but that distant wall seemed to pop back into existence when she tried.

Instead of dwelling or letting herself get worked up about it, Quinn checked how close to bedtime it was and realized she'd almost gone past it. The thing was, she wasn't actually sleepy yet. A bit tired, perhaps? But it had been one of those long days that never seemed to come to an end.

She decided to lean her head back against her headrest, and cross her legs underneath her, and meditate.

Quinn hadn't given herself a good bout of meditation for a while, and she felt herself sinking into a different level of consciousness much faster than she usually would. Perhaps it had something to do with her mind shielding. Finding that new place, the one where she could simply be in her mind and open it to a new level of awareness was sublime.

She could stretch out her senses and feel everything all around her. Where Aradie perched on the back of the couch after being warped there by the Library once Quinn had been deposited back in her office. Right down to the rug on the floor and the different directions the threads ran in.

Quinn could feel as time ticked slowly by, all of it slowed by her ability to condense the time passage in her mind.

In the background, there was the thread of every single person who was currently in the Library. Their borrowing history and their return reluctance, not to mention how the Library had scanned them for threats on the way in. Right down to familial relations, as long as someone from their bloodline had entered the Library in the last five hundred years. Which, in Quinn's eyes, was quite ironic.

Extending herself further, she could feel the species-specific sections as they expanded. It even seemed someone right now was using an aquatic environment. Swimming wasn't Quinn's best talent, but she'd almost be willing to improve if it meant she got a glimpse of an underwater civilization.

Down past every patron, through to the culinary branch, the combat branch, and the alchemical branches. All of them bustling now that people knew they were open. She could focus in on who was on duty in all the branches, and she'd get back an image of the person.

Betty seemed to have completely attached herself back to the Library. The tiny sprite was larger than life.

The dry thought that crossed Quinn's mind pulled her somewhat out of her observations. It was fortuitous that Betty had arrived and taken over much of Jasper's work, or else Quinn and everyone else would be having a much worse time of it. But it also let her realize that she desperately needed someone else with compatible signatures.

Just in case she wasn't as indestructible as the hundred percent cosmicisodracus.

Another deep breath and she allowed herself to sink even deeper. Aradie cooed in the distance.

Quinn sent her awareness down.

It traveled through the floor, through the core chamber below, and continued down until it opened to the cavern below—the filtration chamber.

The blue was practically blinding to her mind's eye.

So many of the pillar had lit back up. Just a few more now and they'd be done.

She could feel the wrongness inherent in Ashiron. It rippled under her skin, threatening to soak through into her body, but she always took precautions, making sure to shield her body. The scales flared, and she couldn't tell whether she'd triggered them by activation or sub consciously just in case.

That was when she realized there was a melody about all the filtration pillars. Right now it was slightly discordant, what with the soul bomb inside the damned thing.

She frowned as she watched it as if she was flying in from above, so she decided to quickly check on the location chamber. Her mark breaking through the one room and rendering the current circle defunct was still there, and the room lay in darkness.

Just as she was about to turn back to study Ashiron in this strange meditative state, a pulse rushed through her.

It ran her over like a tempestuous wave on a beach, stinging without the salt, washing through her as if it was trying to impart all the knowledge possible.

And then it was gone.

But with it came a new sort of clarity.

The connection to the Library buzzed anew—as if it was alive.

Slowly, Quinn opened her eyes.

Everything around her had a freshness to it. Not that anything had changed, not that they'd suddenly got a makeover. But vibrant with its whole history reflected on the surface of each item in the house.

Synchronization complete

Librarian Activation Authorized

Full sensory net initiated

Calibration Time: 48 hours

Lynx popped into being right in front of her, his eyes wild, his smile a mile wide. "About damn time!" was all he said.

Quinn grinned and found that she quite agreed.

12

HARDER TO KILL

EVEN OUT OF MEDITATION, QUINN'S SENSORY REACH SIZZLED IN HER veins—a complete extension of herself, as if she flowed through every part of the Library. It was so much of a deeper connection, she couldn't imagine how the final one would feel.

The sensation was subtle and unavoidable.

Everything around her, even right here in the office, shone like glitter reflecting off the light.

Quinn breathed in slowly for the count of four, held it for two, and then breathed it out again. She repeated the process until the overwhelm happening inside her began to dissipate and the sheen in front of her dimmed enough to separate out her processing.

She knew Lynx was still standing expectantly in the middle of the floor, waiting for a real response from her. And while she totally agreed with his observation of about time, she was still trying to wrap her head about exactly what about time meant.

Calibration was going to take forty-eight hours, and that really made no sense, as she was already synchronized. Or at least that's what she'd thought.

"I don't understand," she finally said, frowning as she still tried to place what had just happened.

80

Lynx watched her, bemused. "But you looked like you agreed."

"Well, I'm thinking that it's a good thing that activation is authorized and that I have a full sensory net activated. Or something like that. But that doesn't mean I know what it means. Why were you so happy that this had finally happened?" She watched Lynx carefully.

Aradie gave a low hoot.

Lynx sighed. But it was the Library who spoke into the room.

The power levels have hit a threshold that allows you to link on a deeper basis with the Library. You're integrating so that everything becomes second nature. You're not fully done yet, but getting close. There's a reason Milaro initially taught you to separate your mind. As the power increases and your sensory net expands, you'll end up needing all that expansion of your mind to encompass the information you'll begin processing.

"Not to mention the power, right?" Quinn asked. Because she knew that wasn't a coincidence. She could feel the rise in energy, the way the tiny hairs on her arms stood up just before her scales began to skim over her skin.

The magic rippled through her lips as she breathed in, down through her lungs, traveling all through her body right into her blood. It suffused with her, completely a part of her body, and yet somehow still separate. Enough that when she used it, her energy and mana centers depleted instead of her life-force.

Quinn knew that instinctively. And yet . . .

She raised her hand and willed her dragon fire into existence. The flame this time was pure white, bouncing from fingertip to fingertip with ease, and a heat she could even feel through her imperviousness. It made her warm in a way she hadn't expected.

The power felt like home.

After a few moments, the Library finally replied. *It's true. Power levels are constantly increasing. Now we have more branches open, more books being borrowed and returned, and more patrons attending. We have a higher rate of energy gathering.* There was a moment's hesitation before the Library spoke again. *I didn't expect your connection to synchronize up like this so fast. Usually, we'd have to be at almost full capacity, but you are clearly not.*

It sounded like the Library was about to say something else, but decided against it.

"Well," Quinn said, flexing her fingers with the feeling of her new scale armor protecting her skin. "I mean, it's pretty obvious, right? My genetics are more than compatible with yours."

Lynx blinked as his eyes went into overdrive.

True. This time the Library sounded contemplative. *In seeking to have our genetic sequence matched so your affinities couldn't help but include those we need in a Librarian, I think this might have been an oversight.*

"But it's a good thing, right? I mean, that I'm so easily able to match up with the Library functions." Quinn didn't like the tone in the Library's voice.

I'm not entirely . . .

Which was when Milaro walked into the room, looking quite harried. His hair wasn't in its neat binding down his back, and for just a second, his eyes appeared wild. That is until he registered they were there and proceeded to smooth down his robes.

Quinn frowned slightly. She'd been sure she'd locked the door. But she'd also been quite preoccupied, so couldn't be certain.

"Took you long enough," Lynx practically growled at him.

"Could have called me sooner," Milaro shot back, a rare scowl gracing his lips. But his poise was back almost immediately. He turned to Quinn. "Okay. What's this about your connection morphing?"

Quinn watched him, taking in all the words, the reactions, and the copious sensations that currently bombarded her body. She knew there was more than just synchronization and calibration. She wouldn't feel like she did if it was just normal growing pains.

"Let me guess," she started slowly. "You weren't precisely sure how I'd interact with the Library as an almost fully engineered cosmicisodracus? You were just guessing and hoping for the best?" Quinn tried not to cringe at the dispassionate way she said those words. Clinical, almost.

Still, it was easier for her to withdraw the emotion from the sensations she'd begun experiencing and look at them analytically. The power coursing through her didn't feel natural yet.

Milaro, to his credit, at least cringed. "Sort of. Our aim was to make sure you had the affinities for a Librarian. The rest was negligible, and this was the only way we could truly guarantee you'd have the compatible affinities required."

"And what . . . 1680-odd others, right?" Quinn cracked a smile, trying to take the sting out of the words. Not wanting to dwell on how insecure it made her feel, she pushed on, effectively changing the subject. "Do we have any theories about all of this?" She gestured at herself and all around her and them.

Milaro narrowed his eyes and then sighed, coming to sit right near her off the side of the desk. "The whole reason we made you was that we needed you. It was imperative, as you know, that you had the correct affinities to even link to the Library with. So when we decided to use the sample as we did, we knew that'd be fine. But without other adjustments, you would have been tantamount to a clone. Which is not what we aimed for."

"I'm not a clone, then?" Quinn's tone was flat as she spoke, as if she couldn't quite believe what they were saying, now he was saying it. Without any emotion attached to it at all. It was her life. She did have a life.

"No, which is part of the reasoning as to why we included other types of DNA into your sequencing, to nudge you toward possessing the perfect skills needed to be the ideal Librarian. Technically."

"Technically?" Quinn raised an eyebrow.

"Well, it's not like you're a robot. You're not programmed for this. You're yourself. All of your life experiences, your relationships, your interests . . . those things all make up *you*. So, the way you interact with your affinities and skills is different to how the Library will do so, for instance." He said it gently, like he wasn't entirely sure how she'd take it.

She took the information in and digested it slowly. "That's good to know. Sometimes . . . it feels like I might be losing myself."

Milaro winced. "I'm sorry. Did you want to guide me in and we can have a look together? See how your protections are keeping up with the overflow of your skills?"

Quinn nodded and closed her eyes as Milaro took her hand. She breathed in and out slowly, guiding herself to clear her mind and accept him into her thoughts. He knew her wards and protections better than she did, so it wasn't exactly difficult.

This felt different to having him in there to help her build protections, however. Instead, Milaro guided her through to her own magical core, and showed her how the magic was called from the outside. How the Library itself yearned for sister magic. Or at least power that could mesh seamlessly with the Library.

Luckily, there was just enough difference that she hadn't yet been devoured. A nagging sensation in the back of her mind cautioned her against developing her skills separately, lest the balance be removed and plunge her into danger of being consumed by the Library as an excess part of herself.

She wasn't going to say she didn't find that scary.

But from the way her affinities and additions worked together in such a seamless way, she was somewhat optimistic.

Milaro helped her add controls into the power that began to overflow. His magic worked smoothly with hers after so long working together. *This way you can regulate. When you feel that power overwhelm, if it feels like you're going to be consumed, then you channel it. You expand your core slowly, but definitively. You use it to strengthen all of your personal protections, and any you have extended to others.*

Quinn nodded, knowing he'd have felt it. She felt around slowly, noticing that not only did her senses extend far beyond herself now, through the entirety of the Library on a constant basis without direction—but she was fairly sure she'd be able to expand on that as well.

Any questions?

She seriously contemplated it. *How far am I supposed to be able to sense things?*

Everything about the Library will eventually be open to you.

I think we've almost reached that.

She could feel Milaro pause. *Interesting. Once this has settled, we might check and see just how far your reach extends now.*

Quinn contemplated if she should tell him. *I don't think it's stopping. I can still feel this strange sensation, like ever-so-subtle expanding. My armor is pulsing out, pushing against my skin. Like it's trying to push me toward something.*

Milaro stilled from his position next to her, and his hand stiffened. All just for a second, but it was enough to give away to Quinn that what she'd described wasn't the norm or, at least, wasn't a good thing. Neither of those options appealed to her.

Can you slow it down, hold it where it is right now?

I thought that's what you'd do? She found it difficult to keep the slight panic out of her voice.

I'll guide you and show you how to feed it back into your personal shielding on a regular loop, so you can check on and maintain it. But I can't be here all the time, so you'll need to continue it yourself.

She nodded again, suddenly feeling hot as the excess magic inside chose to expand.

Milaro dove in with her, this time with a sense of urgency. She thought he was trying to hide from her. That's when it hit her. She wasn't a dragon. She'd never had that form, and she wasn't the Library, which was much larger than a dragon.

How the hell was she supposed to contain power like that? What if more tried to empty into her . . . which it appeared was inevitable?

Breathe. Milaro spoke into her mind, his tone soothing. *Come on, let's divert it.*

They pushed her power through the netting inside to combine with the sensory nets outside as well. After which, he guided her through how to push it into her mind and actual body shielding.

Her arms heated up, her hands stinging, even her fingers felt like they were on fire while her legs warmed up. Reinforcing the shielding allowed the burning to subside after several seconds. She had to hope she'd be able to do this herself if the time came.

Quinn took breaths to center herself, to clear her mind, and hold her goals in her mind. With Milaro's guidance, she created a thread to constantly feed her shielding. It allowed her to finally relax.

That is, until there was a gasp from next to her.

Quinn opened her eyes and looked at Milaro. "What?"

He was staring at her. "You look amazing."

Quinn frowned and looked down, only to realize that her shielding had become a fixture. No more was her armor invisible, but instead slightly blue-tinged translucent scales covered her forearms and hands, and if she wasn't mistaken from the sensations she'd felt, the rest of her body was similar.

"Oh." Quinn wasn't entirely sure how she felt about the change. But she supposed at least she'd be harder to kill.

1 3

———

SO SURREAL

Languid.

It was the perfect word to describe how Quinn felt when she woke up the next morning. Her bedspread was fluffy and cradled her gently. Aradie perched on guard at the top of her headboard, and Quinn never wanted to get out of the warm, snuggly pit of procrastination otherwise known as her bed.

She reached above her head and stretched, twisting her body this way and that in her bed to stretch out the strain in her muscles she could clearly feel as a result of yesterday.

Quinn blinked.

Yesterday seemed important and lingered in the back of her mind. As if there was something she should be remembering about it.

Which was about when the scales covering her arms glinted in the light flooding her room. Quinn frowned as she inspected the gorgeous, delicate scales that now seemed mostly permanent. She willed for them to disappear, and they faded back into her skin. But as soon as she stopped concentrating, they returned.

She wasn't entirely sure what to make of that. So she asked the system. Which only made sense. Wasn't that one of its main functions?

87

Name: Quinn

Age: Irrelevant

Heritage: Earth, Sector 12,942—Infinite reach, pocket Dimensional adaption

*Species: Librarian—of cosmicisodracus origin—determining extent and variations**

Species Power Adjustment: Cosmicisodracus adaption to Library power levels currently at 72%

Power range adjustment: Reaching Capacity

Emergent Involuntary Defensive Capabilities: Scale armored protection, flash fire, targeted enmity clause

Energy Capacity: 6,498/6,498

Mana Levels: 5,432/5,432

Regeneration: Energy Idle: 18 per second, combat 9 per second.

Mana Idle: 16 per second, combat 8 per second

Alignment: 117%

*Affinities: 1723***

Tome Knowledge Expanded: Beginner levels 47% complete. Intermediate levels 19%. Advanced—0.75%—Higher levels not yet available.

Affinity Level: 38

Determination: Extended

**Cosmicisodracus properties established—awaiting additional essence distillation calibration effects*

***As far as the Library can determine*

Quinn blinked at the list. She could have sworn it wasn't that long since the last time she'd pulled it up. Frowning, she tried to leaf through and figure out exactly what had changed.

Species Power Adjustment: Cosmicisodracus adaption to Library power levels currently at 72%

Power range adjustment: Reaching Capacity

Emergent Involuntary Defensive Capabilities: Scale armored protection, flash fire, targeted enmity clause

Well, she guessed that answered her question. She had Emergent Involuntary Defensive Capabilities. That had to be her scales, and since she was technically a cosmicisodracus, then she guessed the scales would present like they were truly a part of her body. It made sense, given her actual genetic heritage.

It just also freaked her out a tad.

But, at least for now, she had some answers. And she'd just have to get used to having this failsafe. But she couldn't get too used to it, just in case.

Aradie finally hooted, and Quinn shook her head, pushing herself up into a sitting position finally. "No, I'm not going to spend all day in bed. I've just had a lot on my plate."

Another hoot, decidedly drier than the last.

"I realize we're all busy, but that's not exactly the point." Quinn dragged herself out of bed, into the shower, and to get dressed, point blank ignoring all of Aradie's attempts to bait her with more strategically placed hoots.

She'd almost forgotten her promise not to warp herself too frequently to travel within the Library. But she desperately wanted food, and then she had to get to the check-in desk and see how everything was running. While she knew the Library was in perfectly capable hands with Betty, Dottie, and Geneva, she still wanted to check over things. Especially since Jasper had passed, meaning some of the tasks required re-homing.

Cook was in fine form that morning. They nodded in greeting, and Quinn felt like their lips moved more in the way of a smile. Maybe the extra added power was starting to perk everyone attached to the Library up.

"I have made hash brown casserole, bacon, and two donuts as a side." Cook pushed the food at her, and continued whatever they were cooking.

"Thank you," she said and pulled out the chair she sat on to each next to their work bench.

It felt more personal, and frankly, it was quieter. While she ate, she noticed they were busier than usual. The whole row of massive stoves had all manner of pots and pans with food cooking in them.

"Did I miss a memo about something important?" she asked around a bite of bacon.

Cook looked over at her for a second after adjusting something on the next stove over. "I was not happy with the standard of the hospital wing's food. For now, until it's sunk in, I am readying the meals here."

Quinn nodded. Nishpa would like that. Which made her think of the Furionas fae and wonder just how much longer she had to stay in the Library's hospital wing.

Watching Cook was almost like entering a trance. They were so methodical, such rhythmic movements were made to chop and dice and cut and stir. It gave her this odd sense of calm as she watched it. Sort of a lulling quality.

In fact, she felt so relaxed she decided to try to test her limits.

Now that they'd set some boundaries and tested some of her senses, Quinn no longer felt like she was about to incinerate the Library at any given moment. It actually seemed easier for her to hit that meditative state she needed for calm, emotional separation, and multitasking. It enabled her to perform everything else at a speed she'd not expected.

Even as she sat there, fully aware that she'd slowed her own time perception down and was working faster than she could comprehend, her reach through the Library was seamless. Power flowed from her in a fluid, sustainable way. Over every shelf, book, nook, and desk, Quinn's awareness swept the Library for any signs of weakness, for any sign of alarm. Neither Milaro nor Malakai were there today, and it did seem that Geneva wasn't rostered on today, either.

A slight tremor that anyone else might have brushed off as a shuddering sigh, or a blip on the radar, spoke volumes to Quinn.

She asked the System for a report on it.

Ashiron Pillar Disturbance Classification E.

Previous Disturbance—18 hours

Frequency has been gradually increasing.

Estimated Time to Collapse of Ashiron Pillar—54 days.

Quinn blinked at the information. Not that it was unexpected, because she'd known there was a timer on it, but that wasn't even two damned months. How the hell was she supposed to figure all this out in such a short time period? Then she found herself biting her tongue, because truth be told, hadn't she figured out much larger problems in much less time?

So far, anyway.

So what if this would totally annihilate the entire Library and its pocket dimension? Surely, she could do it?

Of course, the bravado only went so far when she was willing to believe it herself. Sadly, she wasn't that good an actress.

But she was positive the countdown hadn't been there earlier.

The Library sounded perturbed when it butted into her thoughts. *You'd be correct. It's only just got the calibrations down enough to be able to ascertain just when we can expect catastrophic failure of Ashiron.*

It's okay, Quinn shot back, remembering the plan she'd formed in her mind. She was fairly certain she'd be able to make sure it worked. But to that end, she'd probably have to go down and visit the damn pillar in person. She needed more readings on the power fluctuations and the precise nuance of the magic they'd used to bind or seal it. Maybe it was more important to do this sooner than oh in, like, fifty days and wing it.

She ran a hand through her hair, catching it awkwardly and pulling out the ponytail halfway. With a groan, she reached up and pulled it back into a messy bun instead. The habitual curls still insisted on falling out around her face. If it wouldn't look weird when they grew back, she swore she'd just cut those curls off.

We have a time limit on Ashiron, but we don't know anything knew about how we can get the soul bomb out of there?

Precisely.

Could this be in any way attached to the memories you're trying to retrieve about the time Korradine removed from you?

This time the Library paused before answering. *Technically, it could be. But to be honest, I think it's a total amalgamation of many things. From the filtration system itself, to the sabotage Korradine performed, to the damage caused by the initial insertion of the soul bomb, and then the reinforcement you all provided.*

Quinn nodded, as if it didn't set off her alarm bells. Because she couldn't pay attention to them. *But it says fifty-four days. What I don't understand is that it was fine for almost five hundred years and now all of a sudden it's having a bad day? What triggered it?*

You were there. The pillar has been warded for so long, and the soul bomb itself is unstable. The fluctuations wear away over time and were less with what we have right now. It's not ideal, but we're still standing.

Quinn was starting to think their definitions of survival were a wee bit different from one another. Her scales rippled, as if tugging at her memory. Which was a good point. Didn't she have so much more power right now?

She reached out her senses, focusing down on the filtration chamber and Ashiron in particular. She knew there were ways for the magic around so much filterable chaos to be slightly off. So, she pushed carefully, making sure her grip on her own senses was strong and defined.

There didn't appear to be anything wrong with the seal they'd placed on it, no leakage, nothing that seemed to indicate any type of imminent doom. Still.

Quinn looked up at Cook as she finished off the last bite of donut and grabbed a coffee to go. She walked up to Cook, patted them on the shoulder, and headed out toward the check-in desk. That was first on her agenda now. Go over all the info and make sure the Library itself was actually running at peak performance.

After which, hopefully Malakai and Eric would be around and she could drag them downstairs with Lynx and herself and figure out the damned pillar's riddle. Considering they weren't facing immediate doom, it was probably the best idea.

Aradie swooped down to her shoulder as she made her way brusquely to the check-in desk where Betty and Dottie were deep in conversation.

"I've got everyone organized." Betty, the little sprite, was in fine form today. Her hummingbird wings fluttered so fast it almost made Quinn dizzy.

Dottie, the superellux futora talking bench, simply sighed. "Yes, but we'll need a lot more—"

They both turned to greet Quinn.

"Hey, you two." She was genuinely happy to see them. "Can you give me a quick rundown on where we are with opening the last few branches and if we've discovered any more of the restricted books, we think we're missing?"

Quinn could practically see Dottie's grin as the little bench began in on her report.

Sometimes being the Librarian was just so surreal.

14

NEW TOYS

Somewhere in the middle of discussions with Betty and Dottie, Quinn felt Malakai and Eric's presence enter the Library. The sensation of identifying every single person who passed over the threshold was fascinating. She could have brought up information on anyone who entered the little pocket dimension if she wanted to. As it was, all she had to do was thinking about needing to know when Malakai and Eric arrived, and the wards told her.

"Librarian?" Betty pushed herself closer to Quinn's face, her wings humming as she peered into her eyes. "Are you with us?"

Quinn blinked. "Sorry, just getting used to a few new perks of my abilities expanding." She tried to offer a smile, while still slotting everything into different compartments in her head. She knew it was a time adjustment thing and that it'd get easier the more she did it. But right now, it was still a chore to manage the mass influx of information that kept bombarding her.

It was highly obvious Milaro had taught her those compartmentalization techniques first up because he'd had an inkling she'd need them for more than just multitasking.

"Excellent." Betty beamed and moved away from Quinn's face ever so slightly. "Now, what we need to go over is the current roster status.

I'm in need of several more golems, but with Misha not quite ready and the doctors busy with the hospital, don't you know, it's been difficult to arrange for new golem creation. I'm not suggesting that you take it on, but Lynx has also been busy, and we do need a few to help with the upper levels now that we've expanded and, as you can see, are sure to expand again shortly. Well, might I or Dottie have access to create simple task golems?"

Quinn blinked. It hadn't been long, but she'd forgotten that the little sprite managed to talk almost as fast as her wings moved. It took several seconds for her to parse the information she'd been given. "Yes, I don't see why not." She cringed a little at how long it had taken her to reply, but got straight to it, almost tuning out Betty's thankful reply . . . but only almost.

"Thank you! I knew you'd realize it's the best possible solution. Now don't go thinking we need access to create anything stronger than some of the carts and the shelving golems. After all, we just need to be able to make sure the Library is still running smoothly. You do have so much to do."

Betty sounded like the type of grandma who ushered you over to a table when you arrived and grabbed out freshly baked cookies for you to snack on like she was on a mission to spoil you rotten. Quinn didn't think it possible to frown around the lively sprite.

"There you go," Quinn said as the permissions to create cleaning, shelving, and book transport golems were added to both Dottie and Betty. Though she'd rarely seen them in the Library separately, it was probably best for her to give them both permission, just in case. After all . . . she couldn't be sure how long they'd be there.

The thought was sobering.

Luckily, Betty pulled up some information to share with Quinn and she skimmed over the numbers, glad that they were back to the outstanding book discussion and away from personnel. It was the one thing Quinn didn't feel as equipped to manage: people. There were just so damn many of them.

Main Branch Tome Report

2,895 are still outstanding from the initial overdue amount. 15,147 books returned. No books in reproduction. 321 in repair status. 15 missing restricted books.

Horticulture: 612/720

Bardic Musical: 805/897

Crafting: 682/730

Academy: 679/785

Culinary Arts: 282/282—Culinary Branch Open—2,950 Books of 3,795 remaining, 845 total culinary specialist books returned. Would you like a categorical breakdown?

Yes or No?

Alchemical/Medicinal: 384/384—Alchemical/Medicinal Branch Open— 5,014 of 5,892 remaining, Medicinal ingredients verified and stocked, 878 total specialist books returned, 483 of which are in repair status. Would you like a categorical breakdown?

Yes or No?

Combat: 837/837—Combat Branch Open—8,462 Books of 9,085 remaining, 623 total combat specialist books returned. 212 books in repair status. All books location verified. Would you like a categorical breakdown?

Yes or No?

She sighed and wondered if she could just turn the categorical question thing off as a default. It was likely possible, but she didn't want to take the time right then to figure it out. They hadn't made too much headway since she'd last checked, but the musical and crafting sections were starting to look promising as the next branches to open.

Quinn frowned. It felt like she should be able to obtain more information. Directing her enquiry, she focused on asking the system what else it might be pertinent for her to know with regard to the opening of branches and collection of overdue books.

Note: All branches must be opened in order for the academy to open. Should all books for the academy be returned prior to other branches, then the academy will have to wait. It cannot operate without access to all branches of knowledge.

Please Note: These numbers are those vital books that must were overdue while the Library was offline. Please note that access for all post re-opening overdue books is compiled elsewhere.

Quinn frowned even though she'd known. Now she had it in writing.

Eric and Malakai were approaching, and Quinn turned to speak to Betty. "Just concentrate on crafting and musical if you can? I know Hal isn't currently available to do what he did last time, and I don't expect anyone to go to those lengths again. Just let the books come in organically until we have like a dozen left. Power levels are high enough that it's not the most important aspect we're looking at."

And before Betty could answer, which was a miracle in and of itself, Eric spoke up.

"Might want to rephrase that, oh mighty Librarian." The imp winked at her.

"And why is that?" she asked, proud of the fact that she didn't even sigh when she asked.

"The academy is wonderful, and there are scores of people waiting to get into it." He gave her a wink and crossed one leg over the other while his now fully healed wings hovered him in place, just like he was sitting on a chair in the air.

Quinn counted to three before she spoke. "I'll keep that in mind. Right now, however, I have a ridiculously long list to accomplish and, speaking of which, it's rather fortuitous that I ran into you." It was Quinn's turn to grin.

Eric groaned, and Malakai laughed. "You should know better than to antagonize her by now."

The imp eyed him viciously. "But it's what I do!" he complained.

Quinn supposed he was right. Given the right circumstances, Eric could be rather infuriating.

Before she could say anything else, Malakai moved closer, and took Quinn's hand, lifting it to examine it more closely. She had to fight a blush rising in her cheeks at the action even though there was no real reason for it, because she knew why he'd done it.

"This is really gorgeous you know?" he said softly, looking up at her. "The scales seem so delicate, but I bet nothing will get through this armor on a first or second hit. Probably not even a third. Have you tried it out yet?"

Quinn laughed. Because of *course* her combat instructor's first thought was to test out this new-fangled armor she was sporting. She composed herself and raised an eyebrow. "I haven't yet tested it out. My trainer has conveniently not been here."

Malakai chuckled ruefully as he dropped her hand. "Touché. But we should rectify that."

Eric now hovered around her, checking out all the places where the scales peeked out of her clothing. It just didn't cover her head, although Quinn was mostly sure it would emerge if it needed to. But when it covered her face, she couldn't quite speak, or breathe as well as she'd like. Fine tuning needed to happen.

The imp's entire face lit up. "This is so cool. What else can it do?"

Quinn sighed and extended the shielding to cover both Malakai and Eric. "There we go," she said, showing off a little, even though the effort it took was considerably more than it had been. Her energy and mana levels were high enough now that she could pretty much hold this over the three of them indefinitely if she needed to.

Eric held out his arms in awe. "Seriously? I have like liquid dragon scales?" He frowned and jiggled his arm. "Wait, it's not liquid, just see through?"

Malakai rolled his eyes. "It's scale armor. But it's Quinn's magic. She's protecting us."

"Looks cool all the same." Eric acted like Malakai hadn't mentioned anything new.

Dottie was trotting around the three of them while Betty was already lost in conversation with some of the Library assistants. The bench frowned. "This is unusual."

Quinn shrugged. "I'm not exactly your usual Librarian, right?"

Dottie paused, and Quinn could hear the smile in her voice even before she spoke. "Well, that is an accurate statement. We wouldn't want you any other way, mind now, Quinn. Make sure you don't reduce the efficacy of your own armor in order to protect those who really should be protecting you." Her tone was gentle, but it did hit home.

The thing was, Quinn hadn't ever really been badly hurt. But both

Malakai and Eric had taken substantial injuries for her. Both of which had been unacceptable. "I promise I'll make sure I'm safe as well, but it's always important that I protect whoever I can when we're trying to bring books back."

Which, if Quinn stopped to examine what she was saying, should have made her head explode. Who, in the universe, went out to retrieve an overdue book and had to don armor so they didn't get killed or maimed while trying to collect said tome?

Quinn and her army of vicious Library assistants, that's who!

It was so comical to her in that moment that she had to really tamp down on the laughter bubbling in her throat.

Dottie did that weird movement that passed for a nod. "Just please take care of you. As long as you do, we can all take care of you, too." And then she trotted off to join Betty and the other assistants.

Quinn gaped as she watched her go, trying to make sure what the bench had said actually made sense.

"Close your mouth, Librarian," Eric said as he hovered right next to her. "Don't want to catch flies."

She glared at him, but did close her mouth.

"Anyway!" the imp continued. "Were you just showing off how cool your new group armor 101 is, or did you actually have a task for us today?"

Quinn's glare intensified. "Do you know that sometimes you're not the nicest person?"

Eric shrugged. "Pretty much. I'm an imp. It'd go against my nature."

"I thought I was your wit sparring partner?" Malakai interjected.

Eric rolled his eyes this time. "You've been too slow lately. Quinn is on the ball today, and it's easier to flex my brain muscles with a willing participant."

Despite herself, Quinn laughed. "Fine. Follow me. But don't try to dismiss my armor."

"Why not?" Malakai fell into step beside her while Eric hovered on the other side.

Quinn winked at them. "Because we have to go downstairs and

check on Ashiron, and this way I don't need to get you guys any protective gear because you're already protected."

"That went to her head quickly," Eric quipped to Malakai.

"She does that sometimes. Let her get used to her new toys," the elf responded.

"Just for that," Quinn said, "you two can catch the elevator yourselves. See you there."

And without a second thought, Quinn warped through down to the filtration chamber.

15

A HEARTBEAT

THE FILTRATION CHAMBER SURROUNDED QUINN WITH ITS LOW-LEVEL hum like a hug. She knew she had several moments down there before Malakai and Eric reached her. Unless the imp was racing the elf, but she doubted that'd happen.

Seven pillars were activated.

Just a few more to go.

The serene beauty of the gently flowing mana as it emptied into the lake after filtering lent a soft glow to the massive cavern. The only blip on the radar was the blackened appearance of the one filtration pillar that stood out more than the others. Despite not being powered up, it loomed.

Quinn frowned at the odd vibrations emanating from Ashiron. They were subtle, so much in fact that if she wasn't so concentrated on all the new sensations funneling into her from the Library, she probably wouldn't have noticed. But she did, just like she saw and felt so much more now.

She wished she'd always been this attuned to the whole system before they came down to prevent the last imminent disaster. Because the pulsing from Ashiron somewhat terrifyingly mimicked a heartbeat.

Even from this distance, she could feel it.

Like a subtle undercurrent, pulsing up through the mana, through the energy all around them.

Dum-dum-d-dum-dum.

Quinn closed her eyes to feel the flow in more detail. It was soft, thrumming like a silent guitar, but ever-present. And behind that constant buzz was the thump of a heartbeat.

Is that you? she asked the Library, really hoping that it was.

Is what me?

Quinn wasn't sure how to respond because if that beat wasn't the Library, she wasn't sure what she would do. Taking a deep breath, she worked up the courage to ask. *That heartbeat. Is it yours?*

There was a long pause as she waited, as the Library sought out the sound Quinn had found. *It feels almost like an echo. It's not quite mine, and yet . . .*

But could it have belonged to Korradine? Is she somehow still alive in there and her heart is still beating? Quinn tried her best to keep the panic out of her voice. But on top of having obtained her more enhanced abilities, there were too many negative possibilities for this heartbeat to be a good thing.

Unlikely. The Library at least sounded convinced of that. *But it is very subtle. On such a level that it almost blends with the filtration noise. It means I've missed this for a rather long time.* And the Library sounded put out by that. Perhaps even concerned.

Quinn nodded and decided then and there that a visit to Harish was advisable and not just to see Misha. She wanted to see the diagrams and readings that poured out of the Library's information stream. Surely there should be relevant insights there.

They'd obviously missed something. And she still thought herself enough of an outsider that she could probably see something none of them were looking for, or expect to see.

But again, that was later.

Right now, they needed to focus on the heartbeat and whether it was connected to the soul bomb. Quinn was also quite curious to see if other people could sense it. Not to mention she wondered if it had only appeared or become loud enough to be detected once the energy levels in Library increased.

Malakai and Eric arrived, and Quinn already felt like she'd been down there forever without them.

The elf scowled at her ever so briefly. She could tell his heart wasn't in it. "That warping thing you can do is so not fair, do you know that?"

"Hmm." She wasn't really paying attention to what he said. Not properly, anyway. All the little sounds around them, the vibrations, the smells . . . it all blended together in a new way, a strange way. If she didn't hyper-focus on a specific area, then she ran the danger of overloading herself. Especially down here.

While she'd known the filtration chamber used and generated a lot of power, the sheer volume of it and how it thrummed had been lost on her.

Now, however, it felt alive.

A part of her understood now why a dragon had decided to become the Library. Short of creating another little world or something similar, how would they ever have gotten the concept of the Library off the ground? That Drevicia had basically sacrificed herself to become this—was both beautiful and oddly melancholy.

"Quinn?" Eric sounded irritated. "You can't keep spacing out like that."

She blinked at him, pulling herself out of running too many scenarios and thoughts through her mind. "Sorry, what?"

Eric tapped his foot in midair. Which was an accomplishment and a half. "I said you can't keep spacing out like that. It's rude!"

"Well, you'd know, right?" She flashed him a grin and turned her attention toward Ashiron while Malakai tested his flight jumps a couple of times. She turned to him after a few seconds. "You're able to use mana now, right?"

He nodded. "Fully recovered. Only took me way too bloody long."

Quinn throws her head back and laughs, suddenly feeling rejuvenated—like they would solve all of this. And maybe, just maybe, like not all hope was lost. She wasn't sure how long that feeling would last, but she'd take it while she had it. "Seems like there's no time like the present, right?"

"Obviously," Malakai said and was about to speak further when Eric interrupted.

"Except. What are we doing down here? Did you figure out how to fix it? I know you took Geneva last time, and Milaro—is this even something you *can* fix?" Then the imp got that smug look on his face. "You're overestimating things again, aren't you?"

"Be nice," Quinn muttered as she got her bearings.

"I'm being practical." Eric crossed his arms.

Quinn sighed and turned to face him. "My abilities have increased; my magical awareness is growing, and there are certain things I can pick up on now that I couldn't a month or two ago. We are here because I can feel it every time it hiccups and, while extended, the time we have to shut this down and not blow up the magical filtration system of the universe is slowly running out. We are here to see if I can discover more, and to see if that helps us figure out how to shut this down without blowing the universe up."

"Oh." Eric's hands fell to his sides, and he shrugged. "Why didn't you just say so?"

Quinn counted to three again.

Malakai jumped out first, his flying steps rebounding him higher until he re-initiated them before dropping almost to the top of the lake. Quinn much preferred her own method of flying, which was more of a hovering-through-the-air thing. Much less potential to fall into a lake of mana and probably drown. It looked a lot thicker than water, and she wasn't about to test it out.

The underlying thrum was so prominent when they arrived on Ashiron's base that Quinn almost stumbled. She glanced over at the others—well, at Malakai, since Eric was hovering—and realized that the elf didn't have any trouble. Did her newly deepened perception mean she was more affected by things, too?

She frowned as she walked around the base of the pillar. That black miasma was gone now, but she could feel it, just beyond the surface, waiting . . . perhaps even boiling up, rising until it could leak through the cracks again.

Malakai spoke softly, as if worried he might startle her. "Did you even need us down here?"

"For watching my back. Just in case." Quinn gave him a small smile, but her attention was split three ways to Sunday, and she had to focus on the pillar to make sure she understood what was just out of her reach.

On the tip of the tongue as it were.

"Always got your back, Librarian," Eric muttered from where he hovered to the left of her. He was watching out over the huge mana lake, while Malakai's attention was more on the pillar and Quinn herself.

"Let us know what you need," Malakai said.

The thing was, Quinn wasn't entirely sure why she had brought them with her. They weren't Milaro; they couldn't guide her through any type of magic weaving or affinity combination. They were, however, people she could trust to get her out of there if something went wrong and her reactions were delayed.

They were her chosen family.

She closed her eyes and reached out a palm to place against the pillar.

At first it did nothing. No recognition. Nothing but stone against her palm, filters pulsating with their weird red and black glow that told her she was lucky her scale armor warded her against pretty much everything.

And then the heartbeat pulsed through her fingers.

Gently, and so softly she thought she imagined it at first, that slow, faint drum of a beat echoed through to her.

She focused on it, pulling all the power she'd gained, all the sensory details she didn't need to allocate to anything else and wrapped it around herself like a warm blanket. It allowed her to block out the rest of the world and home in on that beat.

Once she'd caught it, it was easier to trace.

Her mind whirled, creating a web of the runes Jasper had so

lovingly shared with her, the things she'd only just begun to teach her . . . and mimicked the tracking circle in her mind.

It was probably a dangerous thing, but they had less than two months to figure out exactly what this damned soul bomb was about, or else remove it, and Quinn didn't have time to go around being overcautious.

Besides, after the car explosion, she was reasonably sure she could protect the Library from complete destruction if something went wrong as long as she channeled all her power into her shielding.

She followed the beat as it zoomed around, circles and circles that led her nowhere, coming back to settle right inside the Library.

Quinn pulled back ever so slightly, blinking rapidly, a frown on her face. That didn't feel right. There was something she wasn't remembering about the runic circles Jasper showed her.

Surely.

Walking around the pillar again, the beat accompanying her inside her head, she examined all the filtration modules at her level. Nothing seemed out of place.

Or at least it didn't for an overrun, mostly broken, totally derelict pillar of magic filtration.

Because that was a sentence she'd expected to utter in her life.

Just as she closed her eyes again, she got a glimmer.

It wasn't a big thing, and if she hadn't been intent on focusing on her own shielding, she'd likely have missed it, because the spark ignited in her peripheral vision and was barely discernable. But she saw it, and she clung to the image as it dove back inside the pillar.

Where they'd secured the bomb.

Quinn's outer awareness floated over the seal they'd performed, as if she were watching herself doing this from a great height. She examined it from all angles. Running it through a series of gentle tests for the validity of artifacts that had been in one of the books she'd absorbed recently.

Something tugged at her mind all the while. As if she was missing something.

Korradine tried to sacrifice herself and take the entire Library with her. After years of deftly manipulating multiple key players, including the bloody owls, within the place in order to reach a level where she could end, literally, everything. Lynx had thwarted her. In doing so, he'd sealed her away.

She was gone. There was no essence of her around the bomb anymore at all. Nothing.

But what if . . . what if the essence wasn't around the bomb? What if there was something of her inside it? Buried so deeply, so far down, that only maximum power would draw it out again.

Quinn didn't like that thought, because she was fairly sure what maximum power drawing out something like that would mean.

And right then it was only conjecture. She needed to see the others in order to figure things out.

Taking a deep breath, she centered herself again and opened her eyes. "We have to get back up. I need to talk to Lynx and Milaro."

She warped, probably unwisely, from precisely where she stood. But not before she heard Malakai and Eric curse her for making them take the damned elevator.

16

EASIER TO PERCEIVE

Lynx, as always, was as easy to locate as sending out a request for him to turn up. Milaro, however, for once, was back home, actually managing his kingdom. It was the first time Quinn got frustrated by it.

And yet, she understood the why.

Milaro was a king. Despite his obvious enthusiasm for the Library, he did have an empire to run.

Quinn's office had become the regular meeting spot. Lynx, Malakai, Aradie, and Eric gathered therein. With both Hal and Milaro absent, it felt somewhat empty.

"You seem troubled," Lynx stated.

Apparently, Quinn wasn't as good at controlling her facial expressions as she'd thought. "Somewhat. I wanted to wait for Milaro, but I think it's better to go ahead and tell him whenever he gets here." She could already feel the headache starting and knew she'd been overusing her focusing abilities lately. Something about gradually building up endurance in it, which, as usual, she'd paid no attention to.

Diving headfirst into things wasn't usually her style. Or at least, it hadn't been back on Earth. Everything she did was considered carefully. But everything had seemed so rushed, so imminent, so important since the moment she got there, that there really hadn't been much downtime to getting herself acclimated properly to the new skills.

Lynx was looking off into the distance again, his eyes flickering. Even if he wasn't more aware now, his memories were returning, Quinn didn't have the energy anymore to do silly things like balance books on his head. Maybe she would again . . . once this was all over.

"I just need to understand the beat underneath Ashiron. Or perhaps within it?"

"Beat?" Lynx cocked his head to one side. "What beat?"

Malakai shrugged while Erik grumbled out a "No clue. I couldn't hear anything over the waves of the mana lake."

"It's low frequency, soft, almost like it's asleep." Quinn bit her lip as she tried to ascertain if she'd really been hearing it.

She closed her eyes and took deep breaths, centering herself so she could seek it out again. From this distance, it was even more difficult to differentiate. Just that soft blip on her radar, so to speak.

"It's very faint. Sounds like a heartbeat to me. I've only just begun to hear it now my abilities are settling, and the power adjustments are evening out." Quinn looked up at Lynx expectantly.

He frowned while his eyes worked overtime. "I don't believe it's attached to the bomb."

"You can hear it too?" Quinn couldn't believe how relieved she felt. For a while there, she was fairly certain it was in her head.

"Faintly. And to do so, I pretty much just have to access the neighboring pillar. The vibrations are easier to perceive there." Lynx blinked his eyes back from the connection. "I'll look into it."

For a fraction of a second, Quinn hesitated and then squared her shoulders. "Do you think Harish could show me readouts and reports of areas where the Library has missing chunks? Not that I think I'm some amazing sleuth or anything, but I was wondering if a fresh perspective from someone of the only recently magical variety might offer a different viewpoint."

Lynx seemed puzzled more than anything else. "Of course he

could do that. I mean, all the information in the Library is at your fingertips, or even just your brain tips?"

Quinn actually chuckled because that didn't sound anywhere near right, but she knew what he was aiming for. "Okay. I'd like to go and—"

But she didn't get any further as the Library spoke into the room. *I'd prefer to go over the memories that have been retrieved first.*

Quinn balked, not quite willing to believe that the Library had already retrieved said memories. Surely their luck didn't quite hold out to that extent. *Are you serious?*

Why wouldn't I be serious?

You've been known to have a sense of humor occasionally. It wasn't exactly a lie. The Library had become more human than it was before Quinn arrived. It was noticeable too.

In this case, however, I come bearing . . . odd news.

Define odd.

There were a couple of long moments, so long in fact that Quinn contemplated double checking that the Library was still present. Except she could sense it just like she could sense so much more about everything now.

Finally, the Library spoke. *To be honest, it's difficult to. I've continued to reach out to Drivok, but the waking process appears to be almost as slow, if not slower than Drukala's. However, I've also managed to dig deep and trace those memories Dru has and I do not.*

"Well, don't keep us in suspense," Quinn said, starting to get frustrated.

She could almost hear the Library raise an amused eyebrow. *It has taken a while to access these memories. I think . . . I think it might be best if I just share them with you and Lynx at the same time.*

"Share them? Shouldn't Lynx already have access?"

Not to everything, especially not this sort of subject matter. But we are currently all in this together, and we'll need to know it anyway. The Library took in a few seconds before continuing. *Let me know when you're ready, but you should probably sit down.*

Quinn wasted no time in clambering into her massive, comfortable chair and curling her legs up under her. It was probably inviting pins and needles once she was done, but for now she needed comfort and relaxation and that was about what she had here. She closed her eyes, pretty sure that experiencing a memory would be much like dreaming if her own memory recollection was anything to go by, took a deep breath, and spoke. "Ready."

The effect was almost instantaneous.

Her body shifted into a wisp-like substance that felt solid, weightless, and intangible. Yet she could maneuver, and there, she could see the faint human ghostly appearance of the Library when it took human form. Or humanoid form, perhaps?

This appeared to be a run through of many memories, as if showing Quinn what a normal interaction was like as opposed to the altered one. Several flittered through. From when the Library was fresh, and much smaller. With maybe a few hundred books. Drukala roamed around with Drevicia, marveling at the way the doors worked. At being able to open them and gaze upon different terrains and other worlds. Of dreaming about how far-reaching this healing could be, and just how great it would be for the universe.

Quinn's own shade just observed.

The next memory was a visit, just by Drukala with none of the others in sight. reminiscing, talking, meeting another Librarian of a species Quinn's brain couldn't even comprehend. They flashed through more visits, more time passed as the Library grew in size, as branches opened, as the filtration system cavern expanded. Librarians changed constantly. Lynx was ever present.

Owls flew back and forth, all around, their feathers gleaming. The bookworms glowed in their encasements, and it felt like the affinities were alive in every single corner of the building. Quinn wanted to return it to that level of glory. But to do so, she had to fix Ashiron, and she was starting to worry that might not even be possible.

Still, she clung to some hope.

The golems scattered throughout were similar and yet not the same, and the halls flourished, with hundreds and maybe thousands of people visiting at once. And that was just milling around the front entrance, which seemed ten times larger than it was now.

It was larger before I broke.

There was wistfulness in that tone, a rotting sadness that permeated all other sensations.

Quinn pushed back her anger at those who damaged the Library. Their agenda ruined such a great thing for so many, and out of pure selfishness. Quinn wanted to understand their motivations. She wanted to know how to change their minds. But no matter how she looked at it, there was nothing for it.

And finally, Korradine began to cross their path.

Drukala arrived shortly after the new Librarian was integrated into the system.

Korradine's voice had a strangely melodic quality to it. Not unlike a lullaby with a discordant note. Quinn could tell, and perhaps it was because she was looking for something to be off, that every single word out of her mouth was close to or completely a lie.

"I was checking on the restricted vault." Korradine's eye was huge in her face, and her skin shone so brightly she practically sparkled.

And yet, Quinn could have sworn there was a fuzzy dark outline around her, even in this memory.

Next, Drukala visited some vast amount of time later if the state of the Library was anything to go by. Several thousand years, perhaps. Not that it changed much, but it appeared the Library liked to do some redecorating every so often. Subtle changes like colors, book spines, and shelves. The intricate carved work on the pillars also appeared to change semi-regularly. Quinn wondered if it still did that, or if it was a full-power sort of frivolity.

Perhaps it was the crystal clarity with which all the other memories had appeared that made it so obvious to Quinn which one had been tampered with. There was a haze around it as it began, a sort of static interference, and the words were difficult to understand. Korradine and the shade of the Library were in the restricted vault, all on their own. It made Quinn want a lip reading 101 book to absorb. She'd have to check on that later.

She had to pause and motion for the replay of the start of it because she'd missed what it was Korradine said.

Her face was twisted in a sneer, the skin around her eye drawn and strained. "Where is the book?"

The Library pulsated around in the vision, like it was affronted by the tone. Quinn could feel the connection between the two was tenuous at best. Strained at worst, and to a certain degree practically forced. "Which book?" it managed to grind out.

"The Parsneauvian book!" Korradine snapped. "Don't play with me. You know what book I mean, don't make me repeat myself constantly."

"Why would you want that book? It's in my vault." The Library was livelier now, more alert, more aware, even though it still appeared that Drevicia had pulled herself out of an almost hypnotized state. It seemed to be wavering in that consciousness now it had spoken up, as if the drain of all the energy it took to be alert for a moment was all it had.

"I need access to that vault."

"You're not getting it." The words were so clipped, so deep, and so commanding, that Quinn almost didn't believe it was the Library. But then she remembered when the Library sometimes snapped and ordered her to sleep or eat . . . Quinn generally obeyed.

Not the case for Korradine. She looked like she'd been slapped and backed away a few steps, but then her eyes narrowed, and she moved forward again, a sneer tilting her mouth into an unattractive snarl. "You'll regret that."

A console appeared in front of her, all static and lines, and barely discernable to Quinn, but she could see it despite the interference. The scene kept tugging her deeper.

"You'll regret it oh, so much," the former Librarian repeated.

That tone made Quinn's skin crawl, like something had wiggled under her skin and set up a nest. She shuddered.

Sadly, Korradine continued. "Tell me where the book is. Tell me where you put it."

"No! This is not . . ." The Library sounded indignant, irritated, and perhaps even a little bewildered at not being able to get the words out it obviously wanted to say.

Quinn could sense as the energy rippled through the memory, adjusting and adapting things, pulling away from the sides like an old Polaroid being burned. But there, right in the heart of the picture, there was a truth.

Something ripped. As if a photo had been torn apart, one side peeled from the other to reveal the Library's memories. They flashed so fast Quinn couldn't get a read on any of them until Korradine stopped briefly.

A thud echoed through the entire structure, and all around where they stood in the restricted section.

"Ah." Korradine's voice was cold. "Damn it. This was days ago. Weeks, even."

Something about her countenance tugged at Quinn. A memory of being scared, of feeling like everything had been pulled out from under her. It reflected in Korradine's eyes in myriad ways.

"Damn it," she muttered again. "I planned everything so carefully. Why did you have to go and ruin it?"

A tug tore at Quinn's consciousness, just for a split second, bringing a sting of pain as the memory tore and dissipated.

It left her panting there in the office with way more questions than they'd started with.

17

MURDER BOARD

For several seconds, it felt like time had stopped.

Only Quinn knew it hadn't as everyone else was still breathing. They just weren't saying anything. Perhaps, like her, they were waiting for the Library to speak. To be honest, she wasn't entirely sure how much of that Malakai, Aradie, and Eric had gotten wind of, but she knew both herself and Lynx had a full play-by-play.

Finally, a sigh rippled through the room. *That was entirely unexpected.*

Quinn raised an eyebrow.

At least the Library had the good grace to chuckle dryly. *I mean, before you told me, my memories were literally gone. Not just altered, but that some had been removed. It's disconcerting to witness how it happened at such an intimate level.*

Quinn wasn't entirely sure how to approach her next questions. The Library was a massive entity. It had evolved so far beyond anything it had been as a cosmicisodracus that it was difficult to comprehend the scope. However, Drevicia had been a dragon, and there was a part of it Quinn was certain struggled right now.

Now I've seen it, I remember it. The memory slots in with all my others in a surreal sense. The melancholy leaked away from the voice, and it was several seconds before the Library spoke again. *As far as I can tell, I'd been suspicious for a while. Something wasn't adding up. Lynx seemed overly scattered and often not where he said he'd be. Korradine didn't appear to be getting the intricate work done I needed. Managing difficult retrievals, accessing branch expansions, overseeing the modification of personnel rosters . . . there was a lot. I set the Library to record more than usual, to specifically take down her movements. I'd completely forgotten about that.*

The latter was spoken with a detached sort of wonder. As if she couldn't believe she'd forgotten so much. A wave of determination washed through the room now. *Well, at least I'm aware of what that type of memory loss feels like. I'll have Harish help me go over other memories. Actually, we'll just scan all of my memories from 465 years ago and back and see if we can find any more such glitches. I'm quite certain, as much as it pains me to admit, that there'll be more.*

"Perhaps. But you can't blame yourself." Although Quinn knew saying that wouldn't help one bit. Being the Library with a Librarian who was specifically out to sabotage you, that didn't sound like a barrel of laughs to Quinn. It sounded quite dangerous.

I'm only blaming myself for not being more observant. There was steel in the Library's tone now. It had gotten over whatever small pity party it had allowed itself. Now it was down to business. That was another fine quality Drevicia seemed to have.

"Well then?" Malakai asked, piping up for the first time since the Library experienced the memory. "What's the plan?"

That's when Quinn knew they'd definitely all been able to see it.

Before Quinn could answer, the Library spoke up. *Harish and I will scan back and see if there's anything even close to that time involving any of my other siblings. Any memories with the same cadence that would signify a chunk of it missing. Driv is waking up but is still sluggish and has yet to respond in kind. I haven't achieved summoning him here yet.*

Eric piped up. "Hal should be back in a couple of days. He had some things to update us on about Kajaro and Ikeshal."

Quinn felt a lump rise in her throat at the mention of Ikeshal. She'd always had a soft spot for Hal's general. The satyr was a likeable sort. Honest to a fault, and quite blunt, but steadfast.

As for Kajaro? After he'd planted a mind bomb in her head, she wasn't precisely the most sympathetic to anything to do with him. However, when she'd asked him if he had nine lives or something out of frustration because he seemed like a damned cat, he'd indicated the affirmative. Which left Hal, once they'd imprisoned him, to figure out just how those nine lives worked.

So, yes, in her mind, seeing Hal was important. That and Uncle Hal was sincerely one of her favorite people that she'd encountered so far. She quickly calculated the most recent things that had popped up. Figuring out just how Drukala's taking the book had been wiped, and how Sölem managed to track them when Quinn went to retrieve the book. Not to mention taking care of the ritual circle downstairs.

She could practically hear the time limit on the damned soul bomb ticking down.

And there was the dream intrusion by Dro and Drav—and why couldn't they have picked names that weren't so bloody similar?

Quinn pinched the bridge of her nose and took in a deep breath, holding up her hand because right now her working through things quickly wasn't functioning the way it usually did. "Give me just a few, okay?"

"Not going anywhere, darling," Eric said with a smirk, and then frowned.

Quinn laughed at him. "That wasn't quite an insult, was it?"

"No," he said, for once sheepish, "No, it was not."

The tension in the room, however, had gone down a few rungs. Even though Eric might play the fool semi frequently, the fact was that the imp sort of knew what he was doing. More often than not, he provided distraction for those who needed it, levity for situations that required it, and oddly insightful commentary when a puzzle warranted it. Overall, she was grateful he was on their side.

They'd added so many new things to the lists that Quinn felt like they'd have to be completely revamped again.

Settle, the Library said, but this time it was into her mind.

Just between them. It was strange just how easy it was to relax with that voice in her head. Any of them, really. Like she knew, even when her thoughts began to pick up speed and start over-analyzing that she wasn't alone. *Thanks,* she shot back. *Just trying to get my head around the sheer volume of things we need to get done.*

One thing at a time. We just figured out that they did indeed take a memory, and that it was Korradine in specific. This has now given us the signature of a type of memory removal we weren't aware of. By tracking down anything with that signature, we'll now be able to pull any information we can from both Lynx and myself. This one thing we've done has led to solutions for other things we need to do and find out. There was a brief pause, as if allowing Quinn time to digest it. *Now, pick another thing on the list, any of the lists, and make your way through that. Control what you can. Do one thing at a time. Do not tie yourself up in knots. I need my Librarian operating at peak capacity, not floundering because there is too much.*

Quinn mulled that over, seeing the wisdom in it. There was so much truth to those words. And yet . . . *You realize just because you make it sound simple doesn't mean it actually is.*

I know. But you can force yourself to deal with it in a simplistic and manageable way. Life is but the choices we make. Every single one shapes the path we take. We can and will find the way out of this mess.

Well, that was getting rather philosophical, and true. *Yeah. I know you're right.*

I have several diagnostics I need to run over the Library wards and protections. I'm worried I've missed something.

Any idea what? Quinn tried her best not to sound alarmed.

No. It's one of those . . . I believe you call them gut feelings, and I've had so much going on that some of my functions have been running on autopilot. I need to do a precise inventory to ascertain they're all functioning within predicted margins. Frankly, it could be paranoia. But I'd prefer to be safe rather than sorry. Especially since I still feel highly suspicious about many of the actions portrayed in the memories. Almost like they've been altered. Both you and Lynx can contact me should you need to.

Be careful, Quinn said, unsure exactly why . . . but there was the sensation of a nod as an answer before the Library's presence retreated once again.

Malakai suppressed a yawn and flashed a guilty look at Quinn. "Sorry. Standing around is not my favorite pastime."

She raised an eyebrow. "It's not like I'm not doing anything just because I'm standing here. You should try multitasking sometime."

Malakai laughed. "No thanks. I prefer to dive into danger without planning anything."

Quinn wasn't sure why that struck her as funny. Perhaps it was because Malakai always seemed to be the one with the plan when it came to fighting. But it didn't matter *why* it mattered that she laughed. A full-throated, loud and free laugh. It eased the tension in her stomach and allowed her, briefly at least, to regain some clarity of mind. "Thanks. But we should probably try to figure out where Crown's book is. Until we have all the other information we need, all the things we're waiting on, I don't like sitting around twiddling thumbs."

Lynx piped up. "I still have the vague location we got." It was like he tried to avoid saying Jasper's name, which was probably a good thing with it being so raw still. "*The Crown and Fall of Pocket Dimensions Due to Spatial Interference* . . . this one will be tricky. I'm unsure about the location—although we can likely use the same method to find this one as we employed to find the Parsneauvian one."

Quinn was opposed to that. Though she doubted the way Jasper found the previous book triggered her death, she didn't really want to take a risk that it wasn't a complete coincidence in that regard. The lead they had on it, without Jasper to do the tracking ritual, was tenuous at best. Which was an oddly frustrating experience for Quinn.

Malakai spoke up, interrupting her spiraling thoughts. "Wouldn't that book help a lot of the stuff that's going down? I mean, couldn't that even help with the soul bomb downstairs?"

"That . . ." Quinn blinked up at him, surprised. "Maybe, I'm not an expert, but . . ."

"Probably. Very likely actually, once I've looked up what it should be about," Lynx said absently, the bulk of his concentration elsewhere. "I mean, because of its removal from the database by wiping and covering her tracks, Korradine effectively took away most of the information about it. But I have cross-referenced it to other books that have used it as a source and thus . . ." He paused, looking around at the mostly blank faces. "Well, suffice it to say, that could help us."

Quinn clapped twice to get everyone's attention. "Okay! That's all sorted. We try to locate the book with a closer guesstimation, hunt down the last of the books to open the crafting branch, try to figure out the dream thing, and frankly, I think we need to go all murder board on who makes up the Sölem."

Eric blinked at her, a look of pure glee crossing across his face. "Excuse me, did you just say murder board?"

She blinked back at him, slightly confused. "Yeah. You know, a murder board like they use in crimes. Where they pin up all the relevant information in order to link pieces to each other with string . . . or whiteboard markers and try to narrow down leads, et cetera. So we can figure out exactly which factions are against us, and who else might be behind all this, because I have a bad feeling it's not all as it seems."

The imp seemed to deflate ever so slightly. "Oh . . . so not an *actual* murder board, then."

He sounded so disappointed.

Quinn couldn't help but laugh.

OUT THE DOOR

THE MURDER BOARD, AS IT TURNED OUT, WAS MUCH EASIER TO DESCRIBE than to actually plan.

Quinn pulled back, quite proud that the Library had been able to create something akin to a whiteboard. It'd serve the same function, at any rate. So far, however, she had relatively little information on there.

Who exactly is Sölem?

Which was just the problem, wasn't it? Were they the ringleaders? Or was that the name of the conglomeration of different species and factions that made up?

Aradie hooted very deliberately.

Quinn threw her hands up in the air. "I know! That's just it—I still feel like all we have are bits and pieces."

Aradie didn't make a sound, but the stare she gave Quinn spoke volumes.

"I know, I know. Just look at what we do know," Quinn said in a mimicking voice.

Her owl pecked her ear lightly.

"You sort of do sound like that when you speak." The Librarian rubbed the edge of her ear. "But I get it. I'm just procrastinating that

I'm not entirely sure how to approach this." She tapped a finger against her lip as she considered the board with literally no information on it.

Could she have done this on her console? Sure, she could have. But there were such benefits for her making an actual visual list manually. Something about memory retention and being able to see things in different lights.

Eric fluttered up to her shoulder, a bar of some sort of food in his hand that he tore at thoughtfully. "So. This is what you've got?"

She didn't dignify that with an answer.

"No, really," he said. "Looks like you've got it solved." But that was as far as the imp got before he broke character and laughed.

"I'll remember this," Quinn said, narrowing her gaze. But he was right. She didn't have anything.

Yet.

She sighed and moved forward, hoping that the whiteboard type marker the Library created for her would work. First up, she wrote down *Balisor infiltrator? Identity?* Then she backed away and frowned. They didn't have any idea who it was. She'd died while still morphed into Irias. It gave them nothing to go on.

Necromancy wasn't exactly a lauded affinity, but instead an amalgamation of specific ones that had to be established in order to achieve such a result. Rare as . . . whatever was really rare. So it wasn't like they could even figure it out that way.

She added Esposian factions, sedimentites, Aracnios, and a few other species to the list. She'd list the exempt factions on the other side once she had the main stuff down.

"That's all you've got?" Malakai spoke suddenly from next to her, but he sounded like his mouth was full.

Quinn glanced at him and realized he was eating something that looked suspiciously like a tub of popcorn. "Yes," she snapped. "That's all I've got so far."

"Ah," was all he said before he shoved more popcorn in his mouth.

"None of you are being particularly helpful." She sighed as she added her next set. Because she wasn't sure about Korradine's angle.

There was something niggling in the back of her mind about the way the Unusceros Librarian had gone about things. Well, everything. It rubbed her the wrong way, even.

Not that she didn't believe Korradine had acted of her own free will. Oh, no, she might have been influenced, but she'd been swaying in that direction long before. Frankly, Quinn was fairly certain she had been an intended plant all the time. The evidence pretty much said so.

But in that case, was it just Korradine acting in that manner, or were the Unusceros as a whole also a part of the grander plan? Because if that were the case, then didn't they have bigger problems? Ones that reached a lot farther than she'd originally thought?

She moved to the middle of the board and wrote Korradine's name there, with a line and a circle to Unusceros with a question mark. Taking a couple of steps back, she admired her handiwork. It needed pictures and string if she was going to do one of those procedural show murder boards, but . . . she also just liked using lists.

"It's just a list," Lynx said, popping in next to her. He sounded puzzled. "Why did you call it a murder board?"

Quinn rolled her eyes. "Lists are great things," was all she said and frowned, her attention back on that specific list because she knew she'd left something vitally important out.

She continued to add, while totally ignoring Malakai's popcorn crunching, a few more names. Like Kajaro, and the cosmicisodracus. All of them. By Dra, Dre, Dri, Dro, and Dru. Dri was the only one she had to keep a question-mark under. While the others had already divided themselves.

But what for and why exactly? Those were things she still couldn't put her finger on.

That chaotic magic needed to roam free and not be caged by a filtration system? That seemed like such a crappy justification for mass genocide. Even when the argument was extended to include that the weak would be tested and found wanting by chaotic magic and only the strong would survive. None of that made sense. There were no guarantees that anyone would survive chaotic magic, breaking free in its raw, destructive form.

So just where were the guarantees coming from?

She noted that down too, up in the right-hand corner.

Everything had, or if Dravishk's conversation with his sister was anything to go by, been planned since the Library's inception. He'd also added a failsafe. Or at least, he thought he had. Whatever he'd done, it hadn't worked. Was soul bomb what he'd meant by a trapdoor? She didn't think so. Where did Sarila come into all of this? Why were the Balisor's almost wiped out in the way they were?

She pinched the bridge of her nose. The headache was coming on fast now. There were so many avenues, so many paths to track.

"Well." Malakai sort of cocked his head to one side as he studied the board. "I mean, they wanted to stop the filtration system from purifying the mana and leave it in its true form, right? That's their whole schtick?. So why did the siblings allow the Library to be built in the first place? What did that get them?"

Quinn ran over his questions. They were good ones.

The Library chose that moment to speak up. *My siblings, at least, as far as I knew at the time, didn't want to be devoured. We had friends in many other solar systems, too. Thus—it was largely self-preservation, and that of those we knew and loved. Putting them before the chaotic creation elements that were turning on all of us.*

Malakai nodded, still chomping away. "Yeah, I get that. But . . . if Drav and Dro actually wanted to welcome chaotic magic as their overlord and master or whatever, why would they have helped you build the Library in the first place? Especially if they were building in something to hopefully sabotage or destroy it in the future?"

There was a lengthy pause. *I don't know. I never realized they'd done that until Quinn had that dream visit.*

"That's just it," Eric interjected. "They not only admit to sabotage, but in premeditated destruction of you and your system. Why would they have even helped in the first place?"

The Library was quiet for a little while. So long, in fact, that Quinn felt sorry for it. *Like I said. I don't know. But I do know Drukala wasn't involved, and I'm fairly certain my youngest brother wasn't either. But I have to wait for him to wake up to find out.*

"Do you know who was the strongest?" Malakai asked, as if he was idly curious. But Quinn could tell he'd latched onto something. "Like was it you, Drav, Dri . . . who?"

Quinn could practically hear the Library frowning with thought.

Well . . . me, I guess? That's why I was the one to become the Library. I needed Drav's dimensional travel shift. But realistically, I could have obtained that in other ways. His power was just easiest.

Silence fell over the room after that, and Quinn didn't like the connotations one bit. "So, let me get this straight." She spoke softly, gathering her thoughts as she did. Noticing that Milaro had also managed to let himself into the room with food in hand.

"Your siblings and you agreed on this plan to make you into this huge knowledge-and-energy depository that would be effective against the downsides of chaos generated magic—by removing the chaotic element. As the strongest and probably"—Quinn glanced around and nodded to herself—"most stable of the five of you, you all worked together to create the Library. A sharing of magic between everyone, having found a way for magic not to endanger lives?"

Well, I guess? I mean, Hal was there too. He's been around almost as long as us. He has a few siblings too, but they've always been a bit preoccupied with their own wars.

Quinn nodded. "So the five of you and Hal helped build you—helped transform you into this." She waved around behind her and the office at the massive expanse that was the Library.

Quinn, get to the point.

That was just it. Quinn was trying to figure out how best to phrase it. Her thoughts were leading her, but she wasn't entirely sure if she wasn't just being a total conspiracy theorist. "Whose idea was the Library?"

Well, mine, of course. I did have a penchant for all knowledge. I had to know everything. Still do. It's why the memories have been so painful to lose.

"Like the cruelest punishment, right?" Quinn asked softly.

Another pause before a very soft *Yes.*

"Do you think your own magic could have withstood chaotic backlash?"

Likely. Not guaranteed, though. Stopping it from devouring planets wasn't exactly on my agenda, but I'd been looking into ways to modify spatial displacement to help with that. I could always manipulate aspects of it, just not as a whole. That's why . . . And the Library paused. *Ahhhh. That's why Drav suggested it.*

Sadness practically dripped off the last words.

"I'm not saying that's what happened, just that it's a hypothesis."

"Wait." Milaro seemed confused, which was a rare occurrence. "The Library was created because Drav assumed he'd be able to eliminate Drev?"

Quinn shrugged. "Perhaps. It's a theory. Makes sense. Why else would you make the most powerful of your siblings even more powerful?"

"Point." Milaro frowned. "It makes a weird sort of sense, except that it backfired and I don't see why he wouldn't have thought it would backfire."

Superiority complex. Plus, he never looked into the potential of system filtration. I don't think he ever understood just how much power could be gathered and dispersed by the filtration system. Hal and I were quite proud of that, you know.

Quinn smiled as she continued to write down tidbits and theories on her board. It was looking much better now.

"But we haven't learned anything," Eric complained. "We already knew Drav was a dick. I don't get why the why he was a particular one recently makes a difference."

"Because it helps solidify a timeline. I need to know how far back it goes—not only time wise but also person wise." Quinn circled the Unusceros again. "Next, I need to figure out just how long Korradine was a plant for . . . and if she was an outlier of her species or if the entire species was in on it. That's our next stop."

"But we haven't finished figuring out the ins and outs of Drav yet," Lynx said, and then his face lit up. "But that'll come as we put more pieces together. Let me pull up all the history on the Unusceros species for you. They're rather unique, you know."

Lynx's enthusiasm was obvious and slightly contagious. Malakai continued to eat popcorn.

"Keep trying to reach your youngest brother?" Quinn asked the Library.

Yeah.

The Librarian felt a pang for the Library. Sometimes one needed perspective outside of themselves. And the Library had just received a huge dose of that.

Lynx made a whirring sound and pulled Quinn's attention from the whiteboard. His eyes lit up, and he focused on her. "Harish said Misha is about to wake up."

Quinn didn't even think twice about dropping her marker and heading out the door.

19

SUPPRESSING LAUGHTER

Quinn wasn't even out of breath when she made it to Harish's laboratory. Although she wasn't sure that was what she should call it. It felt more like a research and control room.

"Ah, Librarian," he said without looking up.

"Quinn." Siliqua flashed her a brief smile before going back to her console. "We're almost done here."

"Great." Quinn couldn't help the butterflies of excitement she felt in her stomach. This was a good step. To have their supervisory golem back in a functioning capacity would be fantastic. "Will Misha be . . ."

"Be?" Siliqua murmured in response as she divided her attention.

" . . . anything like they used to be?" Quinn finished off. She could sense the others had come in after her. She'd jogged ahead, considering she was eager to see if Misha was already awake and functioning.

Siliqua actually looked up at Quinn. "I thought Harish explained. There will be elements of Misha that are gone because they were never theirs to begin with. But we do have hope that a large portion of their personality has remained because of the time we took to delicately separate the two entities that were intertwined in their core.

However . . . there are now gaps there that will need to be filled in with new experiences."

Quinn wasn't sure how to respond to that, so she just nodded. It was a lot to take in.

Siliqua reached over and tugged Quinn to the massive projected console she stood at. "Look. See this diagram?"

It was a spherical item that looked much like the cross section of a baseball. Quinn nodded.

"See these lines that work their way intricately from the sides and all the way through?" Siliqua waited for Quinn's confirmation before continuing. "Those are the pathways that developed. Where you see blank ones, those need to be refilled in whatever meaningful ways Misha chooses. But, in the grand scheme of things, at least their core was mostly unchanged. Misha fought hard for themself. Things will be okay." She reached over and gave Quinn's hand a squeeze of reassurance.

Quinn was grateful.

"All right." Harish spoke up. "I think we're about ready if you want to go stand next to the pod."

Quinn didn't need to be told twice. She moved over, with Lynx standing next to her, and Malakai on the other side. Both Milaro and Eric hovered around, unsure of their required location.

A whirr hummed through the room and Quinn watched the pod as it began to glow. She looked down and saw Misha's face as it began reforming. Quinn was relieved to see the fine hair spin itself back into being, the moonstone eyes form and the eyelids over the top of them slot into place. The thin line for the mouth and the habitual silver with an underlying black tone as it all came together.

Misha would at least look the same as they always had. Everything else? Well, they'd know soon enough.

Finally, with a brief hiss of hydraulics, the lid opened and slid down.

Quinn stood there, practically holding her breath while she waited. Surely, Misha would remember them.

The golem in the pod sat up, almost reverberating in place. Moonstone eyes flashed through silver and blinked rapidly.

Misha gripped the side of the pod and leveraged themself out within seconds. They stood there, acclimating it seemed, perhaps running through their connection and self-diagnostics, maybe even figuring out who they were and where they were.

Quinn didn't want to break the spell. After all, the golem legitimately looked like Misha. So she stood her ground and waited, as much as she would have liked to bite her nails instead.

"Calibration question." Misha's voice sounded the same. That faint metallic cling to it.

"Proceed," Harish intoned, as if he were accessing base commands. Quinn wondered if that was a thing with the system.

"Data corruption at zero percent. However, there are several data inconsistencies and holes. Clarify."

Harish frowned and his fingers flew over the console as he typed whatever it was he needed to do urgently. There was a brief beep and Misha whirred briefly.

"Much better." Misha moved their arms, stomped their feet, and did several pat downs of themself. Then they turned to Quinn. "Librarian. It is good to see you."

A small smile flickered at the corner of Misha's mouth.

The relief that flooded through Quinn when Misha greeted her was almost indescribable. She hadn't expected this. Wanted it? Of course. But she'd been so sure Misha, who'd basically been there since the beginning, had been taken by this whole damned fiasco of a Library thing too. It was amazing how full of life the last six months had been.

"Misha." Quinn hoped her voice carried how much it meant to her that Misha had returned.

She swore the golem wore a smile.

"That I am." This time there was a slight downturn to the golem's mouth. "Strange there are . . . discrepancies. Several books we need to go over. I do believe I stopped them from being able to retrieve the ones they wanted. But I seem to be at a loss for some of the last few months. I do apologize."

Quinn just blinked at the supervisor golem. "Do you feel yourself, mostly?"

"Yes, but I can find gaps where something has been removed." Misha turned to look at Harish. "What are these, and how do I solve them?"

Harish cleared his throat, reaching back to touch a few keys before facing the front again and carrying on. "You cannot solve them. They are no longer your memories to use. "

Misha frowned again, and the moonstone eyes glittered brightly through many phases and several possibilities. "I do see. He succeeded in taking me over, then?"

There was a defeated tone already in their voice. As if they remembered glimpses of the internal battle they'd endured, remembered standing up for the Library and the connection, and remembered what it was to stick to one's convictions.

The supervisory golem cocked their head from side to side as if testing equilibrium before taking a few very cautious steps. They moved around the pod they'd climbed out of, slowly becoming more sure of their movements with every step they took. Another shake of the head. Several more steps. Expressions flying over their face at a rate of . . . well, fast.

Quinn watched, fascinated by the way Misha was recalibrating, adjusting. The room watched as Misha continued to test limits, push boundaries, and then eventually rolled their shoulders as they turned to face the other occupants of the room.

"Did you remove the invader?" Misha asked.

Siliqua stepped forward. "That we did. How do you feel? How are your pathways? What of your core?"

Misha stood, that same small frown tugging at their lips for a few seconds. "I am missing key memories of my tenure here. But nothing until several weeks ago. Wait." Their eyes turned into darker pools very briefly.

Quinn only hoped that meant they were looking inward or behind or something that didn't mean another core was about to take them over.

"Yes," Misha said. "I believe the glitches I seem to have suffered became substantially more pronounced about three months ago."

Harish let his fingers fly over the console, inputting data, tracking down graphs and information if what Quinn saw on his screen projection was anything to go by.

"And before then?" Siliqua pushed gently.

"Normal. Or mostly normal." Misha paused. "Of course as the Library itself was witnessing some problems, I thought mine were occurring in line with those. I do apologize for worrying people by not reporting them. I never, for even a second, though these were unique to myself."

Siliqua's fingers tapped a soothing cadence into her entries. "That's a good sign. You're being analytical. Not run by anger."

"I do apologize," Misha said suddenly. "I seem to have lost my connection to the Library. I cannot access any of the databases to make sure work has been completed in my absence."

"It's okay. When the Supervisor reared his head, we shut off your access temporarily in order to safeguard the Library." Quinn spoke gently. "It's good to see you back. How do you feel?"

"Wise decision." Misha, it seemed, understood the motivations. But they paused briefly, as if contemplating Quinn's question. "As for how I feel? Right now, without my usual access, I feel sort of distanced. I recognize all of you. And have a certain fondness for most of you."

Their gaze lingered briefly on Eric.

"Hey, that isn't fair! Why am I the only one you don't remember fondly?" Eric grumbled.

"Do I really need to elaborate?" Misha deadpanned. But Quinn could see they were at least partially kidding. Eric's penchant for hefty fines was a running joke, and Misha was more of a by-the-books sort of golem.

"Excellent," Quinn said, clinging to this as a silver lining. After all, at least Misha had been able to be saved.

"What must I prove in order to assume my role again?" Misha asked.

Siliqua cleared her throat. "We just need to run some diagnostics, make sure everything is free of Supervisor, double check your creation was correct this time, and then Quinn can reallocate your permissions."

Misha nodded. "I am ready for the tests."

And just like that . . . Misha was back. Well, sort of, anyway.

"Should I stay?" Quinn asked, unsure of this whole procedure.

"Oh. No. I just thought you'd like to be here when they woke up. You've been worried for ages about this." Siliqua gave Quinn a soft smile. "You're almost as bad as Nishpa with the worrying."

Quinn rolled her eyes. "Fine, I'll be in my office. Come over when you're ready, Misha. I'll get you all set up then."

They left Misha to undertake their tests while Quinn decided she needed to look into the murder board some more.

Something was eating at the back of her mind. Nibbling away at her sanity, taunting her with something she'd forgotten. Milaro said his farewells for now as they approached the office, but Malakai, Eric, and Lynx came along with her. Aradie was preening on her perch when they got in.

Walking up to the board, Quinn frowned.

She hadn't put those weird dreams up there. Not the one between Drav and Dro . . . and not any of the other hints she'd gathered. Because hadn't they said there was a way to get into the Library? That Drav had built in a failsafe, or at least thought he had.

Which meant there were likely weaknesses in the protections placed around the Library, in the very wards. How did they go about finding those in the first place so they could reinforce them?

Obviously, just rebuilding or strengthening wards upon wards wouldn't help if one of the lower or original building blocks was faulty. That would only cause the entire structure to come falling down around their ears.

"What's bugging you?" Lynx asked, prodding her arm with a finger.

Quinn shook her head. "That's just it. I can't quite put my finger on it. I feel like it should be jumping out at me, like it's on the tip of my tongue."

"Share."

She looked at him. "What do you mean, share?"

"Your thought process. Most of us might be able to use telepathy, but your wards are formidable, and you haven't invited us in. So talk to us. Share the thought process so we can all work on it." Lynx crossed his arms and tapped his foot impatiently.

Quinn realized she'd totally forgotten she didn't have to do this all on her own. "Oh. Yes. Of course." And so, she went through her current thought process since she got back to the room and waited to see what the rest of them thought.

Lynx's eyes went crazy, and this time, Quinn did balance a book on his head.

He growled softly. "My glitches have almost been fixed. I'm aware while connected now. Stop balancing things on me."

Quinn laughed and removed the book, oddly annoyed that part of her fun had just been removed. "Ruin all my fun why don't you," she asked rhetorically.

Malakai frowned at her board. "You know. If we strip away the protections and rebuild from the ground up, that leaves us too vulnerable."

Quinn resisted the urge to roll her eyes. "Yes. Quite."

"Don't be like that. I'm sorting through it verbally."

"Sorry." She cringed.

"Anyway. Couldn't we build a second wall, for want of a better word, right next to the original and just get rid of the original after the new one is done?"

"Technically." Quinn mulled it over. "But that might also not address the breach. However, they're getting into the Library, into my dreams, in through the wards to get to the ritual circle and leech off the information . . . however they're doing that? That's what we need to shut down. And while I keep thinking there are more important things out there, anyone with nefarious intentions breaching our security won't bode well."

She sighed. There really was only one thing to do.

"You know what we have to do, right?" Malakai asked, obviously suppressing laughter.

Quinn grinned. "Yeah. I'll see if we can coax Hal over."

2 0

NOT ALL POISONS

Quinn flipped the book over and frowned: *Bahillel's Magical Detection Guide*. Not that Hal would bring poison with him, but she was rather apprehensive since she'd been poisoned by some random person last time she went to visit Halschius. Even though she didn't want to admit it, if someone could get past the wards Hal put up, if someone could reach her there, then didn't it also stand to reason they'd be able to reach her right here in the Library?

Thus, she'd searched and asked and hunted down a book that could help her. It had sections on all types of ailments and hidden affinity afflictions. Some of it was dark stuff. But she figured, while she waited, and because she didn't want to drive herself up the wall by constantly trying to remember what she'd forgotten to add to the murder board, that instead of wasting time recalling whatever it was, she'd absorb the book and see if any of the application in it could help her.

Not to mention that she was the Librarian and her track record of encountering people who wanted her dead was getting longer.

She ran over the directions once again, and focused her eyes, placing herself in a brief meditative state while she took in the information.

Magical Aura Affinity (MAA) allows you to do many things.

Identification. Interpretation. Alteration. Manipulation. Dedication. Nullification.

Should you have all of these, no one will ever be able to cast a spell on you that you can't see coming, poison you with any type of poison, or slip you anything else nefarious.

As long as MAA remains active, it feeds information back to its caster, allowing them to ascertain differences at varying power levels. But even if the detail isn't as intricate as one might expect, it will always flag if the subject is harmful to the MAA caster.

Intermediate books, as expected, had more complex topics. Still, Quinn reckoned with all the affinities she possessed, that this should be relatively simple. All she had to do . . .

But it was more difficult than she'd anticipated.

Aradie hooted one long low note from next to her, and Quinn scowled briefly.

"It's not that easy. I have to locate something and scan it but know what it is that I'm trying to scan or else I won't know if it worked." It sounded perfectly logical in her head. But when she said it out loud . . .

Aradie hopped forward to sit next to her and gave her one of those looks.

"Fine." Reluctantly, Quinn opened her eyes and activated her Magical Aura Affinity in order to observe Aradie.

It was almost like she had one of those weird visors people used to wear in movies as some new-fangled technology. All of these numbers and swirls began to emanate from Aradie. She couldn't make heads or tails of it, but what she did notice was the abundance of blue energy suffusing her.

"Right, then." She stood up, pushed herself back from her desk, and headed out to go get Farrow, Aradie gliding effortlessly after her.

Farrow's appearance always threw Quinn. The Caretaker looked like a living tree, but more in the way of an oil painting tree than a real one. Sort of cartoonish, in fact.

"Librarian." She inclined her head in greeting and waited.

"This will sound really weird," Quinn started. "I need to borrow something poisonous to put in a cup of water so I can see what the aura of poison looks like in order to potentially prevent disaster from striking me."

Several long seconds pass before Farrow nodded very slowly. She walked two terrariums over and plucked a sprig of . . . something out of it and then over to one of the huge washing basins at the other end of the room.

Quinn dutifully followed, unsure how she should act in here. She'd always meant to come and check on this area but things always got in the way. After all, she knew every other aspect of the Library in far more detail. "Your helpers aren't here today?"

"Everyone deserves a day off, Librarian. I do seem to remember you making a point of it." Farrow's smile took any edge off the words.

Quinn chuckled because they both knew she was just trying to make small talk. Which was seriously one of Quinn's weak points.

After running a cup under the water and thoroughly washing it, Farrow placed water into the cup, dropping in a leaf of the plant she'd picked up, and muttered something under her breath that Quinn couldn't quite pinpoint.

Engaging her Mental Aura Affinity, Quinn kept her eye specifically on the cup. A haze formed around it, tinting it ever so slightly red. It wasn't vibrant, so if what she'd absorbed was correct, then it wasn't a deadly poison, but would make her ill.

Still, she wasn't going to drink it.

Maybe she'd just have to get used to constantly engaging her MAA.

"Thank you," she said to Farrow finally. "Sincerely really appreciate this."

"Always." The Caretaker frowned ever so slightly. "Are you all right, Librarian?"

Quinn paused, seriously considering the question. "Yes. Just trying to tick all the boxes I need before I need them."

"Wise choice."

Back in her office after snagging something from the kitchen,

Quinn realized it was late in the day. She was a bit confused about what task to undertake first.

"What do you think?" she asked Aradie, but for once the owl didn't offer an opinion.

Quinn studied everything in her office through her Magical Aura Affinity because it was fascinating. MAA basically gave her different vision, and she could see herself utilizing it regularly. There was a book up in the right hand corner of one of the bookshelves that, if her understandings of the MAA readings were correct, no one should ever touch.

The knock at the door startled her, because was so engrossed in her studies, she barely heard the sound.

"Little egg?"

Quinn's head snapped up to see Uncle Hal standing in her doorway.

"It's good to see you expanding your research into your magic," he smiled.

"Good to see you too, Uncle Hal. How have you been?" Quinn gave him a cheeky grin. "If you'd told me about MAA when I first met you, I'd have superpowers by now."

"Don't you already have those?"

"Touché!" She laughed. "Are you ready to give our place a once over now?"

"That's what I came to see you about." He sounded somewhat hesitant.

That didn't sound ominous at all. "Fine. Spill the beans."

He raised an eyebrow. "I need you to come and check in on Kajaro and Adrito."

Quinn stared at him. She sort of understood him wanting her opinion on Kajaro because he'd been so set on wiping her and the Librarian lineage out. But she wasn't sure what else she could do to help Adrito, not when he was frozen in stasis. Still though, Uncle Hal was one of her favorite people. "When?"

"Preferably now . . . unless you really need some sleep."

"I do need sleep. Lynx will kill you and then me, otherwise."

He grimaced. "How long do you need?"

"Just give me a few hours nap, okay?" Quinn wondered if it was normal to be so excited about traveling to Halschius. Then again, not much about this new life had ever been dull.

21

NINE LIVES

Quinn wasn't exactly sure what she expected when Hal popped into the Library to ask her to come to Halschius, but this wasn't it.

They weren't in the massive dome that housed the strange mind-reading projectors like they had been when Adrito somehow broke through the defenses and attacked her. This wasn't about figuring out what they knew, what hints they might give the Library and allies to help track down the saboteurs and break the hold they still had.

No, this was about figuring out just how Kajaro's magic worked.

Enemies who could just keep coming back to life wasn't conducive to any ends. They needed to put a stop to it.

She didn't expect the sheer white room. And once she realized it was this bright white, she certainly wasn't expecting the cracks of lava that ran along the walls and floors, like veins bleeding beneath the surface. Heat didn't permeate the room. In fact, it was quite cool.

Which was necessary considering Kajaro's ice prison balanced right in the middle of it. He looked just the same as he had when she originally sealed him in it. His forked tongue ever so slightly out of his mouth, his snake-eyes narrowed into almost slits, and his hands positioned as if they were just about to cast.

She had to tamp down on the instinct to throw a damned fireball at his face.

Aradie nipped her ear, having chosen to come this time since so much had gone wrong the last time they visited. It seemed the owl wasn't leaving anything to chance and had spent the bulk of the time getting to Kajaro's room, glaring at Hal.

Malakai stood off to the side, his hand on his sword, at ease, and yet, given their history visiting Hal, constantly aware. Eric hovered next to the satyr, squinting at Kajaro as if that might somehow grant them answers.

And Quinn wasn't entirely sure what she should be doing. "Going to need some direction here, Uncle Hal," she said, trying to get some sort of input. Her nerves were also shot, and a bit of direction would help calm them. Kajaro was well preserved. From scanning him, she knew he was back at full health, but the prison it seemed was more robust now than the initial layer she'd created.

Hal hadn't answered yet, so Quinn kept going. "Look—it's obvious you made some improvements to my makeshift ice prison. Are you sure you can handle him if he breaks out? He's back at full health and everything right now." She couldn't keep that sense of worry from her voice.

Uncle Hal finally looked down at her, as if her words had just registered. That's when she realized he'd been doing much the same as Lynx always was. Communicating with integral parts of his strong-hold, probably organizing troops and generals and whatever it was one did when at war with a bunch of siblings.

He flashed her a smile. "Sorry. Still getting some things sorted on the side. We can handle him. This room has several fail-safes that guarantee he won't be a problem even if he were to break loose. I won't risk a repeat of last time. When I can't be guaranteed of what might happen, I have to plan for every eventuality."

Quinn nodded. "So what am I here for?"

"Aw, little egg, you wound me. You're not just here for the pleasure of my company?" His eyes twinkled merrily, insomuch as blood-red eyes could.

"I promise, when everything is solved, I'll visit for no other reason than to have you make me a hot cocoa."

Uncle Hal threw his head back and laughed. "Excellent." His eyes narrowed and his expression grew serious. "Now we've got that out of the way, we've been analyzing his blood, his DNA, his sequential magic aggregate."

Quinn cleared her throat. "His sequential magic what now?"

"Sequential magic aggregate." He squinted down at her, a measure of shock in his features. "What have they been teaching you?"

"Don't make it worse, just tell me."

"Affinities. Technically that's the official language when referring to affinities—but it goes a little deeper than that."

Quinn crosses her arms. "Then just call it affinities next time."

"Sure. Next time we have another psychopathic, resurrecting snake, I'll make sure to call it that."

The Librarian laughed, and she heard the sound echoed in Malakai and Eric behind her.

Hal looked like he was the one counting to five this time. "As I was saying. We've checked everything. And there are several notable areas in his genetic makeup that don't correspond to what . . . well, to what he is. Or at least to what he presents as."

"As in species wise?" Quinn asked.

"That, and the type of mage he's supposed to be. He appears to have a lot more affinities than registered and on top of that a lot of them are mind based. Frankly, before he placed the mind bomb with you, as far as anyone else was aware, including any of the system that reaches us, he didn't have *any* mind affinities. No mind reading, no mind manipulation, no mental affinities at all."

"Well, I hate to break it to you. But he definitely does now." Quinn watched Kajaro, frozen in his stasis. No movement, nothing to even indicate he was alive except the monitoring station several feet away from him and its infinitely slow beep that showed the slow heartrate of a frozen, cold-blooded being.

The longer she watched him, the more she realized that Hal probably wasn't going to say anything until she asked more questions. Or else he was preoccupied. She took a risk on it being the former. "Fine. What do you need me to do?"

Hal didn't answer for a while, almost long enough for Quinn to wonder if he'd heard her in the first place. When she was about to ask the question again, he finally spoke.

"You've been working closely with Milaro for a long while. I realize you've hit the advanced level in a few of your mental magic capacities. When it comes to shielding and controlling a dream-state domain, Milaro has nothing but praise for you. I believe"—he looked down at her, a rather fond smile on his face—"that this is the one magical area you are no longer quite an egg in."

"Thanks." Quinn fought down a blush. She didn't think Hal metered out praise very often, and it made her proud to have made the cut. Despite him insisting on still calling her an egg. "Go on."

Hal chuckled. "Very well. We believe, that if we set up our system in the right way, which we've been experimenting with, you should be able to either enter his domain, or pull him into your own and figure out his resurrection ability in more detail. He's warier of myself or Milaro. But for you . . . we believe he might be inclined to show off. Even subconsciously. The only way we can stop him from using the ability is to disconnect it so he no longer cheats death."

A shiver of dread ran down her spine. Quinn forced herself to take nice long breaths. Deep and in for four, hold for two, out for four. Rinse and repeat. She had to do this while watching him, remembering how much pain he'd put not only her through, but Escadril and Malakai. And those were just the people Quinn knew.

She'd be willing to bet there were hundreds of thousands or millions of people's lives he'd affected already.

"Give me a bit." She cast around to try and find somewhere to sit, her gaze falling on a set of chairs over in one of the corners behind her.

Sitting down, she closed her eyes with her legs crossed and concentrated. She needed to center herself, and to trace through the information she'd absorbed. Something tugged at the back of her mind, calling to her, as if she should know the best solution for this—right on the tip of her tongue.

Quinn dived into any and all information she'd gleaned on traversing someone else's thoughts without causing them damage. Even with accelerated processing it still took her a ridiculous amount of time to find what she was looking for. It made her realize just how much information on mental affinity-related abilities she'd absorbed and already possessed. A lot of which she'd already used, intentionally, or not.

And there it was.

Cogulatio

Thought walking is an ancient art form that requires an even temper, finesse, and respect of inner sanctums. Winding oneself though the thoughts of others needs to be done with intrinsic levels of trust and consent, lest the mind be hostile. While pure force can overwhelm a mind and retrieve the necessary information, it can permanently damage it. Information retrieved in such a hostile way is also not always trustworthy.

Quinn frowned, pulling herself back out of her head. She knew only a few minutes had passed, but for a second, she had information overwhelm from the amount she'd sifted through to find Cogulatio. It wasn't the perfect solution, but it was the only realistic option for her.

She frowned, unsure if she should risk it. From all the information she had, it didn't appear to be dangerous for herself, just for either Kajaro or the information. She highly doubted he'd hand over information willingly.

Malakai moved closer to her. She didn't even have to open her eyes to know that.

"Any luck?" he asked softly.

Maybe he'd noticed the tension enter her body again once she'd got done. Perhaps he'd just been hanging around her too much for the last six months. Whatever it was, Quinn was glad to have him with her.

"Sort of. I have a possibility." She chewed on her bottom lip for a couple of seconds, letting the couple of sharp stabs to her lip give her a sense of clarity to think over the situation.

"Is it a risky possibility, or a dangerous one?" he asked.

Quinn knew why he asked. Dangerous was bad for the Librarian. Danger could potentially mean bad things for the Library, since she wasn't of cosmicisodracus age yet. How the hell did the other cosmicisodracus survive out there in the wild, put there by chaos to float around while it created worlds?

She shook her head and pushed herself to standing, stretching for a moment, before moving toward Hal and beckoning Malakai to come with her. Flashing a grin at Mal, she shrugged. "You know, I'm not sure. I think it's riskier for the information we'll get, depending on how I approach this."

Hal turned to her, eyebrow raised. "And just how do you suggest we approach this?"

But she ignored his question. "Are you sure we shouldn't wait for Milaro?"

The King of Halschius shook his head. "No, he's busy right now doing his actual job—which is good since we need all the strong empires we can get. Also, Kajaro has a deeper connection to you. He might be willing to part with information to you that he wouldn't give anyone else. Even if all he's trying to do is taunt you."

She nodded slowly. It made sense, even if it did make her feel slightly vulnerable. "I get it. The only thing with this is, I'm going to need his permission, or else any information we get could be corrupted."

Hal frowned at her. "Permission? As in you need to ask him if it's okay to go prodding around in his head for secrets?"

"Technically. There's an actual incantation that if he agrees to it, he'll have to allow me to find what I find once I invoke it. If he declines it, however . . . everything, including my connection with him in there, is fair game."

"Sounds a bit too risky, don't you think?" Eric piped up, concern furrowed his brow.

Hal seemed lost in thought for a second. "It sounds riskier than I anticipated." But after a moment he continued. "How about, if he doesn't agree, if his consciousness tries to bait you or otherwise leads you to believe it could be yet another one of his traps . . . we'll wait for Milaro before going in again?"

Quinn mulls that over. "Fine. Just let me make some preparations."

She didn't tell them that she had to calm her nerves before she did anything. Quinn couldn't tell if it was fear, or anticipation. She hoped it was a healthy dose of both.

2 2

NO IDEA

"Are you sure, Quinn?" Malakai spoke softly, a hint of steel in his voice. Like he'd figure out another way if he had to.

She shrugged. "It makes sense. I'll be careful."

And before she could second guess herself, Quinn took a couple of steps forward, leaving a few feet between her and the ice prison. Close enough that she could feel the cold emanating from it. Just a breeze of it, but it was there. The constant chill.

Quinn allowed her mind to softly brush against the outskirts of Kajaro's. No response. Which was pretty much what she expected. She backed out and went over her own shielding again. She filled in cracks, strengthened and expanded walls, and did everything she could think of to keep her own thoughts out of the equation.

To protect herself.

All she had to do was meet him in his own thought space and keep the upper hand. Shouldn't be too difficult, right?

"And you're sure the wards and shielding around this space won't let him trigger anything external, correct?" Quinn was proud of speaking without an obvious waver to her voice.

Hal turned to her. "I promise. We've been over it with multiple experts, multiple reinforcements. And I'm here and have applied my wards. This is the safest way to do this short of transporting him to the Library, and then there's potential danger to all the patrons. This will be fine. I'm right here."

Quinn nodded and took a couple of deep breaths. "He's not conveniently hanging out on the surface level of his thoughts, just so you all know. This'll take some digging to get to him." She pushed down the nerves, locking them away. There wasn't time for her to second guess herself, and there wasn't room for fear past caution. She locked everything away that might interfere, closed her eyes, and let herself sink into a semi-trance.

The surface of Kajaro's mind was desolate. Windswept granite, with nothingness echoing through. His walls were sturdy. She could have walked along them for eons and never made her way in. No, she needed to intrigue him enough that he'd be willing to talk to her. Lying mind to mind should be difficult. For both of them.

While his consciousness was deeper than surface level, she could feel a sort of presence. Very faint like a netting overlay for mosquitos. There but not obtrusive. She willed herself to seek a door. But nothing happened.

Not being her own mind, of course, that didn't really surprise her. But she pushed further, deeper, recalling the strange, castle-like structure she'd found herself in so many months ago after which Milaro had to help her expel the mind bomb. That whole area was filled with stone walls and floors, sconces and dark corners. There were nooks and crannies, and so many places to hide.

She visualized it, and moved slowly, asking for the wall to let her into that mindscape, that dream world where Kajaro had tried to trap her, where she'd managed to eavesdrop on him. His internal one. Quinn didn't let herself think about whether it would be a wise thing to do, or if she should take another approach.

Her gut told her to go with what she knew, so that's what she did.

A click resounded through her head, echoing like a dropped pebble in a church.

The wall rippled, and an opening showed itself. Right there, a ways down, a crack appeared.

Quinn didn't hurry, she didn't run. She maintained a sedate pace and made her way over, pushing against it, getting a sense for it. Her magic couldn't detect anything malicious, thought she knew that could be deceiving, she stepped toward it, pushing it open.

The hinges creaked, like they hadn't been oiled in a while, and she guessed he'd been stuck here for a couple of months by now, so maintenance on his own thought space probably wasn't up to par.

Taking a figurative deep breath, Quinn crossed the threshold.

She'd expected that door to slam shut, for the floor to collapse out from under her and plummet her into darkness. Any manner of hostile actions crossed her mind.

But nothing happened. The door remained partially open, the floor nice and solid, and beyond where she entered, she could see thick stone walls all around her.

Quinn moved in, slowly taking stock of things. The decorations were sparse. A bench here. A banner there. She moved through the space, making her way toward where she'd first encountered Kajaro and his friend. She also knew the door was closed now, but she didn't feel trapped.

Rounding the corner, she hadn't expected him to just be sitting there. But there he was. Right smack bang in the middle of the seating area she'd eavesdropped on last time.

His scales, once such a vibrant green, had a grey hue washing them out. Or perhaps that was the dream altered state they were in. His snake eyes looked straight ahead, and he didn't seem aware of her presence quite yet.

Quinn glanced around, relieved to see that Hal had spoken the truth. There was no one else here, and Quinn couldn't see how that would even be possible. She moved a few feet closer, able to feel the cold emanating off the figure in the middle. Cold mist stretched out toward her, reaching with cold tendrils.

She paused, just out of reach. "Kajaro, we should talk." She said it softly, and in here, her mouth moved. She wondered if it did outside as well, in her trance.

A flicker of recognition passed through him, a shudder of sorts. But he didn't respond verbally.

Quinn repeated herself. "Kajaro—we need to speak." Her words sounded forceful that time.

Kajaro's tongue flickered out, like he was tasting the air directly in front of him. A hiss escaped his throat, in a long sibilant note.

She waited several seconds, or it could have been minutes, she wasn't quite sure. "Kajaro."

This time, his head turned ever so slightly in her direction. But she could see it cost him effort. Whether it was fighting the cold, or he had a stiff neck.

Kajaro looked at her. "It's you."

"Glad we've established that," she said, still waiting for him to agree to speak.

"Well," he said, his voice raspy and unused. "Speak, then."

Quinn wasn't sure what she'd expected. Perhaps an argument over why they should speak or even a discussion of what they should speak about. But not a command to do so. It left her floundering a bit. So, perhaps unwisely, she started with what she was burning to know. "Why?"

If possible, he did manage to raise an eye ridge. "Why what?"

She had to tamp down on the brief surge of anger that tried to get out of its box. "Why all of this? Why chaos?"

"Ah," he said, and went back to looking at the wall in front of him. Only a slight ghost of steam from his breath gave away he breathed, and his tail swished ever so slightly against the ground. "That is a long story."

"I have time," she lied.

He actually chuckled. "I did not expect it of you. For you to reduce me to this." He gestured slowly at himself.

Quinn wasn't entirely sure how to respond to that. So she didn't. She just waited, uncertain how time passed in here versus out there.

"Stories is where it started, I suppose. Dragons are a part of our reptilian family. Did you know that? Their eternal lives offer us a faint look into possible futures. Of what power could bring us."

"Us as in the Serpensiril?" Quinn asked softly.

Again, another pause before Kajaro answered. "Partially. Us as in the strong. Us as in those who want to be powerful because we're recognized. And us because . . . have you ever wanted to belong, young Librarian?" He finished the last of that off with an oddly intense stare.

The thing was? That last one hit home for Quinn. She'd been outside for almost a decade. Jumping from home to home, keeping her head down, never truly belonging anywhere, until she came to the Library. Perhaps the former was what Kajaro counted on to reach her. Maybe it had been a gamble he wanted to take.

Quinn smiled at him, a surge of pity rising. After all, six months ago she might have been more intrigued. Now? No, now the Library had given her a home, and a found family, and even a way to keep in touch with her old family and friends from her original world. Kajaro didn't understand her the way he tried to project. "I used to. But now I do belong. I wish everyone had such a place."

A flash of something passed through Kajaro's eyes. She thought it might have been confusion. His information probably outdated since he'd been in stasis.

He yawned, the movement taking him by surprise. "It's cold and lethargic here. I can't hear the voices I'm always in contact with. I'm not used to spending so much time with just my own thoughts."

Maybe he should have thought about that before he helped ambushed them all, killing Escadril, two imps, and almost killing Malakai in the process. That was what she wanted to say to him. But she didn't. He wasn't being cooperative. She wasn't getting any information they didn't already have.

"Tell me," he asked. "Since I seem to be stuck here, have you figured it out yet?"

"Obviously not," Quinn said, rolling her eyes. She'd give him that.

"What have you learned?"

"That the Library was always supposed to fall, but the trapdoor Drav built in failed. So he's had to resort to other means."

This time Kajaro looked impressed. "That's a lot more accurate than I'd have given you credit for."

"Thanks . . . I think," she said, wondering why he didn't seem to have that sibilant echo to his words when speaking mind to mind.

"And have you discovered the others yet? Because that's when the fun will truly begin."

"Others . . . other dragons?"

"Ah." He rolled his shoulders and then they sagged, like all his energy had been sucked out of him. "No . . . the others. I'm not sure if destroying the Library itself was a goal, but . . . Sölem truly are not the only people you have to watch out for. Some of them—some might even be closer than you think." He cackled and closed his eyes, his tongue flicking out involuntarily.

Quinn parsed the information, desperately trying to make sense of it. Perhaps making too much sense of it, in fact. She didn't want him to be telling the truth, but every part of her said he'd not been lying.

He seemed to have gone still, and she wasn't entirely sure what to do except leave. She turned as if to do so when he spoke back up.

"Going so soon?" His tone held defeat, and a rawness that was surprising.

"I'm not a fan of staying in hostile minds," was all she answered.

He chuckled. "I am, aren't I? Hostile. It's odd. I wasn't as a child, you know. And here, where it's so cold, where you stopped me from resurrection? It's like I'm perpetually between the two planes. How very odd."

Quinn filed that away, marveling at how she felt sorry for him, even though he'd killed people right in front of her. Half of her wanted to warn him that once Hal was done, he'd never resurrect again. But she didn't want to give him a chance to prepare a plan. Desperation caused mistakes.

"Thank you for chatting," she said, turning to head back the way she came.

"No problem." He laughed, and he did sound ever so slightly maniacal. "Come back any time. Not like I'm going anywhere."

She half turned to look back at him, only able to see half of his face now from her angle. "If I have time."

Which she wouldn't. But didn't everyone need hope?

Just about to disengage, Kajaro spoke up once more. His voice more of a whisper as it crept over the stone halls toward her.

"Be careful, Librarian. Some things in the mirror might be closer than they appear."

She released the connection, having no idea what to make of that.

23

UNPOISONED TEA

IT TOOK SEVERAL MINUTES FOR QUINN TO ACCLIMATE BACK TO THE room when she exited Kajaro's head. The complete brightness hurt her retina. Kajaro's last words kept echoing through her mind, bumping off corners like an old-fashioned screensaver.

Some things in the mirror might be closer than they appear.

Like that made no sense at all. Wasn't that on side-view mirrors in cars back on Earth?

She sighed. And shook her head, clearing out the last vestiges of the damn thought walk.

Hal's voice spoke softly from her right-hand side. "You feeling okay, little egg? I've got some unpoisoned tea for you."

Quinn chuckled despite herself and opened her eyes to accept it. "That'd be great." It felt warm in her hands, which were surprisingly cool right then.

She was grateful they gave her time to recover. A part of her felt weak, as if all her energy had drained out of her.

"Tired?" Eric asked, with none of his usual sarcasm.

"Yeah. Oddly so."

"Not odd," said the imp. "Normal. You used the thought walking trigger as your entry point. You weren't invited or tricked into the space. Entering someone else's mind—and you would have had to go past the surface—is supposed to be taxing. Or else everyone would do it. I haven't done it myself . . . but I've seen people who did. And they all looked as tired as you do."

Quinn nodded, taking some solace in the fact that she wasn't the only one to look like death after thought walking. "Thanks."

"He's right, you know," Malakai said. "Grandfather always looks like crap if he has to help someone who is sick and he can't speak to them before obtaining access. It's draining."

Hal clapped his hands together. "Okay, let's leave the snake in here, and head somewhere more comfortable now, if you're up for it?"

He glanced at her, making sure she was well enough to move now.

Quinn stood up, still holding her nice warm cup, and followed Hal as he left the room. She wished Milaro was with her right now. After all, she was pretty sure he'd know what to make of that whole conversation.

They made their way up levels and through to a different sitting area from the one Quinn was poisoned in. Perhaps he even did that deliberately, which was kind. Its couches and armchairs reminded Quinn of a more Victorian-era vibe, and the Oriental-type rug seemed slightly off style. She sat down anyway, sinking into the couch cushion comfortably.

Once everyone had taken a seat, she spoke. "Okay. Everything was even more cryptic than I expected." And she recounted the entirety of her encounter, after which she waited.

Hal frowned, Eric scowled, and Malakai perched on the back of the couch with his bow on his knee, concentrating on the string.

"That's so"—Hal suddenly laughed and then finally finished his sentence—"unnecessarily cryptic!"

"Right?" Quinn groaned and fell back against the couch cushions. "Infuriating."

"We should probably try to dissect the ridiculously vague clue." Malakai sounded tired. "It'd probably help to have my grandfather with us."

Hal shook his head. "Milaro is reinforcing his wards right now. He probably won't have time for a day or two. We should see what we can do and get Nishpa if we need to."

Quinn frowned, recalling the words in her mind again, trying to figure out what to focus on.

"Shouldn't we focus on the fact that there is a backdoor in the Library, courtesy of her brother, from basically creation or something?" Malakai asked.

Eric shrugged. "I rather think the Sölem not being the only one's thing is pretty important."

"No." Quinn shook her head. "We've had suspicions since the Bardocian root incident and the death of thousands of Balisors that there's more than one potential adversary out there. Although I think Sölem were allied with Korradine. From my understanding."

"The 'closer than we think' part is the one that's bugging me," Hal grumbled. "Frankly, all of it bugs me. You said he sounded out of it?"

"Of course he did." Quinn laughed. "He's a reptilian species in ice. I'm amazed there's enough blood flow to his brain for him to have communicated anything."

"Does him being stuck between two planes mean anything for us?" Mal asked. "I mean, that's pretty weird. Does it mean he can slip between dimensions or something?"

"No. I wouldn't think so." Hal stood up and began pacing. "He's bound corporeally. We halted his resurrection process."

Eric laughed. "It could all be crap, then, you know? Because why would he give us information when he's all in limbo?" He cackled gleefully until Quinn threw a pillow at him.

But there was something weird about Kajaro in his own thoughts. Something nagging at the back of her mind. A lot of things did that lately. It was as if he gave her answers, not only reluctantly, but as if she was drawing him out. And yet, at the same time, he'd been capable of twisting things into such cryptic words. She realized their knowledge of the backdoor and the hibernating dragon had surprised him. But the rest of it . . .

"What did he mean by the mirror? That's the weirdest phrasing

I've ever seen before," Malakai said, pulling Quinn out of her thoughts.

"The mirror?"

"Some things in the mirror might be closer than they appear."

Quinn shrugged. "Yeah, that was really odd. Makes no real sense unless you happen to drive Earth cars . . . sort of."

Hal perked up. "What do you mean Earth cars?"

"Cars. Automobiles. You know they have a motor and fit generally like four or five people. Take you from place to place. Run on petrol or electricity . . ." Quinn raised an eyebrow. "Cars."

Hal paused his pacing and looked at her. "But why does the mirror make sense in this context?"

"Oh!" Quinn felt a bit sheepish. "In your side-view mirror when you're checking to see if someone is in your blind spot, sometimes there's a sticker that says, 'objects in the mirror may be closer than they appear.' So you don't think they're further away than they are and accidentally sideswipe someone's car when you change lanes or something. There's always a blind spot."

"Um . . ." Mal moved to sit next to Quinn, putting his bow back in storage. "Are you okay?"

Quinn blinked at him. "Yes. I'm not disturbed by a car changing lanes. It's just on the mirrors for safety."

Mal looked around the room, obviously making brief eye contact with both Hal and Eric. "But Quinn. Weren't you and your parents in a car accident when you were a kid?"

"Well, yes." Quinn could feel her breath start to come in shorter gasps. "I mean . . ."

What did he mean?

"Well, we know the collision was engineered by Sölem, right?"

She nodded.

"And couldn't it . . . might there have been others too?"

The memory flashed through her head, but not in a way she could access and study, just sudden and complete. She clenched her eyes shut and tried to get rid of the vision. "Maybe others? People?"

"Yeah." Mal gave her arm a squeeze. "Perhaps visible in that mirror and thus closer than they appeared?"

Quinn ran it through her mind. Even with that vision, she'd need to take it and dissect it. But she didn't feel confident doing it herself. "I mean, you could have a point. I didn't even recall the memory until recently."

She really did try her best not to be forlorn.

"It's the only thing that makes sense if you pull on your Earth experience. I mean, he would have known you were from there, right?" Mal asked, gently.

"Probably." Quinn didn't like this. It'd been traumatic enough to recall the accident the first time. Doing it again . . . but needs must. "Is there a way for me to recall that memory in more detail? Like vivid detail I can dissect and examine? I know I've gone into it before."

Hal placed his hand very briefly on Quinn's shoulder, exuding warmth and sense of safety. "It's okay, little egg. Let's get you home, and see if we can't dig up a Milaro or Nishpa."

Relief flooded Quinn. She'd been taking so much on, and she should be, considering she was the Librarian. But sometimes, having someone else direct her was just a nice vacation.

———

Back in the Library, however, Quinn didn't feel comfortable. With Kajaro so far away, the thought walking almost seemed dream-like. As if it had never happened.

A strange level of trepidation began to form in her gut, too. She wasn't sure what to make of it, even though deep down she knew why. Delving back into that memory wasn't simple. She'd have to watch her parents die again, and her grandmother, blood suspended in the air, glass shattering and cutting flesh—depending on where she had to pause the memory to examine it.

Her stomach roiled at the thought, and she rebelled against the idea of doing it.

The scenario ran rampant in her head, around and around in a loop. It took a concerted effort to remember to breathe, even sat in her big chair in the office waiting to do this. Even with Aradie right next to her, owlish concern on her face.

Quinn closed her eyes and tried to force herself to relax, her hands resting loosely on her desk.

She wasn't sure how long past as she allowed her breathing to slow and meditation to kick in, centering her. As long as she didn't allow a panic attack, things would be okay.

A hand covered one of hers, resting loosely on the desk. She didn't need to open her eyes to see who it was because the magic signature was a dead giveaway, but she did anyway.

"Hey," said Milaro, his voice full of warmth. "I hear you spoke to a snake."

"Yeah. Weird conversation, too."

"He is frozen."

"True."

He squeezed her hand, taking the seat opposite her. "You sure you want to do this? No one will blame you for backing out."

"But it's one of the best leads we have."

"Or it could be a practical joke by a sick and twisted fellow who has killed more people than I can count." Milaro raised an eyebrow.

Quinn laughed. "Touché. Okay. Is there another way, and what is it?"

Milaro seemed to ponder that for a few. "I could try to extract the memory and examine it myself, but it's not always reliable, and I'm unsure what the state of the memory would be like when I try to return it. But that way you would avoid more trauma from having to relive it."

For some reason, that scared Quinn more. "No, I don't want to lose it."

He considered that for a few seconds. "Do you want me to try to blur them? So that anything you see of them in particular is just a blurry image?"

"Oh, yeah. That . . . that would work much better." The relief she felt rushed through her like an energy drink. "Thank you."

"Don't thank me yet."

"Wait, aren't you supposed to be warding something?" She suddenly realized he wasn't supposed to be here.

"Done."

Her eyes narrowed. "Then shouldn't you be recovering?"

"I had a power nap. We'll tackle this memory and I will crash for twelve hours. Happy?"

"Not really. But I do appreciate you."

"I know," he said simply.

"Okay, we'll send for some food, get you settled, and then dive into that memory."

Quinn nodded, nervous as hell. Luckily, Milaro kept a hold of her hand, grounding her.

So much that she almost convinced herself she was ready for it.

24

INTERNAL REDIRECTION

HER SEAT WAS COMFORTABLE.

This was an important distinction. A grounding one. Something she needed to cling to as a reminder of where and what was real should she need to pull herself back to reality if something went awry.

Quinn was fully aware of this, and yet somehow found herself fidgeting.

"Are you sure you're ready for this?" Milaro asked again, pushing the calming tea toward her, even as he reached out his other hand to hold hers.

"No. But this is necessary." Quinn didn't want to dive into that damned memory. And if that snake was having her on, she'd gladly pay him another visit for screwing with her head like this. Two could play at that game.

However, she was certain on a strange level that he'd told her the truth. And that meant they had to follow this up.

Food in her stomach, calming and focus tea in progress, and her mentor sitting in front of her holding her hands and ready to go through the whole thing with her? That was about as good as it could get.

Milaro nodded. "Okay, first up, I need you to recall one of the exercises from a book I think Lynx gave you."

Quinn raised an eyebrow. Over the last several months, the manifestation had given her a whole slew of tomes. "You'll have to be more specific than that."

"*Swebby's Path of Cognizant Deliberate Memory Management*," he began, but Quinn interrupted him.

"Oh, the IR book? The Internal Redirection book?" She sounded eager. She knew it. After all, it was one of her favorites so far. It had helped her focus on Eugea's healing in such detail that she'd forever be grateful. Speaking of which, she'd seen that spell cast. She still had to get Milaro and perhaps Nishpa to look at it.

Milaro smiled. "Then yes. The IR book. I believe you should use those techniques to pull us into the scene we need to examine in your mind."

Quinn took in a deep breath and nodded. It made sense, of course. It was the most efficient way for her to dive in and get the best of this. Thing was, she wasn't entirely sure how to just pull up that recovered memory. Closing her eyes, she dug deep. But she couldn't bring herself to relax. There was a part of her just too wound up.

"Breathe, Quinn." Milaro's voice was gentle and if she didn't open her eyes, she could concentrate on her breathing, on her mind, on her memories.

In and out. Counting it down.

She remembered being back on Earth. That little storeroom with Malakai. The sudden memory.

And there it was.

———

"QUINN, COME HERE, SHOW ME YOUR REPORT CARD," HER MOTHER CALLED. *Quinn walked over and giggled at her mother. She had to be, what, twelve?*

"Mom, it's online, like it always is. What are you talking about?"

"Fine, fine, give me the hard copy anyway." Her mother attempted to smile sternly, but it was, as always, just filled with contentment.

Quinn handed over the hard copy to her mother with a big grin on her face.

"You did it again! All As, I'm so proud of you." The smile her mother gave her showed both love and pride.

———

Nope. That was too early. She frowned as it slipped out of her grasp, only to catch it briefly and try to locate the portion she wanted.

———

Dad laughed, her mom laughed, her grandmother laughed. The sounds were like music to her ears.

They headed through the intersection closest to the ice cream shop.—they were so close she could practically taste it. The lights were green. They had the right of way.

And then time seemed to slow down for her . . .

———

Quinn froze the image right before the crash.

Milaro's voice was like a breeze speaking into her mind. *Did you mean to stop it here?*

She nodded in her head but then realized that wouldn't help. *Yes. I don't . . . I'm unsure what would be in the side-view mirror during the accident. Wouldn't it just be the car behind us? I feel like others would have braked, would have avoided it. I only remember the car getting hit from the side.*

You're not just trying to avoid the actual accident? he asked gently.

Maybe a bit, she admitted, *but it's more than that. If we don't catch something this way, then I'll give in and look at the actual crash. I'll have you blur out their bodies. But right now you don't need to yet. I just need you to sit with me. Here, in this scene. The side-view mirrors are at each side in the front. We won't have the best angles for them.*

He stiffened ever so slightly as she felt him move in her awareness. And then she remembered he'd known these people. He'd sent them with her, to take care of her. He'd thought her dead with them almost a decade ago. This would be difficult for him, too. Maybe that's why he chose to guide her instead of Nishpa.

Quinn pivoted around in her head, watching the frozen scene before them. Smiles on faces, ice cream expectant, joy and love. She'd had a pretty good first twelve years, after all. The memories weren't difficult to recall. Just this one. This bad one.

She could feel Milaro over in the vicinity of her mother in the passenger seat, while Quinn maneuvered to look at the one next to her dad, who was right in front of her.

In the still image, just about to pass the line at the green lights ahead of them, Quinn's face was frozen in laughter at her father's joke. She'd been shaking her head, calling him out, and laughing in that carefree way. Which was probably the only reason she'd even had the side-view mirror in her vision at all.

It was strange stepping outside of the car in her vision. Beyond the car was nothing. Just a big, open space where the image of her memory faded out to nothing but space. Quinn moved carefully to the side-view mirror and frowned. She needed to enlarge the picture, to pull it out.

With a shrug, she grabbed the mirror, and it detached with relative ease. She rotated it, trying to see the image in detail. But in her mind, where many things were possible, she simply asked it to enhance and enlarge. She remembered vaguely that the IR book had many ways to make the most of memories. Accessing them, controlling them, finding their secrets.

There was something in this one, but the blur was so severe, Quinn couldn't be entirely sure. She squinted even harder at it and frowned.

Found something? Milaro asked, looking over at her.

I don't know . . . was her only response. Because it wasn't clear. There was something there, like a sphere or an eye. *Any luck on your side?*

He hesitated. *Not entirely, but maybe we should have a look at each other's and see.*

They met in the middle and looked. The object in Milaro's was much the same as Quinn's. *What do you think it is?* she asked.

He shrugged. *Right now, it's a circular blur. Perhaps spherical. I think you should go back and see if it's clearer before this juncture of the memory. Maybe fifteen seconds, even?*

Quinn nodded. It made sense. She dismissed the memory, clenching her hands around Milaro's in the real world as she recalled another portion of her memory.

"So, Quinn, tell me, did you cheat?" It was almost like a ritual question, a joke shared among all of them.

Quinn remembered those jokes. She remembered the way they all reveled in them. She felt tired. Couldn't she stop everything for just a moment?

Milaro's presence by her side was warm and calming. *This works,* he said.

Quinn knew immediately upon approaching the side-view mirror this time that their idea had worked. The image was already clearer. So clear, in fact, that Quinn gasped. Mainly because it still didn't make sense. She walked around with hers to be closer to Milaro's presence. *This doesn't make sense.*

No, it really doesn't. Not when we didn't detect any traces of other magic here. We locked down your parents, too. There was no way to scent them.

Quinn had known that, at a certain level, but it helped to have it confirmed. *Well, then . . .*

But neither of them had an answer, and so Quinn just studied the image closer and committed it to memory. *I swear it's a moon-like eye.*

In some ways, it looks like a dragon's eye. And in others, it feels more like a golem eye. But both of those creatures require great deals of magic to exist on a world like Earth. It wouldn't be sustainable.

Quinn pondered that. *But would it be momentarily sustainable? In that, perhaps this is how they got the actual drivers to the scene? A dimensional teleport?*

You're really taking my 'with magic anything is possible' speech to heart, aren't you?

Quinn knew if he was standing next to her corporeally, he'd be raising an eyebrow. She sighed. *But why is it just an eye? I can't see any other attachment. And it takes up most of the mirror.*

Milaro was peering closer. *You don't think . . . can you feel that?*

Quinn leaned closer to the mirror and its expanded image that already took up most of it. A strange pulse of warmth. *This . . . whatever this is, isn't hostile. It's warm. It's watching all of us.*

At that, Milaro frowned, and his presence seemed lost in thought, even though she could remotely feel he was still there.

Her curiosity piqued. She was fascinated by the eye thing that reminded her ever so slightly of Lynx and the golems as they communicated with and through the system, that it was a presence in her memories.

She had an idea. Ducking back another ten seconds in the memory, she quickly checked the mirrors again. But there was nothing in them other than the cars that should have been. Not even a shadow of a sphere or eye or whatever it was. Pity the details were too blurry in the other ones.

Which meant she should also check the actual impact memory. Only. She chose the split second before impact.

Quinn could feel herself shake as she stepped around the still intact vehicle, squeezing herself to see the reflection in the passenger side. Nothing was there. Nor was there anything on the driver's side. Finally, she dismissed the memory and allowed Milaro rubbing the back of her hand to pull her back to reality.

She blinked, even as thoughts ran rampant through her head.

Milaro simply watched her, as if he was making sure to let her come to her own decisions before he jumped in and offered any insight.

She ran a hand through her hair, pulling strands free and tangling them around her fingers in thought. "First up. How the hell did Kajaro know anything about this?"

"I don't have an answer for that." Milaro spoke carefully, still watching her. "Maybe put that question to the back of the line."

Quinn scowled, then sighed. He was right. "Fine. They weren't the same eyes. You know that, right? If they were eyes. They reminded me a bit of Lynx, a bit of Misha . . . golems and all."

Misha popped into the office, a look of surprise on their face. "I . . . I am not supposed to be in here," they said, looking around. "Did you need me, Librarian?"

The hopefully soon-relegated-back-to-full-supervisory duty golem's appearance made Quinn smile. "No, I don't need you right now. But I had mentioned your name, and so . . . here you are."

"Ah. Well. Then I will warp back to Harish, then."

With a slight pop, they were gone.

"It's good to know something's working like it should again," Quinn grumbled.

"Stop it," Milaro chided. "Two different synthetic eyes. Watching the whole scene take place."

"No," Quinn corrected him. "They weren't there upon impact. And they weren't there another ten seconds in the past. Just for about twenty seconds right before. What, do we have dragons who only show us their eyes following us? Golems created to travel intergalactically to, I don't know, make sure they finished the job?"

Milaro shrugged and Aradie gave her a wing hug. Neither of those things helped.

"I'd suggest we see if you can project the images. Might help to have some reference. Could ask Carafax with all his chronicling." Milaro sounded like he was grasping at straws. "I'm sorry I'm not more help. From Kajaro's phrasing, I thought this would be a revelation."

Quinn pursed her lips, running it all over in her mind. What had he wanted to tell her? Was it really a wild goose chase? "Perhaps we're not looking at it from the right perspective?"

Milaro laughed. "Well, let's see if we can discover which perspective it's from. After I go and have a bloody good sleep."

"Thank you," Quinn said suddenly. "For being there with me."

"Anytime." Milaro smiled and took his leave.

Quinn watched him go, closed the door behind him, grabbed a pillow off the couch, and screamed into it. Just what she needed. More stuff she didn't know.

Aradie swooped down to land gently next to where Quinn lay on the couch and hooted in commiseration while offering a brush of her wing.

2 5

LITTLE STOWAWAY

EYES.

Mamoria, that shapeshifting species that helped kill off so many Balisors.

Korradine.

Sölem and their oddly self-destructive wish to be judged by raw chaos energy.

So many factions.

Eyes.

Or were they moons?

Artificial eyes?

How did Kajaro know about them?

Quinn groaned as she jotted down the information running rampant in her head. But with each word, her handwriting got worse, and she just wanted to stab the pages in front of her.

She slept fitfully after diving through her memories and sifting out the specific side-view mirror elements. What bugged her more was that she'd even dived back in briefly on her own and frozen the image back in place and looked at the rearview mirror, thinking perhaps it had caught something else.

To no avail.

Which made no sense whatsoever.

It could only mean one thing—magic. But as their visit to Earth showed them, mana and energy basically couldn't be replenished. So anything they used while there would have been quickly depleted and taken years to fill back up.

Literally.

"Thought I'd find you in here." Mal's voice was soft and full of concern as he placed a nice hot cup of tea on the desk in front of her. He stood at the desk looking out through the massive window of the restricted vault, gazing at the millions of stars beyond the Library's doors.

Quinn took the cup gratefully, feeling a slight chill for once. Sometimes she just liked it better in here. Not as many people knew to find her, and generally, the Library kept them out. It must have realized that while Quinn wanted to be alone, she was also feeling marginally vulnerable. Mal was a good antidote to that.

"Thanks." She sipped her own cup, thankful for the heat against her chilled hands, and turned to look at the stars too.

For several moments, they just sat there, enjoying their tea, each other's presence, and the view. It lent a level of calm to Quinn's mind that she'd been sorely lacking. A clarity of mind which allowed her to not be alone.

Mal scooted down and sat at the opposite end of the bench, his tea easily in reach. "What are you working on?"

Quinn tapped her pen against the paper in front of her and sighed. "That's just it. I don't know. The murder board helped a bit. Let me get some of my thoughts in order. But it's such a huge task, all of this. Isn't there a book I can just absorb and use wish magic to say: Hey, make this all better? And it's done?"

Malakai chuckled. "I don't think that's quite how this works."

"Should be," she grumbled. "Thought magic could do most things."

"With a bit of direction? Yes. With vague gesturing? Probably not a good outcome."

Quinn laughed. He had a point. "I know. I'd just like an easy way out of this . . . shitstorm?"

"Very apt description." Malakai nodded in approval.

Instead of writing it out, Quinn began to talk. "Sarila is the wild card here. It's infuriating. The Balisor massacre is basically the odd thing out. Before that, I'd never considered anyone else being responsible for any of this."

"How do we know it's related to the whole Library sabotage?" Mal asked, continuing to sip his tea.

"What do you mean?" Quinn couldn't quite grasp what he meant.

"How do we know it wasn't a revenge plot on the Balisors by one of the Jenishu clan of Salosiers?" He looked at her over the rim of his cup.

She wasn't sure how he'd ever manage to look more like an elf. But she also didn't like the implications of what he said either. "Because they said we'd never recover from a chaos backlash if we didn't have Salosiers to fall back on. Since the magic binding their bodies involuntarily fights raw chaos energy as is. At least for a while, right?"

Mal frowned. "Technically, I think. But would that be a reason to almost wipe out an entire branch of a species?"

Quinn threw her arms up in the air. "That's just it. You tell me! I have no clue."

Lynx popped up in that instant, startling Quinn so much she screamed, a short, high-pitched yell.

"Damn it, Lynx! Don't do that!"

"The Library said you were distraught. I got here as soon as I could." He narrowed his eyes. "You don't seem upset. Just irritated."

"I'm all the above," she grumbled. Then she perked up at the thought of asking Lynx what he knew. "Are there any eyes in species that you can think of that resemble moons?"

Lynx raised an eyebrow. "That's an oddly specific strange question. Does this have to do with the mirror thing?"

She nodded.

"Many of us can have moonlike eyes, I guess? Depending on whether we're working in synchronization with the system at the time." He frowned as he thought it over, morphing his eyes into various shapes and colors to make his point. "Some fae species, most golems. Probably some sub-species of sprites too, dragons . . . a lot."

Quinn groaned. That wasn't the answer she wanted. "I can't figure out who or what it was that showed up watching us in the side-view mirrors. Which is just . . . I thought it could have been headlights at first, but it was the middle of the day and even the running lights I could see outside of that freeze frame looked nothing like moonlike eyes."

"I'm sorry." Lynx leant forward and patted her hand.

She shrugged. "I just wanted to figure out exactly who was responsible for the accident so I could make them pay when the time comes. I really hope they have like five overdue books so I can fine the hell out of them."

Lynx looked at her for a couple of seconds before speaking. "You've been spending too much time around, Eric."

Quinn laughed. "Did you just come here because the Library told you I was having a breakdown?"

He chuckled and his eyes flickered briefly. "No. I didn't. I have information I thought you'd like. First up. The trace-back is yielding results and we've begun to narrow down the area the signal accessed Jasper's ritual circle from."

Quinn perked up. "Seriously? Like where? Should we go . . ." She slowed down at the look Lynx gave her. "What?"

"I said we're narrowing it down, not that we have the location. Give us a bit more time. But I wanted to make sure you knew we're making progress faster than I anticipated, given the strength of power behind the trace and behind Jasper's initial runes and wards."

Quinn had to take a deep breath. Just hearing Jasper's name so frequently caused her chest to tighten. She really missed her Alyenarvor friend. "Yeah, all right. What's the other thing?"

"Memories. We're almost there. Or at least, I hope we are. Library and I should have most of our memories with regard to Korradine at least, in the next few days."

Quinn blinked. She wasn't about to get super excited about this. Because it could be that there'd be another hiccup. Just like there always seemed to be when they got even remotely close to anything. "That's great." She hesitated.

"I hear a distinct *but* there," Malakai observed.

"I don't know . . . it feels so surreal. There are Drav and Dro—Library siblings. Then we even have Korradine and the Supervisor. After that there's the Sölem comprised of Aracnios, Esposians, Sedimentites, and more. And to top it all off, Sarila appears to be playing two sides? Or two attackers of the Library?" She waved her hand around, trying to encompass everything. "It's just a lot of stuff with many moving parts."

"Were you hoping it'd be easy?" Mal asked softly.

"Of course!" She wasn't exactly sure what she'd expected. But it hadn't been so complex. "It's not that. I just didn't expect to second guess myself at every turn."

"You don't have to, you know?" Mal said.

"What do you mean?"

This time, Lynx shrugged. "Your gut feelings, I believe, is what you call them? You should pay more attention to them. It's one of those things where, when your gut, or perhaps even innate magic, reaches out to warn you of something . . . then you should pay attention. You haven't steered us wrong yet."

Quinn knew he meant that to sound bolstering. But the *yet* echoed through her head as if someone had put a pot on it and rapped it with a wooden spoon. He was right, though, wasn't he? She hadn't steered them wrong yet. She frowned. "Hey. Can you give me a second? I need to scan my shielding. Keep watch?"

She didn't wait. Because she knew both Malakai and Lynx would do exactly that. Her self-doubt didn't often creep in when she was in analytical mode. And she had been for the past several hours. Which meant there had to be something inside her shielding, or because of her shielding, that crept through and was bothering her. It meant something had probably come through the memory analysis with her when she came back.

She'd known she shouldn't have gone into it again without Milaro present. It wasn't that he found things she couldn't anymore, but he was there as a safety net and backup.

She scoured her walls. But each of them was as tight and inter-woven as it was supposed to be. Smooth, seamless walls rose up to meet each other, slotting perfectly into place, and only activating as she wanted to pass through them to view the rest. They melted before her, only leaving enough room for her to pass perfectly through them.

No seam, no singular brick was even out of place.

Quinn frowned and pushed through, heading to where she'd viewed her memory of the damned accident. While sick of viewing it at all, she knew she had to check. And that's when she saw it.

At the corner of her peripheral vision she could see one of those little eyes, or well, not so little eyes that had been hovering in the mirror. She realized it wasn't attached to anything, either, and that she'd been way off about all of her guesses. It watched her, obviously removed from her memory, yet still attached enough to observe her while she figured out what was happening.

In short, there was a stowaway in her head.

It'd be tricky, but she needed to capture it, keep it contained within her mind until perhaps Milaro or Nishpa could help her out with it.

But she had to move swiftly. Biding her time as she walked around the car on the way to its doom again, Quinn conjured a cage within her mind. It wasn't too small, but there were holes an eye could get out of. And if that wasn't the weird sentence ever ...

Since it had what she thought of as wings, she couldn't quite bind it, so she chose to imprison it.

It took several passes for it to stop following her like a starving puppy. Finally, she turned around, struck it with a targeted shot of Gravitas and levitated it into the cage, which she then locked.

Levitating the cage, she moved it out of the memory ahead of her. The eye flitted about on its odd little owlish wings, the moon-like orb watching her as they moved, it's eyelids blinking ever so slowly.

It seemed familiar, yet at the same time, it felt foreign. Like perhaps she'd seen other eyes like this before.

She frowned as she got to the threshold of her mind and glanced at the little thing. Would it be okay to take with her? Could she even take it with her? She'd not transferred anything out of a memory.

But this wasn't technically from a memory. Instead, she was fairly sure it was a trespasser and had been sent to gather information on Quinn's past or perhaps just her thoughts and movements.

After a lot of effort and some shrinking of the cage and its occupant, Quinn pulled back her awareness. It was more of a struggle to manifest the cage and its occupant into her office as well, but with a discordant plop, the eye and the cage landed on the desk.

"What in the universe is that?" Malakai asked.

"I think I have a little stowaway." Quinn grinned, a harsh set to her jaw. The flying eye pulled back into its cage and cowered.

"That's odd," Lynx said, and he visibly swallowed. Considering he didn't need to, Quinn found that telling.

She waited.

"Why do you have an eagle eye, Quinn? And how did you pull it out of your head?" Lynx asked.

26

EAGLE EYE

Quinn looked down at the little eye in her cage. Immediately wondering if it could transmit location or frequencies from where it was. It'd obviously been in her head to do something specific. She made quick work of erecting both mental and normal shielding around it too, just in case it had a nefarious means of communicating outside of the Library.

It hovered there, its gaze fixed on her, following her every move.

"Eagle eye?" she asked, moving just to make it bob around following her. "What the hell is an eagle eye?"

Lynx transformed into his feline form like he could get a better view up closer. "It's very focused on you."

Quinn felt a pulse of power exit the manifestation, rippling the air around the cage.

"Good move, restricting what it can send. Although I don't think it's been able to send much of anything while trapped in your mind. Your shields are hefty." He padded around the cage once more and then sat back on his haunches. "Was he in the memory of the accident?"

Quinn nodded.

"Probably locked away until you recalled that memory. Your

innate cosmicisodracus self-preservation probably initiated shielding until you regained energy, too. Those memories were buried deep initially, right?"

She nodded again, checking for any feeling that might have been her transmitting information involuntarily. But she couldn't find anything.

Malakai cleared his throat, trying to grab her attention. "My grandfather or Nishpa would probably be best to help you with that." He gestured at the eye. The constantly following-her-every-movement eye. It was decidedly creepy yet sort of cute in its own way.

Aradie pecked her ear as if to say, *That is not cute.*

"Yeah, you're probably right." And she knew he was right because it had been her first thought, too. She wanted to cover the cage so she couldn't see the eye following her every movement. The unblinking way it looked at her sent shivers down her spine. Almost like it waited for orders. She just wasn't sure who from. "Got anything to cover the cage until I can get to one of them, Lynx?"

He sighed as if he was most put upon. But the next second, a cloth covered the cage.

Quinn got the distinct impression that the odd little creature could still see her, regardless.

"Right." She clapped her hands, looked mournfully at her spot in the restricted vault, and realized she'd have to abandon that project in favor of figuring out just what this meant. "Nishpa's in the hospital, right?"

It was more of a rhetorical question, since she could feel that out herself.

She picked up the little cage from the ring at the top, still covered, and made her way to see Nishpa. Malakai and Lynx moved with her.

They heard Nishpa before they saw her.

Which wasn't unexpected, but it was marginally entertaining.

"The food is fine, Dr. Miles. It's your understanding of mind healing that's lacking." Her voice held such an authoritative air, Quinn couldn't help but be impressed.

The doctor, on the other hand, spoke with a level of patience

Quinn attributed to saintlike. "I am trained in all aspects of healing, but mind healing, as I have already explained to you, is not specialty based, unlike the rest of my skills."

Quinn could practically feel Nishpa scowl from out in the hall.

"Be that as it may, you'd do well to allow me to tend to the Balisors still suffering."

"As soon as you are cleared and fit to leave the hospital, I would gladly accept your help," Miles said in an even and calm tone of voice. It was like he dealt with Nishpa every day.

"I know you're out there," Nishpa practically snapped.

Quinn blushed, and even though she couldn't see Malakai as she walked in, she was pretty sure he did, too. Lynx was still in feline form and trotted into the room, jumping up on the couch to groom himself.

"Sorry. We didn't want to interrupt," Malakai offered smoothly as he took a seat.

Nishpa frowned. "The doctor was just about to release me, weren't you, Dr. Miles?" She gave him a very pointed look. It might have been successful with her own kind, but Miles didn't seem to care about her glare.

"Dr. Miles was not about to release you," he contradicted her, completely unflappable.

Quinn decided golem doctors were the best.

Nishpa scowled and crossed her arms. "What do I need to do to be released? I've been here for ages now."

"One more day. I am happy with all the grafting progress most of it has taken. It is the membranes on your left wing I am not entirely happy with. While to outward appearances, they seem completely healed, they still exhibit a modicum of weakness when I magically scan them." His tone never wavered once.

The Furionas fae looked like she was about to say something else and then thought better of it. "Fine. But tomorrow, I get out of here and help you treat the ill."

"I would appreciate your expertise. There are several patients who could use a specialized mind healer once your magical center is realigned. Which, by tomorrow, it should be." He sounded kind. Patient, even.

Nishpa looked like she wanted to say so much more, but then she caught Quinn's eye again, and noticed she was carrying something. "I can look at whatever it is the Librarian has brought for me to, right?"

"As long as it does not require for you to overexert yourself." Dr. Miles then turned to Quinn. "Make sure she does not overdo it, please. I have other patients to take care of."

"Will do," Quinn said, just as the doctor turned to leave.

"Well?" Nishpa asked as soon as Miles was out of the room.

Quinn hesitated, not entirely sure how to broach the subject.

"Tell me. I've been cooped up in here for days."

"You were mortally wounded. I can't believe you're whole enough to even be having this conversation," Quinn said, glaring at her defiantly.

Nishpa paled ever so slightly, which was tough because she hadn't regained the darker golden shimmer of her skin yet, and so appeared paler than usual. "I know. But I am recovered. Milaro made sure of it. I shouldn't have been protecting him."

"As far as we know, that's why you're in here in the first place." Quinn's voice was soft, gentle even as she tried to comfort the older fae.

"Yes. Well. All that aside." Nishpa seemed oddly put out by the fact that she'd taken her injury while protecting Milaro. Or at least, while fighting by his side. She pointed at the covered cage. "What do you want me to take a look at?"

Quinn lifted the cage and placed it on the edge of the bed. "I don't think it'll do anything, but . . . you might want to sit back." Then she paused and glanced over at Malakai.

He shrugged. "I mean, do you want to tell her about where it came from and why you know about it first?"

Quinn shrugged and told Nishpa about the encounter with Kajaro and her visiting his mind-space, and him referencing the mirror, and discovering the eye reflections. Although she had to make sure Nishpa knew that Quinn didn't think the eye in the mirror was the same as what Quinn was about to show her. But that she'd gone to inspect the memory and had pulled out this thing in the cage.

Nishpa raised an eyebrow. "Wait. You pulled this out of a memory . . . of your own?"

Quinn nodded.

"Literally pulled a physical thing from your memory and manifested it into the Library?" Nishpa still sounded incredulous.

"Let me just show you," Quinn said. And she removed the sheet.

The eagle eye was still glued to Quinn. Watching her. She was fairly certain it had even been able to watch her through the cover the entire time.

Nishpa's gasp was loud in the silence. Even the evil eye's wings were silent as it hovered. Its gaze concentrated solely on Quinn.

"I'm not sure what to do with it. But it came from my mind, so I figured . . . maybe I should talk to you or Milaro, and he's not here." Quinn shrugged uneasily.

"So here you are," Nishpa replied absently. Her eyes had grown larger with anticipation, and she bit her lip in concentration as she walked toward the cage, examining the creature. "You manifested this into the real world."

"Sort of? I mean, I caught it in the cage in my mind."

"In your mind. It was sitting there watching that one memory?" Nishpa frowned, like something was off.

"I think so? I mean, it sort of seemed more intent on my presence."

"That makes no sense. They're spies, messengers, carriers."

"Carriers?" Quinn asked.

"You know, letters, small packages."

Quinn bit her tongue to stop from answering where they'd put a small package. She was sure magic would be at least part of the answer.

"And Kajaro told you about this. Or hinted that this existed."

"Actually, I'm not sure about that," Quinn said, thinking it over. "He told me about the mirrors and the reflections—or sort of, I assume. I'm unsure if he knew this was there."

Nishpa nodded. She cast several glowing incantations, spells, and something that looked like a diagnostic of some sort. "Hmm." She scowled. "It's attached to you. Like . . . a lot. You're its total focus. Let me just check something."

Another few incantations.

"Odd." Nishpa pursed her lips and waved her hands slightly in a symmetrical pattern.

Quinn glanced at Malakai, who was no longer sitting but standing with his hand on one of his swords. She desperately wanted to ask what it was that was odd.

"Well, I can say, quite accurately, that this little eagle eye was almost certainly supposed to keep a watch on you after the accident. But your innate defenses severed the connection with its original creator and trapped it inside the memory which was, in turn, buried deep. That meant the eagle eye didn't have a chance to do more than observe from a distance. Since it couldn't transmit or move . . . you've been its sole focus."

She frowned, casting another beam of light in a burnt orange this time.

"See there?" she asked, a triumphant tone to her voice. "Whatever happened over the last what . . . nine years since the accident?"

Quinn nodded. "About that . . . almost."

"Well, it's neither really here nor there. At that time, with no other contact, it's become yours. This eagle eye is yours and pretty much just awaits your commands." Nishpa shrugged. "Fascinating, really."

"What do you mean, it awaits my commands? It's like a pet?" Quinn seemed flabbergasted.

"No, not a pet. It's a tool of sorts. They don't have much sentience. Because of the lack of ambient magic floating around your world, and because your own was in no state to substitute, it basically imprinted on your persona to survive." Nishpa looked up expectantly, as if she thought this was the best news.

"But who put it there in the first place?" This was what Quinn wanted to know.

"Oh," Nishpa said, seemingly disappointed. "I'm not sure about that. You'll have to give me a few moments to see if I can trace its activity, or former activity. It's been several years now, so that might be difficult. You should probably lie down."

Nishpa moved to the other side of the bed, motioning to Malakai to move the cage.

He did and placed it on the little roll-y side table that usually held food for the patient. Quinn pulled her legs up and lay back on the bed.

A warmth suffused her as Nishpa's spell took hold, sweeping through her mind with a beautiful golden wave of comfort. It sought out any pain and anguish, any confusion, anger, and all her self-recrimination and left behind a calm Quinn wished she could bottle and drink from regularly.

"Odd," Nishpa said again. "This is highly irregular and completely unexpected."

"What is?" Lynx jumped down from the couch and morphed into his human form, peering over at the eagle eye curiously.

"Originally, it seems to have belonged to the Darigháhnish bloodline."

Malakai gasped this time. "What?"

"Well, more specifically, to whom, I would think?" Nishpa sounded like she was miles away. Like she was thinking out loud.

Quinn cleared her throat, and the fae snapped out of her contemplations. "Right, right. Ardenil, you know—"

"My great aunt?" Malakai choked out. "Why in the universe would that even be possible?"

No one answered him, and Quinn could feel his shock from where she lay. After all, his great aunt had been responsible for removing one of the books from the Library—in a roundabout way, anyway.

"I guess that's something we'll have to ask your mom since your great aunt hasn't been seen in years," she said.

Malakai paled.

Quinn couldn't help but think there'd be no good answer.

27

A REAL DRAGON

Malakai groaned and let himself slump in his seat. "Please tell me this doesn't mean what I think it means?" He sounded so whiny, Quinn couldn't help but chuckle at his misfortune, before she sobered up and realized just how serious this was.

Nishpa clucked her tongue, her brow furrowed in thought. "Do you know where your aunt is?"

Mal shook his head and brought it to rest in his hands with a huge sigh. "No. Also, don't know anyone who does."

"I thought she was dead," Quinn said, and realized she'd said the thought out loud. "Sorry. I just . . ."

"No, it's fine. I don't know her. I've never met her. My mother has, but that doesn't necessarily mean she knows where she is." It was like Mal was trying to convince himself.

"We should probably go and ask her. Make sure we can track Ardenil. Perhaps even go through the memories of the Library to check when she was last here. Anything to help us locate her." Quinn spoke gently, not wanting to alarm Malakai.

"Fine. When will we head out?" he asked sullenly.

Quinn raised an eyebrow at Nishpa in inquiry.

"Let me check this little eye out first. I have several tests I'd like to run. It really is fascinating." She sounded totally preoccupied.

Quinn peered at the eye. "You're truly fascinated by it?"

Nishpa blinked at her. "Of course. You pulled it out of your mind space. You manifested it in reality. It's not . . . that's not how they usually work. And they're never this large."

Quinn shrugged. "I didn't really have a basis for comparison . . ."

"When you decided to pull it out?" Nishpa looked at her incredulously.

"Well, of course. I wanted to take it with me and guessed it would be sort of like these flying eyes with bat wings from this computer game I played way back when. And then I sort of guesstimated just how big that would be. And I moved it to here using the affinities Dru mentioned when she moved our camp back in the cave . . ." Quinn petered out. She wasn't entirely sure why she felt the need to defend herself so vehemently.

"Ah." Nishpa's eyes narrowed. "That makes a strange sort of sense. They're usually about the size of your thumbnail."

"Oh," Quinn said. She made a mental note not to base anything on her computer game experiences again.

"So you're saying we don't have to go and see my mother in the next twelve hours?" Malakai asked hopefully.

"I would think not." Nishpa frowned. "It's more that I need to understand elements of this eye before I'll even have the questions we need to ask. I'm also curious why it wasn't flagged as a foreign element when I gave you that scan what . . . a week ago or so? I gave you the all clear, with no foreign elements in your system. And yet . . . I wonder."

Quinn waited. And then she waited some more. After which she chose to poke Nishpa. "Wonder what?"

"Oh." Nishpa wrinkled her nose as she mulled over the right words to use. "Since it seems to have linked itself to you now, its integration was dependent on you as its sole source of energy for so long, it probably registers as an extension of you now. Thus, it isn't recognized as a separate part to you, because now, it's technically part of you. Make sense?"

"In a weird, I'm-stuck-in-a-magical-universe sort of way, yes." Quinn sighed. Couldn't be easy, could it? "So we will need to find Ardenil?"

Nishpa shrugged. "If you want to know her connection to your accident, and why there was a damned eagle eye in your head? Probably."

Quinn nodded and shot a glance over to Malakai where she could see he was relieved. "In that case, I'm going to visit Drukala and see how she's doing." She hadn't been to see her aunt in days and felt like a pretty terrible niece.

"She'll like that." Nishpa gave her a warm smile. "You could tell my niece to take a page out of your book." And the Furionas fae turned back to the eye, her fascination still evident in her barely contained glee.

"Coming?" Quinn asked. Mal pushed himself up and trudged after her. "It's not that bad. if we have to go see your mom, you know I'll be right there too."

He glanced at her. "True. It's just that I fought her not two weeks ago to avoid going back there for healing. I don't want her thinking she's won some kind of battle."

"Would that really be so bad?" Quinn couldn't help but feel sad that she no longer had her mother to go to, regardless of whether they were blood related. But she also understood that not all parents deserved to be parents, and Malakai's relationship with his mother was set for a reason.

"Probably not. But she gets very superior when she thinks she's right." He shook his head. "Besides, I'll make it clear I didn't come back for her wants."

"Good plan. I can reiterate it for you." She grinned and pushed open Drukala's door.

Warmth permeated the room in a tropical and glowing sort of way. Quinn couldn't help but feel proud of the Library and the way it could contain and cater to its guests' every need. This wasn't much different from the species-specific rooms they put together in the Library for those who needed their environments like home in order to study at maximum efficiency.

Drukala lay in a nest of what looked like clouds, even though Quinn knew that wasn't possible. Her scales glistened and her moon-like eyes fluttered open, fixing her with a gaze full of curiosity. The scarring on her face appeared to be mostly gone, and Quinn felt a surge of relief she hadn't expected.

"It's frightfully dull here," Dru complained, "But also extremely comfortable. Which gives me a conundrum of sorts. Tell me, what brings you here, to seek my company?"

"I wanted to check on you," Quinn said, feeling oddly flushed for some reason. "Wanted to see if you needed anything or had any other thoughts."

Drukala watched her closely. "I've been talking to my sibling."

"Dri?" Quinn asked, hoping the other dragon had woken from his hibernation.

Dru chuckled, and it wuffed out in a strange gust of hot, sea-salty air. "No. The Library. Been trying to make sense of a lot. Stitch the memories back together. We've been making progress."

Quinn felt a surge of contentedness through her link to the Library. That must have been a nice catch up for them. She couldn't imagine having to go so long without speaking. But then again, most age and time references in the Library broke her brain.

"I sort of wanted to ask you a few questions, if that's okay?" Quinn asked tentatively.

"Of course. As I said. It's rather dull here. I'm almost healed up, so I'll be able to go soon. Better ask me any questions you have now rather than later." Dru shifted. Her form began to shrink down ever so slightly and morph into a humanoid shape. Her hair grew as she morphed like liquid metal, legs turning into arms and legs, before she finally stood before Quinn, just as she had briefly back in Naka Region Gate 73.

The burn scar was indeed less noticeable now, just a faint distention of her face through her collarbone.

Drukala winked at Quinn. "You should see the other girl." And grinned before settling herself on the bed in the corner of the room.

Quinn found herself laughing softly. She'd love to spend more time around Dru, but she got the feeling that her aunt wasn't exactly Library material. If anything, she didn't think Drukala would be able to sit still for long. Ever.

"Now. Tell me. What brings you to me?" She leaned forward, her pearlescent eyes large and alert.

Quinn hadn't come in with some huge plan or anything, but figured it was a good opportunity to take advantage of, anyway. "Have you ever met Ardenil?"

Drukala blinked very slowly. "Ardenil . . ." She said it in a way that sounded like she was going through years of files to find a reference. "Oh. Ardenil Irishan . . . Darigháhnish, yes?"

"That's her." Quinn couldn't help but be relieved given she realized even Ardenil's more than a millennium of living was nothing but a drop in the ocean for Dru.

"I recall having met her once, I believe. Why? What happened?" She leaned forward as if eager for gossip.

"Well, she seems to have implanted something of hers in one of my memories, and I was curious about her." Which was the truth, but Quinn wasn't entirely sure how much she should be sharing yet.

Drukala's eyes blazed. She'd obviously taken affront for Quinn. "That's low. Do you need to find her? We could probably sniff her out. Heck . . . if she's ever removed a book and returned it, you should be able to track her through her scent of magic."

"What?" Quinn asked. "I don't even—"

"Has no one taught you about your heritage? It's one of the best parts ever. You can sniff stuff out like you wouldn't believe. Trust me, no one will ever hide cake from you again." Impulsively, she leaned forward and hugged Quinn.

Oh. The Library actually sounded embarrassed. *I completely forgot about that. It's been so long since I was me that I forgot that aspect of our genetics.*

Quinn recalled always having a good sense of smell. Although she'd sort of lost it a bit since coming to the Library, what with everything else overwhelming it.

"Wait," Drukala said. "Have you been listening in?"

There was another sheepish pulse from the Library. *Well, of course I have. I am everywhere in here. I'm just occasionally preoccupied.*

"And you didn't think to teach her about her heritage?" Drukala sounded so offended on Quinn's behalf.

Of course I thought of it. I just haven't had time. We've barely been able to get her fire and scales under conscious control. You know, the important things. She's only been here six months.

Drukala looked at Quinn. As in *truly* looked this time.

Quinn bore it, but it felt like an examination.

"You're not . . . exactly like us." Drukala pursed her lips. "But you're so close as to be negligible. They've added . . . a few mixes in there. Totally agree with those, by the way. That was some smart thinking right there." She leaned back, her smile contemplative.

What are you doing? The Library sounded wary now. As if it was backing away slowly into a hedge.

"I'm contemplating doing what it appears you haven't done," Drukala said with a bit of snark.

"Wait," Quinn interjected. "What are you talking about? What hasn't the Library done?"

It's not a bad idea, said the Library. *Actually, it's probably one of the best ideas Drukala has ever had. I'm no longer corporeal. I haven't been for so much longer than I was. I can barely recall it, to be fair. I'm unsure how I'd teach you to be a true cosmicisodracus. Drukala would be much better at that. My memories are . . . well, suffice it to say I agree.*

"Fantastic!" Dru said, her eyes shining brightly as enthusiasm infused her. "I'll get myself all healed up, and we'll get you singing like a dragon in no time."

Quinn laughed. "I hope not. I get the feeling that'd be loud."

"Of course! What's the point otherwise?"

Well, that's lovely, the Library said. *But as to the reason I came to find you in the first place.*

"Oh, I just thought you were eavesdropping." Quinn grinned.

No, well, also. But . . . Misha is ready to resume their role as supervisor.

"That's wonderful," Quinn said, when all she really wanted to say was *about time.* "I'll go right away."

And Harish has those reports you asked for, the Library called after her as Malakai and she left the room.

"So, you're going to learn how to be a real dragon?" Mal asked on the way to see Harish.

"Apparently."

"That's so cool."

Quinn really hoped it was.

2 8

LIKE AN AFTERTHOUGHT

MISHA LOOKED MOSTLY LIKE QUINN REMEMBERED. STILL THAT blackened silver, those moonstone eyes, the oddly expressive slit that passed for their mouth. Even their bearing was the same.

But there was a difference in their aura, one that Quinn now recognized as a wholeness she hadn't realized was missing before. Which was quite a surprise in and of itself.

"Hey," Quinn said as Aradie hooted like an echo.

Misha bowed their head slightly. "Hello. Thank you for coming. I do believe I am ready to resume my duties if you see fit to trust me."

A small pang in her chest made Quinn analyze the words for what they were. She had the odd feeling Misha didn't entirely remember Quinn's friendship. Or well, perhaps Librarianship was more accurate.

Harish beckoned Quinn over to his consoles. He pulled up information and shared it with her. "See these waves here? Those are indicative of Misha's core health. We've removed the Supervisor's influence, and the core itself is completely new. All we did was transfer the relevant personality strains into it during creation."

"Sort of what the old core did?" Quinn asked.

Harish half scowled. "Not exactly, but similar. That was a matter of

191

using an old core as a base instead of infusing it with a specific persona instead of allowing it to establish one itself."

Quinn nodded slowly, mostly understanding it. "So we should be good?"

"Yes." He flashed her a rare smile, which was barely an upturn of his lips, but for Harish, it was practically beaming. "Misha is as healthy as they could be and is ready to resume their duties within the Library whenever you're ready for them."

One of the benefits of Quinn's upgrades sensitivity was her access to the HUD. She could pull it up anywhere, anytime, and did so right then. Accessing the golem directory, she quickly highlighted and reactivated Misha's supervisory capacity.

Their eyes went through myriad colors, creating a very brief rainbow effect, before settling back on the moonstone appearance.

Misha took several steps, a slight whirr emanating from them, and then nodded. "Excellent. I now also have assistance for the hospital, as well as the alchemical and medicinal branch?"

"Yeah, the doctors know best what they need and were created for that purpose anyway, and they make use of a lot of the alchemical branches stuff." Quinn shrugged. "Made sense."

"Of course it makes sense," Misha said. "Just checking my parameters. I will double check storage and the state of our stock levels, and then I will attend to all branches."

They looked up at Quinn and gave a small smile. "Thank you. For fighting to keep me."

"Of course!" Quinn wanted Misha to know she'd needed to fight for them. "Couldn't let my first supervisor wither away, could I?"

Misha regarded Quinn seriously for a few seconds before speaking. "Not everyone would react that way. I appreciate it. I will also work with the assistant supervisors at allocating resources to retrieve the books we require for the crafting branch. Do you need anything else from me?"

Quinn shook her head.

"Then I had best be off. There are several things that have fallen by the way since I went offline, despite the hard work of others. Should you need me, you have but to call my name." And Misha popped out of sight.

"I'd forgotten they did that." Malakai laughed from the doorway, startling Quinn.

"I didn't even realize you'd followed me."

"Should be more observant."

Quinn laughed, but at the same time was slightly worried that her enhanced senses hadn't picked up his presence, and hinted as much to the Library.

He's always there. Like a shadow. I thought you just expected it.

Quinn wasn't entirely sure how to respond to that, either. Especially not the element of truth in the statement.

With Misha reintegrated into the system, Drukala resting up so she could teach Quinn how to dragon, Nishpa working on the eagle eye trace, and Betty and Dottie running the damned Library as far as patrons went, Quinn felt oddly out of place.

"What's wrong?" Malakai asked, nudging her.

Quinn shrugged. "That's just it, I'm not entirely sure. I feel like there's so much I should be doing. And I feel like I've very specifically missed something."

"What would that be?"

"If I knew, I wouldn't feel like it was missing." She rolled her eyes. "But it's right there, on the tip of my tongue, and it's like I went to get something from another room and couldn't remember what it was once I got there."

"Oh, I hate that."

"Everyone does."

Entering her office, she threw herself back in her chair as Aradie landed on the back of it, hooting irritably.

"Yeah, yeah, you're fine. You've got wings." Quinn searched around on her desk. She knew what had jogged her mind was on there. Like an afterthought. She frowned and glanced up at the murder board. Which also didn't enlighten her as to what could be missing.

Writing things out by hand always helped Quinn master them better in her mind. But right now, her desk was a graveyard for so many lists and theories, so many notes about the books from the restricted vault. Books that they knew had been there once but had no way to trace.

"Wait a second." She rifled through farther and found a couple of lists she specifically sought. Then she leaned back, looking at them, and smiled.

Ririn's Dimensional Distortion Through Sacrificial Means

The Parsneauvian Theory of Spatial Dimension Manipulation

The Crown and Fall of Pocket Dimensions Due to Spatial Interference

Machmüller's Theory of Dimensional Dissolution and Disintegration Through Ritual Sacrifice

DeKarlyle's Thesis of Spatial Distortion

And just below, she'd written the word: *TRACKING? Possible to trace?*

Underneath that, bolded and underlined, was a note *Relationship to each other?* followed by a few more book names. Books that Milaro had flagged for her what seemed like an age ago.

Seveshall Lineage of Mind Healing and How to Break It

The Ashelan Mind Capitulation Device

Chmilenko's Guide to Dimensional Complacency

She looked at the note, and then at the murder board. Then back at the note again. *Machmüller's Theory* was their starting point. Technically. Because *DeKarlyle's* had turned into a sort of trap for Quinn. But no . . . Machmüller's was different.

It hadn't been a trap for them. In fact, it had been a complete fluke they'd discovered it. She didn't think they'd been meant to find it. At least not when they did.

"Lynx!" she called out and tapped her foot while she waited for him to appear. He didn't drop everything, like Misha always did for her. He was a little more stubborn.

Malakai watched Quinn from the couch, arms crossed, and she offered him a very slight smile. Too much of her concentration was on what she wanted to ask Lynx.

"I'm here, I'm here." He seemed grumpy.

"Did I interrupt something important?"

"No, just the middle of a rather tedious task. I'll have to restart now." But Lynx shrugged and turned to her. "What do you need?"

"Tracing. Like tracing magical signatures. That's sort of what Jasper was doing with her ritual circle, right?" She was proud that her voice only cracked slightly on Jasper's name.

"Yes. Sort of. She sent a calls for a specific tome by name and by description to locate it using the magic inherent within it." He paused and then added sheepishly, "I guess it was tracing a magical signature."

"Okay, so if someone had to activate a book's magic, would their magical signature be evident in that book . . . or on that book?" Quinn tried hard to downplay her level of excitement. She didn't want to be wrong and have her idea dashed.

The runic bands around Lynx's hair extended out to encompass his body as his eyes began to glow in that strange static way. It took several seconds, but he cleared again, the runes slowly seeking their usual spot, and he grinned as he spoke. "Technically, we might be able to find a residue." Then he looked a little sad. "But we've had the book back for some time now, and I'm uncertain if the echo on the book will allow us to go that far back now. It's been through so much of the new Library magic."

Lynx looked apologetic. But Quinn shook her head. "I don't think that's a problem. See. The thing is, I wasn't thinking we'd use the book."

"Sorry? You've completely lost me now."

"My thoughts are jumping around." Quinn calmed her mind and sorted out how to say what she thought. "The book was placed and activated on that isle we visited for the cookbook. Remember? With the death tree and everything."

"But we destroyed the tree," Malakai said, leaning forward, his hands steepled.

Quinn nodded. "Precisely. We destroyed the tree, but the magical signatures should still be there, right?"

"Technically, maybe?" Malakai seemed doubtful, but not fully against the idea.

"We have all these suppositions, all these traps they've laid for us, all of this conjecture." She gestured toward the murder board. "For once I'd like something concrete. Like oh, this precise magical signature was involved in stealing and activating this book, and here is the culprit."

"You know it's not going to be that easy, right?" Mal said gently.

"Of course she knows that." Lynx sighed. "But it still makes a bit of sense."

"Plus, it's not like we have trouble flying. And we can still use those doors, right?" Quinn smiled and began pulling up information on the island area of the rabid tree they'd killed.

"I can come with you," Lynx said softly. "Power levels are approaching optimal. It might do me good to analyze the area you got the book from, anyway. But I need you to tell me why you thought of it?"

Quinn was only too eager to do that. "These are Hal's important books, right? The ones he entrusted to us and we lost spectacularly?"

"Accurate," Lynx said, his brow furrowed, as if he was trying to figure out where she was heading with this line of information.

"Well, *Seveshall Lineage of Mind Healing and How to Break It, The Ashelan Mind Capitulation Device,* and *Chmilenko's Guide to Dimensional Complacency* are all ones I believe Milaro mentioned that his family entrusted to the Library. Or at least the first two, while the other one seems to fall into the same vein as Hal's books." She paused, trying to make sure she'd get her point across. "And two of them are particularly overly specifically to do with mind healing or just the mind."

Malakai and Lynx simply watched her, waiting expectantly.

"You know . . . the memories." She nudged their thoughts incredulously.

"You think they used techniques in those books to alter the memories of the Library and me?" Lynx asks incredulously.

"Well, we don't know when the books went missing, do we?" Quinn shrugged. "Our best-case scenario for the *Seveshall* and the *Capitulation Device* is sometime after Milaro wrote the damned things."

"I hate to burst your bubble, but Korradine was around by then," Lynx said gently.

"True, but had she already begun to alter the memories?"

Lynx paused. "I couldn't say."

It was all the concession Quinn needed. "I'm willing to bet she had. I'm headed to see if there are remnants of magical signatures still left with the murder tree remnants. Does anyone want to come?"

Mal stood up. "Of course I do. Although I'm concerned that you've started naming everything with murder."

Quinn laughed. "I promise, it's just apt right now."

"I'll come too. Might want to bring Eric—"

But Quinn interjected. "Geneva. She's more suited to go against Esposians should we run into them, and was with us last time."

"Geneva it is," Mal said. "I'll go let her know. I supposed you want to leave as soon as possible."

"Of course. I'm going to go get food from Cook."

"Do we need acclimatization?" Malakai asked, raising an eyebrow.

"Nope. I'm just hungry." Quinn flashed him a grin. She refused to wonder if it was wise to eat before going to visit the Hostile Copse.

2 9

DECAY

THE DOOR THEY PUSHED THROUGH WASN'T AS ROBUST AS QUINN remembered. Its flimsy hinges threatened to buckle under the pressure of being opened.

"Be careful," she said to the rest of the group as they followed her into the Esposian Furionas settlement. A chill wind passed over her, as if confirming her idea to come here.

When they'd arrived last time, the rainforest had been teeming with life, even if it had ominous undertones. Magic thrummed through it regardless.

But now, it felt wild, and bereft, and perhaps just a bit unstable. So much that awareness reflected in Geneva's face as she crossed the threshold.

Malakai frowned, bow drawn, as he scouted around the area. Lynx scanned the entire isle from the looks of it, his eyes flashing through myriad colors as he did so.

Quinn's own system overlay surprised her. With the filtration power expanded, the rudimentary options she'd had available to her last time had increased tenfold. She was able to bring up information about the door they'd just come through.

Entrance Door to Treeway 6 Dwellings

Status: 47%

Caution: Repair necessary. Complete degradation and incompatibility with Library System in seventeen days.

Quinn raised an eyebrow at the message and turned to scan everything else. The walkways above hadn't fared much better. Not to mention the gardens and the other dwellings below.

Malakai sighed and walked back toward them. "Can't find any life signs," he muttered as he leaned a hand against the door and exerted a sliver of his power.

Quinn watched as the wooden door regained solidity.

"Someone needs to reinforce the hinges. I can't quite swing metal creation. It's too far gone for my restoration to work." He grinned at Quinn.

Filing through her own catalogue would have taken too long if she didn't know what to look for. As it was, she reached over and touched each hinge, just allowing some of her earthen metal restoration to leak into it. Fine. She'd never really read a book on it, but she got the gist. And she did have the affinity, right?

Most of her stuff seemed to flow from her will anyway.

The whoosh of power that gusted out of her surprised her. She stumbled back a few steps as the hinges doubled in size and reattached better than they'd ever been.

"See. I knew you could do it." Mal grinned at her again, crouching a little as he began to blend back in with the scenery and turned toward the village. He paused, calling over his shoulder. "We're supposed to be headed to the copse, right?"

Quinn frowned and looked around at them. She could still sense the endless waterfall off to the other side of the floating island. Memories brushed at her mind. They had more than one option here, but first, she thought Mal was right. The copse was the first place they should look. Nodding, she headed off after him.

To say she regretted the decision to see if they could find magical traces here in order to find the actual base of operations behind the Sölem and its members would be mostly incorrect.

Decay spread through the grass, leaving crunchy black leaves in their wake. The vegetation smelled like a fetid, rotting swamp without the liquid to go with it. Stench reached them all in varying waves. Not only was the plant life dying, but there were still remnants of bodies strewn amongst the rotting flora that had been revealed because it too was now coming undone.

Bones broke through the ground coverage, scattered all around them. Hands reached out toward whoever passed, bony fingers grasping at nothingness.

Quinn barely managed to keep down the bile.

They moved cautiously, even though Quinn couldn't sense any living people around them. They'd also had a crew of Esposians out to clear everything up—but that was before the Ishiposan Isle trip, and Quinn was willing to bet whoever came out didn't do a bang-up job of it. Now they knew exactly where those loyalties lay.

"Keep an eye out," Lynx said, his words soft, almost as if he was speaking mind to mind. "There's something still here. I just can't get any life signs."

That didn't remind Quinn of a horror movie at all. "Something is here, but it doesn't have life signs. You realize you're just asking for zombies, right?" She sighed.

Lynx paused, a scowl on his face. "Well, now you've gone and said that . . ."

Geneva scowled at them. "Enough."

When she said it in that tone of voice, Quinn was pointedly reminded of how she'd halted those Esposians in their tracks last time. They settled down and continued scouting out the area, drawing ever closer to where the blood tree remnants were located.

The copse was up ahead. All the trees swayed, as if their boughs were made of melting rubber, leaking down the sides and making it impossible to stand upright. Any leaves were shriveled and blackened and hung from equally dead branches.

The stench, however, roiled in Quinn's head. She strengthened her personal shielding around herself, allowing plenty of room for the air filtration, and did so to the rest of the group as well. Except Lynx, of course. Somehow, instinctively, she knew the air reaching them right then was dangerous.

Malakai initiated mind communications. *I thought they cleared this area of toxins and potential danger.*

We also didn't expect Adrito to try to ambush our Librarian, but here we are. Geneva's tone dripped with anger.

Quinn couldn't help a small smile as she crept forward, reaching out with her sensory abilities to make sure they weren't running into anything they couldn't handle. Flashes of corpse pieces sticking out of that damned tree trunk dashed across her vision. Her memory appeared to enjoy tormenting her. *It'll be in the actual copse. Don't let your guard down.*

Lynx snorted softly. *Didn't need to say that. This place is creepy.*

Malakai motioned them forward, and they walked through into the copse together.

After destroying the tree once Quinn had disentangled Machmüller's book, she hadn't really given it much attention or even thought.

The trunk itself was mostly destroyed, and the rest of it and what had been contained within it was rotting. However, rising up from the center of the dead trunk was a sludge-like ooze that vaguely reminded her of the sludge in the filtration chamber back when they'd had to repair a pillar and she'd discovered how to use Gravitas. Chaos sludge.

It oozed out, creating a little pool around the erstwhile tree. Everything it touched melted into it as it began to trickle toward them.

"It'd be scary if it could move faster . . ." But that's all Lynx got to say.

From behind the stump, a figure rose out of the sludge. It pushed up and through, taking on a vague creature-like shape. Short and blocky, it reminded Quinn of a squishy toy covered in slime. Black, tar-like slime.

That stood about four feet tall.

It lumbered out, shambling through the pool of sludge toward them, reaching out with stubby little arms, trying to wave menacingly in the air.

An arrow of pure light shot it right through the middle of the head, dissipating it entirely and even clearing some of the pool.

Quinn blinked and turned to Malakai, her mouth open in shock.

"What?" he asked and then shrugged uncomfortably at the attention. "It moved slower than a slug. It wasn't a hard shot. Did you want me to leave it alive or something?"

Quinn shook her head. "No. It just seemed scarier than that."

"Quinn." Lynx prodded her from the side. "If you want that signature, you need to scan the area. I've already done it, but right now, you have a little more power behind yours. It'll enable us to make comparisons of readings if you do it from a few places around here."

Quinn proceeded to scan the area, getting minor readings, not recognizing anything immediately, but slowly becoming distracted. She frowned, taking a wider berth with her scans, making sure she was meticulous about all of her readings. Not only that, but she clamped down on her shielding of the group even more, making sure none of their own magical signatures leaked out.

Something in her rather reliable gut told her it was just as important to know who'd been here as to keeping their own identities a secret from having been here. Several more minutes and she was frustrated beyond belief.

Her sensory abilities were fritzing. Or else she apparently wasn't sure how to interpret them properly.

"What's wrong?" Geneva asked, placing a hand on her shoulder gently. Her huge golden eyes seemed full of concern, and the gentle hum of her wings helped calm Quinn's frustration.

"Thanks." She acknowledged the help, even if that wasn't what Geneva intended. "It's more like . . . I can feel something. There's something around here. I know there is. I felt it as soon as we opened that damned half broken door. I thought it would be here; this made just so much sense." She frowned, scanning the area once more.

Once again, it remained oddly indifferent to her opinion.

Mal had been weaving in and out of the trees that lined the copse and he paused just across from her. "This wasn't the only area, though. What about where the Esposians disintegrated?"

Quinn blinked at him. "That's so true. There was so much magic used there to kill them. Surely there'll be residue Harish can analyze there."

"He can analyze what we have already. The Library will be able to once we're back as well. But I don't see how more samples could be a bad thing." Lynx smiled, pocketing the actual samples he'd taken before he turned into his lynx form and began to pad out of the copse.

The others followed. They moved faster now, through the trees, past the decaying dwellings and tree paths that nature had already begun to reclaim, past the door they came through and toward the waterfall.

Quinn couldn't believe how much duller the surroundings were. Gone was the vibrant rainforest. The vines were brittle, and the life had been sucked out of every leaf, every staghorn fern that had amazed her with vitality last time. This was what chaos did, and the amount on this island was but a fraction of what the Library filtered.

She shuddered to think just how bad the unmaking could be if chaos had free rein. Imagine it with no constraints.

They reached the area at the start of the forest, just beyond the shore of the lake.

Magic lingered, thick like syrup. Choking the air away from them. Quinn adjusted her shielding appropriately.

"Whoa," Lynx said, his eyes brightening as his runes began to whirr in response, winding their way all along his feline body, glowing as they took in the information.

The magic here tasted similar, yet different to what she'd gathered in the copse. However, it was much more potent. After all, even all these months later, that magic had to travel and reach in order to disintegrate the Esposians it tried to coerce. And yet . . . it felt directed, deliberate. That book had almost had a life of its own.

Quinn frowned. Now that she'd adjusted the filtration around her face and compensated for the cloying magic around them, she could still feel a pull. It grabbed hold of her, just behind her navel for some reason, as if trying to tug her in a direction, tug her toward something.

"Quinn?" Mal asked, grabbing onto her hand.

She shook her head. "Just follow. This is . . ."

And she stumbled the first few steps, but then managed to walk with confidence, all the way to the edge of the island. "The tent. We visited the tent to get that damned cookbook, remember?"

Geneva rolled her eyes. "How could I forget?"

Quinn didn't understand. But she knew what her instincts were telling her. And the last few times she hadn't listened to them, people ended up injured or dead. Before she could give it too much thought, she stepped off the island, the roar of even the cascading waterfall next to her blending into the background as she flew across to the small island and the tent.

The others followed, and Quinn made herself wait as she touched down right next to the campfire. Mal landed a split second later, and then Geneva hovered into view, with Lynx shifting out of a bird form into his human one to stand next to her.

Somehow, the tent appeared larger than she remembered, and Quinn narrowed her eyes. This was different. Unexpected.

The flap pushed open and a round, quilled body pushed the flap open. The slothilis chronicler flashed them a huge smile and winked at Quinn.

She rubbed her eyes to make sure she wasn't hallucinating.

"None of that now, Librarian," Carafax said in his slow drawl. "I must confess, I didn't think it would take you so long to get here."

30

CEMENTING THE MEMORIES

Quinn blinked again. But he was still there. Large as life, which was pretty damn big, all things considered. She'd never seen Carafax's quills in the sunlight, but they glinted with the occasional golden highlight, giving him a light dappled look. The slothilis smiled gently at her, as if he had all the patience in the world.

Her imminent danger gut feeling faded and gave way to relief. Perhaps she was just meant to remember to visit this small island.

"What are you doing here?" she asked, even as she felt Malakai scanning the area warily, Aradie flew over them with a deep hoot, and Geneva and Lynx practically vibrated with nervousness next to her.

Something about the image flickered. "I am not precisely here, Librarian. I do apologize."

She barely resisted the urge to rub at her eyes again and just took in the slightly grainy appearance of the chronicler in front of her. "How am I seeing you right now, then?"

She couldn't pick up anything substantial when scanning him, either. The system just glitched. She wasn't entirely sure if she should be worried about that. Her gut feelings appeared to have taken a hiatus.

Quinn felt torn between action and inaction. Surely there was something she had to do here.

Carafax chuckled in that languid way of his. The large, all-knowing eyes took in all of them. "I'm not actually here. This is a sort of memory of myself, though I am glad you are here now, as otherwise I would have had to refresh this enchantment soon."

Looking around herself, Quinn realized the tent was larger than it was last time, and she could glimpse past the slothilis to see there were no remains on the little cot anymore. Suspicions tickled at the back of her mind, but weren't reinforced by her usual sense of foreboding. In fact, her sensory abilities didn't pick up anything untoward. She crossed her arms and narrowed her eyes, trying to see if her net caught a glimpse of aura or anything else.

Carafax's smile stayed on his face. "I left this copy of myself here on my last hiatus from the Library a couple of months ago. I assumed you'd make it here much earlier than now, but am still relieved to see that you did make it back. Magical signatures are one of the few things we can trace definitively. I am glad you realized this."

"And that's why you're here?" Malakai asked this time. Quinn could hear the skepticism practically dripping off the words.

"Yes, and no. There are . . ." The image paused, as if it was searching for the correct phrasing.

But Geneva spoke up before he could say anything else. "What is a chronicler doing out of your jurisdiction? Why were you here in the first place?"

Carafax's eyes twinkled, but not in a realistic way, sort of like a recording. "Chroniclers may travel. We are not assigned a place and never leave. There were messages left here, echoes of occurrences, especially magical ones that weren't fully investigated."

Quinn felt a wave of guilt wash over her. It'd been one of her first excursions. One where she hadn't understood much of what she was doing.

It was like Carafax's visage could understand that. Or whatever he was. "I don't mean that as a slight, Librarian. I mean that as an important piece of information for you."

"We came for the signatures." Lynx sounded defensive, and Aradie swooped down to sit on Quinn's shoulder, hooting like an exclamation mark.

"But time dissipates them. They are here, in a much better concentration." Carafax hesitated before handing over a small satchel. "Do not put them in dimensional storage. It will wither the signature."

Quinn squinted at him. "How are you able to hold that if you're just a memory?"

"You haven't got around to the memory control portion of your mind training yet. Milaro will tell you in good time," he said with measured words.

But it was Malakai who shuffled forward to take the satchel. It clinkered sweetly, proof there were several glass sample bottles in there.

Geneva hovered, and Quinn could practically feel the nervous energy rolling off her. "What aren't you telling us?"

The Furionas asked a question Quinn hadn't had the guts to ask yet.

But Carafax frowned. "Ask Jasper to help you with the tracking of those."

"She's dead." Quinn didn't even realize she was going to speak, but once she did, the dispassionate tone of her voice startled her.

Carafax's memory blinked. "I apologize. It has been a while since I placed this memory here. I am sorry for this loss."

Quinn nodded. There was so much she had to ask. "How are you able to be so direct? Everything you've usually helped me with has been in hints and puzzles and figuring out things ourselves."

But he flickered once more and held up a hand, as if to forestall a barrage of questions. "There is limited time now I am active, but there are things you must know. First. I am able to tell you because . . ." He cocked his head to one side as if referencing something. "Because others, shall we say, have broken rules."

"Rules?" Quinn blurted out.

"Rules that govern how the universe works."

Quinn suppressed a groan. This was more like Carafax. Superbly cryptic. She waited for him to continue.

"Because of this, the chroniclers have some leeway. That is likely the best term. With Jasper's death, it might even open up more." His eyes glowed briefly before he continued. "You do, in fact, have two opponents. Ones that wish to destroy the Library, and ones who wish to commandeer it. Though the latter is less dangerous, you should still be aware of them."

"Commandeer? Take over? Usurp?" Lynx asked, his eyes flickering, his runes erratic.

"Precisely the definition," Carafax said without an inflection of facial movement, and then continued. "I am here because the Library is not safe. Safe communication within the Library is no longer guaranteed. Mind speech has never been one of my fortes. It is not something I felt comfortable attempting. Thus, I am here. I found new information, contradictory information to that which has been set up within the Library. Bringing this book into the Library with me would alert those who do not want it found. However, with sufficient mental protections, your thoughts should be safe. You must keep this information to yourself. Do you understand?"

Quinn shook her head. "Not entirely. You wish me to take what information and keep it safe? Can we discuss it, read it, what do we need to keep it away from?" So many freaking questions.

Momentary flickers ran through Carafax, and Quinn could have sworn his visage was beginning to fade. "I am unsure where your skills are. Reinforce your office. Use your heritage to do so if necessary. Keep it that way."

"Got it." She took the satchel off Malakai and slung it over her shoulder. "Anything else?"

Carafax offered her a smile. "The Library grows in power, but the situation is still dangerous. These signatures are taken from the tree, the Esposian walkways, the attack point, and this camp. They are marked and should hold sufficient strength of magic to track. You will need to use the ritual circle in the Library, if you can."

Quinn nodded, making mental notes. She was glad the others were there. Right now her paranoia ran rampant enough that she didn't believe making notes into her HUD was a good idea.

"Find what is hidden. Find who is hidden. Find the heart of the matter."

Quinn blinked at him. He'd never been quite this cryptic before.

"Deep down, you know who you can trust," he said the words softly, locking his projected eyes with Quinn's while holding an odd intensity for a memory. "Analyze everything, everyone, and you will find the inconsistencies. Remember that everything has a source."

There was a pause, a brief gust of wind that fluttered the tent around him.

"It is too dangerous for you to speak to me about this at the Library. This exception will not be welcomed."

And then he was gone.

Quinn wasn't entirely sure what to make of it. She'd meant to ask him where the bones were, where the body had gone. Why he'd chosen this specific island to come to instead of . . . but then again, at lease this place didn't have the stench of rot and death lingering around it.

"That was . . . unexpected," Geneva said, her expression thoughtful. "I've always loved the slothilis. Chroniclers are notorious for being cryptic. This encounter was no exception."

"Yeah." Quinn still watched the crack in the front of the tent where the flap blew. Not for the first time, she wished they could use the tent flap as a door to return to the Library. She'd always liked Carafax, and at first when she saw him here, she'd been worried he wasn't on their side, that he'd lured them here for a nefarious reason.

Not that he'd been waiting there for them in person.

"What did he mean? Others have broken the rules?" Malakai asked.

"I'm sure our saboteurs broken some rules," Quinn answered absently. Her mind wasn't there. She ran over every single word he'd said, trying to find more of a hint than the cryptic. Cementing the memories so she could recall it and dissect it later when she had time in her office. She could freeze her memories now and work through them. This whole conversation had multiple layers of meaning to it, and Quinn would figure it all out.

Already compartmentalizing, she catalogued the final surroundings. Noted the firepit, the strange little pond. How nothing had changed except the tent being larger, and the bones being missing.

She glanced over at her friends who were scouting in their own way, making sure they hadn't missed anything else.

"We should get going," she said suddenly. The breeze brought an air of unease with it. She crinkled her nose, suddenly certain they'd almost outstayed their welcome.

"Across and back to the . . ." But then she remembered her impossibly large power pool. She recalled her massive amount of mana. And all the affinities she had. "Bugger it. I'm taking us directly back to the Library from here."

Lynx raised an eyebrow. "You sure?"

Quinn nodded, because suddenly, she was certain she could do this. Glancing around, wrapping her power around her, she sought out the best surface. Which, it turned out, was the tent flap. Mal, being the tallest, would have to duck through it, but he'd live.

She touched the fabric and muttered "Solidify" under her breath. It obliged in the same second it also followed her "Create a door" command. Creaks echoed around her, battling her will as it created a small five-and-a-half-foot-tall door. The fabric stretched, giving it the grooves equal to the ones that led into her office. A part of her could tell it wouldn't hold indefinitely, but they had a good few minutes to get into the Library. This was akin to the doors Escadril could create. The one that ultimately took him to his death.

Quinn sighed and placed her palm on the outside of her makeshift door, its creation barely having tapped into any of her mana at all.

"Library, I need you," she whispered into it.

It wasn't the first time she'd meant every syllable of the words.

She hit the ground into her office and immediately began warding the room, even before anyone had followed her through. Her mind stretched, grasping at all the details Carafax's memory had mentioned. She expanded her quarters by sheer force of will, the Library obliging her.

Pushing her own power into the shielding, she kept it thick around the entire circumference of the room. Not to mention the outer walls. Quinn extended her heritage that far too, making sure anyone who wanted entry would have to pass her stringent list for access.

And then she sat down at her desk and looked at the others in front of her. "We're going to be in here a while for me to attune the room to me and those I trust."

Mal sat on the couch, Lynx hopped up on the sofa, Aradie flew to her perch, and Geneva crossed her legs and sat on the corner of the desk her legs dangling off the side. None of them seemed perturbed. They all took her at her word.

Quinn grinned and began to make her list, with those four at the top of it.

Carafax was right. She knew who she could trust, deep down, if she analyzed everything. Now she just had to admit it to herself and set the shielding appropriately.

31

NOT THE ANSWER

Lists were obviously the best thing, which was exactly what Quinn proceeded to make once she'd settled down in her office. She knew, as Carafax had so subtly put it, who she could trust, at least out of those people around her right now. Lynx went without saying, and the Library. Mal, Nishpa, Eric, Hal, Geneva, Milaro, and of course, Aradie. Eventually they'd need to gather to discuss the whole bizarre Carafax situation, but first, she had to make sure that what he'd had given them even held viable information.

Speaking of him, she allowed her senses to extend identifying those people in the Library. He was there, in his species-specific room. At least, if they needed to question anything, the source was right there. It only made her worry more about the security in the Library if he hadn't felt safe enough to approach them inside.

She took the satchel Carafax had given them back on the island and opened it carefully. The vials were suspended in a type of cushioning she didn't recognize. She pulled each of the vials out of the bag and placed them on the desk in front of her in a line, and frowned at them. The magical signatures shifted in the bottles. Magical signatures that were hopefully not as degraded as the ones they'd attempted to pull from the remnants of that bloody tree.

She frowned at them. Aradie nudged her head with her beak.

"No, no, it's okay," Quinn said. "I'm just trying to gather thoughts."

There were several vials, and the closer she looked, the more the substance within them shifted. All of them had slightly different color sheens. She sat them in front of her, examining them.

"Do you have any idea what you're doing?" Malakai asked from where he sat on the couch.

"No, I don't, but I'm assuming the system and therefore my HUD will know what to do with these." Quinn was taking a lot of guesses lately. At least they were fueled by gut feelings, but she knew she needed to get better at making informed decisions instead.

"Probably," he said. "Just let me know if you need anything." And he went back to the book he was reading.

Quinn withdrew the chronicle from the satchel and placed it on the table in front of her. It looked just like a notebook, like any special sort of notebook that she could have got back on Earth. Thick, leather-bound pages from what she could see without opening it. There was writing on the front of it, a script she didn't understand. She activated her HUD to engage the translation protocols, not only for listening, but also double checked that she had them engaged for reading. Which it said she did. She frowned, looking back at the journal. Nothing had changed.

"Can you read this?" she asked Aradie.

Aradie paused as well, a look of concentration in her eyes, and shook her little owl head.

"Hmm, well, at least it's not just me." Next, Quinn leafed through all the HUD menus, seeking out analysis sections, gas analysis, text analysis, performance analysis. Magic analysis, magical signature analysis . . . That was exactly what she needed. There were so many other analysis options when it came to magic, it'd be easy to get lost in research. She thought at the Library, *I need for the console to allow me to insert samples within the wards that I've placed in my office.*

Of course you can do that, Quinn. We have plenty enough power. Restrictions really only applied during emergency or low-power mode. You can ask me to perform pretty much everything now.

Oh good, Quinn said, *because we now have magical signature residue from the bloody tree isle.*

That's a good thing. I may have to engage Harish's aid.

Quinn had thought as much. The desk opened up, and a tube appeared. It looked like those she'd seen at pharmacies where it sucked a tube through piping up and over to the pharmacists. She placed the first magical signature vial in it and after what sounded like a hydraulic *whoosh*, the vial was gone. Words flickered in front of her eyes.

Magical signature sample accepted.

Processing time: 72 hours, Pending Verification

Ouch. Quinn hadn't realized processing time would take that long. Considering it had a database that spanned the entire universe, she probably should have. She obliged and fed the next five tubes into it, making it the total of six Carafax had given them.

Now she had time to read through the journal. But she paused, thinking. Frankly, it was more important to do an in-depth check of the Library shielding. With that backdoor lurking about, her nerves were fraught.

"Librarian?" Geneva said, hovering in front of her. "I think it might be best for now if I help in the Library."

"Oh yeah, that's a good idea," Quinn said.

"I'm sorry, I'm a little preoccupied," Geneva added.

"Understandable."

"Look, I can't help you with any of your system things. Our interactions with the system aren't the same. But if you need any analysis done on texts, then I know that Nishpa, Narilin, and I can probably help." Geneva seemed so eager to help and yet perhaps a bit embarrassed that she couldn't actually look into the magical signature element they'd gone to retrieve in the first place.

"Thanks," Quinn said. "Gonna go help Betty?"

"I might go relieve Dottie of Betty's over-exuberance." The Furionas flashed a grin at her and flitted off.

Lynx sat curled on the floor in cat form, his eyes flickering constantly.

"Are you supervising the magical signature readings?" Quinn's curiosity was piqued.

"No," he said. "I'm endeavoring to scan through the shieldings to see what I can find, or if my perception is off as well."

Quinn nodded, not wanting to point out that if the Library thought it was part of the original system, then it was likely Lynx did by default too. "Good plan. Hey, Mal, I'm going to have to concentrate a lot now."

He raised an eyebrow but nodded. "I'll stand guard." And even though he didn't move, she could feel the way the pulse of his magic shifted around him. More alert.

She wasn't entirely sure how to describe the connection that she felt with the Library. It was deep and involved, and it was gonna suck her in, and even though she knew she'd be able investigate and discover any holes probably in record time for anyone else, she knew that this time it wouldn't be as easy to get her attention as quickly as usual.

"Thanks," she said.

Quinn adjusted the warding on her office to include everyone she trusted who might need to enter the office. Just in case. Either way, with Malakai there looking out for her, Quinn felt an odd sense of safety.

The Library's shielding was ever present. Always there in the back of her mind, a gentle humming. Stronger ever since they'd adjusted its parameters after the whole Tenejo Serpensiril incident a few months ago.

She'd grown relatively accustomed to the shielding by now. She could sense, on a surface level, how the Library was protected from so much outside interference. Quinn understood how every single dimensional door that opened keyed into those security defenses. She knew that each time a door was opened to the Library it initiated a scan to protect everyone within it and the Library itself.

While she was familiar with the shielding, she wasn't intimately connected to it. At least, she hadn't been until her last synchronization. Now, while analyzing it, she could see her connection was not only deeper, but more personal. Maybe it had something to do with her heritage, her relationship to the Library as a whole. It was just the sort of thing she needed to discuss with Milaro.

Quinn tried to let go of the thoughts rushing through her head. There were always so many, not always easy to separate or quantify. Ripping herself away from tangents, she focused on the energy all around her. She could feel the entire security web pulsing with power, almost like a grid, but more intricate. It was vast.

The term "pocket dimension" was deceptive, considering the Library's size and its inborn capacity to adapt, adjust, expand, and grow as needed. And since it would eventually include an academy, it would only keep growing.

Still, she couldn't initially find anything wrong with the shielding as a whole. It was smooth, well maintained, and dense. How could there be a backdoor? How would Dravishk have installed one during the Library's construction? How much forethought had he put into sabotaging his sibling's endeavor? According to his own words, quite a lot. She was determined to find it, but her initial scans showed nothing. Which only made sense, considering even the Library hadn't detected anything nefarious.

It made Quinn wonder if Dravishk was laying yet another trap. Was this some sort of lure? After all, it was coincidentally fortunate that the backdoor had essentially backfired.

Quinn frowned as she examined the shielding that covered every floor, every entrance, and exit. This time around, she set her senses to scan the protections on a deeper level. To find anything even slightly out of sync with everything else. And there. Just a bump. The slightly differential. She could feel it. Something was off. She called to the Library, *Can you feel that?*

Feel what? the Library asked.

That, she said, pointing at the slightest hiccup in the shielding. It wasn't something she could see, but something she felt.

The Library paused. *That's minuscule, Quinn. But it is there. It's not just you. It's something, I guess.* The Library sounded unsure. *Sometimes there's just a blip, you know, where my shielding or my magic hasn't been as smooth as usual. It happens sometimes.*

How often does it happen?

I don't know, a couple of times?

In your existence?

Yes, in my existence. The Library sounded reluctant to admit it.

Quinn pushed her senses even deeper into that exact spot. The bump was almost like a ripple where a heap of strands came together and braided themselves for strength, attached to each other like spiderwebs, plugging every single hole in a massive cascade of protection. There was one strand that wouldn't smooth down, woven through several others. Quinn frowned and prodded it. Nothing she tried smoothed it out.

I think I found it.

You think that's the backdoor he mentioned?

It reminds me more of a trap door. Like, they'd hook their finger into this thread and open it. But I can see how they might not have been able to maneuver it the way he'd originally intended. Quinn frowned at it, trying to figure out how the mechanism would work. She couldn't very well go to the other side to figure it out. *There's probably something very similar on the other side. I just don't know how they would have connected it so that they could access the other side from anywhere. I'm betting he didn't think it through enough. For the concept of entering through a dimension side door he didn't know the precise location of.*

The Library spoke after a few seconds. *He did initiate the dimension. That's the whole point. He has spatial manipulation. That's why I needed his help. Probably the most out of everybody.*

But you combined your magic, right? I'm not sure how that would translate. Do you agree this is it?

The Library probably would have shrugged if it had been standing in front of Quinn. *I always just thought the weaving was off in this area. It's been there forever, Quinn.*

She wasn't quite sure how to respond to that.

It's always been there. It's always been this one little ripple in the whole thing. There was heat in the Library's voice now. *Can you pull it up?*

Probably, Quinn said, but she'd extend the warding first, which she did quickly. It turned out to resemble a groove in the floor with a pull-up ring. Quinn yanked, and it budged ever so slightly.

Oh, she said, *that's not good.*

No, it's really not, the Library agreed. It sounded defeated.

At least we found it, right? On the bright side, it does seem to be malfunctioning and won't open properly. Quinn desperately wanted to cheer the Library up. *And now we just need to seal it to remove it from the equation, right?* Quinn lowered it down and began the process of amalgamating it with the rest of the shielding. *I . . . it's not working. It's not working.*

What do you mean it's not working?

I mean exactly that. It's not working. It's not going away. It didn't seem to matter what Quinn tried. The damned thing wouldn't melt into the rest of the shielding. The door stayed put, even if it was only able to be opened a fraction. It didn't seem like a good backdoor to Quinn.

But it has to, the Library whispered.

You tell it that, Quinn said, frustrated with the lack of a solution. *I can't get it to go. Usually, this is instinctual.*

And it won't even go back with the magic driving you?

Quinn shook her head, at a loss for how to proceed. The threads wouldn't change to allow the redistribution of the bump. *Nothing is working.*

How do we keep him out if we can't seal off the exit?

Quinn really felt that should have been her question to ask. *It doesn't open far, and we might be able to weave a net over it? Brainstorm together?*

The Library's silence was not the answer Quinn was looking for.

3 2

SMALLER NUMBERS

Sometimes, Quinn wished the Library had eyes she could watch, like she did with Lynx, to know whether it was actually paying attention or trying to multitask too many things. She steadied her breathing and rephrased herself as calmly as she possibly could, considering the current trapdoor situation. "We can problem-solve this together, right?"

Sorry, the Library said. *Of course we can. If we can't absorb it, then we just need to seal it, and tie it in to security alerts.*

But we can't seal it completely, right, with the way it's built? Quinn said. It didn't matter which type of sight she used for that portion of the shield. There was no way to eliminate the actual door. For some reason, it was a sticking point for her brain.

No, the Library said. *I don't think we can remove it yet. Knowing my current luck as it stands, it's probably a Death of a Caster thing or something. I can't figure it out.*

Quinn could practically feel the Library frowning. An idea occurred to her. *Well, how about we tie the alerts into the standard golem security patrol?*

That's an excellent idea, the Library said. *Perfect.*

Reaching out, Quinn gathered her energy. She had no idea which exact abilities, affinities, or anything else she was using for this, but she did need to seal it from the other side. She pondered it. She already knew she couldn't just go through it and seal it. She didn't even know how she would breathe on the other side in an empty dimensional space, among many other things.

With power gathered, she closed her metaphorical eyes and touched the gaps in the shielding. She imagined herself using an energy blowtorch to weld underneath the trapdoor, pulling and pushing the fabric of the web of shielding and making it a part of the reverse side of the trapdoor. She wasn't entirely sure why the backdoor that he'd built into the system of the Library was an actual trapdoor, but Quinn got the symbolism.

She could feel the Library feeding her energy, the thrum of the filtration chamber echoing with it. Fresh mana. It suffused her entire body, refreshing, tingling. Finally, she finished the last portion of the trapdoor. *Okay, it's encased solidly inside the web. Even though they couldn't use it as intended before, it's doubly secure now. However, I feel like there's something I'm missing about it. Might want to tweak the entrance wards and shielding too. Make sure we're taking everything into consideration. We've already had enough infiltrations.*

The alarms should help with that now, but it's easy enough to adjust the scanning parameters. The Library sounded distant, like it was doing several things at once.

Quinn shrugged. *Now if anybody from this side is about to betray us like Korradine did, then at least we'll have forewarning.*

The Library didn't seem particularly focused. *Golem synchronization initiated. The security golems have been tapped into this specific alert on a high priority.*

You need to let me and Lynx handle some of the more mundane tasks.

Excellent, the Library said. *And in the meantime, I will add it to my—*

No, Quinn cut it off. *You're doing so much already. When I first got here, I thought you were a machine. And now I realize you're not. You're an organic being with an amazing brain that is very encompassing, but you can't be all-encompassing. You're not a god, right?*

The Library actually chuckled. *No, I'm definitely not a god. I don't have all the power or all the knowledge . . . yet.*

Quinn laughed. *Good to know. That's the shielding done, I think, right?*

Yes, of course . . . The Library paused before continuing. *Quinn. You feel more attached than you were.*

Yeah, I've noticed that, too. This last synchronization was a doozy.

There . . . The Library paused again. *That heartbeat . . . the one you could feel in the filtration chamber?*

What of it? Quinn blinked at the rapid subject change.

I think . . . that might be you.

What?

The Library let out a sigh that felt like a rush of wind through Quinn's head. *Obviously, I'm not completely sure. This is all new to me too, but I can feel it in here, behind the shielding. It's safe. I'll look into it more.*

Sure. Quinn wasn't entirely certain how to react.

After an excruciating moment, the Library spoke again, bringing the subject back to where they'd been. *We need to open another pillar. I believe you'll need more power soon.*

Really? Quinn checked several of the information tabs she kept open—one of them being the filtration chamber status. She was glad of the distraction. *We haven't even opened another branch yet.*

But this time the Library butted in. *In anticipation of. There's a lot of power sitting here. I don't think we're getting through it fast enough.*

Okay, I'll add that to my list.

Just about to send herself back into reality, the Library spoke. *You know, did you want me to have Harish look over those samples?*

Quinn, about to answer in the affirmative, second-guessed herself. *Actually, he's not on the list of people I trust most. So right now, that's a no.*

You don't trust Harish? the Library asked, obviously curious.

I don't not trust Harish, with the extremely sensitive information we've given him and Siliqua. But it's more that I have to be careful and gradually check who I need to add. Quinn was happy she'd figured out what had been bugging her since she'd made the list. *And after Misha's problem, I just—I'm really hesitant to involve a lot of people.*

Understandable. Maybe you'll feel like you can add them in a few days and they can still check the samples, the Library said. *What about Cook?*

Oh, I trust Cook.

What about Narilin?

Narilin's and my relationship isn't exactly what I would call even-keeled.

The Library chuckled. *That's an understatement.*

While I trust Narilin with the books, I'm not entirely sure that I trust Narilin with, well, the security of the entire Library.

Valid point. I'll leave you to it, then.

Quinn pulled herself out of her trance. Her shoulders were stiff, and her neck had a crick in it. She rolled the former and cracked the latter.

Malakai looked up when she moved. "You're back."

"Don't sound so excited."

Mal chuckled. "No, no, just you were gone for a couple of hours."

"A couple of hours?" No wonder she felt stiff and sore from sitting in the exact same position for so long. "Anything exciting happen while I was away?"

"No, no, just the usual. You know, Library almost burnt down. Got sabotaged."

"Shut up." She couldn't help chuckling.

"You feeling okay, Quinn?" he asked, serious this time.

"As good as I'll get for now."

"You realize we need our Librarian, right?" His tone had turned somber. "You can't run yourself ragged. We don't have any other options right now."

About to answer flippantly, Quinn realized not only was he correct, but if everything ran its course, technically—genetically, even—the Library would never need another Librarian. She wasn't entirely sure how she felt about that. She nodded at him and spent several minutes working out the kinks in her shoulders and neck.

"Do you think Milaro will have time to come and see us soon?" Quinn asked Mal suddenly.

He blinked at her. "Well, probably. I'm not sure whether he's here talking to Nishpa at the moment about that eye thing you pulled out of your memory, or—"

"He's not here," Quinn said, her senses reaching out on command.

"Okay. Or he's at home fixing a few things that went haywire. If it's of dire importance, you know he'll come back, right?"

Quinn sighed. "Yeah, I know he will. To his own detriment. To your entire people's own detriment, just because we need him."

"Well, that's okay. He's one of the guardians of the Library." Mal's voice was soft and even, endlessly patient. "Essentially, that's what they are."

Quinn leaned back against her chair. "I know. I know. I just don't like always having to depend on people. Never had to depend on people back home."

"Yeah, and look at how that turned out. Got you sucked into a magical universe, didn't it?"

"Technically," Quinn said. "I've always been in this magical universe, right?"

"You're being pedantic today." He barked a laugh.

"I am a little. I've just realized several things that make me slightly uncomfortable."

"What? You've realized you're succumbing to my fantastic and whimsical charms?"

"Yes. Yes, that's it," Quinn deadpans. "Oh, no. However, will I live with your wit and charm?"

They laughed softly together, some of Quinn's tension easing.

Mal sobered first. "Seriously, though, Quinn, what's up?"

"Well, no, I just . . . since I really have the Library's, I don't know, genetic code, doesn't that mean I'm going to be like a forever Librarian? I mean, I won't ever be able to retire, right? Because I'll always be."

"I guess technically," Mal said, "as long as we found somebody else with the Librarian affinities, which hopefully now they're done massacring you all, we should be able to find one, right?"

"Theoretically," Quinn said.

"See?" he pushed, but she just watched him, her brow furrowed with confusion. "Because you're a cosmicisodracus, and you're probably going to live a very long time, if not forever, then your natural lifespan would kick in once you retired, you know, in like five thousand years."

Quinn chuckled. "True. Then I could just float around the universe, depending on whether or not I can actually turn into a cosmicisodracus by then."

"Exactly. Otherwise, you could just, you know, sit in the academy and read books."

Quinn pushed herself up, suddenly restless. Her back was cracking, her shoulders were sore, and her stomach rumbled like a rockslide. "I do believe I am starving."

"You know you're not actually starving, right?" Mal goaded her.

"I know I'm not actually starving. Thank you for being the pedant this time, but I *am* hungry, and I feel like talking to Cook. I'll be back soon. Does anybody want anything?"

Aradie began to hoot, and Lynx blinked up at her. "Nope, I don't eat."

"That's really sad, Lynx," Quinn said. "You don't know what you're missing. I find it tragic that you can't taste the donuts I love."

"I'll take whatever they're willing to give you for me," Mal said, flipping through another book. Quinn couldn't see the title from where she stood, but she was too hungry to care.

The culinary wing, per usual, was extremely busy, yet Cook stood at their massive set of four stoves, preparing a plethora of meals. Quinn watched. They were very efficient and ran their culinary branch with methodical competence. Even patrons who came to utilize the branch were well versed in their rules.

"And what can I do for you today, Librarian?" Cook asked, not even turning to look at her.

"Lunch, or I don't even know when we are right now. Is it dinner time?"

"How about we call it food time?" Cook said. "How about I make you a lamb ragu? I do believe that is one of your favorites."

"I haven't had a lamb ragu since I was like ten. How did—I'm not going to ask. I remember what you told me and thank you. That's definitely a meal I'll enjoy." Quinn couldn't even keep the smile out of her voice.

"Excellent. I have already had it cooking for a few hours. It will be ready shortly. Just give me a few minutes, please." Cook busied themself.

Quinn sat down next to their stove section and waited. It was calming, sitting in the kitchen. All the smells, and the bubbling, and the background noise, and the steam. It was quite delightful. Quinn was particularly fond of the scent of herbs and spices that wafted all around. Her nose had always been sharp, able to define different smells. And lamb ragu was one of the best. She wondered where they'd found a bay leaf to simmer it with. Her grandmother . . . Quinn was resolved to calling them her parents and her grandmother. That's what they'd been; that's how they'd treated her. Her grandmother had been a damn good cook, and she remembered the dish fondly.

"There you go. For you, Malakai, and some treats for Aradie. I do believe I owe her." Cook deposited a small thermal bag directly in front of her.

"Thanks, Cook." She stood up, grabbing the bag and getting ready to head back.

"Quinn?"

"Yeah," she said, looking back at them.

"Stop second guessing yourself. You are doing a wonderful job. I will be proud to cook for you for many millennia to come."

"Thanks," she said, unsure how Cook always knew what she needed to hear, and not only what she needed to eat.

She made her way back into the office, plopped one of the containers on Mal's lap, who squealed as the heat hit his skin through his pants. She chuckled as she sat down, savoring the scent.

"This smells amazing," he said, already recovered from the light singeing.

"Yeah, Cook had already started my food for me." She hummed as she unpacked her cutlery and took a smell of the aroma, closing her eyes.

"You sound content. Food makes you happy," Mal observed.

"Food is a wondrous thing," Quinn said as she dug in. They were quiet for several moments as they began to devour the meals.

"What do we do after this?" Mal asked.

"I don't know about you, but I have a book to read." She flipped through the journal with her left hand. "And it's got a lot in it. Luckily, I think the translation spell is working on it now. I don't . . ." She paused, a name catching her attention just a few pages in. "The Unusceros? Weren't they Korradine's species.? I didn't think there were many left."

"Well, comparatively to a lot of the other species, they've always had smaller numbers," Mal said, shoving food in his mouth so much he was barely audible.

"Oh," she said, flipping a few pages back and forth to check something. "This book chronicles a Unusceros council session."

"Oh," Mal said. "That should be interesting."

33

ALMOST ARCHAIC

QUINN KNEW SHE WAS RIGHT, BUT JUST HOW RIGHT, SHE WASN'T exactly sure. The minutes Carafax had given her were old, as in ancient, in an almost archaic tone. She found it difficult to interpret their meaning properly.

She'd obviously been quiet for too long because Malakai cleared his throat before speaking. "So either it's really interesting or it's so dreadfully dull that you've fallen asleep with your eyes open."

Quinn barked out a laugh, and the rising tension she'd been experiencing seemed to dissipate with the laughter. "No, no, I'm actually awake," she said, shaking her head. "Just, I'm not entirely sure how to interpret this."

Mal frowned and stepped over to where she sat on the desk. "Well, how do you mean it's difficult to interpret?"

Quinn shrugged and spread the journal very carefully so that he, too, could see its contents. Although the journal was old, magic kept its pages pristine and whole, so she didn't feel like she was in danger of damaging the journal to spread it open. It was one of those Librarian instincts, the knowledge of how best to preserve any book she touched.

She indicated two sections on the page. "Do you see this? First

227

here, *to the order of time allocation of Korradine's tenure* and then there's some legal jargon I'm really not understanding here. But then there's also"—she pointed further down the page before continuing—"*a close race between Korradine and Sarilia to be the next Librarian, not approval-based, voting-based. Sarilia withdrew.*"

Quinn looked up at Mal very excitedly, expectantly.

Mal frowned. "Do you think it's the same person as Sarila, Quinn?" he asked incredulously.

Quinn continued her nodded encouragement, and he paused. "But how? I don't think the Salosier lived for ten thousand years."

"Do we really know that she was a legitimate Salosier? We came across people who camouflaged themselves as the Balisor clan." She paused. "Do you see what I'm getting at?"

Malakai nodded. "Well, it makes sense," he said, "In a weird round-about sort of way. You think Sarilia is really Sarila, and it was a spy, or do you think Sarilia could be a relative?"

Quinn shrugged. "I don't know. That's why I'm asking you to help me interpret it."

"But I'm not knowledgeable." He paused. "Sorry, I'm also not helping by arguing the point."

Quinn chuckled. "We should probably ask somebody who knows." She hated that Escadril and so many Balisors were dead because of Sarila. It made her feel all sorts of empty whenever she thought about it.

"No, you're right," Malakai said. "Do you think we should ask Narilin for help?"

Quinn sighed. Narilin had been extremely close to Sarila. She probably needed to check on their book doctor. After all, she'd just lost not only her grandfather of sorts, but also somebody who had been a parental role model for her. It had to be difficult and yet she was constantly repairing the Library books lovingly and efficiently.

"I really—I don't know," Quinn said. She ran a hand through the hair that had fallen out of her ponytail, pulled it out and twisted it around the elastic band in her hair, trying to get it out of her face. She suddenly felt a bit overloaded. "I really don't know how to go about figuring this out," she said, suddenly somewhat defeated.

Malakai shrugged. "Well, you're the Librarian, and this is kind of the stuff you have to deal with." While the words were sort of harsh, he did say them kindly.

Quinn sighed. "Yes, but you've been here—like as in this world, universe, whatever—way longer than I have."

He chuckled. "Well—"

But Lynx interrupted him. "You could just ask me," he grumbled.

Quinn raised an eyebrow. "I guess I don't need to because you just offered to take a look at it," she teased, her tone light.

This time, he glared at her. It was probably the most unimpressed look he'd ever given her before. He sighed, sounding very put-upon, and picked up the journal reverently, closing it very carefully. "Fine, I'm going to take the journal with me and gather Dottie and we're going to go over it. Oh, don't look at me that way, Malakai."

Malakai raised his hands in self-defense to either side of his head. "Hey, I'm just worried about the journal. It's been entrusted to us."

Lynx raised an eyebrow. "You don't think Carafax gave us the *only* copy of this one. There's no way he did that. Their annals aren't for public consumption. This is, as far as I can tell, a very rare stepping in by the Chroniclers. They gave us a copy, not the original. It has protections. Can't you feel them?"

Quinn let out her magic senses toward the journal, which she probably should have done earlier, she realized. It could have had traps in it, for all she knew. It could have had anything in it. But this didn't. She really needed to start being more cautious.

"Oh," Malakai said, "well, you make a good point."

"Anyway, I'm going to get Dottie." And then Lynx was gone.

Quinn blinked after him. "Oh, well, I—I guess we can go over the results of the security scan I did with the Library." She felt a little off kilter. Overloaded. Overwhelmed. Suddenly very hot, and the room around her felt smaller than it was. And it wasn't a small room at all, which she knew. She paced her breathing: in for four seconds, hold for two, out for four seconds. She did it multiple times, while Malakai looked on somewhat concerned.

"Are you feeling unwell?"

She shrugged. "I'm healthy, just a bit . . . it hasn't been that long since my last synchronization, and I don't think I have quite wrapped my head around the changes that were made this time. Everything is more vivid, more alive, more connected. Especially me."

"Well," Malakai said, "how about you take a breather, while I go over the information you gathered? Can you share it with me?"

She smiled at him. "That I can do."

For several seconds, Quinn just watched him. There was a lightness to her thoughts now, to allowing Mal to take a look at the things she'd already seen. Right now, she couldn't see the forest for the trees and that was a big problem. Compartmentalization was a great thing as long as she could keep track of everything. But with Jasper's death, the revelation about the Library's siblings, the little eyeball hijacking her memories, the core, and the other plethora of things . . . the separations she'd created to keep everything on track were slowly fading.

She couldn't afford for things to meld back together. It'd be chaos.

Her only option was to slow down, analyze everything again, and make sure the lines she'd drawn were strong.

She pulled the breathing trick again. Four seconds in, two seconds hold, four seconds back out. It was amazing how calming that could be. She went through all the memories she had, examining each section of the compartmentalization, and found there were things in there she hadn't paid the proper amount of attention to that she probably should have.

The main thing was the eagle eye everybody had been so shocked she'd pulled out of her head and manifested in reality. When she thought about that, it was bizarre. That she'd dismissed it as something so normal felt odd now. Perhaps there'd been magic to make her not notice it, or else not recall what she'd done with it. How did they shrink the eagle eye down to get into her memory in the first place? Had she blown it up? She shook her head and laughed.

"Everything okay there, Quinn?" Mal asked, looking up from his HUD.

She smiled. "Just realized I dropped the ball on something."

"Do tell." He grinned at her.

"Not yet, figuring it out first."

He returned to the information in front of him and Quinn continued to figure out what was bugging her about the eagle eye and its tie to Ardenil. If Quinn had an eagle eye, what was to say that other people in her vicinity didn't have an eagle eye as well? Didn't it stand to reason that it could be a way to track them and perhaps thereby also the Library? No, not exactly because Ardenil had lost possession over the eagle eye. She really needed to talk to Nishpa. It was probably her next stop.

And just when did they even insert the eagle eye? Just before the accident? Quinn groaned ever so slightly.

"You know, you could just take a break."

She looked up at Malakai. "I don't think a break will help. I'm more stuck. It's like I need something to kickstart this thought I have in the back of my head and help me get my brain around it."

He perked up at that. "Is there anything I can—"

But the door burst open, and Nishpa floated into the room.

"Shouldn't you still be hospitalized?" Quinn asked.

"Obviously not, because I'm already here," Nishpa said in her sort of overbearing but kind of sweet way.

Quinn raised an eyebrow. "I see you're here. *Should* you be here?"

Nishpa pondered the question for a second. "I do believe Dr. Miles's exact words were that he couldn't keep me there if I insisted on leaving. Therefore, he didn't keep me there, as I insisted on leaving."

Despite herself, Quinn chuckled. That sounded exactly like the Nishpa they'd all come to know and love. And she heaved an internal sigh of relief at the fact that the little Furionas fae she'd befriended was back to her old self after her horrific encounter with Sarila. Which was part of their problem and one that she didn't really want to bring to Nishpa's attention right then.

"Why the frown, Quinn? Talk to me." Nishpa's gaze was clear, determined.

"Why are you here? Why did you insist on leaving?"

"Oh, I was absolutely fine. I'm healed. They don't need to keep me there anymore."

This time, Quinn's raised eyebrow had absolutely no effect on Geneva's aunt.

But finally Nishpa capitulated. "Fine. I wanted to speak to you about your eye."

That was when Quinn noticed that the eye was hovering behind Nishpa. Peeking out and glancing at Quinn before it ducked back behind the hovering fairy as if it was shy or perhaps unsure of its welcome.

"Hey," Quinn said. "Come here."

It poked its head out, blinked twice and looked up at Nishpa, who nodded. And then it hovered over to where Quinn was. Its little wings beating rapidly.

"You . . . can you tell me when you were put in my head?"

It blinked at her and sort of held itself at a diagonal. Which ended up being weird with the way that its wings beat, because it sort of went in this weird circle. Quinn couldn't help but laugh at it. "Can you just sit down?"

"It can't, Quinn," Nishpa said. "It's not able to stop its wings."

"Oh." That surprised Quinn. "How did I pull it out of my head, then?"

"I don't know. I would literally have to have a look at your memories."

"Well, you can." Sometimes magic made things so much easier.

Nishpa studied her for a few seconds. "I know I can. I just . . . I think you've had so much crap in your head that I should probably leave well enough alone just for a bit."

Quinn nodded. "Probably."

"I think we have a couple of things that we need to do, Quinn."

Malakai had sat himself half on the desk, his arms crossed as he watched the Furionas fae speaking to Quinn. His body language was receptive, so Quinn was less worried about what Nishpa might say. Despite Mal being very close to her own age, compared to the rest of people around her, she always felt like he'd been there so much longer that he had better instincts than her around magical creatures and beings.

Nishpa sighed before speaking very forcefully. "I think . . . I think we need to go and visit Ardenil."

Malakai grunted. "We don't know where Ardenil is," he said. There was exasperation in his voice, as if he just . . . he knew that it was tied to a portion of his family and he was irritated that he couldn't be more help.

"That's not exactly true," Nishpa said, practically cringing at the admission.

"And how is it not exactly true?" Quinn asked.

"I meant exactly that. It's not exactly true that we don't know where Ardenil is."

"Then why have you been keeping it from us?" Quinn blurted out.

"I haven't been keeping it from you." Nishpa winced as she spoke.

Malakai swore.

Quinn didn't even know what language that was, but she knew swearing when she heard it. Her translation protocol had failed. "Tell us how you really feel, Mal."

He turned around, his eyes blazing. "You realize, that since I don't know and Nishpa doesn't know, what that means, right?"

And then Milaro was in the room, his hands on Malakai's shoulders. "We all realize it, Mal." His grandfather spoke gently.

And that's when it clicked for Quinn. Of course. That meant Arnekai had known all along and hadn't told any of them, even while she'd been in the Library treating her son.

34

POTENTIAL PERKS

QUINN BLINKED AT NISHPA, MILARO, AND MALAKAI, STRUGGLING TO comprehend how they knew Arnekai had withheld the truth. It wasn't uncharacteristic, but it hadn't crossed her mind initially, which was odd. Her own mother, even the foster parents she'd had, hadn't lied. The latter had been a bit abrupt and occasionally harsh, but she felt like all the adults in her life usually gave it to her straight. She couldn't imagine what Mal might be feeling right then.

"So you want us to go find her now?" Quinn asked, admitting that they could. She had grown stir-crazy in the Library and desperately needed an escape. Meeting Carafax on the island hadn't allowed her to stretch her wings as much as she would have liked.

Nishpa laughed. "No, gods no, we can't do that yet. I have no idea how to confront her. Arnekai is far too foxy for that. I need to plot this. Probably in a day or three."

Quinn sighed. "Fine." She refused to count how many things she had happening over the next few days. Maybe some of them would have a delay.

"What do you think, Milaro?" Nishpa asked, turning to the elven king.

"I think that probably sounds like a fantastic idea, but are you sure

Arnekai knows the whereabouts of Ardenil? I've spoken to her briefly about it recently, and I didn't believe that she knew . . . but she's never been an easy read."

Nishpa gave him a look of considered commiseration. "She had practice with your son."

"I know she had him wrapped around her finger," Milaro said, clearly not amused, but obviously reticent to say anything else in front of Malakai.

"Look," Nishpa said, her tone softening, "it's not like she's betraying you."

"Oh, no, she's not betraying us at *all*. If Ardenil is the one who's responsible for all of this—"

"No, I don't think Ardenil was responsible for all of it, just perhaps . . ." Nishpa seemed to be searching for the right phrase, and Quinn was utterly captivated by the golden hue her hovering wings created. "She didn't orchestrate this. It's not in Ardenil's wheelhouse, but she would definitely have taken the ball and run with it. I think that's the right analogy."

"Do you really believe this?" Milaro asked, although he sounded like he already did.

"Well, I think it's highly likely. I mean, her magical signature is all over this." Nishpa waved her hand around vaguely.

"You mean the eye?" Milaro asked.

"Yes, the eye that literally belonged to her before Quinn's accident triggered her innate powers and cut off its connection."

Milaro looked at Quinn long and hard, like he wanted to say something but wasn't quite ready to. He turned his attention back to Nishpa after a few seconds. "Well, for what it's worth, I don't think she's dead."

Nishpa laughed. "She's way too stubborn for that."

"I also don't believe for even a moment that she's away on some special trip." Milaro's words were clipped with annoyance.

Nishpa shrugged. "All the more reason to figure out our approach and find her."

"Okay, so we'll go in a few days," Quinn interrupted, fighting back a huge yawn. Everything they'd just said spun around in Quinn's head, leaving her dizzy and blurry.

"You know," Malakai said, "you should probably go to sleep soon."

Quinn blinked rapidly at him. He had a point and it was one people constantly pointed out. She couldn't even remember exactly when she'd last slept decently.

"Anyway," he said, as Nishpa and Milaro continued to converse in softer voices in the background, having pulled slightly away from Quinn's desk to do so. "This Library alarm grid? I don't see how else they could approach the security, but I'm no expert. I mean, the experts are obviously the Library and Harish, probably Siliqua. You might want to have Siliqua pulled back here for this."

Quinn watched Malakai as he dove further into the information she'd passed over to him. He had a good point. Quinn only had instinctual knowledge, none of the factual basis. Nothing that wasn't simply reflex and reaction. Things that she hadn't learned and had no idea if they'd be effective or not. She only hoped they would be.

Malakai cleared his throat. She'd managed to space out again. "Um, does the Library have analysis assistants?" he asked.

"Well, Lynx, I guess," Quinn said, thinking about it. "And Harish and Siliqua."

"Yes, but Harish and Siliqua are my grandfather's friends. They're not just beholden to the Library."

"Well, no, but they worked with the Library on and off for centuries before it shut down, right?"

"I think so."

Quinn wished she knew and could fill in the blanks for everything she had never been here for. Maybe she could retrieve some of the memories contained in the fabric of the Library. If that *was* a thing. It sounded like it could be a thing. Magic could probably *make* it a thing. Reading the past waves of being or some such. It wouldn't surprise her.

Malakai hummed under his breath for a few moments while Quinn thought over the web as she'd experienced it until she was pulled out of her own trance by him speaking. "This just looks so messy. Didn't you notice how messy the security was before?"

"I'd not gone that deep before. I could only reach the ones that go all the way down to the filtration system on my last synchronization." Quinn pondered that for a second.

"Hmm," was all he said. "I think I need a bit longer with this. I might take it to Harish. Is that okay?"

Quinn sighed. She was about to expand that list of trusted people considering everything they needed to get done. At this point in time and after the Library's reaction, she didn't think she had much of a choice. Harish and his wife were list adjacent anyway, but something held her back. She was still hesitant and it wasn't a gut thing. "I think I probably do mind. We might want to call Lynx in on this, maybe?"

"He's busy right now," Malakai said, "so let me just go over this again."

She watched again as his face shut down and he began concentrating in earnest again. Her gaze drifted across to Milaro and Nishpa, having their discussion, when a thought struck her that wasn't something she'd considered before.

Maybe it was tiredness making her think that way, but she locked her shields down tightly, just in case. She wanted her own thoughts to remain private. Quinn wasn't entirely sure why she suddenly had this massive distrust for almost everyone around her. It might have been because being told she knew who she could trust left her second guessing herself.

Even with the memory gaps, there were still protocols and system analysis and alarms and all measures of security that weren't just alarms. There should have been lists and specific sequences and routines where the Library had to complete regular maintenance. Shouldn't there?

The Library might have been organic in a way, and not actually a machine, but so many of its system integration particulars resembled computers and machines. How had it overlooked so much? Just what did the memory loss really mean? And had it all just been Korradine?

Overall the information loss, the attacks, the missing

books . . . they all appeared sporadic and confusing. She felt like it defied logic. Maybe the hints were in those missing books. The ones that vanished from the restricted section.

The more she thought about it, the more that mind capitulation book called to her. Was it instinct or desperation? Only really one way to find out . . .

There was a poke in her shoulder and she blinked, shooting a glare at Malakai who had his finger raised to repeat the action.

"Where did you go?"

"Just thinking . . . sort of." At least that's what Quinn thought she'd been doing. Speculating might be more apt.

"Anything you want to share?" he asked.

"Not yet." Quinn wasn't about to give voice to her paranoia until she had some facts to back said paranoia up, and right now, that's all it was.

"You," Malakai said, pulling her attention again, "need to get some sleep."

"People keep saying that," she grumbled, knowing all too well they were right. "I'm fine,"

"Quinn, sincerely, you look like crap. You look tired, you look worn, and really stressed."

Quinn threw herself against the back of the chair, causing it to creak, and sighed deeply. "I know, I know, I need to sleep. It's just that I worry."

"You worry about the dreams you might have?" Malakai asked pointedly.

"Yes, I'm worried I'll have another dream that shows us more things we have to investigate, which gives us less time to do every-thing else we already need to do and research and figure out before somebody decides to pull the plug on the proverbial bomb that they've planted in the Library, and we're all just going to go up in smoke—the whole universe, everything."

She found herself short of breath and hadn't realized how fast she'd been speaking, nor how into her speech she'd gotten. It managed to pull the attention of Milaro and Nishpa away from the conversation they'd been having.

"Quinn," Milaro said, coming closer, "are you feeling quite all right?"

"Actually," Quinn said as she examined herself closely. Some of the tension had escaped her shoulders, and she felt marginally lighter. "You know, I feel a bit better than I did."

Malakai grinned at her, "Of course you do. Sometimes it needs to get out of our system."

Quinn raised an eyebrow and Milaro laughed. "It's good to see you listen to some things I've taught you," he said to his grandson and then he turned to the Librarian. "Now, Quinn, have you been doing your meditation?"

Her shoulders flagged. "When I remember."

"I guess that's better than never?" Milaro asked, raising his own eyebrow.

"I've done it a bit. I just use it when I know I have to." She shrugged, feeling uneasy.

"It's probably better to get in the habit of using it regularly. It might help. Now, what was this about you not wanting to sleep?" His tone had changed, and his mentor mask was back in place.

Quinn sighed again. "It's not that I don't want to sleep. I don't feel endangered or anything. Aradie's there if anything happens." The owl buried her head at the nape of Quinn's neck for just a second, lending some warmth and strength. "See, she'll protect me. She'll pull me out any thought or dream space if I need help. It's not that I'm worried, it's more that I just don't want more information than we've already got because we have enough threads to follow. I'd like to tie off some of these loose ends, some of these investigation avenues, before we take any more on our plate. Stretching ourselves too thin seems like it's asking for trouble."

Milaro nodded very slowly, his eyes seemingly distant. Nishpa fluttered next to them. "Go to bed, Quinn," he said gently.

"Easy for you to say." She pouted and then caved. "But I will."

Nishpa smiled and placed a tiny hand on Quinn's. "I can help with that. I am a mind healer."

"I know, but I would prefer to develop the ability to sleep myself."

Nishpa chuckled. "Of course you would. But sometimes we all need help."

Quinn wondered if she was letting her tiredness interfere with her perception of the information she was currently navigating. She saw shadows where there shouldn't be any. "It's okay. I'm a little worried about the security, so I want to call Misha and Lynx."

She called out, waiting while they popped into existence right next to her. "We need to talk about some security measures the Library and I tried to implement. I'm not entirely sure if they worked."

Milaro cleared his throat. "You know you can delegate, right?"

"I've delegated," Quinn said. "Everyone's running the desk. They're getting to do all the fun work and talk to the people and recommend the books and get the fines and go and retrieve books and I'm stuck here trying to figure out who else is trying to kill my Library and why."

"Once you've figured it out," Nishpa said, "and we've gotten rid of the problem . . ."

Nishpa nudged Milaro, who continued. "Then you can do all the fun Library things you want."

Quinn glowered at him. "I'm sure I'll be able to do that, eventually."

She tried to keep the bitterness out of her voice. After all, she'd landed in a magical universe and did kind of love the potential perks. Right now, she knew she wasn't being fair, but at the same time, nothing about the situation was fair.

To calm herself down, she closed her eyes briefly, concentrating on the heartbeat she could feel through the core, right through to the filtration system. She could feel a faint connection tugging at her. While Quinn wasn't sure if it really was an echo of her own heart, it felt reassuring.

"What do you think?" she asked Nishpa and Lynx.

Misha blinked at her with her moon-like eyes.

Lynx raised an eyebrow. "I think it'll take us a while to go through every strand of the security screen, the security web, you know. Make sure everything's working as intended, and better. Misha and I will find the loopholes."

Misha cocked their head to one side. "There is the uneven area Lynx has shown me. I do not remember this previously, but that could have been with the former resident of my old core."

Quinn was impressed. She hadn't been aware that Nishpa was so aware of the passenger in their head,—of the supervisor. It made things a bit easier. At least everybody knew why certain memories and mannerisms wouldn't be present.

"Anyway," Misha said, "Lynx and I shall endeavor to find a solution. Was that all a progress update?"

Quinn nodded. "And just to check in on how you're recalibrating."

"Excellent. Much better than the first time around." There was a small uptick at the corner of Misha's mouth, and Quinn thought it might just be a smile. "Very well, thank you."

Lynx rolled his eyes and popped away directly after the golem.

"Well," Quinn said, blinking at the spot they'd vacated. "That's a thing off my plate."

Before she could say anything else, she felt a surge of power emanating throughout the Library as a door was opened, and she knew who'd step through that door before he even opened it.

Hal popped into view, a chagrined smile on his face. "Ah, Milaro, Malakai, and Nishpa, good to see you. Can't stay. One of the two, three, or seven wars I take care of right has popped back up. Just wanted to let you know that Kajaro is down to one life now. We figured it out."

35

HOT CHOCOLATE

QUINN FELT LIKE SHE DID A LOT OF BLINKING LATELY.

"What do you mean you figured it out?" she said to him. She wondered if everybody she knew was planning to suddenly turn up in her office with a lump of new information to dump in her lap and leave it for her to take care of.

Hal laughed, interrupting her not-so-helpful thoughts. "Right, little egg. Basically, we found and isolated the genetic graft that allowed him to, you know, cheat death with his nine lives." It sounded strange coming from Hal.

A thought struck her. "Wouldn't removing it have made all of the previous reincarnations, like, moot?"

"Ah, they weren't reincarnations, they were more like resets," Hal explained.

"Resets," Quinn said, "like we had to reset the Library."

"In a manner of speaking," Hal said. "More of a body creation conscience and soul transfer."

Quinn raised an eyebrow. "Only with magic," she said.

"Only with magic." He nodded.

"And you've removed this nine lives graft?"

"Affirmative," Hal said, a grin spreading across his face. He probably wouldn't appreciate that Quinn thought his eyes were twinkling, but they were. He seemed far too amused by this.

"How can you be sure you've removed it? Did you try to kill him?"

"No, we didn't."

"I guess if you tried it out and it worked that he'd be dead. You'd have confirmation though." It felt odd to be talking about killing someone so casually.

Hal laughed. "Don't worry. We ran all the simulations, Quinn. Trust me, when he dies the next time, he'll be dead. He'll *stay* dead."

Quinn frowned. "Do we have any more answers out of him yet?"

"Very vague ones. You and your eagle eye are probably the best answer we've gotten out of him at all."

Quinn wasn't sure she liked that, but then Hal glanced at his arm where a watch would be if he had one and said, "Well, I just need you to keep an ear out, see if there's any trouble. I mean, I don't think there will be, but . . ."

"What do you have to do that's so important you're leaving your home base when it's got somebody like Kajaro there? Isn't he gonna get desperate not having nine lives now?"

"Frankly," Hal said, "I wouldn't be surprised if he doesn't get more cautious. I mean, he doesn't have a free-for-all on lives now."

"True," she admitted grudgingly.

"Anyway," Hal said, "I need you to keep an eye on any alerts coming from my sector because I have to run."

"You need us to babysit because you don't trust Kajaro without you there to oversee him?"

"Precisely, and I'm going to be gone. This is the perfect time for something to go down while I'm away."

"And what will you be away doing," Quinn said very slowly this time. Maybe he hadn't heard her earlier.

"Oh, sorry, I did mention the wars, right? Didn't I tell you that?" He did seem slightly less perfectly poised than usual. "You know, the two, three, or seven wars I constantly have between all of my siblings at once?"

"Oh, those," Quinn said. "Funny that."

"Anyway, one of those has cropped up and I need to deal with in person. Doesn't usually take more than a few days. I'll come back with crazy stories and all the time to tell you the information about the nine lives and how we got rid of it. You'll love it, Quinn. Your human-raised brain will love it."

Quinn chuckled. "Fine. Go take care of your wars."

Hal laughed before he disappeared. She watched the spot he'd stood in for several seconds before cocking her head to one side and wondering out loud, "I don't think we're supposed to just be able to disappear from inside the wards, are we?"

"It's fine," Malakai said. "Hal is attuned just like my grandfather, Nishpa, any of your close circle of advisors."

Quinn nodded slowly. "It makes sense." But it also meant if somebody had the same magical signature as a person who'd been added to the wards and security, then couldn't they also get through? How close a match would a magical signature of a sibling or even a child be? Magic was great and all, but it was magic and she still clung, in a way, to a little bit of logical evaluation.

"What are you thinking?" Mal asked and then paused in thought. "I seem to be asking that a lot lately."

"I'm just . . . do you think he came here to tell us to keep an eye out? Like that was his reason because he was going. Or do you think he came to tell us that they'd removed the nine lives from Kajaro?"

Malakai shrugged. "I have no idea. But the point is he did come, and he told us both of them and now we know."

"Yeah, something just feels . . . I don't know."

"It was probably the latter," Milaro said, speaking up for the first time.

"You mean he wanted to tell us about the nine lives and then the war stuff popped up?"

"Yes, that's what I'd say." Milaro pursed his lips in thought.

"Hmm."

Milaro smiled and moved closer, patting her on the shoulder very briefly. "You know, those wars are in constant flare-up around him. It always exacerbates when it shouldn't, when he doesn't have the time, doesn't have the will. But he needs to take care of it."

"Kind of like you and your regions' wards?" Quinn asked.

"Yes, sort of like me and my wards, in a way." Milaro's eyes twinkled.

"Is Hal's empire bigger than yours?" Quinn asked.

"You just don't go asking people about their empires, Quinn." Milaro put his hand on his heart in mock shock. "But since you asked so nicely, yes, a lot larger. The layers of Hal's just are . . . well, let's just say I'm glad that I'm in charge of what I'm in charge of."

Quinn wasn't sure how right they were, but be that as it may, there were things to organize and things to do. She cleared her throat. "I should probably send for Narilin. I need to speak to her about her aunt and uncle."

"If I may," Nishpa piped up, "do you think it might just be best to visit her yourself?"

"Go to the book infirmary? Sure, I mean, I can do that," Quinn said. The more people that came to her office, the less she had to get up and out of it.

"It's difficult to talk to people about grief," Nishpa said. "You know that, I know that, and frankly, having the comfort of the books that she repairs around her will probably go a long way to making Narilin more susceptible to whatever other questions you're hoping to sneak in there."

"Not really questions, I just kind of want to know if Sarilia and Sarila are the same people."

"Well, that"—Malakai looked troubled—"that would make things a lot more dire than I hope they are."

Quinn raised an eyebrow.

Malakai chuckled. "Come on you, let's go see Cook and Narilin, and you need to actually sleep."

"Fine," she said. "I was heading to bed anyway, right?"

"Yeah." Malakai nudged her. "Considering how you were so rudely interrupted just as we were about to send you to sleep."

She laughed at him, and they left the room. Quinn didn't feel bad about leaving Nishpa and Milaro behind to return to whatever they'd been discussing. Aradie, of course, flew along with them. She hadn't let Quinn out of her sight much in the last several days. It made Quinn wonder if there was something the owl sensed that she hadn't shared with Quinn. If it was dire enough, Quinn was sure she would. But that didn't stop her from wanting to know now.

They made their way to the book infirmary, where Narilin stood at her workbench, methodically and efficiently taking care of the books. Quinn stood there for a couple of minutes watching, even as Narilin spread the pages lovingly, such care and reverence in every move of her fingers.

The way her magic stitched the spines, examined the leather, stretched it perfectly, embossed the lettering. It was magical to watch. Well, of course it was magical to watch. But Quinn and Narilin now had somewhat of a truce, a working relationship, and the Librarian realized just how lucky they were to have somebody who loved their work to that extent.

"Hey," Quinn said, as she stepped further into the book infirmary and noticed that there were a couple of people there that she hadn't met before.

"Oh, Librarian," Narilin said. Her eyes widened in surprise.

Now that that she was closer, Quinn could see there were shadows under her eyes. Was it even possible for bags to form in bark-like skin? Quinn had no idea, but Narilin was doing a very good job of impersonating the bags under a human's eyes. "I just wanted to see how you're feeling."

"Oh. I'm getting by each day, one after the other."

It was then that Quinn could appreciate just how honest Narilin was. "I'm glad to see that you're getting by. If you need anything at all, I hope you know we're here. I'll try to check on you more often." She'd been about to offer for Narilin to just simply ask them when she needed something, but Quinn remembered asking for help was a lot more difficult when you were grieving, when you were sad, when you were depressed, when everything felt like it was going wrong with the world. So instead, she took it upon herself to make sure she checked on her book doctor.

Narilin brightened ever so slightly and then balked. "I don't believe you've met my new assistants, Librarian. I interviewed them with Betty recently."

They turned around and waved. "This is Myron." She pointed to someone who Quinn couldn't define. They had four arms, but only two very humanoid legs, even if they sort of scuttled instead of stepped. His face was blocky and yet humanoid in nature. Quinn inspected him.

Age: 85

Background: Book Doctor Assistant (newly created position)

Species: Dwindler

"And this is Fane." Narilin indicated the other person who just looked human, just like Quinn, just like Savinth. When she inspected him, it came up that he was genetically human, and in good standing with the Library. Quinn grinned.

Age: 64

Background: Book Doctor Assistant (newly created position)

Species: Human Genome Variety 79285

"Nice to meet you both. I'm the Librarian." She couldn't help noticing that Fane's specific human genome variant apparently aged like elves.

Fane laughed. "We gathered that. We have a lot of work to do. Your branches aren't in the best condition when they open."

Quinn cringed. Not that it was her fault, but she did take it personally. It was her Library. Sort of. Kind of. If you didn't count the siblings trying to take it over.

"Is there anything else, Librarian?" Narilin asked, as if she could sense something.

But Quinn shook her head. "No, I just . . . actually, I do have something else. I wanted to know if Sarila was ever known as Sarilia."

Narilin's face went through a few quick emotions and settled on mild confusion. "I am uncertain. I am only a couple of hundred years old. It could have been before my time. Sounds very similar. I am so sorry I cannot help with that." She seemed genuinely disappointed that she couldn't help.

"It's fine," Quinn said. "My brain's just fixated on finding answers."

Narilin chuckled. "That I can believe. Okay, well, just if you need anything, you know where I am."

Quinn nodded a goodbye and left.

"That wasn't uncomfortable," Malakai said as they headed toward the kitchen.

"Stop it. That's literally the most comfortable conversation we've ever had," Quinn grumbled.

"Seriously? She's not hard to get on with." Malakai sounded genuinely surprised.

"Well, apparently she's hard to get on with for me."

"Hmm," he said. "Are you hungry? Why were we going to see Cook?"

"Because you suggested it and then I decided I wanted a hot chocolate."

"What's this hot chocolate?"

Quinn raised an eyebrow. "You know what chocolate is?"

"Yes."

"And what would happen if you made it hot?"

"It would melt."

"It'd become liquid chocolate, right?" Quinn asked.

"You're being condescending now." Mal crossed his arms and shot her a glare as they walked.

"I know." She flashed him a grin. "You just add milk and make it warm and it's a hot chocolate."

"I'm sure there's more to it than that."

"Of course there's more to it than that. You can mix in cream and cinnamon, nuts and whipped cream. It's just fantastic." Her mouth was practically watering. "And then there are marshmallows."

Mal smiled. "Well, I look forward to tasting it."

"Oh," Quinn said, "we're here." She stopped just inside the kitchen.

"Librarian?" Cook greeted her. "You look like you could use a hot chocolate."

"Did you hear me or are you reading my mind?" Her eyes narrowed as she contemplated them. Cook was way more attuned with every single day.

Cook chuckled. "You tend to forget that the halls echo sometimes."

Quinn watched them and nodded. "Yeah, just so you know, I've got my eye on you."

"Excellent," Cook said. "Maybe you will learn how to make yourself a hot chocolate."

Quinn laughed. "I can make a hot chocolate. It's not hard. I just don't have to use the kitchens now. You're a better cook than I am."

Cook, per usual, knew exactly what she wanted. Quinn wasn't entirely certain they'd heard her coming through the halls. Ever since they'd explained about her leaking magic telling them things about her preferences for food, she'd sort of understood how they'd done it. But at the same time, she wasn't completely clear on how they continued to do so since her walls were much better and her control over her magical power had increased tenfold.

"Thanks," she said, taking the mug in her hands and letting them warm her up as she sipped it. "See you tomorrow."

Cook nodded absently, already intent on his work again.

"Okay," Mal said as they walked toward the staircase. "You're going to sleep."

"What about you? Your quarters are upstairs."

"I've a few things to do, and then I'm going to sleep because I sleep more consistently than you do."

Quinn couldn't argue with that. She made her way up the stairs, walking this time, taking the time to sip her hot chocolate. She got dressed for bed and collapsed into it. Despite her reticence to do so and her absolute certainty that something was wrong, she fell asleep almost immediately.

3 6

THAT'S-WHAT-SHE-SAID

Quinn didn't dream. In fact, she fell into such a deep sleep that all she felt was comfort, safety, and a sense of belonging. It was wonderful, and she could have slept forever. Or at least until she was supposed to wake up.

A sense of wrongness wafted into her dreams, in through her mind, coaxing her to wake up. She struggled to do so, to push through the fog, and finally blinked her eyes open, disoriented in the darkness.

Something felt off. A dire sense of wrongness about everything around her. She took stock as well as she could, sensing, realizing that she was in the Library. She wasn't caught in a dream. She wasn't in somebody else's dream. Why was she awake?

Something hit her. A sense of unease so foul that it sucked her through what felt like a slimy sewer tunnel, from the tips of her ears all the way through her body, right down to each individual toe. And frankly, the sensation elicited a scent like a sewer, too. Quinn pushed herself up, coughing, retching, feeling violently ill. Aradie even jumped down from the bedhead to sit next to her, cooing softly, looking up at her in concern.

"I'm okay," she rasped out, unable to figure out just why her throat felt so spent and smoky and heated.

And then the alarm sirens blasted. The sound blared through her mind like a tornado siren, practically knocking around in her skull. It hurt to even try to think, to orient herself. But it wasn't the Library alarms. No. Those alarms remained eerily silent.

The ones blaring in her ears right about now were connected to Halschius. Apparently asking her to keep an eye on his home world, it had been an invitation for crap to hit the fan. She'd thank Hal later. The sound blared in and around her. *Top priority. Danger. Meltdown imminent.*

They were the panic-inducing sort of alarms.

A meltdown imminent, for a place that was pretty much a lava paradise, didn't instill much hope in Quinn. Not that it really mattered.

"Oh," she said. "Well, hell."

Before she consciously realized it, she'd directed her body to move. Quinn was up and diving for her wardrobe. In a matter of minutes she was dressed, dragged a brush through her hair, and called to Aradie to head down to her office, which, if she was being honest, had probably turned into more of a murder board situation room sort of thing.

That wasn't as bad a situation as she had first thought.

Quinn was there. Milaro stumbled in shortly after her. Misha and Lynx already stood in the middle of the room. Dottie trundled in.

"Betty's not here," Dottie said. "She's not on duty today."

"Everybody gets days off," Quinn muttered absently.

"Oh, I wasn't complaining," Dottie said. Her feet tapped a soft staccato beat against the tiled floors, showing her nerves. "Not everybody can be a superellex futora. If you have to leave, I'll make sure everything is taken care of at our end."

"Thank you, Dottie." Quinn still had an absolutely soft spot for the bench. She never thought this would end up their relationship. The talking bench, who almost threatened to bite her butt off when she first met it, so long ago now.

Quinn continued to flick through her HUD, pulling up every bit of information she had from the databases of Halschius. She frowned. "This doesn't look good."

"No, it really doesn't," Malakai said, walking into the room. "Can we reach Hal?"

"I don't know," Milaro said. "I've tried. Nishpa's tried. So far, nothing. Really depends on which world he went to. There are so many of them his siblings fight over."

Quinn nodded. "This must have been planned. They had to have known. Maybe, maybe the war declaration was a trap."

Milaro considered her words carefully. "No, the wars of the Halschius siblings have been raging for millennia. I don't think this specific one—"

"No, I mean the event that pulled him away from his home base today. I could have maybe helped." She wasn't too sure about herself now, but Milaro watched her, a fresh look in his eyes, like he was seeing her for the first time.

"You know, that would be a logical step to take," he said. "Maybe we can send somebody."

And that's when Eric flew into the room. "Send somebody to get what? You've got to get to Halschius. Those alarms aren't screwing around." He seemed ever so slightly panicked, which was how Eric showed he cared. The more snark, the more he liked you.

"It's okay, we're going," Quinn said. They headed to the storeroom, Misha blipping in front of them to meet them there.

Misha clapped their hands and looked around at the group. "Time to get you all geared up." But she looked at Quinn and frowned. "You can just adapt to the environment. Check for atmospheric influences, make sure the mana in the area is stable, and activate anything you need to help adjust."

"Are you sure that's wise, Quinn?" Eric asked. "To head in without protective equipment."

"Why wouldn't it be wise? I did it last time." She flexed clenched her fists, bringing her scales to the fore.

"True, I'm just being over cautious."

"What awaits us there?" she asked, her tone soft.

"It's chaos." His eyes smoldered, and he cringed. "Our soldiers are overrun. They were already spread thin, what with the new threat looming. We're being invaded by some of the factions. It's a concerted effort."

"Let me guess, something started inside the fortress?"

"Yes."

"Would it be in a cell of a certain enemy of ours?" Quinn asked, pushing a little further.

"Yes."

"I knew it. Doesn't he realize he only has one life left?"

"Probably why he's trying to escape," Eric said.

"We can't kill him," Quinn said. "I still need answers. We can't let him die before he gives them to us."

"Wow," Eric said. "Aren't we feisty today?"

"I'm not feisty, I'm being driven and determined," she said. "Don't be so obnoxious,"

"Can't say I agree with that," he said. "I'm always obnoxious."

Quinn laughed, because it was true, and her mood lifted some-what. Finally, they were ready. It might have only taken them about fifteen minutes to get prepared, but Quinn felt like it had taken an absolute age. What all could have already gone wrong in Halschius in fifteen minutes? What were they already screwing up?

"Do you think Hal's okay?" Quinn asked Eric as they lined up to take the nearest door into Halschius. If there was fighting raging over there, it wasn't the best idea to open the main doors of the Library, despite how much Quinn preferred to use them.

"I think he'll be okay. Hal is made of, well, stuff you couldn't even begin to imagine," Eric said. "Or maybe you could. You've always had a pretty good imagination."

Quinn laughed, but she could hear the nervousness in the sound. It was more the need to expel a noise.

"Okay," she said, "let's set the destination links." She concentrated hard on the door and remembered Hal's quarters they'd visited last time. He had a warded door in there that worked. They couldn't afford to have their approach to his home seen. She closed her eyes and prepared to project the image and location.

She finished her visualization and placed her hand flat on the door, channeling the precise image into it. A thrum echoed through the door, and she opened her eyes, opening the door with a twist of her wrist. The handle was brass and felt hot to the touch.

"The handle is hot," she said, trying to keep the panic out of her voice.

"That's . . . unusual," Eric said. "I've never had it be hot before."

"That's-what-she-said," Malakai muttered, under his breath, barely audible.

"Not the time," Milaro admonished him.

All Quinn had to do was glance at the younger elf and she knew he was thinking that it was definitely the time, because she could have cut the tension with the knife. She caught his eyes and gave a brief nod, hoping he knew she appreciated him.

"Door's hot too," Eric muttered from closer to her ear than she realized. But she was used to the imp's presence by now and managed not to jump.

"Is that a problem?" The last thing she wanted to do was to open the door and unleash some sort of hellfire into the Library with all the damn books. Because that wouldn't be a disaster or anything.

Eric shrugged uncomfortably. "Probably not. I think it wouldn't let you open it if it was dangerous or deadly on the other side. I mean, it'd either melt or destroy his magic. Pretty sure just the heat regulation is off in his room. Likely the whole castle. It'll be hot, but it's nothing your dragon can't withstand."

Quinn nodded. He had a point. The others had protective gear from Misha. Quinn reached out her senses to double check. And while she was wary, no immediate panic came, no feeling of impending doom. She took a deep breath, turned the knob, and opened the door.

And with that, they stepped through the doorway and straight into Halschius.

The room was not on fire, but it was hot as hell. Quinn's scales slammed into place all over her body. She scanned the area while her friends adapted to the current climate.

With her senses reaching out, she could see the groups gathered in multiple places, but not on the upper levels. There were probably fifty people here, all told. Way too many for her little group to take care of.

Keeping all the calm in her voice that she could. Quinn turned to her group and grimaced. "Not exactly sure what to do now. There are dozens of others out there . . . I'm open to ideas."

She wasn't even surprised when no one else had any.

THIS TRICK

THE SILENCE IN THE ROOM WAS SO CLOYING THAT WHEN ERIC SPOKE, IT sounded like a thunderclap.

"We could use the old servant passages," he whispered.

Quinn cringed at the way the sound rebounded around the entire room. But she needed to clarify. "What do you mean, servant passages?"

"There are secret passages within the walls," Eric said, glancing about furtively. "We should all be able to fit. They don't seem to be locals, so they shouldn't know about the passageways."

Quinn was inordinately glad that Aradie had come with her this time because she was sure she'd seen movies about exactly this—people getting stuck in secret passages in walls or chased through secret passages in walls or something. Quinn wasn't the best in enclosed spaces. Having Aradie with her helped.

Eric, however, didn't seem to notice her reticence and continued. "Can you share the intruder locations with me? Accurate locations?"

Quinn nodded, happy that Eric seemed to be taking this seriously as opposed to his usual flippant nature. But she wasn't entirely sure how to translate the information from her sensory net through to the HUD. She pulled it up in front of her, glad that the Library had enough power for the full system's reach to be restored. It took a bit of finagling, but her HUD allowed her to create an in depth map she could share with the whole group.

"This is exactly what I need," the imp said, his brow furrowed with concentration. "I can try to get us there."

Quinn waited for him to examine the map and where the groups that made up those fifty-odd people were. Although there seemed to be another one moving into range now, maybe it was more like sixty. A shiver ran down her spine. They probably should have brought more backup with them.

Malakai hovered near the door, his head angled as if trying to hear something in advance. Quinn didn't have the heart to tell him that she would know. Her sensory data expanded in the world outside the Library too. Milaro stood with his eyes half-closed, obviously concentrating.

Eric cleared his throat. "Just give me a few. I'll use the tunnels to scout this out. I won't be long. I know my way around." As he left, it looked like he ran straight into the wall but disappeared through it.

Secret passageways on top of magic made her grin despite the gravity of the situation. Magic was awesome.

Milaro let out a sigh. "I could only see one group without your map."

Quinn cringed. "Better than none."

"Wait," Milaro said. "I think there's another one approaching."

Quinn nodded at that too. "Yep, definitely." She felt apprehensive. Milaro managed to avoid scowling.

Malakai reached over and squeezed her hand. "You know there aren't any innocents here that we need to protect, right?"

"Aren't there?"

"No, they seem to have cleared most of the Halschius imps and other residents out."

Quinn nodded slowly. That made sense. "What's your point?"

"You haven't seen him fight full on yet. He's always concerned with collateral damage. Just wait and see. He's a lot more powerful than he looks."

Quinn glanced over at her mentor. "He's always looked pretty powerful to me."

"You're no fun," Malakai said.

Tingles ran down Quinn's back. Just as Eric re-emerged from the wall, his eyes were narrowed. "Technically, we should be able to eliminate five of the groups as long as we act quickly. Before any of them find the basement entrance."

Quinn nodded. "That makes sense. It makes a lot more sense than doing it as part of a takeover attempt."

"I think they're here for him," Eric said.

"Why?" Malakai asked, his expression thoughtful.

It was as if he answered his own question in his head at the same time that Milaro answered it. "Well, if they also couldn't kill him before, because he wouldn't die? Now that he doesn't have extra lives anymore, he's just as vulnerable to his former allies as he is to us."

"Why do you say former allies?" Quinn asked.

"Because he's been in Hal's custody for months now. You think they'd actually trust him anymore?" Milaro chuckles ruefully. "They've probably been waiting for just such an opening."

"You think they're here to silence him?" She didn't think that was fair even if he was a bit of a git.

Milaro grinned. "Exactly. I don't believe the Sölem are particularly loyal, and Kajaro has seemed mostly after his own interests. Now that he can't come back from the dead."

"How would they know?" Eric asked.

"I'm not a mind reader. Oh, wait." Milaro chuckled. "I am. I'll see if I can figure that out."

Quinn almost volunteered to do the same, but Milaro held up a hand. "No, you need to concentrate on guarding us. Your protection spells? I've got a bad feeling we'll need them. And if we want any information out of Kajaro, it's looking like we'll have to protect him from being massacred by his own side."

For just a split second, Quinn had a flash of guilt. That Kajaro didn't deserve to be hunted by his previous allies. But she squashed the pity immediately. She remembered everything Kajaro had done.

And she remembered those who'd been hurt in the crossfire and knew how many more people over however many millennia had suffered because of him. They might need information, but she wasn't going to cry over spilled Kajaro blood if they didn't make it in time.

"We should get going now," Malakai said. He was starting to get a little antsy. She could see his foot tapping ever so softly in a staccato beat.

"Wait," Quinn said, her sense prickling with the approach of the wandering group. "If we go now, they'll find us. They're too close to the passageway entrance."

"Well, we can't have that," Eric said.

"The group that's approaching us," Quinn said, "has about twelve people in it just like the others. So we're looking at about sixty people all up. I'll have mana and health regenerations running."

And she paused because Aradie was speaking to her. *Make sure you put up your shield.*

Okay, what sort of radius do you want me to put it up in?

Protect the group and the battle. Close it off. We don't want people over-hearing it and coming to join in.

Quinn visualized it in her mind so she'd be ready when they needed it.

Don't worry about filling the walls around us. I'll make sure it's as soundproof as we can make it.

Quinn followed her night owl's instructions, running through all her abilities to prepare.

Malakai didn't step into the corridor to engage the enemy. Instead, he let the door fall open slowly. The only thing that would have made it better was if the hinges had squeaked.

It made the intruder scouts hesitate. Peering into the room, they called out to their group mates, "They're here! Quick!"

All of them entered the room, not nearly as cautiously as they should have.

Quinn pondered briefly how gullible they were, before she needed to concentrate on the two to one odds. She placed the barrier around the entire room once everyone was inside the large antechamber.

She funneled power into the shielding to give her group some physical protection. After which she threw up her mana distribution overlay to filter the ambient mana through to all of her group.

It punished her for its usage but replenished slightly more for her than it took. With her regeneration buff in place, she hoped it meant Malakai wouldn't have to perform more than rudimentary healing.

She wished they could have brought Nishpa with them, but the mind healer was still recovering.

It only took Quinn a few seconds to make sure the barriers and mana, and health replenishing buffs were in place. Then she turned and took stock of the situation.

She felt like everything moved in slow motion, even though it was just as her perception sped up, allowing her to absorb the information in the surroundings. It fed into her just like the Library tomes did. She didn't recall it being this vivid before, but she liked it.

It allowed her to recognize their opponents in far more detail. There were imps, eerily similar to Eric, yet with an oddly green undertone. The way their magic vibrated reminded her somewhat of Adrito, the Esposian who'd tried to kill them multiple times with a golem that sent islands crashing through the air.

She managed to dodge an incoming physical spear attack, barely rolling to the side as she inspected the strange creature in front of her, which was not an imp. It stood about six feet tall and looked oddly like a thorny devil lizard that was humanoid and had four arms instead of two. She inspected it, species Spinoboli, and frowned. That was all the information it gave her.

That's all the time she had for it. In the middle of a battle, she shouldn't be reading her HUD.

Quinn shifted and intensified her focus, making sure that she didn't get hit.

Watch for bladed instruments. Milaro's voice came through their mind connection, brushing against her, asking for permission to speak to everyone. He already had blanket permission from her.

Poison? she asked, extending the reach to all of them.

Very likely. I wouldn't put it past them. Make sure you protect your airways, he directed everybody.

Quinn could thank her dragon physiology for the fact that she didn't need to do extra, but then she couldn't afford to be distracted any longer.

She gathered flame around her fists, her scales working overtime to protect her skin, to protect her body. Incoming attacks began to pick up. Luckily, she only had two of the Spinoboli focused on her. The imps had gathered around Eric.

Are they on Hal's side? Quinn asked as she parried another spear with a blade of air. And then managed to roll out of the way of a sword strike. She shuddered. Fire. She needed fire to melt the metal.

She grinned to herself as Eric managed to gasp out over their minds, *Nope. These guys don't belong with Hal. These guys belong to Hulishars. His sister's never been a very nice person.*

Aren't satyrs known for tricking each other and not being very nice? Malakai asked. Even in mind voice, Quinn could tell he was out of breath. He employed evasive maneuvers, and she could barely see him. It allowed him to take on aspects of stealth and fire from areas their enemies weren't expecting. But she was fully aware that it also took a lot of power and energy.

Don't stereotype, Eric huffed.

Quinn was even more convinced that this whole thing had been a setup to pull Hal away so these intruders could get to Kajaro. How the hell had they gotten the information when even Quinn had only just found out a day ago? She wondered if those imps could have disguised themselves. She asked as much over mind channel, just as a sword nicked a strand of her hair, knocking off a lock. Her scales couldn't protect her hair.

Damn it, she said, angry. She needed to concentrate more. *Our senses are too good.*

Other illusions?

No, probably just somebody who has a vendetta or, I don't know, got a lot of money. Bribes, perhaps. Hal doesn't exactly inspire defection.

Quinn didn't have time for any more banter because the spear hit her shoulder. She let out a scream and yanked it out, realizing her scales had prevented it from cutting into her body. It only pushed sorely against the bone and tendons. She grabbed the spear with her scaled hand and activated a white-hot heat, dropping the weapon before the metal dripped down.

The Spinoboli looked up, startled. "That's not possible."

Quinn glanced down at the spear as she gusted wind to slam her opponent into a wall. "I don't think that word means what you think it means."

The sword wielder was next. Quinn rolled back, barely avoiding a strike, a hundred percent certain that if she didn't have her cosmicisodracus scale reinforcement, there was no way she'd have avoided that injury.

There was a scream next to her, but it wasn't one of pain. It was of frustration and came from Milaro.

She wasn't exactly sure what she was seeing as she loosed another white-hot ball of flame at the sword, effectively melting the tip, and sending her other attacked back into the wall with a gust of wind too.

Milaro stood in the middle of three of his attackers, while his grandson rained arrows down on all of them. Her mentor had them stuck in place, crouched on the ground, weapons at their sides, clutching their heads as if they might otherwise come off. Blood dripped out of their eye sockets, nose, and ears in great globs. Their eyes rolled up in their heads as they fell to the ground and in one of them, the drips became gushing liquified brain matter.

Milaro looked up and grinned at Quinn. "I'll teach you this trick next time," he said.

38

RENDER THEM

QUINN WAS SO DISTRACTED BY MILARO'S DISPLAY OF STRENGTH, THAT she narrowly avoided a blow to her leg. Had her scales not automatically protected her with one of the thickest shields she could imagine, the blow might have severed her limb. Just because it didn't cut through flesh didn't mean it didn't hurt. She screamed, a short, strangled sound, before pushing her opponent back with a violent gust of wind that threw them into the opposite wall.

It was becoming her signature move to give herself space.

Testing her weight on the leg, she realized she'd probably bruised the bone. She funneled magic through her system so she could at least function with the injured leg. Quinn pulled her compartmentalization back a bit to concentrate on her own battles more closely. The throbbing throughout her body from the bone bruise reminded her to focus.

She honed her focus on the two Spinoboli in front of her. Scales reinforced around the injured area, making sure it was doubly protected in case somebody wanted to go for the weak point they'd created. At least with healing applied, she could move freely again.

Quinn utilized wind to push away and destabilize her opponents, keep them off balance, and caught the flat of their weapons with the element, taking away immediate dynamics. She also utilized a small gravity well to trip them, as well as modify intermittent sections in the floor regularly to upset their footing.

Applying heaviness here and there to their weapons also enabled Quinn to keep them off balance. They couldn't approach her without tripping, falling, or even swinging themselves off axis because of the gravity and wind attacking them.

She could use fire, but within the room, it wasn't a good idea, considering there were flammable drapes and couches. Inhaling smoke was never fun. While she loved fire and just how well she'd managed to melt some of the initial weapons, she chose the wiser option.

Even though she was intent on paying attention solely to her own battle, Quinn kept a portion of her mind focused on the rest of her party members and their attackers to make sure that she wasn't immediately needed. It also helped notify her when she needed to reinforce shielding. Most of all, she was aware of Aradie flying through the room, dive-bombing wherever she could, those laser eyes disarming their opponents. A laser to the hand will make almost anybody drop the weapon they're holding.

The owl aimed to disable them, because as much as they might not like it, they needed to question their attackers to find out the information they needed. Who was spying from Halschius? Because Hal wouldn't be impressed. Quinn didn't want to be in that person's shoes when he found out.

Quinn reiterated that point and did so through internal communication. *Just make sure you don't kill them. We need them alive enough to answer questions.*

She could almost feel Eric's glare, but couldn't spare the attention to double-check that he really was glaring at her. *You're no fun,* he said, grumbling even in her mind.

Quinn groused herself. *Well, this isn't meant to be fun. It's meant to be fighting.*

Aradie cooed throughout the link and added, *We never said they had to be unharmed, just not dead.*

Quinn suppressed a chuckle, focusing on her own fight. She gritted her teeth. Just how far could these attackers push things?

She knew Eric, Aradie, and Malakai were dealing well enough with the green imps and the two Spinoboli attacking them. But that was a lot of attackers for the three of them. And it was really only the speed of the trio that allowed them to keep up with the attacks.

Traveling with only five people including Aradie had been a mistake. Quinn should have anticipated that the alarm meant that Halschius might actually be in trouble and require more forces than just five of them. Still, she wasn't a mind reader, especially not of alarm systems.

Checking mana and health levels, Quinn was surprised to see that they were holding well within the parameters she'd set. And she blinked as two of Hulishar's imps fell to the floor, effectively bound by chains that, well, looked like they'd originated in hell. Their links were thick and mostly black with what looked like red hot lava flowing through them. It helped maintain immobility in its victims. The imps cringed, but their faces went slack, as if they were unconscious, their chests rapidly rising and falling.

Quinn glanced at Eric. "Alive?"

"Of course."

And that's when she noticed *his* chest rising and falling rapidly. She hoped the imp was okay. She barely managed to focus on the next incoming attack, keeping all of her buffs up over the team, the healing, the mana regeneration, the shielding.

The shielding. She double-checked its soundproofing. As long as they could prevent others from coming to this group's aid, they should be relatively safe. Maintaining so many things at once began to drain at her power and overwhelm her senses. She popped an energy ball into her mouth when she had a fraction of a moment to do so.

Aradie's voice spoke in her head. *You don't need to worry about the soundproofing. Just stay alive and don't let your opponents kill you.*

Wasn't planning on it, Quinn responded in kind. A slight snark to her tone, considering she didn't need to be told the bleeding obvious. *That whole being alive thing is kind of addictive.*

I'm just looking out for you, Aradie said. *It's a lot to keep in mind.*

Quinn grunted. Her owl wasn't wrong. And Quinn had no idea how they were supposed to take on another four of these groups and protect Kajaro. She also wasn't entirely sure why they *should* be protecting Kajaro. It seemed such a weird thing to come full circle.

This time, both of her attackers decided, apparently, that it was a good idea to attack Quinn all at once. A part of her thought all enemies should take a page out of their book. One on one was always easier. They were ever so slightly out of sync, so when Quinn accessed her earthen powers this time, she caught the first one in a block, yanking their feet into a tight rocklike hold, lurching them forward to twist and fall on their arse as one of their calf bones shattered, piercing the skin. A scream rang out, and Quinn cringed.

Luckily, the sound seemed to distract the other attacker, who failed to dodge their own bit of earthen binding. As they ran through it, the earth rose higher, grasping their knees and thighs. When they toppled over, their thigh bones splintered from the force of their run. Their head hit the corner of one of the jagged earth shackles that held their teammate in place. The sickening thud upon impact was a crunch of flesh and bones—wet and hard at the same time.

Quinn refused to look, but she knew at least one attacker was no more. Two down, not exactly the way she intended, but accidents happened. She pushed it to the back of her mind. They weren't done yet; she could reflect later. At least utilizing the earth was an efficient way to dispose of people, or at least to stop them in their tracks.

Her living Spinoboli opponent was trying to free themselves, all four of their arms now working on it instead of holding a weapon. Quinn thought it'd been unlucky on their part. With four arms, they could usually catch themselves, but that one had been dual wielding. Maybe she'd pushed a little too much power into that last attack. Quinn turned briefly, ensuring her shielding was strong enough to fend off any potential projectiles the still-alive Spinoboli might fling her way in anger.

She blocked out the sound of the hysterical Spinoboli trying to push the body of their fallen comrade off them and concentrated on her HUD. She tried to send a message through to Lynx, knowing her current group would barely survive the next four groups of these guys with their current resources. They needed at least another hand on deck.

Lynx, are you able to come through and help us? We overestimated our proficiency and underestimated their numbers.

She wasn't sure how long it'd take for him to reply or react, but she didn't expect the Library manifestation to literally appear next to her within seconds of sending her message. She raised an eyebrow when he appeared almost instantaneously.

"I'll talk to you about it later," he said. "Just remember you and I are effectively a part of the Library." He shrugged and left to survey the area.

Quinn turned around and realized that almost everyone had been taken care of while she'd dealt with her own attackers.

Malakai and Eric were handling the last of the Spinoboli who'd been attacking them. All four imps lay bound on the ground, unconscious, their chests rising and falling rapidly. The other Spinoboli attacker also lay bound, but it was obvious the chains Eric had used were causing this one pain. Quinn had nothing against hurting them in defense, but this seemed unusually cruel.

"Isn't there anything else you can use to bind that one with?" she asked.

Eric raised an eyebrow in her direction. "Sure, I'll just go get rope and do it manually."

"No need to be sarcastic," Quinn retorted.

Eric coughed. "There's always a need to be sarcastic."

Quinn supposed he was right. Once Malakai had their last opponent down and out, the elf went about binding them.

"Anything you can tell me about them yet?" Quinn asked.

Malakai looked at her, just short of a glare. "No. Not yet. As you can see, I've only just managed to subdue this one. I hope that's okay."

"Not you too. You've been hanging around Eric too much." She left him kneeling next to his prisoner and turned her full attention to Milaro. He crouched next to his attackers, and Quinn realized there'd actually been four of them. The one whose brain matter liquified appeared to be dead.

"When did he . . . ?" she began.

"Immediately," Milaro said. "I may have been slightly overzealous with the first attempt."

Quinn frowned watching him. "There's really no coming back from liquified brains, I guess."

He moved along the survivors with a soft chuckle, watching their faces. Blood still seeped out of their eyes, nose, and ears. So much blood made it look like their faces had been pummeled in, but she knew better. There was no physical damage to them. Not outwardly, anyway. If anything, Milaro's damage would be less noticeable once the blood was cleared away. She shivered. She was not okay with any torture, including this, even though sometimes she realized it was necessary.

Milaro frowned, and there was an edge of anger seeping through the mask he wore, as if he was trying not to let on how deeply disturbed and irritated he was.

"What is it?" she asked, not entirely sure she wanted to know the answer.

He glanced up at her, and it looked like he was fighting with himself, like he couldn't decide whether he wanted to tell her what he was actually thinking, or if he was trying to find a way to cushion the facts. He sighed, his shoulders falling, the tension leaking out. "They don't have anything more for us. No new information, no new names, no new locations. They were just simply under orders here. They know nothing."

"How do you know that?" Quinn asked. "I didn't hear them speak."

Milaro raised an eyebrow. "They didn't have to. If you're skilled enough with mind magic, like I very obviously am, I can get into any thoughts and pull them out if they don't know how to shield against me . . . sometimes even if they do. I knew exactly what I was looking for, and frankly, we need the information. They just don't have it."

Quinn nodded, and a thought struck her. "Is that the mind capitulation device?"

She wasn't entirely certain, but the grin and nod that Milaro gave her unsettled her slightly. That book would come back to haunt them.

Eric cleared his throat, interrupting her thoughts. "Let's render the rest of them unconscious for a bit, Milaro."

The elf stood and nodded, wiping his hands on his robes. "Yeah, we still have a few more groups to get through."

39

RIGHT OR WRONG

By the time they'd trussed up the rest of their makeshift prisoners, and Milaro had ensured all their attackers were slumbering peacefully for several hours, while Eric bound them with a different method of restraint. Sweat, blood, and a faint scent of death lingered throughout the room. Quinn closed her eyes and swallowed, trying not to taste the smells in the room. When she opened them again, Eric was motioning them all into the passage.

She stepped forward, unsure how to navigate, and realized the door opened in such a way that it made the entry seem invisible. Being a hidden door, this made complete and utter sense. As they moved, Quinn reinforced her own shielding, as well as that which she extended to those around her. Her mana and health-regen continued to utilize the ambient mana around them and top everyone up.

Lynx followed next to her. He whispered into her mind, *You all seemed to have that perfectly under control.*

Quinn shrugged and turned to him as they made their way slowly through the passage. *Maybe. It's just that there's another few groups of this size, and then we must get to Kajaro and make sure nobody has already interfered with him. Even though my mana regeneration sincerely helps with everything, I don't want us to be so low on magic and health by the time we get there that it's dangerous for us to do anything, or for us to be confronted by something.*

Lynx watched her and nodded. They continued through the path, slowly, silently, their footfalls making no sound at all. Aradie perched on her shoulder, surveying everything. She was grateful the night-owl extended a silencing shielding.

Eric's voice rang through her head, skimming over the top of her thoughts. *We need to work methodically,* he said, more serious than she'd ever heard him before. She guessed he'd probably performed this type of reconnaissance previously for Hal's armies.

Anyway, he continued, *there are groups of them working their way down. We can overtake them and snipe out each of them without alerting other groups. As long as you can put that shielding up again.*

Malakai piped up, *But don't you think they'll be making their way straight toward Kajaro?*

That's just it, Eric said. *I'm not entirely sure they know where Kajaro is from the way they've spread out. It seems like they're searching for the location of him.*

Quinn frowned. *What about hostages? What about everybody who lives and works in the palace?*

Eric shook his head, moving ever slowly down the corridor. *That's just it. I haven't seen anybody yet, nobody. Not even any bodies. So they've either evacuated them, moved them to somewhere else, or disintegrated them.*

Quinn shuddered at the thought. *Disintegration? Doesn't sound like the best way to go.*

Eric shrugged. *Quick and painless.*

Point, Quinn acknowledged. *We don't have any hostages to worry about, and Hal probably won't hate us if we do some not-permanent damage to the palace?*

Milaro chuckled. *Well, he won't hate* you. *I don't think he could ever hate you, but he will probably ask you to pay for the repairs.*

Quinn shrugged. *I'm sure the Library's coffers are deep.*

Milaro's sigh echoed through Quinn's mind. *What we need to take care of is making sure that none of them can alert another group to our presence. They need to think we're still clueless as to their presence here.*

What if they're waiting on communication from the group we just put out of commission? Malakai asked.

Can we intercept their communication? Quinn asked.

Not exactly, Milaro said. *We have to be aware and make sure we're blocking any communications.*

You can do that, right? Quinn said.

You're already doing that with your shielding, which should show up as interference and not just a block, so . . . But Milaro didn't continue. Eric and he paused, listening for several seconds, and Lynx ended up next to Quinn in the overly narrow passageway.

Quinn didn't understand how creatures like the satyrs and some of the other inhabitants of Halschius would ever fit in these spaces. Then again, she didn't think the satyrs were the type of species that *served* the King of Halschius. She might have to ask him about that. The path seemed inordinately narrow, but it served its purpose. It allowed them to seamlessly move from place to place within the building as if they were ghosts.

After several seconds, Eric's voice rang in her head again. *Once they find Kajaro, I believe they'll send out an alert to each other that he's there and make their way down. We simply have to keep them unaware of his precise location until we wipe out a few more groups.* He fell silent again.

Quinn wasn't entirely sure why he'd reiterated their point, except that it sounded as if he was trying to convince himself. This was his home, after all.

It was several seconds of waiting before Eric motioned with his hand. *Everybody gather around. They're approaching. Once they pass us, we'll go out behind them. It's the best way for us to file out and appear instead of doing so gradually in front of them. It gives us a slight advantage; I believe.*

Quinn nodded. This wasn't exactly her area of expertise, this whole strategizing thing.

Milaro spoke softly. *We don't want to pull them anywhere near the passage. We can't risk them knowing about it and somehow getting a message out. There could be a way that they do, but I'm fairly certain the barrier Aradie is assisting you in maintaining blocks any type of telepathic speech beyond it as well. It should be enough to prevent any type of outside communication.*

Quinn nodded. She didn't feel ready for this. She didn't like fighting other people, but she knew she could. And she knew if she let herself go, she'd be lethal. She could hear their opponent's feet shuffling if she concentrated truly hard, sending out her senses to double check. There were ten of them this time, as opposed to the dozen they'd had before. Five of them were imps. Five of them were Spinoboli. She frowned. Their group should be able to neutralize them. Aradie and Lynx could easily work together to take two down. Quinn reinforced her mana and health regeneration and waited for the signal.

Now, Milaro uttered, his words echoing through Quinn's brain, ringing like an alarm.

They tumbled out of the passageway, though Quinn thought it was probably closer to stepping out less than gracefully. Quinn slammed up the shielding around them and the group that was several meters past them now. Their footfalls were still silent, and they managed to creep out of the passageway without alerting the group that had just passed them. It probably helped that the group was talking in hushed whispers with each other, and thus any slight noise Quinn's group made wasn't heard.

It was tricky timing, and she wasn't sure how they managed it, but it did seem that Aradie had filled the spaces in Quinn's shielding walls with the right soundproofing. Quinn's group glanced at each other. Milaro counted down in their heads.

Three . . .

Two . . .

One . . .

It was really amazing what the element of surprise could do. It was the safer option, the better option, and in this case, appeared to be the quicker option. It served them well.

Two imps went down immediately. They were bound by Eric's glowing chains, dragging them into the floor with a clink that set

Quinn's nerves on fire. Those imps dropped effectively, becoming useless, thrashing in the chains, which only made them pull tighter.

At the same time, Milaro dropped two of the Spinoboli immediately. They clutched at their heads with both pairs of hands, falling to their knees, to the ground, completely rolling on it as their eyes and ears and noses bled profusely. If Quinn wasn't mistaken, she was sure some blood even exited the pores of their skin. She shuddered, not entirely sure she should let Milaro show her this little trick. They needed to get that capitulation device book back as well, because this, this wasn't a skill Quinn wanted in the hands of her enemies.

In that same moment, Quinn also used her ability to command the stone under the feet of the Spinoboli. Just like before, it caught them unawares. The one that she took out on the left managed to trip and face-plant badly enough that she was sure he'd knocked himself out. This time, however, there didn't appear to be any broken bones poking through perfectly good skin, and the lack of a crunch made Quinn feel slightly less queasy. That first one had a sword which fell out of their hand as they tumbled over without control. It was amazing what happened when you couldn't right yourself because your calves were locked into the ground.

But her second attacker, the one on the right, had a bow and arrow. Luckily, because they'd attacked their opponents from behind, it was very difficult for the Spinoboli to activate whatever spell or skill they were using to aim the arrows behind them. After a couple of misfired shots, Malakai took out his opponent of the same weapon with an arrow through the wrist. Quinn whisked the bow out of their hands with a particularly harsh gust of wind. It left only four more opponents needing to be dispatched who were still grasping around trying to understand the situation because everything had happened so fast.

A voice in the back of Quinn's mind kept whispering that this was far too easy, that she couldn't take this for granted because, obviously, something else was lurking. She couldn't help but agree. As the rest of them were trussed up, Milaro went from body to body, double-checking, making sure that they didn't have any information.

"Nothing," he said, throwing his hands up. "Again, they know nothing."

"Well, they're all just henchmen, right?" Malakai asked, running his hand through his hair. He glanced at his grandfather. "I mean, surely you can't be that naïve."

Milaro raised an eyebrow. "I'm not naïve. What I am is frustrated that they haven't even sent a competent person to any of these groups so far."

"Well, that could be," Eric ventured. "I mean, it could be because they didn't expect these groups to find Kajaro. Maybe the next ones will be more challenging."

The idea occurred to Quinn that perhaps these groups were more of a decoy. Maybe they were meant to keep any potential rescuers occupied. She was certain everyone else wondered the same thing. They just couldn't risk not taking care of the outliers.

After Eric and Malakai moved their bound prisoners into a room not too far off and Milaro made sure they'd all sleep for hours on end, they went back in the passageway to make it to the next group. This time the passageway cut over and it took them a few minutes to round on the next ones.

Eric frowned while they waited for them to pass. *These guys are completely out of the way of their patrol.*

The third group they subdued took about the same time as the second, and Quinn was left feeling like there was something she'd missed.

Do you think, Lynx interjected, *that this is all a trap and they're just wanting to lull us into a false sense of security and are triangulating to ambush us?*

They turned and blinked at him. Lynx shrugged. Quinn knew he was a manifestation and thus probably had a different perspective on a lot of stuff. The thing was, Quinn really agreed it was too easy because the second and third groups fell so easily.

She put her hands on her hips as they bound their captives up, had Milaro put them into slumber for the next half day or so, and began to move them toward another room.

"You know, Lynx might be right," Quinn said, hands on her hips, as she surveyed the area. There was no sign of life from anywhere else in the castle. Nothing at all. Just an eerie heat that permeated the entire building, and being in Halschius. Of *course,* it permeated the entire building. She frowned. "I don't understand. It shouldn't be this easy."

"To be fair," Eric said, "they're sending groups of ten to find one man."

Quinn shook her head. "One man guarded by, what, ten people? One on one wouldn't even faze them."

"I don't think," Malakai said, "that they're worried about one on one. I get the feeling there's something much bigger at play."

Quinn shrugged. "Maybe." She still felt uneasy, perhaps even more so now.

They made their way back into the passageways, silently moving through to find the next group.

Lynx nudged Quinn, and she looked at him as he spoke into only her mind. *You know you didn't really need me, right?*

No, we did. We'd probably be much worse on the mana front otherwise.

You thought all the fights would be the same as the first one, didn't you?

Quinn nodded, *I feel like they're baiting us right now.*

I think you're right.

Luckily, they were almost at the next group. Quinn wasn't sure if she wanted to find out just how right or wrong she was.

4 0

ELECTRIC VOID

QUINN HAD WANTED TO BE WRONG, DESPERATELY WANTED TO BE wrong. Yet when they came upon the next target, creeping out of the passageway to ambush them from behind, she couldn't deny the truth. They absolutely annihilated them in such a way that it was almost painful. It wasn't the most sportsmanlike way to defeat their opponents, but Quinn thought it was warranted considering they were yet again outnumbered almost two to one.

For infiltrators, intruders, who'd cleared everything out, who'd rid the place of everybody there—these people just weren't skilled enough.

Milaro's frustration was palpable. Their opponents knew nothing; they had nothing. She thought he might tear his hair out.

Eventually, he sighed and pushed himself back up to standing. "But at least now we know how they had managed to clear everyone out."

"How?" Quinn asked.

"Well"—he indicated loosely around them—"they came in as a group of sixty, which is pretty imposing when there are only scattered groups of three or four in the palace. It appears that Hal only had a perfunctory guard on the palace. If everything outside of it was taken care of, those people infiltrating the inner sanctum won't have to worry about it."

Quinn mulled it over. He was right. They'd made it in, despite the odds. They should probably be grateful that the intruders hadn't chosen to massacre everyone in their path. She watched as the others bound the infiltrators, setting them into another room where Milaro made sure they'd stay asleep for hours. Now she wanted to tear *her* hair out in frustration because even with this dozen down, there was still another dozen left that they had to face. She could only hope that they'd get answers from the last twelve people. Otherwise, this was all for nothing.

After tidying up behind the fourth group, they decided to enter the passageway again. But Eric stopped and frowned after a couple of minutes. He looked around back and forth, obviously checking the map that she'd sent him in the HUD.

"No," he said, "we can't get to them from here. These passageways don't go down to the dungeons. They veer around to the kitchens."

Quinn reinforced her senses and looked at Milaro for reassurance, but he just shrugged in his own irritation back at her. She reached out, feeling around, but also came back annoyed. "I can't pick anything else up out there. Only that this last group feels more solid."

Malakai grunted. "Yeah, that probably means they're stronger, right?"

Milaro groaned. "Likely."

"But that's good, right?" Quinn asked. Because wasn't it? Hadn't they just been complaining that this all felt too easy? Too good to be true? "I mean, it's better that these are people who've been sent here to do a job rather than just to distract us from something we haven't discovered yet, right?"

Milaro shrugged. "Yes and no," he said.

"What do you mean, yes and no?"

"I mean, it'd be really nice having an easy go of it."

Quinn rolled her eyes. "If we just want it to be easy, we should ambush this group, too. Let's time our attacks through telepathy, and do what we do." She wondered if she came off as impatient as she felt.

Probably. She wasn't really fussed right then. The others blinked at her. "Anyway, how do we get there?"

Eric spent several more seconds studying his HUD before he spoke. "We'll have to take this passage a bit further, up to where it breaks off to the kitchen and disappears. Then take the hallway to the stairs." He hesitated, narrowing his eyes as he followed the map. "I think the group is actually getting closer to Kajaro's holding cell."

Quinn, having been there to see Kajaro already recently, tried to figure out where they were according to the map in her head, but needed to pull up the HUD again. Quinn knew that if this group got there . . . well, it wouldn't be pretty.

Milaro stretched his arms above his head, cracked his knuckles and said, "I guess there's no time like the present?"

Eric butted in before Milaro could say anything else. "Speak telepathically once we're closer. They won't hear us for now. There's too much interference between us and where they are, even if they have enhanced hearing."

Lynx piped up. "Regardless of their species, I doubt they can hear through the shielding anyway."

"True. While we're out of combat it's not even a drain." Quinn sighed with relief. She liked speaking telepathically, but then she couldn't take facial cues properly, and that always led to misunderstandings.

Eric nodded. "Excellent."

Moving ahead, they exited the passageways, coming into the gorgeous hallways shaped by the igneous rock sculpting, opulently decorated with carpets that Quinn thought probably cost an arm and a leg. There were sconces along the walls, lit with low-yield flames that somehow still illuminated the corridor in a beautiful, shadowy way. Some of the rock glistened as if there was glitter or some sort of precious metal embedded inside. But when scanning Quinn realized the sparkliness was magic residue.

Which just made her appreciate magic all over again. She chuckled internally because it didn't seem like the right time to be chuckling externally. The whole palace or castle reminded her of medieval dungeons that she'd seen in movies or even in documentaries. The paths wound around in ways that belied the size of the palace she'd seen from a distance, but then again, handwavy magic made the impossible happen.

Just when she thought they'd come to the end of the corridor, another one popped up, a winding chicane away from the previous one. If she'd been alone without a map, she'd have been lost for years. Maybe it would have behooved her to take the course cartography 101. She couldn't even follow the map on her HUD easily.

The surrounding conversation moved on to mild speculation and discussions about why these intruders were after Kajaro in the first place.

"Why would they want to silence him, do you think?" Eric asked.

Quinn raised an eyebrow. "Because he knows everything they've done and have planned, plus where they live, where they train, where they hide. Probably."

Milaro continued the list without missing a beat. "And how they recruit, how they insinuate themselves into people's lives in order to give themselves leverage to lure others to their cause."

"My, my, Grandfather, that sounds like you have had first-hand experience at this," Malakai teased, although Quinn noted there was a hint of trepidation in his voice.

Milaro did not chuckle in response. Instead, his voice grew grave. "Well, I've been around for thousands of years, and I've seen some crap in my time."

Quinn realized that while she knew him as old, he rarely acted like it.

"Anyway," the elf king said, "I am quite certain it's to stop him from spilling secrets. He's bound to know too much.

"Why didn't they kill him before?" Eric asked and then hit himself in the head. "It's okay, don't answer it."

"No, let me clarify it for you," Malakai said, "because your poor little brain hasn't been able to absorb the knowledge."

"Shut up, Malakai," Eric said, a little snarkily.

Malakai ignored him. "You see, it's because he had all these lives and could just pop back up wreak havoc on his attackers. That only had to happen once."

"How did they get word," Milaro started this time, "that he no longer has those lives?"

Which was one of the biggest problems Quinn had with the whole thing, because they hadn't even known before yesterday afternoon. "I have no clue. How did they manage to get an entire contingent of people ready to move and out the door? Even if they somehow overheard it in the Library yesterday when Hal came to visit, or somehow defected it from here. Didn't they know Uncle Hal will just track them down? I don't understand how they moved this quickly."

"Well," Milaro said, "their team was probably already organized and waiting for Hal to break through and remove the magical graft. They likely didn't count on him having not only guards but also a backup plan in place."

Quinn supposed that made a lot of sense. So Malakai changed the subject and turned to Eric. "Did this group just head straight here? Were the others decoys?"

"No," Eric answered. "I don't think so. I think they all started at different points in the castle, and unluckily, they didn't locate his cell yet. So they basically did it by process of elimination. I'll leave any damage here to Hal and Ikeshal. I'm just glad the basement is so well hidden."

Quinn perked up, remembering the satyr general who had helped them back in the battle where they captured Kajaro. "Is Ikeshal well again?"

"Mostly," Eric answered. "He is back to about eighty percent of his duties. He's gone to oversee the campaign tent with Hal."

Quinn nodded slowly. "They should be back once they realize it's a diversion, right?"

Eric shrugged. "Maybe? Depends on how deep that so-called diversion runs. I wouldn't put it past his siblings to take advantage and for him to have to make it a lesson on why they shouldn't have."

Quinn didn't like it. She didn't like Hal or any of her friends in danger. Especially not herself.

"Anyway," Eric said, "I can tell where they went because of their magical signature. I followed it."

"Wait," Quinn said. "Magical signature? We should bottle a sample in case we need to compare it to the magical signatures we got on the Esposian Isle."

"Not a hard thing to do," Eric said. "I'll do it before we leave."

They all came to a stop at the top of a very long staircase. Quinn looked down into the gloomy lighting below them. She frowned. They were quiet as they descended the stairs. Eric held his finger up in front of his lips in a request for silence. They pushed open the doors, luckily on oiled hinges, which made no sound at all, and proceeded through very carefully.

That was more like it. Everything around them had a smooth, white, sterile feeling, but it wasn't bright. The light in the area maintained a golden hue that softened as it hit her vision. She took stock, seeing similar holding cells up ahead, just like the one that she'd originally seen Kajaro in.

Quinn frowned. It didn't smell right. It didn't feel right. Nobody spoke. Eric simply led the way. But there was nothing. No people. No speaking. No messages. Nothing scrawled on the walls. Yet with each step she took, her sense of foreboding grew.

I don't like this, she sent out to everybody. Aradie pushed in next to her neck, making herself smaller. *We should be on alert.*

Yes, Milaro agreed. *This feels . . . wrong.*

She looked at him. There were tiny beads of sweat on his brow. Another sign that Quinn knew not everything was all right. Only silence and emptiness greeted them. And that's when the itching in the back of Quinn's mind began. She couldn't reach it. It wasn't like she could scratch inside her brain. She put it down to a gut feeling.

Definitely be on alert, she warned the others. *Milaro's correct. There's something not right up ahead.*

They turned the corner, and this time, Quinn saw the door she'd entered through on her last visit, where they'd avoided this long corridor of sterility. They opened the door in front of them, the one that led through to Kajaro's section, just in time for a severed arm to smash into the wall as Quinn entered. She blinked as a trickle of blood hit her forehead and ran down the side of her face.

The room in front of her was filled with chaos. There were, as far as she could see, three Spinoboli and two imps still standing, hovering . . . whatever. Around her, there was a massacre of medical professionals in their scrubs, as well as the intruders. Bits and pieces of bodies, entrails, blood, and viscera made the floor a shiny, slippery mess.

And Kajaro stood at the end of the room opposing his attackers in all his electric void glory.

4 1

WORSE FOR WEAR

Kajaro flashed a self-satisfied smirk at all those who entered, as well as those who were already there. However, if Quinn looked closely, she could see shadows around his eyes and his skin. His hollowed-out cheeks left him gaunt and skeletal like. She also barely resisted the urge to send him careening into the wall behind him.

As she took in the rest of the room, she realized that more healers and staff were actually cowering behind him, as if he protected them. Not everyone had combat affinities, and these healers were likely among those who didn't.

She knew there'd been a staff of about ten people around him. She wasn't entirely sure of how many lay strewn around the floor, but from all the body parts and bits and pieces that she could see, she was quite sure that about half of them were dead. It wasn't a pretty sight.

Quinn wished there'd been carpet. It might have made some of the entrails more difficult to see. She frowned down at the arm whose blood she had on her and scowled.

It was a lot to absorb inside just a few seconds as they came upon their intruders already occupied. Kajaro flashed them a half smile, hope flickering around the edges of it. Quinn noticed that the Spinoboli, upon closer inspection, seemed sturdier than the ones they'd fought in the hallways. They were larger and had paused, watching the newcomers, probably weighing their options.

They were a wee bit scary.

Kajaro bled from a couple of gashes along his body. Quinn frowned at the sight, and Kajaro broke the silence.

"Do you mind helping?" he asked in that weird, sibilant way. "This whole having one life thing is terribly overrated and mildly terrifying."

Quinn knew they didn't have the luxury of time. While they weren't outnumbered right then, per se, she could sense the power rolling off their opponents. These Spinoboli and different variations of imp appeared to be much more robust than the previous ones they'd encountered in the halls. She glanced around quickly, trying to get other people's input, but nobody met her eyes, all focused on the interlopers.

She offered Kajaro the barest of nods. She couldn't bring herself to speak to the homicidal bastard, but decided to extend her shielding around him. They needed information she was sure he could give and made sure to include the mana regen and health regeneration buffs.

Malakai apparently sensed her thoughts. He gave her a pointed look, raising an eyebrow in question. It was good for the Serpensiril to know exactly where he stood right now. Less of a temptation to turn on them as soon as the others were stopped. She shrugged at Mal. "Can't exactly interrogate a dead person."

Both Kajaro and Milaro looked like they wanted to comment on that. Quinn was glad that neither of them chose to.

The lull was over. Two of the Spinoboli and one of the imps turned away from Kajaro, leaving only two to face him. His shoulders sagged with relief. The stronger versions of the Spinoboli now faced Quinn's group, splitting off to separate the group and fight them.

Mal leaned over, his bow safe in his hands. "These are so much stronger than the last ones we fought. My arrows won't penetrate. I can tell from here."

Quinn frowned and muttered under her breath as she watched the others approach. She wasn't entirely sure how to instigate combat. "Can't you use some of your specialty arrows?"

He glared at her. "I can, but I'm not sure it'll do any good against these guys."

"We can at least try, right?" His glare intensified. Quinn shrugged. "Look, I'm not trying to be nasty. I'm just saying come prepared for the fights, Mal. I hope you've got more than one arrow up your quiver."

She was aware that some of his arrow types had high-end components, and sometimes he needed to replenish their fuel. But in the long run, at least he could heal for them.

That's the moment when Quinn realized these new Spinoboli were more caster-oriented than combat. She barely twisted out of the way of a fireball aimed directly in the middle of Quinn and Malakai. Her magic shot out on instinct, allowing for both of them to barely avoid it. The remnants would have hit her if she hadn't reflexively sucked the oxygen from the fireball, effectively nullifying it. In removing the air from it, the structure winked out of existence.

The Spinoboli who'd fired it laughed. It sounded like metal grating on metal and made her eardrums ache. Then it smiled, showing off multiple rows of tiny, razor-sharp teeth.

"Ah," it said in a strange accent she couldn't place. "It is challenged." It cocked its head to one side, studying her, and Quinn felt like an insect under a microscope for just a split second. The grin remained on its face. "And a Librarian. Two of my favorite things to squash. It would seem that in this case, I can eliminate two problems with one stone."

"But apparently not with a fireball," Quinn muttered, only realizing taunts were unwise.

The Spinoboli grinned again, this time wider, and dove toward her, surprisingly fast and nimble. Quinn realized this one wasn't a grunt. No, this one held power on a totally different level to what they'd fought before.

A wave of that power hit her as the Spinoboli moved. She didn't even need to extend her senses for it.

That's when Milaro whispered in her mind. *I hate to break it to you and be the bearer of bad news, but my usual tactics won't work here. At least not until they've been beaten down some.*

Quinn tried not to let the worry show on her face. Down Milaro's ability to make them bleed from every orifice put their chances of success on shaky ground. That didn't mean they couldn't still attack and defeat these guys. It just meant it wouldn't be extremely easy. He'd warned her, and now they could be prepared.

She'd been using the igneous rock around them to tap into the earth and force it to push up through and use it as a weapon. However, right now, they were positioned in an indoor hall with marble settings. She didn't understand the makeup of marble well enough to commandeer it. Manipulating these earthen materials was currently beyond her. When she initially tried to tug at the ground, it resisted vehemently.

She sighed, cracking her neck from side to side. *These guys are tough,* she thought at the group. *We need to be cautious. Avoid draining your energy too fast.* She activated her fire, rolling it around in her palm, her scales adding protection. She wondered if these Spinoboli knew she had fire abilities and fire immunity.

Since their opponent had an obvious preference for fire, it stood to reason they were therefore also somewhat immune to the element. Fire, as an attack, wasn't the best choice. The Spinoboli was done with its amusement over Quinn's predicament. It didn't wait for any of them to have the first go. Both attacked at once.

Eric, it seemed, met his imp attacker halfway. Considering they were roughly the same size and could hover off the ground, the fight involved a lot of flight and darting around, making it difficult to follow. Malakai began to dig deep into his arrow repertoire so he could assist both Eric and Milaro from a distance.

The other Spinoboli approached Milaro cautiously. It was likely the one Milaro had tried to brain fry. That explained the caution.

The flurry of attacks by the imp toward Eric gave Quinn pause. It wasn't easy to fight the imps, and she knew for a fact Eric had taken several of them down in the hall easily. These were more robust. And Milaro had enough on his plate with his own opponent.

Quinn had Lynx and Aradie to help her. Although Aradie flitted between all of them, swooping at their targets, she was currently focused on Quinn's opponent, who was now circling her. She didn't have time to worry about the prisoner. All she could do was focus on her own opponent. She'd worry about Kajaro later when they'd survived this attack.

Look at her being all optimistic. *When* they'd survived. She was proud of refusing to contemplate defeat.

She threw spell after spell toward her attacker. Any fireball sent her way got deflected by a simple oxygen deprivation. Fire without air didn't work. Several attacks came far too close for comfort, and despite her own fire resistance, Quinn chose to create sand to extinguish the fire despite the drain to her core. She only used it rarely.

Her hair got singed. She smelled that horrible burning human hair scent lingering around her head. Asking her scales to mold around her scalp lent her more protection. She just wasn't sure how long it would hold.

At first, this Spinoboli appeared to be a type of earthen and fire creature. Quinn really hoped that was their main affinity. Ice spears as weapons didn't work, regardless of her own proficiency with the element. Given the marble surrounds, the earthen element was most difficult to access, and creation simply drained her too much.

Out of the corner of her eye, she noticed that the imp Eric and Malakai fought began to flag. A few areas of its wings were shredded, which left it lumbering down on the ground. Even with minor lacerations, Eric seemed in much better condition than his opponent. However, it appeared that its partner, still facing Kajaro, noticed its state and moved over to join it.

However, that meant Kajaro only faced one opponent now, and that Quinn could worry less about protecting him.

She managed to sidestep a strange spell she didn't understand. Instinct made her duck an attack that warped the air. If it could warp the air visibly, Quinn hated to think what it could do to a body. She reinforced her shielding as she glanced over at Kajaro. He'd taken a breather when the imp left, accidentally letting his guard down.

It was like she could see the split second the attack happened. The Spinoboli attacking him got in a very clean shot. A gasp rang out through the room as Kajaro stumbled.

Quinn's energy levels plummeted as she extended thicker shielding over Kajaro. In the space of time it took her to pop another energy replenishing ball, Quinn's attention waned for a split second. Just enough time for something to hit her in the gut, whooshing air out of her. It punted her back into the wall behind them. Pain exploded in her gut with the impact, and she realized with some shock that her opponent hadn't used any of the expected elements based around fire, earth, or air.

A steel spike ran through her side, almost pinning her to the wall. Luckily, her shielding had saved her.

She felt blood gurgling up and channeled her healing toward the wound. They couldn't afford to lose. She dropped down to one knee, reinforcing her own and everyone else's shielding. Pushing the spike out, she attempted to knit what flesh she could around it, but she was no healer, and while slowed, blood still seeped out.

Eric's imp opponent finally fell to the ground, the second one already worse for wear. Aradie swooped at the Spinoboli who'd hit Quinn, distracting it. Laser eyes focused while Lynx joined her, attacking in avian form. Kajaro's Spinoboli challenger seem on its last legs.

But Quinn's heart beat in time with the playlist in her head. The whole fighting scene in front of her felt like a slow-motion music video with her bleeding out on the side.

The Serpensiril began to cast one of his electric void circles. Quinn only hoped he'd succeed in taking his opponent out.

Blood continued to seep down Quinn's side, and wave of dizziness hit her. Her vision began to blacken ever so slightly as the Spinoboli Milaro fought fell to its knees.

The moment that happened, Malakai left his station next to Eric and dove for Quinn. Healing magic suffused her, even as her vision blackened.

4 2

REGENERATE

Burning pain shot through Quinn like it tried to ignite her. She struggled to maintain consciousness. Those spikes were a nasty surprise, seemingly specifically tailored to go through cosmicisodracus scales. It was only her magical shielding that meant it didn't pin her to the wall. If the weapon used by the Spinoboli was created in conjunction with the other cosmicisodracus siblings, Quinn didn't like the ramifications of it. If she fell unconscious, her shields would fall, and they weren't done fighting. Passing out wasn't an option.

Mal sat next to her, funneling healing into and around the area. His healing was steps above the rest. From the way it knit back together, she thought he might have read up on cosmicisodracus physiology.

Slowly but surely, the darkness at the edges of her vision receded. Quinn heaved a sigh of relief and gently pushed Mal's hands off the wound. She held them and looked at him, in the brief respite. "I'm okay. You can't give me all your energy. Keep some in case he needs it." She gestured over her shoulder at Kajaro. "We lose him, and we get nothing out of all of this."

Malakai gave her a withering look as he turned to look at Kajaro.

Greenish Serpensiril blood dripped down Kajaro's body. Although "dripped" was probably generous; it was more like a sluggish flow.

Malakai sighed. "Are you sure you're healed enough? Because if you keel over dead, it's worse than if we get no information from him."

It was easier now to funnel her own energy into the shielding, reinforcing it since she didn't feel strong enough to fight right then. She sincerely gave it some thought, and nodded. "I'm fine. Or, I will be."

Sequestered behind an overturned desk, Malakai and Quinn observed the current state of the fight. He made as if to go back into the fray, and she stopped him. "You're the only one who can heal. Get to him as soon as you can. Regenerate mana while you can."

Serenity settled over her. A certainty that they'd survive with some scrapes as she watched her group fight. They engaged their opponents with surety and teamwork.

Blood flowed, but more of it from their opponents. Eric and Milaro took minimal damage. Their flying combatants evaded everything, adding an aerial component their enemies couldn't counter.

Quinn suddenly shivered as certainty that things were way too easy crept down her spine. Down to the second that their opponents fell and didn't get back up, she still expected the other shoe to drop.

Now that Eric, Aradie, Lynx, and Milaro seemed to have polished off the last two attackers. The one concentrating on Kajaro seemed far more formidable. Maybe that was the other shoe.

Malakai's gaze darted between their group and Kajaro. But the Spinoboli was never out of reach. The elf seemed antsy, trying to get to his patient to be close enough to allow his heals to work.

Pain permeated Quinn's entire abdomen, and she suppressed a groan, not wanting to worry anyone. She was certain some kind of toxin had been on that spike and closed her eyes briefly, basically begging her body to seek out such intrusions and take care of them. Once they got back to the Library, she'd be fine.

When she opened her eyes again, she saw that Milaro, Aradie, Eric, and Lynx were attempting to lure the other Spinoboli toward them, away from Kajaro. Like Quinn previously noticed, this one was an advanced version. Perhaps a captain or some other rank.

It moved fluidly, aware of every one of their movements. Eyes narrowed, arms at the ready. When it turned, it didn't allow a clear path through to Kajaro. Like it knew that they needed to reach him. Just as they knew that the Spinoboli was there to finish him.

Since the Spinoboli had four arms, she thought they'd be much more difficult to kill and had been mildly disappointed at the easy victories they'd had so far. This captain though, it danced fluidly, its arms reaching practically 270 degrees. It could extend its limbs across in different ways, bending at unnatural angles. It seemed to be completely and utterly dual-jointed and wielded not only weapons in the upper two arms its spell workings and magic workings cast from the bottom two. Something about it reminded her of a marionette. Quinn knew, though she didn't understand how, that it could also cast while wielding weapons too.

Quinn watched, entranced. As if the captain had switched into high gear, it flowed like a dance with multiple partners all having to dodge each other and their opponent's multiple arms and weapons. The Spinoboli moved in an agile fashion, arms rotating widely, taking the focus of each one of its attackers. Fireballs, ice, spears, and any measure of spells that Quinn couldn't yet identify, a lot of them earth-based, piqued her interest and made her wish she'd absorbed way more books.

She frowned as Eric missed a dodge and took the first hit. It slashed into his thigh, sent him tumbling to the ground, but he managed to pull his wings in and not damage them badly. Even so, at the same time, the creature slashed out with a throwing knife from one hand and a spell from another, aimed at Aradie and Lynx, who dive-bombed it. They only narrowly avoided the attack.

Milaro, on the other hand, danced with it. Hundreds of tiny cuts began to appear on its arms and legs and torso. It screeched in anger, sounding like an excited piglet. Quinn couldn't reconcile the sound with the appearance of the Spinoboli. It doubled down its focus, mostly on Milaro, yet he didn't even blink.

Quinn understood now what Malakai meant. His grandfather was a force to be reckoned with. He moved like an assassin, like something she'd only seen in movies and computer games before this. His spells arrived at their targets without needing to be launched from him, and yet she could also see the hint of fatigue emerging. The way the skin around his eyes crinkled with concentration. There was also discomfort in the way he held his shoulders, filled with tension and worry. She couldn't blame him for feeling exhausted, but at least he was making a dent in the Spinoboli captain.

It didn't take long for Quinn's healing regeneration to kick in and get Eric back on his . . . wings. Back up in the air, he was more aware, his movements and spells showing far more agility this time.

Aradie and Lynx dove in and out of the combat area, distracting it for crucial seconds. Meanwhile, Quinn sat there, trying desperately to infuse more healing into her body. Whatever the pike injected into her system meant her regeneration barely kept up with the damage. As long as she maintained the buff until they got to a healer, she'd be fine.

That's when she noticed a red blip in the corner of her HUD. Kajaro's alert blinked at the side of the screen. She turned, gasping softly, hoping the noise hadn't drawn the wrath of the remaining Spinoboli.

She poked Malakai and gestured to the Serpensiril, who'd fallen to the ground by now. The elf's mana levels had crept up enough to where he could use his abilities again. Combat always made regen slower. She could barely even tell if Kajaro's chest was moving. She aimed her thoughts directly at Mal, hoping the Spinoboli wouldn't be aware of their telepathy. *Can you make it to him, Mal?*

He looked at her as if he wanted to say *Only if I have to*, but then he sighed and answered. *I'm trying, but right now I can't get past the Spinoboli. Right now, it'll see me if I move that way.*

A little bit of distraction? Quinn projected to the others. She could almost feel Aradie's grin in response.

Don't worry, Milaro said, sounding strong and confident. *We'll tug it over for you. Just make sure you pay attention and duck out as soon as you get an opening.*

Malakai nodded, and Quinn suddenly felt uneasy. She couldn't help the feeling they'd been too late, and they'd run out of time. Quinn stayed where she was, wedged behind the overturned desk. She was mostly hidden, so technically safe. Despite the fact that her wound was closed, Quinn was in an inordinate amount of internal pain.

Black spots kept trying to cover her vision. For her regeneration to kick in fully, they had to get out of combat and back to the Library as soon as possible. None looked promising right then. She reached out with her senses to double-check that there weren't any other groups doubling back to join this one, but it appeared the captain was the only one.

She followed Malakai's slow progress toward Kajaro, the elf dodging blocked spells, body parts, and the rest of the detritus. He'd inherited his elegance from his grandfather. The staff behind the Serpensiril appeared to be doing their best to hide and blend in with the wall, leaving him to die without putting a foot or a spell forward.

Quinn pushed her anger away and concentrated on keeping the shields strong and her buffs alive. As Mal got closer, Milaro taunted the Spinoboli even more, pulling it away from his grandson to keep him safe.

Finally, Malakai was there. From the way the staff paled, he'd obviously berated them. They moved forward to help with Kajaro, but from the way Mal's brows pinched, Quinn knew the Serpensiril wasn't making it through this. Ironically, they needed his help to understand exactly what they were up against.

It worried her that she was too callous, being concerned only with what they could get his help with instead of that he was dying. Then again, homicidal sociopaths didn't really deserve sympathy, did they?

Just as he was about to reach Kajaro, a rain of ice spikes beat down suddenly on Malakai and the rest of them. Quinn funneled as much energy as she could into the shielding. It held after only wavering a bit. The captain screamed with rage.

Luckily, in the distraction of the ice rain, Milaro took advantage of the opening and went in for the kill. Quinn watched.

The Spinoboli, who was no longer concentrating intently on its opponents, clutched at its head. It moaned and screamed, and blood emerged, black as night. It came out of its nose, its mouth, its eyes, and ears, dripping like melted tar.

Milaro frowned, made several complex motions with his hands, and suddenly the Spinoboli was encased. Not in ice like Quinn, but in a restrictive binding that looked clear and impenetrable.

"That'll do it. We need at least one of them alive for questioning," he said, sounding angry. Quinn couldn't blame him. None of the weaker ones had any information for them. This stronger one had to have something.

She struggled to push herself up as it became evident that the fight was finally over. Finally, it allowed her regeneration to kick in at full speed and help her recover easier. Eric limped. Lynx and Aradie were fine even if the bird was exhausted. Milaro looked like a small wind would knock him over, and still, he came to Quinn's side and assisted her over to Kajaro.

She stumbled to toward the Serpensiril, noticing how his snake hood flared around his face. His eyes had already begun to glaze over.

"You can't die yet, you bastard," she said through gritted teeth.

"Seems you are incorrect," Kajaro sputtered out, green blood oozing from his lips.

"No! We need you to give us the information," Quinn said.

Kajaro sighed. "You know I only have one life now. But since my allies came for me, to shut me up . . . I have no allegiance to them. So you, Milaro, can take whatever memories out of my head you want. I give you full access. You just don't have long."

His breath became raspy there toward the end of his speech, and Quinn could practically tell he had minutes at most. Milaro moved closer.

"With me, Quinn," the elf king said, gripping her hand.

Kajaro looked up at her, blinking, his eyes slowly clouding over. "Permission granted for her too, then."

Milaro took Quinn's hand and placed it on Kajaro's head, and his mind sucked them both into a maelstrom of thoughts.

43

MAELSTROM OF THOUGHTS

THE FIRST THING QUINN NOTICED ABOUT KAJARO'S MIND WAS THE surrounding green-tinged darkness. She heard dripping, as if someone had left a tap on, overflowing for days, and the drips were falling into the widespread puddles that had been created. In a way, it was almost like a clock ticking.

Tick. Tick. Tick. Tick.

Steady.

Constant.

Slow.

Yet ever gradually slowing more. The drips echoed through her mind, through this world they found themselves in. The silence between each drip and tick was deafening. It built up until Quinn thought her ears might burst. It gave her a distinctive sense of time running out. She didn't have a lot of it right then for contemplation, for figuring out the mind of a dying man, snake . . . Serpensiril.

Images swirled around them, around her, brightening in areas, giving the darkness and dim surrounds a sudden glimpse of life.

Chaotic.

Hectic.

And sad.

The images held flashes of people she'd seen and others that she'd never known, likely never would. They flew past her so fast she couldn't grasp them all. As far as she could tell, Milaro was genuinely pulling all the memories Kajaro gave them access to into his own mind as fast as he could to make sure none of them slipped by. That way, they wouldn't lose even one piece of information Kajaro might have imparted had they made it in time.

A heavy sensation of pettiness lingered in all the thoughts. Quinn guess it was Kajaro's way of taking revenge on those who betrayed him.

Images flew past her vision included some people they were trying to stop or prevent from destroying the universe. General everyday sort of stuff as well. Kajaro and Dravishk in heated arguments multiple times until one of them settled and made Quinn pay closer attention.

Demanded her focus.

Kajaro and Dravishk stood in the middle of a room of some sort. It didn't seem to have furniture in it, and was small and private. She got the sense from Kajaro's memory that it was secure and sound proofed. Dravishk, in his mostly human form, appeared highly agitated, irritated. In the back of her mind, Quinn thought he seemed rather mundane. Nothing like the beauty Drukala was in her human form ...

Even his words sounded impatient. "If Korradine does what she said she would."

Kajaro raised one of his eyebrows. "Why wouldn't she?"

"It could be a reverse trap," Dravishk said. "Or else maybe it's for her amusement."

"You don't really believe that," Kajaro said.

"No, I don't. This is what she was groomed for, after all. The entire species agreed on it."

Kajaro laughed. The sound set Quinn's spine on fire. "You make it sound like it was against her will."

Dravishk let out a strange grimace and scoffed. "Hardly. She practically dragged us into this. I was prepared to wait it out."

"Not necessarily," Kajaro said. "You've been on this kick for a very long time, and don't you forget it."

She could feel his irritation with his collaborator. After all, in Kajaro's mind, they were both as in charge of this as the other. Oblivious to how Kajaro currently felt, Dravishk carried on. "Her sacrifice will mean nothing if a Librarian remains to take the spot we so painstakingly cleared."

Kajaro shrugged. "True, but if the Library is destroyed, will it even matter?"

"If there is any part of my sibling left," Dravishk said, "then it can be resurrected. Any part at all. Then it can be re-established. We don't want that."

"True." Kajaro frowned. "Would definitely interfere with the spread of chaotic magic again."

"It's an imperfect science," Dravishk said. "Either way, as long as we get in there and modify what we need—"

But the image stuttered as if it was an old television with bad reception. Lines began to grow across it and she could no longer hear. Had it been modified? Had Kajaro hidden it? Was this another memory tampering that the Serpensiril wasn't aware of?

A smoky grey mist began to spread all around and through, touching on some of the images, infecting them. That's when she realized Kajaro was probably closer to death than they'd realized. This was simply the brain fog that came with that.

As the images began to rush past her again, some now with frayed edges, she realized the dripping had slowed significantly. Darkness crept at the edges of everything. Even though images continued to bombard both her and Milaro's mind. The ticks grew even more lethargic. Slow, like blood pumping sluggishly through veins. More and more images passed through her. More and more memories simply shooting past that she couldn't grip onto. She knew, instinctively, that they'd be contained in the compartment of her mind she'd automatically begun to place them in.

Another one shot to the fore unexpectedly. This crinkled around the edges, as if he hadn't really wanted to withdraw this. Because some of the images flashing by her showed representations of Sarila, Kajaro, and Dravishk in one room.

But the one that unfurled to her was only of Sarila and Kajaro. She seemed on edge, snappy. Her bark-like brow furrowed. Her hand clutched at the hem of her sleeve, worrying it, fraying it. "We can't keep doing this. They'll suspect us."

Kajaro tried to soothe her. "Just keep playing the daughter and grandmother. Make sure you blend in. Be friends with their friends."

"You expect me to lower myself to this?"

"You agreed to it," Kajaro said, his tone no longer nice. "There are only two ways this can happen. This one is more difficult. You said you could handle it."

"Fine," Sarila snapped. "I can. I just don't want to."

He ignored her protest and carried on. "The Balisor infection is imperative."

"I know." Sarila glared at him. "But the destruction?"

Kajaro sighed, interrupting her. "I don't have any clue if the destruction will work yet. I can't even tell if the shutdown will work. This is just us hedging our bets."

Sarila laughed. "Don't you worry. I'll see to it. I can keep up my end of the bargain."

Kajaro watched her for several seconds, confusion clouding his thoughts. He couldn't tell if he could trust her. He couldn't tell if all the plans that he'd made were coming to fruition, or whether they'd crash and burn. It all came down to whether or not Korradine could execute the plan the way she'd indicated. Having contingencies in place was only good business sense. Either way Library control would be gone, or his. He flashed Sarila a grin that he didn't mean.

"Either the bomb eventually works, or we simply take control of the whole Library and work from there. It's a good plan, if we can make it work." Sarila sounded more confident this time.

Kajaro nodded slowly, agreeing with Sarila. And yet, at the same time, he wasn't sure if he wanted the path of least resistance and more death, or the plan B path where he could control every single outcome.

The sound and recollection fizzed again, as if somebody had dropped sherbet into water, creating that strange bubble effect. The surface next to the vision began to shimmer, even as the images themselves began to fade, as if the world around them shook, sending ripples back toward the center, disturbing the images.

Tick . . .

Misremembering.

Tick . . .

Unremembering.

Tick . . .

Fading.

Tick . . .

The dripping had all but stopped.

Pressure built up in Quinn's head, as more and more of the images made their way into her mind in a last-second mad dash. Pain ripped through her with the speed they entered her compartment, but she persevered. Milaro and Kajaro obviously aimed to leave no memory lost. Milaro wanted the information, while she sensed Kajaro wanted revenge.

Pettiness: the great motivator.

Quinn didn't like Kajaro.

None of the memories she'd seen inclined her to like him in any way. However, she wasn't partial to people being as cowardly as his former allies. She might do a lot to protect a secret, but she didn't think she'd kill. That was one moral high ground Quinn hoped to maintain. Turning on an ally seemed so low.

She could feel Milaro at her side, within Kajaro's mind, as well as next to her out in the real world. Heat surrounded her, a steady thudding of his heart, and a cracking of his psyche as his mind began to fade.

Milaro had been right. She had so much more to learn about the mind and its magic. She'd devour every single book as soon as she could when she got back.

Quinn felt out of her depth and at the mercy of Milaro's good nature. While she knew he wouldn't let her get hurt, she needed to be strong enough to defend herself, whether it was imagination, mental-based, or physically tangible.

Kajaro's consciousness shook, fracturing. Milaro reached for Quinn's hand and tugged her with him, providing an anchor that pulled them back to the real world. As they fell out of Kajaro's head, she came out of the memory share gasping for breath, momentarily blinded by the whiteness of the room after the dim and dark nature of the memory space. Her head pounded, and she knew, without a fraction of a doubt, that Milaro had tugged her out of those thoughts at the last second.

Her eyes adjusted quickly, and she found herself looking directly at Kajaro. Blood settled on his lips, dripping down in the strange greenish-black hue. Sluggish now, it no longer poured freely, and the glazing of his eyes was practically complete. She liked him even less after seeing his thoughts, but she admired that soul of vindictiveness to pass on as much information as he could to his former enemies.

"The enemy of my enemy is my friend," she muttered under her breath.

"What are you saying now?" Malakai asked.

She shook her head as she watched the way lifelessness entered Kajaro's gaze and the last breath pushed from his lungs. A grey hue began to settle over his deep green scales at an alarming rate. One glance at Kajaro right now would let anybody know he was dead.

She liked that finality, visceral evidence that death had come to him, not a guessing game where you tried to take a pulse, where you tried to see with a mirror to see if they still breathed. It was a stark contrast to how she'd perceived him in life, larger than evil and despicable.

She backed away and groaned, her gaze falling on the only other opponent in the room who managed to survive their attack. The Spinoboli's eyes were closed, breath coming evenly, but its wounds were still obvious, denoting a lack of personal health regeneration. Quinn supposed she should be glad for that. Still encased in Milaro's bindings meant it'd be easier for Hal to interrogate the captain.

But right now, Quinn stretched and groaned, Milaro echoing her.

He looked haggard, tired, and drained. Then again, they all seemed exhausted. Even checking her own energy levels, they were far lower than she would've liked. Not to mention she could still feel the poison running through her system.

The others watched them expectantly. Malakai spoke. "What? Anything?"

Quinn sighed, pushing her pounding head out of her mind. "Lots of things."

"And I take it too much to share?" he asked.

She shook her head. "Not necessarily that. It's too much information for me to process right now, or even on my own. I'll need Milaro's help to go through them."

Milaro flashed her a wan smile in acknowledgement.

They left the room to head up in the palace, so they could use one of the three doors to go home, Quinn's energy flagged. Still, she felt lucky that her whole group was going home with her this time.

Alive!

4 4

MOOT POINT

The door back to the Library deposited them directly in the middle of one of the hospital rooms. Quinn turned and frowned at Eric.

"I'm really fine," she said, trying to put emphasis on *fine*, even if it was about as bold-faced a lie as she could tell.

Eric simply raised an eyebrow, crossed his arms, and blocked her escape. Despite his imp size, she didn't like her chances if she tried to leave and she didn't have the composure currently to warp her way out.

It was only a few seconds before Dr. Miles stepped into the room, glancing at a something on the screen in his hand. "How about I be the judge of whether you are fine or not, Librarian?"

Quinn groaned. She felt wiped out. Just keeping her health regeneration still active to offset the poison in her system drained her. The wound ached, even though it was technically healed. The sensation of weakness permeated her body. She'd hoped to delay the treatment so they could go through the memories, but deep down she knew her health had to come first.

She sighed. "Fine."

"I'm going to visit Nishpa and get a head start on these memories.

Heal up so you can help me go through them." Milaro ruffled her hair and left before she could say anything.

Miles frowned after him and then gave everybody a perfunctory once over to make sure none of them had lingering injuries. He healed Eric's limp and worn wings in a second.

The imp headed to the door. "I've got to tell Hal, Quinn."

"Even if it means going to a war front?" she asked.

"Especially since it means going to a war front that was probably staged as a distraction and thus is absolutely pointless. Lives are lives. Even if they're on the supposed opposite side" He spoke seriously for once, not even a trace of a smile on his face. "Senseless death is avoidable."

She cringed and nodded. Sometimes she got a bit distanced from the facts about some of the species the Library served.

Lynx took that moment to speak up as well. "I'm going to leave and talk to the Library."

"But you can talk to the Library anywhere," she said, trying very hard not to pout.

"I know," Lynx interrupted, his eyes flashing as he delved into communication. "But there are several tests we need to run together. Diagnostics work better if we're in proximity to one another. Heal up! I'll see you soon."

And Lynx popped out of the room. Aradie nipped Quinn's ear, leaving the message that she was off to find food. As she left, Quinn realized her owl probably meant just for herself. and her stomach rumbled. That left only Mal.

"Are you leaving me too?" she asked sulkily.

He laughed softly. "No. I thought I'd watch you squirm since I know you're not overly fond of people fussing about you."

"Thanks."

Malakai was right. Quinn wasn't overly fond of doctors. They were great when they were healing *other* people, discovering cures, and keeping the populace generally not dead. But she'd never liked them much herself. Not since her parents' accident. Not since waking up after six weeks to find there was nobody left who loved her.

She sighed at the morose turn her thoughts took.

Dr. Miles frowned, pursed his lips, and went over the readings that were in the files in front of him. He looked up at her briefly, mild surprise in his eyes. "Before I forget, just to put your mind at ease, your Supervisory Golem?"

Quinn nodded.

"They are back at full functionality. We double-checked to make sure."

Quinn didn't realize she'd been waiting from an all clear from the doctors. They had been the ones to initially notice the problem and give it a cause. It gave her a sense of relief, right through to her bones. She was about to say something to that effect when Miles continued.

"You, however, are not in the greatest of shape. Probably shouldn't have hopped through the portal with that toxin in your body. Dimensional residue can exacerbate this specific toxin, which they probably knew and thus had multiple weapons tainted with it. The others didn't fare as badly."

"They probably dodged most of them," Quinn said, still trying to recall exactly how she'd managed to get impaled. "This went through my dragon scales, like it was made to slip through their defenses. What does this mean?"

Malakai squeezed her hand, which she didn't even realize was shaking ever so slightly. She inhaled the comfort he offered and took a deep breath. "How long is this gonna take?"

Miles considered her, going over the charts again, casting several other diagnostics he looked back at her and shrugged.

"You have different physiology. I also don't have a vast database on cosmicisodracus genealogy or physiology even if your current form is deceptively human like. Thus, I can only guesstimate and my best guesstimation is one to two days, up to forty-eight hours. I can do a test in about twenty-four hours to see how close it is to vacating your system."

"Malakai." Miles turned his attention to the elf. "You did a great job. Otherwise, she'd be much worse. I recommend that you look into enhancing your healing side, perhaps even focusing on it. It may come in handy if you're constantly running into incidents like today, which, given present company and the present predicament . . . is likely."

Malakai blinked. Quinn could almost see the cogs turning in his head as he thought over the idea. "Thank you," he said. "I'll give that some thought."

He said it in a way that made Quinn certain he'd switch focus to healing. It'd definitely help them out when they left the Library. She wondered which type healing affinities he had, but they could check on that later.

"Do I have to stay in the hospital to heal?" She hated the way her voice sounded small and weak, perhaps even a bit scared.

Miles looked her over, and for a second, it felt like he could see how much the idea of a portal-triggered illness disturbed her. But he shook his head. "No, you don't have to stay here, provided you follow my medical instructions to a T."

Malakai piped up. "I'll make sure she follows them and takes any medication you give her." He looked pointedly at Quinn. She glared back at him or at least tried to. It was half-hearted at best.

Miles stayed and gave some instructions, as well as observing her first round of medications.

"Okay," he said, lining up tiny bottles for Malakai to take with him. "She needs to take and ingest several of these potions at very specific intervals. I will send the information to your HUD."

Mal nodded, taking the vials, popping them in a special carry container the doctor provided, and then tucked them into his dimensional storage. Quinn was relieved he took the initiative to take charge of her meds since her brain was still mush from the onslaught of memories.

All in all, it was mostly painless, even if most of the potions she took left a lot to be desired in the taste department. She grimaced at Miles. "Couldn't you have made it taste appetizing?"

"No, I couldn't. We don't want people excited to take the medicine. We only want them to take it when they need to."

She got it. She would have nodded if her head hadn't felt like it was about to explode. It was like Miles could read her mind. Maybe he got inklings like Cook because of their connection to the Library. He gave Malakai two more bottles. "In case her head hurts too much."

Malakai nodded. She grabbed one of the headache potions before he could put it away. As soon as she'd downed it, they left.

Quinn didn't realize that they'd actually spent a couple of hours in the hospital wing. By the time they made it to her office, everybody else was there as well. It seemed everyone's energy levels were low. Nishpa hung out in the corner with Milaro, creating an inclusive and welcoming atmosphere. Quinn's office had apparently fed off that sensation, because the Library had reconfigured it, allowing for less of a conference room atmosphere and more of a lounging-about comfortable hangout with extremely nice sofas.

Quinn settled into the corner of one of them. It was soft without being too soft and plush without being furry. She could get used to this. She made sure to direct her thoughts to the Library in regard to it.

But it didn't respond. Probably still sequestered with Lynx, doing whatever they were up to. Or maybe it was in a mood. Again.

Nobody spoke. Frankly, nobody really moved apart from Milaro and Nishpa in the corner as they talked. Their whispered conversation didn't appear to be about their current predicament. Malakai simply sat with her in a comfortable silence.

Thus, it was startling when someone cleared their throat from the doorway. Quinn jumped slightly, even though she knew only those she'd let through the wards could get through them.

Dottie poked what amounted to her head around the door and peered into the room. "Librarian!" She sounded a little nervous. "There's something we need to discuss."

Quinn glanced around at everyone else happy they all still looked relaxed. "Okay, just give me a second." She pushed herself up and moved stiffly and slowly over to her desk.

Miles hadn't been kidding. The wound, or at least the site of the wound, was inflamed and painful. While she could endure pain, she didn't like it. This was a fiery burning of her intestines. She could quite safely say she wouldn't even wish it on her worst enemy.

Finally, after what felt like an age, she let herself fall back into her office chair and brought up her legs to cross them in front of her. "Come on," she said to Dottie. "Tell me all about it. What is it you're here for?"

Dottie trotted through from the main door past the rest of them and made her way toward Quinn. But as she did, Mal tapped her on the back and handed her a vial. Dottie, with however her magic worked, balanced the vial without any spillage and brought it over to Quinn. She chugged it down. She wasn't even going to ask what this potion was for. After all, Mal had the instructions, and she had the wound in her stomach.

Being able to trust someone to that extent sat well with her. Around Malakai, her paranoia level barely existed. He was the last person she thought would ever betray her. She really hoped she wasn't a bad judge of character.

Dottie finally sat next to her, waiting.

"Okay," Quinn said. She grabbed a glass of water and washed the vile taste of the potion away. "You've got my attention."

She tried to smile but the aftertaste lingered. Luckily, it worked much faster than something like paracetamol or ibuprofen. From her reading of Dottie's aura, Quinn could tell the bench was somewhat concerned, or maybe nervous was the right word. Excited was probably in there too.

Which seemed to be quite right because Dottie could barely stand still. She looked at Quinn.

"Why did you take the potion?" she asked, surprising the Librarian with a question unrelated to whatever news the bench had to share.

"I got hit by a projectile capable of cutting past dragon scales," Quinn said. "Anyway, Dottie, focus. What's up?"

"Oh yes," Dottie said, seeming a little off center now. "Well, you see, you did entrust Betty and me with the task of gathering more of the tomes. We have, of course, enlisted our own aid, and as you know, we've been gathering many of the overdue tomes included in the original batch overdue after the initial opening."

"I know," Quinn said, trying to be patient because sometimes Dottie could be so scattered.

"Anyway, I just wanted you to know that we're extremely close to opening another branch."

Quinn blinked. Another branch? Did they have the power for that? Did they have the people for that? She tried to take a few breaths, but counting in for four and out for four wasn't working.

"Quinn, are you okay?" Dottie asked very seriously.

"I'm fine. I just need to recalibrate right now." She breathed a few more times nice and deep, counting all the way, focusing her attention on a spot on the wall on the other side of the room. "Okay, so which branch are we close to opening?"

"Oh, a couple of them, the bardic one and the crafting one. Those two are probably the closest. You might want to look at numbers and pick which one we're going to go after."

The thing was, Quinn wasn't concerned about the number of books. Opening new branches sounded great in theory, but in reality they still had a few pillars to activate. Not to mention the trouble with Ashiron. The countdown was active, ticking down even as they spoke. If they couldn't take Ashiron out within the next few months, everything was going to be a moot point anyway.

45

FLUMMOXED

DOTTIE SEEMED DISAPPOINTED BY QUINN'S REACTION, OR LACK thereof, to the news. Quinn tried to be more upbeat about it, but she couldn't get over her worry about Ashiron. Her smile turned into more of a grimace while thinking of the soul-bomb timer ticking down. She attempted to appear more harried than panicked before she spoke. "I'm sorry. Opening another branch means we need more power, and I'm trying to figure out the logistics of that."

Dottie appeared confused, or at least that was the sensation Quinn read from her aura, considering Dottie couldn't make any facial expressions.

Quinn sought to clarify. "The power levels, you know, like from the pillars, pumping through the mana, doing their thing? The branches require more and more energy the more of them we open. We seem to be close to opening two branches, correct?"

"Right. Yes," Dottie said. "I'll worry about the components that allow us to open the branches, and you can do your Librarian thing and take care of the power levels."

Dottie made it sound so simple. Quinn wished it were only that easy. "Have you got some numbers for me?" she asked.

"I thought you'd never ask," Dottie said. Several seconds went by, and then there was a strange blip in Quinn's ear. "There you go. It's all in your head now. You just let me know if you have any questions, and I'll be right here to answer them."

Dottie turned around and preened, her aura fluctuating with what could only be curiosity. She turned back to Quinn before Quinn could pull up her HUD. "Everybody seems rather tired."

"We just had a very long day," Quinn murmured almost absently as she sent her request to the HUD.

"I'm so sorry, I should have waited till tomorrow."

"Nope, it's all good. No time like the present," Quinn mumbled as the numbers pulled up in front of her eyes. She stared at them for quite some time. Her brain really did feel slower than usual. Maybe she'd overused her abilities while fighting the Spinoboli in Halschius. However, as long as she shocked herself awake, she should be fine.

Main Branch Tome Report

1,875 are still outstanding from the initial overdue amount. 16,167 books returned. No books in reproduction. 287 in repair status. 14 missing restricted books.

Horticulture: 664/720

Bardic Musical: 882/897

Crafting: 721/730

Academy: 712/785

Culinary Arts: 282/282 - Culinary Branch Open – 2,563 Books of 3,795 remaining, 1,232 total culinary specialist books returned, 23 of which are in repair status. Would you like a categorical breakdown?

Yes, or No?

Alchemical/Medicinal: 384/384 - Alchemical/Medicinal Branch Open – 4,628 of 5,892 remaining, medicinal ingredients verified and stocked, 1,264 total specialist books returned 395 of which are in repair status. Would you like a categorical breakdown?

Yes, or No?

Combat: 837/837 - Combat Branch Open – 7,423 Books of 9,085 remaining, 1,662 total combat specialist books returned. 241 books in repair status. All books location verified. Would you like a categorical breakdown?

Yes or No?

Note: All branches must be opened in order for the Academy to open. Should all books for the Academy be returned prior to other branches, then the Academy will have to wait. It cannot operate without access to all branches of knowledge.

Please Note: These numbers are those vital books that must were overdue while the Library was offline. Please note access for all post-reopening overdue books is compiled elsewhere.

When she'd first arrived, they'd needed just over eighteen thousand books. She'd never understood why people wouldn't return books that didn't belong to them. The problems with Ashiron overshadowed the excitement of opening new branches. With a ticking clock literally timing them down, she couldn't help but feel the pressure.

Depending on Betty and Dottie's retrieval process, the Library would likely have the branches restored sooner rather than later. In moments like this, where people were quiet and still, she could feel at peace. At home.

She looked at the waiting bench and smiled. "Thanks," she said to Dottie, and meant it. The bench watched her for a few seconds and then spoke softly.

"You know, we're here if you need us. You just let us, Betty and me, know if there's anything we can do to help you. Anything at all, dear. We're right here."

Quinn looked at her for several seconds and nodded.

"I hear you," she said, and Dottie trotted out, as if everything was right with the world.

Quinn watched her go and glanced around the room. Dottie had been right. Everybody seemed to have melted into their couches.

Malakai slumped, about to doze off too. Aradie sat on her perch, had her head tucked under her wing. It was rare for Quinn to catch Aradie sleeping. She wondered if she could just curl up and sleep too. A Librarian's work was apparently never done.

The curse of a comfortable couch.

Quinn sucked it up, unable to summon the energy to move back to her couch manually, she warped there.

Which saved her having to contact the Library.

Did you just warp yourself ten feet? The Library sounded incredulous.

"Yes," Quinn said speaking out loud because she had a slight headache. Voices reverberating in her head didn't help. "I did. I'm so tired."

But it took more energy to warp than to move, the Library said, toning down the echo so it wouldn't hurt Quinn.

"Not necessarily," Quinn mumbled. "I've drained all my physical energy, but I still have a lot of magical power left."

But still, that was so much energy...

"Well, it's good you're talking to me, again" Quinn piped up, "You've been pretty quiet lately and I really need to talk to you. I have questions."

Questions, the Library said, sounding suspicious. *What sort of questions?*

Questions that only you can answer, Quinn said, deciding telepathy was the better choice. The subject matter was rather sensitive.

Very well then. The Library sounded irritated. *Fire away, I'm all Library ears.*

Quinn chuckled at the pun as it washed away the initial annoyed tone. Then she turned on serious mode and approached the topic head on.

The pillars, she said, as if that should explain everything. Then she remembered the Library didn't necessarily listen in to every conversation in the Library. *We only have three more pillars available to us before we're at peak power-producing capacity, right?*

Yes, the Library said. *Ten is the maximum. Once all ten are activated, they can boost themselves, extend the chamber to up capacity. That sort of thing.*

Great, Quinn said. *I learn something new every day.*

It's not something you needed to know before now, the Library said, in a teacher-lecture voice. *Since it wasn't something you had to know, I didn't tell you because it didn't affect the activation of all the pillars. If we can't fix Ashiron, then that's going to be a moot point.*

That set off a chain reaction in Quinn's gut that she really didn't want to talk about. *I understand. It's good to know that as long as they're all activated, the power output can increase.*

Yes. As long as all ten are active. If the filtration chamber is optimized and operating at peak capacity, the magic allows it to expand. I didn't foresee somebody sabotaging one of the pillars when we created the Library.

How dare you not foresee millions and millions of years in the future.

The Library actually chuckled. *Ah, it seems you have encountered foresight and how uncompromisingly inaccurate it can be the further out it gets. Well put.*

Quinn paused and pondered the Library's words. It still didn't change anything, it didn't give them any time. So Quinn tried to figure out how best to phrase it. *How do we go about doing this? Being on a timer is nerve wracking.*

I've been working this out for months, the Library said, *ever since we realized Ashiron was broken. We still have two more to activate before we need Ashiron.*

But we've only got, like, four branches left to open. We'll need them all sooner than later.

The Library made a clucking noise as if it was clicking its tongue. *Power levels are doing well. If you check your HUD, you should see. For another branch, we probably need to open at least one.*

Quinn sighed, *Yes, maybe two?*

They both sat in silence for several seconds. It began to feel awkward. Quinn didn't even know what to say.

I guess, since we're opening two more branches, we have a little bit more time?

Perhaps, the Library sounded sad.

Quinn rushed to try and turn it around. *We don't want to procrastinate for too long. We can't afford to leave the solution to the last minute, right?*

But the Library still didn't answer directly. Something about its reticence to address the Ashiron problem directly really grated on Quinn's nerves. *Is there something I should know?* she asked. *Is there something, like, that you haven't told me that I should know?*

It isn't like that, the Library said, sounding exasperated. *I don't want to waste time with this back and forth while we don't have a solution. It's not getting us anywhere. We'll talk when we need to.*

Quinn narrowed her eyes at the shift in tone. *We're not stopping other things to look into Ashiron. Right now we're multitasking everything. But we have to get it back to working order again. If we don't, we're all gone.*

Including me, snapped the Library.

Quinn couldn't place the tone with which it had spoken. Just that it wasn't telling her something. *I mean, from the way you're reacting, anybody would think that you want Ashiron to obliterate you.*

The Library scoffed. *I do not. It's just not the only problem we have to solve. I still can't remember things. Lynx is still missing elements. Speaking of which, I have several problems on my plate that need to be dealt with now. They don't have eighty-day timers. I'll leave you to figure this one out yourself, Quinn.*

And the Library's presence was gone.

Quinn huffed, unsure what to make of that weird interaction. She was flummoxed. What did the Library even mean by that?

4 6

RABBIT HOLE

QUINN HADN'T EXPECTED TO FIND HERSELF DOWN A RABBIT HOLE OF crafting information. Hearing about the crafting branch opening soon made her want to look into how it worked. Everyone in her office was dozing or working quietly, as if the room was a small safe haven.

Eric still hadn't returned from briefing Uncle Hal, and Quinn wasn't worried at all. No, she wasn't.

Quinn hadn't expect Dottie to tell her they were so close to opening not one, but two branches again. She knew the bench took pride in it and the Librarian was grateful.

Quinn was exhausted. She could have warped herself up to her bed, gone to sleep, and tried to replenish her levels that way, but the Library had been right. She *was* low on energy, and it did take a chunk as well as way too much concentration for her exhaustion levels to manage safely. Instead, she decided to stay where she was, studying information about the branches they were about to reopen.

Music was food for the soul. It gave people an outlet for frustration, happiness, sadness, and love. She didn't see the immediate impact it could have when they were essentially in a type of war with the saboteurs. Crafting seemed more beneficial in the long and short term for both the Library and universe as a whole.

Weapons, gear, and even instruments the bardic branch would need to use. It made far more sense to open the crafting branch first. It also, numbers wise, looked like that'd happen.

Then she went into a spiral researching all the types of items the crafting branch made. It left her knee deep in her HUD's information section. After a few hours of lost time, she had a solid understanding of how the branch worked and just what it could bring to the table.

Crafting, as it turned out, was all sorts of awesome. From simple garments right through to clothes that provided defense, offense, and protection. From the simplest of blades through to ones that could cast their own spells.

There was also the gathering materials, which was also a part of crafting. To skin animals, to cure leather, to gather any of the woods, and to refine them, carve them. Crafting had such a huge scope it almost made her giddy.

At least, when all of this was over, she'd hobbies she could pursue. Crafting didn't seem like something she'd be able to master, even if she managed to live forever. Which, as long as she didn't die in the next few months, or get blown up by a rogue Library bomb in the filtration chamber, she might actually get to do.

It took amazing willpower to pull herself away from retrieving all the crafting books to memorize.

Quinn frowned, looking at her HUD. Learning to craft now wasn't pertinent to their current problems. She repeated that over and over in her head. So much that she almost believed it. She sighed and briefly contemplated snuggling into her couch again, but wasn't sure how much time she'd lost in the HUD going down the crafting trail.

Mal had fallen sideways and was legitimately fast asleep on the couch, with a blanket draped over him. She had no idea where that had come from, but he looked peaceful and a lot younger when less stressed. His hair was in slight disarray. That's when she realized she also had a blanket draped over her. She hadn't been asleep, just in the HUD. It might have looked like she was in a trance.

Looking around, she noticed that Nishpa and Milaro had left at some stage. Aradie was still asleep. If she wanted to be responsible she should sleep instead of procrastinating and letting her mind run away with her into crafting spirals.

However, Quinn was tired, but not sleepy. Her mind ran in circles listing everything over and over again. There was so much left to figure out, to take care of. Ashiron and the pillar bomb, the tracking problem, the trapdoor traitor, the Balisor conspiracy, the magical signature tracking she'd started. Memories, dragons, and Sölem, oh my!

On top of everything else, because of what they had to deal with right now, she still had to learn her cosmicisodracus abilities, because they weren't just affinities. She couldn't just grab a book and absorb them; she needed to be *taught* them. So basically, if she didn't try to sleep, she wouldn't have the energy to do half the things she needed to.

Even just thinking that, her contrary body suddenly felt wide awake and partially rejuvenated. She glanced down at some of her stats to make sure that she wasn't just fooling herself.

Name: Quinn

Age: Irrelevant

Heritage: Earth, Sector 12942 - Infinite reach, pocket Dimensional adaption

*Species: Librarian - of Cosmicisodracus origin - determining extent and variations**

Energy Capacity: 6,128/6,128

Mana Levels: 4,972/4,972

Regeneration:

Energy Idle: 17 per second, combat 9 per second.

Mana Idle: 15 per second, combat 8 per second

No, her energy levels were up and pretty much full, although every now and again, the energy number dipped slightly. Her mental defenses pulled negligible energy constantly. Her energy pools were much larger than she'd been led to expect. It probably had something to do with her heritage.

Drukala was still in the hospital. Had it only been a week? Was she still healing from the dragon fire scars? Probably. Her aunt wouldn't have left without talking to Quinn. Surely.

Hadn't she promised to teach her about cosmicisodracus powers? Quinn knew she had and chided herself for being so busy she hadn't yet made time to seek her aunt out yet.

Not only could Drukala help Quinn with the dragon side of her and the powers that had nothing to do with affinities and absorption from books, but they could also compare notes? She'd be able to find out things like energy level normalcy, mana levels, shapeshifting possibilities, and how not to burn others to a cinder accidentally.

The very idea gave her a physical energy boost. She hadn't seen Drukala anywhere else, so she assumed she was still in the hospital. Quinn had sort of lost track of the days since Jasper's death. They all flowed into each other.

Not wanting to wake Aradie and Malakai, she tiptoed out of her office and reached for the door handle. They all deserved their rest, and the other two seemed to be sleeping so peacefully. She exited the room, into a cacophony of sound outside her door that she couldn't hear in her office. Got to love those silencing wards. It was loud only because of the sheer number of people. They huddled in sitting areas, multiple different species with each other. There were Ilgonomurs and centaurs and several species that Quinn had never seen before.

It all gave a sense of camaraderie and simply wanting to discover knowledge for the sake of revealing information and discoursing about that knowledge. All of the reasons she'd ever wanted to be a Librarian in the first place.

Golems patrolled the floor. Some were in charge of returning books to their shelves. Some interacted animatedly with people. Not all of them were like Tim and Tom, the shelving golems, who were constantly silent and had never found a need to magically speak.

She watched the hustle and bustle of the Library, books coming and going, the learning atmosphere that suffused everything around the main hall.

She turned toward the check-in desk where there was a line and many of her assistants were helping out with a smile, answering questions, checking books in. Quinn was fairly certain she saw fines pass hands even without Eric there to oversee them so strictly.

The Library System worked. It flowed. It welcomed. Everybody loved being there.

She wondered if people who didn't have magic affinities, if they resented the Library. But then again if they didn't have a magical affinity, that meant their world probably didn't have magic, which meant they didn't even know about the Library, which meant they weren't aware that there was something that they could be resenting in the first place.

Logic 101.

If she concentrated on the sensations through her link with the Library, Quinn could sense where people were located. The sheer amount of people traversing all of the branches—and not just the main one—warmed her heart.

It was all her fault in a roundabout sort of way. Something she'd gladly take the blame for.

She turned and headed to the kitchen to grab something to eat on her way to the hospital to see her aunt. Her senses told her she was there.

Luckily, the Library's personal mood didn't lessen the effect of Quinn's own magic. The Library's connection to her was still dulled in the back of her mind. It seemed that this time the Library was sulking. Not all conversations went its way. It didn't mean that Quinn wasn't willing to listen, just meant that she'd weigh all pros and cons. She'd give it a bit of time and then if the Library still hadn't come around, she'd see if she could figure out what was wrong.

Cook wasn't in the kitchen for once, which felt odd. How was the culinary branch a culinary branch without Cook? She grabbed a snack off the grab-and-go shelf and took a big bite of what looked like a churro. It was all cinnamon crispy on the outside, fluffy on the inside. Pure goodness. Even in Cook's absence, it appeared that the culinary branch knew exactly what Quinn wanted. She decided to take a couple with her for Drukala. If Quinn was a dragon and liked these, that stood to reason that her aunt would as well.

She made her way through the halls to Drukala's room without running into anyone. She knocked on the door and waited. Shuffling could be heard from inside.

"Come in," Drukala called.

Drukala lay on the floor in tiny dragon form like she had the last time. Her scales were white and beautiful, and it appeared that the injury on her face had healed.

"Hey, Dru," Quinn said. "How are you?"

"Healing up. But I don't think you came to ask that."

"You said you'd train me and teach me about our species. I've had a lot on my plate and was hoping the offer still stands?"

"Of course it still stands. Give me a moment." Right before Quinn's eyes, Dru morphed back into human form. The eyes set her apart. They were still white and gleaming, like she could see everything and anything, especially what you didn't want her to.

Quinn smiled. "Thank you. Where should we start?"

"Do you have any burning questions?" Drukala asked, smiling.

"Do you have a lot of energy?" Quinn started and paused. "Like magical energy, not physical."

"Definitely."

When she didn't elaborate, Quinn did instead. "When you say a lot, how do you mean a lot?"

There was a beep in Quinn's HUD, and stats flew up in front of her.

Information sharing enabled. Specifically defined statistics only.
Name: Drukala
Species: Cosmicisodracus original
Energy Capacity: 895,723/904,835
Mana Levels: 492,084/492,084

Quinn blinked. Did a double take. That *was* a lot of energy.

"Wow," Quinn said.

Drukala chuckled. "I'm the least impressive, and Drev doesn't really count now. Hope that helped."

Quinn nodded, her thoughts racing. "I really am an egg."

The dragon watched her for several seconds before continuing.

"Keep in mind I'm a lot older. Your capacity will keep growing with age and knowledge absorption. Now what is it you'd most like to know?"

"Everything," Quinn said firmly. "I only know very basic things with fire and shielding and some flame control."

Eagerness shone through Drukala's expression as she launched into a spiel. "Oh, it's easier than you think. It'll come to you like second nature."

Suddenly, something shuddered against the wards. It was hard and quick, but luckily there was no sense of violence evident. At least, not that Quinn or the alarms could detect. While it shook the ground, Quinn didn't think they'd be in danger.

Drukala's eyes grew wide, and there was a knock at the door.

Quinn activated her shielding just in case.

"Come in," Drukala called.

A tall, lanky man entered the room, his eyes blazing.

Drukala grinned, a ripple of delight emanating from her. "Brother, what a surprise."

47

BRIGHT LIGHT

"It's hardly a surprise," he snapped.

Dru grinned. "Nice of you to grace us with your presence, Driv."

Quinn did a double take, looking at the door. After all, the time between the shielding wavering and Drivok's appearance was minuscule. She had no doubt he'd been the brief disturbance as he'd crossed into the Library. It made her think given that he'd had part in creating the Library, it allowed him access regardless.

She took a breath and slowed her thoughts down. She observed the newcomer as he engaged in an apparent staring contest with his sister. His human form was tall but shorter than Milaro, probably a bit shy of seven feet. He was strong and lean, but then as a shapeshifter he could pick his likeness. His aura reminded Quinn of a stalking jungle cat, all coiled and ready to strike at its foe. His eyes were bright green, sort of like an emerald, and his hair was a deep burgundy that glistened. In the lights of the infirmary, golden highlights were scattered through his hair and his eyes. Even his skin, or at least the forearms that she could see, glittered bronze under those same lights.

He was dressed in such a human fashion that Quinn had to blink rapidly to make sure she wasn't hallucinating. Jeans, a white T-shirt, and white sneakers. Bizarre. Why would a dragon dress like a human?

Drukala looked away from her brother with a sigh.

"Why did you wake me?" He'd won the staring contest and finally spoke angrily. His anger was smooth, like a warning.

"Because shit hit the fan?" Drukala said, unimpressed, raising an eyebrow and then gave a bored and deliberate look at her nails.

He frowned. "Why?" And then he glanced around, as if really seeing the place for the first time. "How were you injured? Why are you here, specifically?"

Then his nose twitched, like he was smelling something. He did it a couple more times. It made him look a bit like a rabbit, far less like a jungle cat, and momentarily, nothing like a dragon. He turned and looked at Quinn for the first time. She couldn't tell, but something flickered through his eyes. Maybe recognition? She wasn't sure.

"And what is this?" he said, gesturing up and down at Quinn. She wasn't entirely sure how to take that. But his tone was condescending enough, she was pretty sure it contained intended offense.

"I'm not a what, I'm a who." She bit off the words, deciding to take offense.

His eyes narrowed. "You're whatever I say you are."

Quinn almost growled at him. "And *you* are rude."

He looked slightly taken aback, like nobody had ever told him that he was rude before. Well, Quinn took pride in being the first.

He cleared his throat, narrowed his eyes again, and studied her. "You're not quite right," he said, looking completely and utterly confused.

Quinn was immediately irritated. She'd finally had time to get herself the cosmicisodracus heritage training that she so desperately needed, so she could handle all the raw power that went hand in hand with her species, and this happened. She scowled. Affinities that she'd been learning about since she got here had nothing to do with her innate dragon powers. And right when they were about to start her training, this other dragon barged in? Just before she could say bite out an angry response, he abruptly turned in a full three-hundred-sixty-degree circle.

A soft hiss emanated from him. "What's wrong with it?"

"It?" Quinn asked. He'd better be talking about the Library, or Quinn wasn't forgiving anything.

"This, here." He gestured around to the Library at large and turned to his sister, who had finally positioned herself up on the bed. "This, Dru, the Library, what's wrong with it?"

Drukala sighed. "Yeah, that's gonna be a very long story. Are you sure you have time?"

He stood, watching his sister carefully, and then he turned to Quinn again. "You smell just like Drev. Sort of. Mostly. Why?"

But Quinn cut him off. "People keep telling me that, and I'm a bit hazy on the precise details., but I'd assume it's because my genetic sequence contains the Library's DNA."

He raised an eyebrow and opened his mouth to probably ask a lot more questions, but Quinn cut him off.

"We shouldn't do this discussion in the hospital. Dru, are you up for moving?" Quinn asked, trying to be gentle.

Drew grinned. "Yes. I scarred my face, not my skeletal structure."

Quinn felt a little flicker of presence in her mind. It seemed the Library wasn't sulking anymore. Its moods had been a bit back and forth recently. She was just glad it wasn't dwelling anymore. She was never quite sure how to handle a temperamental ancient being.

Your siblings are here, she told it. There was no response, just another flicker. *Do you think my office, or the Core?*

The silence took so long Quinn didn't think it would break. Meanwhile, the others occupied themselves with another staring battle.

No, not the Core. I'll reinforce your office. Do you want others present? Mal? Aradie?

If you don't mind, Quinn said.

"What are you doing?" Dru's curiosity got the best of her.

"I'm talking to the Library, which you could probably do too, but it's been a little preoccupied lately." She didn't want to tell them it'd been sulking. From what she knew, siblings used that sort of thing as ammunition.

Driv looked like he was pondering that. There was a sigh that echoed through Quinn's head. *Hey, I'm sorry about before. Sometimes I feel not as strong as a pocket-dimensional intergalactic Library dragon probably should.*

Quinn had to suppress an actual chuckle at that, because the apology did her good. It made her feel appreciated. *You know, it's okay.* She got that sometimes even the Library might have a tough day.

Drukala smirked.

"What?" Quinn asked.

"Nothing. This is just coming together much better than I imagined."

Quinn's eyes narrowed.

"Oh, don't get your knickers in a twist. I just meant adding Driv. I was *mostly* certain he wasn't a traitor."

"What do you mean I wasn't a traitor?" Driv said.

Quinn crossed her arms and said, "We'll fill you in once we reach my office. Follow me."

Tell him to behave himself on the way through the Library, please, the Library said.

Quinn relayed the message, and Drivok grumbled under his breath about how he always behaved and how dare his sibling feel the need to remind him.

These two might technically be relatives, but the weight of time lent them intimidation. Their mere presence as primordial beings made their auras sing. They were billions of years old. It gave her such a vast sense of inferiority to stand near these creatures.

She knew that when she'd initially met Drukala, there'd been a lot of adrenaline. She blamed the sheer adrenaline rush she'd been experiencing for not feeling the weight of her presence earlier. Not to mention they'd been so preoccupied with battle, escape, and then death that she hadn't checked her other emotions.

Now she was relatively calm, and the sheer magnitude of these people was weighty.

Drivok's enormity, the way he held himself and spoke with such conviction only exacerbated the sensation. She wondered why she never felt that with the Library. And so she decided to ask. *Why don't I feel this pressure around you, like this overwhelming pressure of time, experience, and force?*

Well, the Library responded, *my power is spread out through the entire Library, from the atrium up there, right down through to the filtration chamber and beyond.*

Hmm, Quinn said, *makes sense. You're saying your majesty is sort of being distributed evenly over a massive space?*

Yes, how about we go with that, the Library said, which gave Quinn pause, as they were almost at her office. She realized all the differing functions the Library performed, even if some was subconsciously. If Quinn really thought about it, she was surprised the Library had maintained a grip on sanity over all the years.

Quinn continued to guide them. Their auras drew the attention of everyone they passed. All of them stopped to look up at their little procession. Finally, they entered her office. She was somewhat relieved to see Aradie was still fast asleep in the corner. Malakai had made himself scarce, but she knew he'd come back later. She made sure to send him a message to that effect.

Gesturing for them to sit, she cracked her neck from side to side. She was about to speak up when she noticed they were watching a spot slightly behind her. Lynx popped into view, too, and joined them, but not before the Library coalesced into its shadow form.

"You'll have to excuse me. This is the closest I get to a form other than the Library. I'm still the same."

Its siblings watched, thoughtful looks on their faces.

"Are you sure this is your most solid form?" Dru asked, her tone hard to read.

"Of course I am!" The Library snapped the words out. "Sorry. I've been very busy."

Dru shrugged.

"You're not really still the same, are you?" Drivok said to the Library. He watched the shadow, his eyes flickering in a way that reminded Quinn very much of Lynx, who stayed in a corner with his eyes downcast. Quinn would have to ask him what that was about next time they were alone.

"The Library's not quite speaking the truth. You know it was closed down for, like, five hundred years, right," Quinn said, getting to the heart of the matter, because if Drivok didn't realize that, then they were in a bit of a pickle, really.

"I know that now," he said, seemingly confused. He pinched the bridge of his nose with his fingers. "Can we start from the beginning, please?"

"Well, that's a really long way. How about we just start with the sabotage of the Library?"

"The Library was sabotaged." He sounded surprised.

"Keep up, Driv," Drukala said. "Sabotaged by our very own other brother and sister."

This time, Drivok looked at her as if he was trying to find the lie. "You couldn't have put that in one of the wake-up messages?"

"I wasn't sure how safe that message would be."

"Well, of course it'd be safe, because it's me." Drivok sounded affronted.

"Drav and Dro already turned against us. How could I be a hundred percent sure you hadn't done the same thing?" Drukala's argument was valid.

Drivok went to open his mouth with a retort, and clearly thought otherwise. He clamped his mouth shut and nodded. "No, I see the logic. What about you?" he said to the Library.

The shade shrugged. "It's not really about me, is it?"

"I beg to differ," Drivok said. "It's precisely and completely about you and the Library, and the fact that I think we've all known that Drav has always been sketchy."

"Yeah," Quinn sighed. "He put a backdoor into the system, although it doesn't seem to work properly."

"Have you already fixed it?" Driv seemed genuinely curious.

"Sort of," Quinn said.

"Drav never did anything straightforward. There will always be tricks." Drivok's tone was serious.

Quinn nodded watching the younger brother. Drivok gave her a weird feeling. As if everything was too easy. "You say you were woken up from your hibernation?"

"That was several days ago, now. Took me a bit to adjust myself," he said. "But yes, I was. I was woken prematurely, by about fifty years, which I don't appreciate." He glared between the Library shadow and Drukala, alternately. After several seconds, the Library spoke up.

"I really thank you for coming. I wanted to make sure I had some allies."

"What's he trying to do?" Drivok crossed his arms.

"Oh, you know, release chaos back into the universe," Drukala said in a sing-song voice.

He waited as if expecting a punch line or continuation. "You're serious? I thought that was a joke. He's been going on about that, for millions of years. I think he went on about that when we were still fighting chaos, originally. He's always been very bad at jokes." He paused, tapping his chin thoughtfully. "Well, carry on. What's this Librarian's deal? How does she have your DNA?"

"Ah," Lynx said. "That was a council decision. A last stand of desperation, when all those with Librarian compatible affinities were massacred."

"He did that, too?" Drivok asked, and a hint of revulsion had crept into his voice. Anger glittered in his eyes. A slight red hint rose up within the green. Quinn was fascinated.

"Quinn was created to embody all the affinities and thus be a perfect match." Lynx offered a small smile in the Librarian's direction.

She rolled her eyes.

"How did you keep her hidden from detection?" He seemed enthralled by the concept, the look in his eyes one that showed he needed to know how this had worked.

"Hid me on a non-magical world," she murmured.

"Excellent. That would do it!" Drivok practically glowed with excitement. "And let me guess. You don't know how to use your cosmicisodracus powers properly yet, do you?"

"Nope. Got it in one." Quinn wasn't sure why his eagerness made her wary.

His eyes shone with a bright light, and Quinn regretted seeking this out immediately. "Then I do believe I can help."

4 8

PRACTICALLY FALL

Not having had close siblings or even really a family for most of her life, Quinn wasn't sure what to make of her new quasi aunt and uncle. Especially, since it seemed both of them wanted to take on her training. The Library, given it hadn't *actually* been a dragon for longer than it *was* one, appeared only too eager, or perhaps apathetic enough, to hand over the reins of training to its siblings.

The banter between Dru and Driv was just short of nasty. These two fought like cats and dogs. But deep down she could tell they didn't really mean a word of it.

"You can't teach her that yet," Drukala said.

"Whyever not?" Drivok gave her a glare. He had a really intimidating glare.

Drukala threw her hands up in frustration. "She needs the fundamentals first. You can't just jump out of the frying pan and into the fire."

"I beg to differ," her brother said. "Jumping into fire is exactly what dragons can do."

Their arguments began to fade into background noise.

The doctor *had* wanted her to rest for a while, so she sat back and watched them. Considering how much information she could absorb, they could teacher a considerable amount if they got past arguing about what and who should teach. Their discussion seemed circular, and Quinn was about to tear her hair out.

They likely expected her to stay put for a whole heap of training, except she had a million things to do. Her head pounded. Kajaro's images screamed for attention. They desperately needed to leaf through those memories. But Milaro hadn't returned yet.

Quinn didn't even know what time it was. Should she be asleep?

She sighed and decided to stand up for herself, quite literally.

She held up a hand, hoping it would stop the three-way sibling discussion that appeared to have forgotten she existed. When that didn't work, she put her fingers to her lips and wolf whistled once, very loudly.

She'd forgotten being a cosmicisodracus meant heightened senses. The whistle didn't help her headache, but it got the chattering to stop. Thus, her aim and goal had been achieved.

Quinn's uncles, aunts, parents, whatever they were, looked at her expectantly. Which served them right for talking around her and not to her.

"I'm right here, you know. How about talking *to* me? I'm a whole entity that can operate all independent and stuff. Not one of you makes me excited to learn about my heritage." She gestured around vaguely. Quinn glowered at them and found herself ever so slightly out of breath, but she felt miles better. At least Drukala and Drivok looked at each guiltily.

But then they did that thing where they were like communicating with their eyes.

"Nope," Quinn said. "we're not doing that either."

They looked at her like *Doing what?*

"That whole you having a discussion while I'm here without me knowing about it? A: I know about telepathy. I can do it too. B: That's just plain rude. And I know we've already talked about you being rude," she said, pointing at Drivok. Which, technically, if she'd been taught correctly as a human child, was also considered rude. But right now, she wasn't concerned with any potential double standards.

"And . . . I expected better from you," she said to Drukala.

Dru hurried to clarify. "We didn't mean anything by it. We were just trying to—"

"What? Do what's best for me? How about you consult me? I'm not a child. You pulled me to this place to fix stuff. You're supposed to be teaching me aspects of my heritage that can help us resolve all of this. Stop wasting my time." Quinn stood up and made as if to leave. She was far too tired, and way too stressed for all this crap.

Except the Library spoke up. "Quinn, wait."

With them finally being back on speaking terms, Quinn didn't want to jeopardize that. So she turned around . "Fine. You've got ten seconds."

The Library didn't waste any of it. "We haven't seen each other in person for a *very* long time. We got a little carried away. There's always been a slight rivalry between all of us. You know, friendly rivalry."

"So friendly that one of your brothers decided to try to sabotage your entire being?" Quinn narrowed her eyes. "You haven't explained that part to them in full yet, have you?"

"Well, no," said the Library, "because we've only just started catching up and you're here and we're trying to solve the problem of getting you up to speed on your abilities. We're just not the best at agreeing on things."

Which was a plausible explanation, Quinn thought. It also impressed upon her an element of sheer dumb luck. How the Library ever got to exist with all this bickering was a miracle.

Drevicia and Drivok looked absolutely horrified at the casual comment about destroying the Library and universe. Completely and utterly taken by surprise. At least meant that they weren't in cahoots with the other brother, unless they were superb actors, which their auras didn't indicate.

"So I take it," she said, "you weren't aware of your sibling's machinations."

"No," Drukala said, and when Quinn turned to Drivok to get his opinion, he looked like he was going to break something.

"Definitely not." He bit out the words like he wanted to take a bite out of his brother.

Quinn wondered if she could let him. "Well, now we've settled that, maybe we can talk like real grown-ups."

The Library chuckled. "You realize that you're still an egg, literally. That's why Hal calls you it."

"I know, I'm young. Give me a break."

"Yeah," the Library said softly, "you've done pretty well so far. I should."

There was a knock at the door, interrupting whatever other compliment the Library was going to give her. Quinn turned as the wards filled her in. She knew who it was. When she saw Mal's face as he opened the door, a ripple of contentedness swept over her. It allowed her to relax, and she didn't realize she'd been so tense. She'd missed Malakai.

"Am I interrupting?" he asked.

"No," she said.

"Anything I can help with?"

"No," she said, "but you're welcome to stay. They're gonna teach me how to be a dragon."

"Oh," Malakai said, grinning as he stepped into the room. "Sounds fun."

"Mal, this is my uncle Driv and you know Dru. Everyone, meet Mal." She didn't wait for a response before she dropped back to sit on the couch with Mal.

He plopped right down on the seat next to her. To be honest, these new couches were way too comfortable, but the talking seemed to have woken Aradie. She squawked and launched herself from her perch over to Quinn's shoulder. If Quinn wasn't mistaken, she also shot Malakai a withering look, as if he was on her preferred side. Then she settled on the back of the couch instead, her owl eyes observing everything.

Driv cleared his throat and nodded at Mal before he spoke. "I apologize. I wasn't expecting a new hybrid version of our species to appear. Ever. You're a bit of a surprise. And I was awoken from my hibernation early, might I add." He glared briefly at Drukala and the Library's shadow.

"To be fair," Quinn said, "I wasn't expecting for you to simply burst into the Library either. So, you know, we both had a surprise."

Drivok chuckled. "So," he said and clapped his hands for attention, "what do you need or want to know about our species? How can we help you do the job you were summoned here to do?"

Faced with the actual question, Quinn balked. She really had to think about that. How could knowing this potentially help her apart from control? What did she want to know? She gathered her thoughts. "Well, apart from being able to use fire, having apparent atmospheric differentiation immunity, and being mostly immune from fire, I'm not sure. What else *can* I do?"

Drukala raised an eyebrow, but it was Drivok who answered. "I'm not sure how to go about it, but—" He glanced over at Drevicia's shadow, just to make sure he wasn't veering completely off target, or at least that's so it seemed. Once it nodded, he continued. "You should also have innate water and ice control, regardless of whether you had the affinities."

"But I've got all the affinities," Quinn said, "so how does that make it any different?"

"It just means when you're using any of the innate genetic skills your hybridization offers you, the draw on your energy and mana will be small if not nonexistent."

"Oh," Quinn said, recalling how when she fought with Kajaro originally, she'd been able to do more than she'd imagined. As a human, she wouldn't have come out on top.

"Yes," Drivok said, "so given that Drevicia is your main donor of genetics"—he cleared his throat and continued—"you should a hundred percent have those affinities locked down. It should also enhance any innate control you have of any affinities. Not to mention your shielding abilities."

Quinn perked up at that one. "Shielding? Like when I project my shielding around myself and my allies type thing?"

"Exactly," Drivok said. "We have built-in automatic shielding in the form of our scales. I believe you've already had first-hand experience with this?"

Quinn nodded, trying immediately to avoid recalling her parent's accident. "Okay, so I've got automatic shielding. I know this, but I appreciate knowing why."

Drivok studied her for a few seconds. "When you extend your shielding out, do you notice that it doesn't pull much on your energy reserves?"

"I just assumed it didn't take much." She shrugged.

"If anybody other than you or us were to attempt that type of shielding, it would drain them so fast they'd be empty in minutes. We, on the other hand, have innate shielding. It is, I guess you could call it, a will to protect. It's also why the dragon fire didn't do as much damage to Drukala here."

Dru nodded. "He speaks the truth. Those are automatic defense capabilities can be extended. There's also speed and agility. I know when we're in our original forms, we don't necessarily look like the most agile of beasts, but I can guarantee you we are. Which is why agility has probably transferred into your human form. We're lucky you've avoided as much damage as you have. It's not just luck. Part of it is your innate dragon mobility."

Quinn perked up. "I assume there are ways I can foster these?"

"Of course there are. We'll put you through some exercises with fire, heat resistance, and shielding, to gauge where we are and what we need to do. Eventually we want every innate ability to become an automatic reaction."

"Like muscle memory?" Quinn asked.

Driv cocked his head to the side in thought and then smiled. "Exactly."

But Dru wasn't finished. "Also, as you grow your mana and energy pools will increase exponentially until you'd never have to worry about running out unless you're fighting one of us. It doesn't make us completely invincible, but it should make you pretty close to it. I'd like to get started as soon as possible."

Quinn smiled. Even just knowing the theory gave her a direction in which she could target herself and her evolution as a cosmi-cisodracus.

"Oh," Drukala said, perking up. "At your current level, you can increase the number of books you absorb. It'll help you get stronger faster."

Quinn nodded at that too. Books sparked happiness. She mentally made a list of books to have delivered to her quarters later on.

Mal was reading a healing book when Quinn stood up to join Drukala and Drivok. Some of her strength had returned, and she was eager to begin. She already understood fire levels, the different atmospheric pressures, and above all, she knew she was getting faster and stronger at her shields. Now she just had to learn how to wield it all with finesse, speed, and strength.

There was tug against the door as if whoever tried to open it had difficulty gripping the handle. It pulled her out of her contemplations. Her senses automatically flared. It wasn't dangerous, but the person trying to come through was injured. She strode to the door knowing who it was but not wanting to believe it and pulled the door open just to watch Hal practically fall into the room.

He looked like a wreck.

IN ANY CAPACITY

A DETACHED PART OF QUINN THOUGHT IT TYPICAL OF HAL TO STUMBLE through the doorway just her dragon training was about to begin. Then there was the part of her aghast that her first thought hadn't been about his injuries.

Malakai and Drivok supported the satyr as he staggered into the room, practically before Quinn could even blink. The Library conjured a size-appropriate recliner for the satyr in the middle of the room, and they dropped Hal into it.

"What happened?" she asked, surprised to hear how shaky her voice was.

She couldn't downplay how much she liked Uncle Hal. He'd done so much for her. He'd helped them all. He might be the King of Halschius, but he'd always made time for them and helped the Library when he didn't have to.

Hal's face was battered, and he grinned at her through the black blood dripping down from a gash over his eyebrow. "You should see the other guys." He gave her a wink with the non-blood-filled eye.

Quinn couldn't help the smile she gave and the glee she felt that she'd made the others pay. Relief flooded her, and at the same time a portion of shame at the fact he still felt the need to make her feel better even when he'd been hurt.

"What happened?" she repeated slowly, not about to let him off.

But before her question could be answered, Eric appeared, towing Dr. Miles behind him. Quinn activated her wards to allow them entrance. Her worry nipped at her heels like a puppy, making it difficult to wait patiently.

Eric fluttered over to her side, his face pinched with concern as he watched the doctor attend to Hal. Quinn brushed his thoughts, asking for permission to speak to him mentally. And in response, heard a mental sigh from him. She tried to figure out how to phrase what she wanted to say without sounding completely and utterly insensitive. But she didn't have to, because Eric spoke first.

You don't even understand how bad it was. His voice, even through thought, sounded like it was cracking, almost breaking.

She had no idea, nor could she picture it. *It's not something I can imagine.*

Eric chuckled very dryly across the mental connection. Even though outwardly it looked like he was a complete wreck, maybe there was a slight hint of paranoia to that laugh. *They were mid-skirmish when I got there with the news. Usually, Hal is one of the most calm and collected people on a battlefield. He's ruthless and efficient, and he never lets anything ruffle his feathers. He knows exactly what needs to be done, who needs to do it, and what needs to happen to bring a battle to its end.*

He has been doing it for millions of years, right? Quinn said.

I guess practice makes perfect. Still, the news set off his temper.

Quinn waited while they watched Miles attend to the king. The gash above his eyes appeared deeper than she'd thought and more difficult to close than anticipated. The doctor motioned to Malakai, who put his healing book down and came over to watch the process and assist the doctor where he could since they hadn't brought a nurse with them.

In the meantime, Eric remained silent. So Quinn broke the mental silence. *Well, what happened?*

Eric raised an eyebrow in her direction, but his gaze never wavered from Hal's treatment as he spoke. *The only way this distraction could have occurred was if his sister helped arrange it. She knew they meant to deliberately distract him with this specific fight and probably knew about the end goal. This skirmish was aimed at helping someone outside of the family take down Hal's defenses. The method, the strategy. It was all her. She instigated it.*

Quinn thought she understood or at least had a glimmer of understanding. Luckily, Eric carried on.

It's just not done. The siblings and Hal just fight. It's what they do. But the fights are between their families. They team up against one another or against Hal constantly, but they never bring in outsiders. It's not an outsider's problem. These skirmishes are unnecessary anyway. Their wars are succession wars. Bringing in someone from the outside to assist . . . crossed a line.

Quinn cringed. That didn't sound very honorable, but then she'd never thought that demon-like creatures would be honorable. But wasn't that, like, speciesist? She wasn't sure. It did make sense, though, how blasé Hal was about the two, three, or seven wars constantly being waged in his territory, about his strange fondness for fighting family when he'd say, "Oh, got another war to go to."

He must be so very disappointed, she said.

Eric shook his head. *You have no idea. I've never seen him this angry. I thought he was going to break things. He could have melted rock himself. He was so incensed.*

Quinn swallowed. *Is everybody on his side okay?*

Mostly. He would never hurt anybody who's loyal to him. Usually that includes his siblings.

Why? I don't understand, she said.

Look, Eric continued. *He allows his siblings quarter. They have their wars, they end them, the others go back home and lick their wounds. Hal leaves them in peace until the next time they attack. But this time, Hulishars screwed up. He caught her. He'll interrogate her and leave her in the house indefinitely. She betrayed a way of life that's existed for millions of years, Quinn. This was a bad outcome. A totally unexpected outcome.*

Quinn frowned as she watched the doctor continue to work on the satyr's back. Wounds she hadn't even noticed before gaped with a sickly green hue. She wasn't so sure she blamed the sister having to constantly fight her siblings. *Wait a second. Do they have to fight him or die? Lose everything if they don't try to take more? Is it a weird, convoluted thing like that?*

Eric looked at her, and she could hear the derisive laugh in his head. *No, they all have estates on their own worlds. It's just that Hal is in charge of the region.*

Quinn was still trying to wrap her head around that. *So they have their own places that they're in charge of, that they make the rules for, with subjects that look up to them?*

Exactly. How did you think it worked?

I don't know. I thought they were all annoyed that he got to rule over them, and kept waging war and they all hated each other.

Well, Eric said, *I'm not sure hate is the right word, but they're all extremely competitive.*

They decided to start wars and throw their armies at each other because they want to be the ruler of the region? To be bigger and better?

Pretty much, Eric said.

Quinn needed more clarification. *He doesn't imprison his siblings or annihilate them or torture them or take their soldiers and torture them?*

No, that's not really Hal. Although he's extremely good at interrogation. It's one of his main strengths. He just doesn't use it against family. Eric grinned quite impishly. *People hire him for that. He's got a reputation.*

Quinn didn't think she sympathized with Hal's sister anymore. *So she basically screwed him over, trying to take over everything despite already having her own world and people.*

In a nutshell. Eric shrugged uneasily. *Hal is strong. He was made as the ruler, forged specifically to rule. Defeating him would upset balance in hundreds of quadrants. It'd also take a concerted effort of multiple forces. You haven't seen him when he's in his true combat form.*

Quinn nodded, knowing instinctively how formidable he'd be. She turned to watch Miles and Malakai finish working on Hal's injuries. They seemed almost done. The cuts, blood, and abrasions all along his body appeared to be healed behind pale scars. He breathed better, his aura less aggravated and jagged.

"Thank you," he said, and pushed himself to standing as the other two scattered. Hal grimaced as he moved, flexing his arms and his legs as if trying to gauge just how bad the damage had been. "I owe you thanks. Thank you, doctor. Thank you, Malakai. I'll tell your grandfather that you don't suck."

"Thanks," Mal said dryly.

And then Hal turned to Quinn, a sort of smile on his face. "Hello, little egg. I believe I owe you thanks." He said it seriously, and Quinn grinned up at him. "How can I show you I appreciate all you've done?"

Quinn seized the opportunity, even though she didn't think he owed her anything. "You can't call me little egg anymore. That's my ask for having come to your palace's aid when it needed me."

Hal threw his head back and chuckled. "No can do. You'll have to pick something else. Maybe I can give you a nice little lava pool or something attractive for the Library."

"That's not fair," she said, pouting. "And here I helped save your damned palace."

"Everyone evacuated safely, Quinn. Don't act like you had to do an amazing feat of . . . actually—"

Mal butted in. "Might not have been an amazing feat, but we used all of our freaking energy and mana reserves for your crap, and she got a major injury she's still taking medication for. Be a little less flippant, uncle." Malakai tried his best to look stern, but Quinn could see the twitch at the corner of his mouth.

Hal glared at him, the fire in his eyes flaring brightly. "I don't think I'll tell your grandfather anything."

"Excellent," Malakai said. "Didn't want you to."

Hal turned back to Quinn, effectively ignoring Malakai. "I won't stop calling you little egg, but I will owe you a favor."

"To cash in any time?" she interrupted, narrowing her gaze,

"To cash in any time." Hal laughed heartily, even if it sounded a bit thinner than usual. Healing took a lot out of the injured body. "My favors are solid, so whenever you need me, I'll come for that favor."

A part of Quinn wanted to ask what made it so different from how things normally went. But she refrained because it'd be rude. Plus, she felt guilty for not having saved everyone in the palace. "I'm sorry we didn't manage to get Kajaro's medical and guard team out in one piece."

Hal shrugged. "You know, I'm just happy as many got out as did. The last thing I expected was an ambush. An attack perhaps, but a full blown invasive ambush, no. It's my fault for being ill prepared. I thought Kajaro would try to break out. I should have anticipated they'd come for him. I'm sorry I left that in your lap."

"It's okay, we dealt with it," Quinn said. "We dealt really well with it."

He gave her a real smile. "I believe you have some memories to go through."

She nodded. "Milaro and I do. I think it'd be better for him to do the extraction, since my expertise with handling such an influx of memories is minimal. At the moment, it's all I can do to confine them separately from mine."

"Very well," he said. "Let me know if I can help in any capacity, and not as a favor. There are some things we are all allies for. I should be going, though."

"Where are you going?" she asked.

"I interrupted you, and I stole your healer, because mine was on the battlefront tending wounded." He grimaced sheepishly. "I thought I'd go and double check how things are progressing back in Halschius. I'll return and visit you as soon as I can."

Quinn's eyes narrowed. "Be sure that you do because you owe me a nine lives explanation."

"And that would be my cue to leave." Hal laughed as he disappeared.

Quinn wasn't sure what to think of the interlude, but she smiled after him and turned to her trainers. "Let's finish what we started."

5 0

NO OFFENSE

Sweat dripped into Quinn's eyes. She'd have thought that being immune to fire would prevent her from sweating. But she was wrong.

Training her heritage given abilities wasn't anything like Quinn expected. After her initial couple of weeks with the Library, she'd accepted there were simply a few innate abilities. Those included fire and her scales. She'd thought that was all it entailed.

She'd been so very wrong.

Drukala and Drivok had entirely different approaches than the Library. Given they were corporeal and Drevicia wasn't, that probably had something to do with it.

Not being a pure cosmicisodracus made things somewhat different. The elements from other species in her genetic makeup were for specific evolutionary reasons Milaro had never fully explained to her. Both the siblings she'd officially met so far seemed enthralled at her ninety-seven-odd percent cosmicisodracus genetics.

Drivok snapped at her, pulling her out of her thoughts. "Your shielding is flimsy. Anybody could break through if they used half their brain."

Quinn sighed and crossed her arms, willing herself not to snap back. Her instruction from Drevicia had been drilling in the basics. "Cantankerous" described Driv to a T. He snapped out clipped answers, making most of his training counterproductive. He didn't understand why she couldn't "feel" the things they could.

"My shielding has withstood and withstands plenty of attacks." She tried her best not to get defensive.

"Then those attacks haven't homed in on your weaknesses. You got lucky," Drivok said. "If I was attacking you, there's no way you'd come out unscathed. You'd all be dead, and the Library would be gone and the universe would implode."

Quinn wanted to tell him he didn't need to be so mean about it. But he was also right. Fate of the universe and all.

The Library's shadows sighed. "It seems I've forgotten more than just my memories."

"Don't be so hard on yourself," Drukala said. "You've been away from your dragon form forever. A lot longer than you ever were a dragon."

"True," the Library said. "I just . . . I never realized how much I'd lost." The Library sounded contemplative, with a side of melancholy. It sounded world-weary, tired, and a bit lost.

Quinn wished she could give it a hug. The Library really hadn't been a cosmicisodracus for a long time. Comparatively, at least. Just how far removed was it? She shook herself and focused instead on extending and reinforcing her shielding.

She saw what Drivok meant, even if she didn't like it. Her points of weakness stemmed from her scales. Where they joined to her body when she extended out her shielding. Making it larger to encompass more area or people made the barrier weaker at the points where her scales joined one another. If aware of the shielding structure, those weaknesses could be targeted. So far she'd been lucky.

Quinn hated that Drivok was right.

Instead of dwelling on it, Quinn focused on smoothing the shielding out. She barely listened to Drivok's instructions and followed her instincts on how to adjust with subtle differences in the shield construction. Once she'd mastered that, it'd allow her to shield more people effectively.

"Excellent," Drivok said. "You're a pretty fast learner. You'll need to practice that until you can activate it and hold it in your sleep. For yourself, for others, for everyone. There's no reason for you ever to feel vulnerable. Just practice makes perfect, as they say."

Apparently that was a universal saying. Literally.

She nodded at Drivok and concentrated again, this time extending her shield to specifically encompass only Aradie.

The effect was almost instantaneous, just a blink, and suddenly the casing covered Aradie, who hooted.

Quinn liked to think it sounded like approval.

"Much better," Drukala said. "Nice quick learning, quick adaption."

Even after minimal practice, there was definitive growth in her shields. She'd been putting everybody in danger because she didn't know what she was doing. As if he could read her thoughts, Malakai looked up at her, caught her eye, and grinned, pointing to his stomach, while the other hand still held the healing tome he was reading. Quinn marveled at the fact that he was taking the doctor seriously. If they'd had a devoted healer earlier, perhaps Jasper wouldn't be dead.

This way, maybe no one else she'd come to care about would die.

She blinked as her stomach growled in response and realized she was ravenous. Driv caught the sound and grinned, backing off slightly. "That's enough for now. You've utilized a lot of energy, and it's getting late. I should've made you eat dinner a while ago. I apologize for that. I got a little carried away. Wasn't expecting to come here and find a niece."

The Library's shadow nodded.

Driv continued. "Exactly. I wasn't expecting to find a niece to train, either. Which, it turns out, also helps me refresh some of the skills that I haven't used in a long time." He paused, frowning as the door opened and Milaro walked in. "Ah, just the Areiltháhnish that I wanted to see."

Milaro rolled his eyes. He looked tired. "And here I am," he said. "All yours. Haven't seen you in a couple of thousand years, right?"

There was a hint of something to the tone that Quinn couldn't place. But since she was absolutely starving, she wasn't about to look a gift horse in the mouth.

Driv turned to her. "Go eat. Get some rest. We'll be back here first thing in the morning."

Quinn narrowed her eyes. It sounded like a dismissal, Too hungry to argue, she thought she might have skipped a night's sleep. Then she realized he attempted to kick her out of her own domain.

She put her hands on her hips and glared at Drivok. "You realize this is *my* office, right?" she said, mentally directing the Library to make a training room for her to learn this dragon stuff nice and close to her office so the guests wouldn't have to move too far. A room that wouldn't restrict Milaro, Malakai, Aradie, or anyone who wasn't a cosmicisodracus from entering. As long as they were on her list. It'd make this much easier to have a dedicated training space. While she could get over her office constantly being used as a meeting place, she didn't find being kicked out of it acceptable.

She kept her voice even as she spoke. "After I've eaten, I'll return, here, to my office because I have things to do before I sleep. When I come back, I'd like it to be my office, not a training room."

Drivok, at least, had the common decency to look sheepish. "I'm sorry. I got a bit heavy-handed, didn't I?"

Quinn nodded. "Just so we're clear, the Library created another room that we can use for combat training, but this here is my work space."

"Perfectly understandable." Driv inclined his head in apology.

"Why, Quinn? I guess you're not such a little egg anymore," Milaro said, a genuine smile on his face.

"That's what Hal calls me, and you know I hate it. Did you want me to hate you a little bit, too?" she asked pointedly.

"You do have a point." Milaro laughed and his eyes twinkled. "Thanks for arranging somewhere else."

Quinn narrowed her eyes. Even now they still babied her.

She left the room with Malakai in tow. He followed her out as Aradie swooped after them, landing on Quinn's shoulder. She sent a questioning inquiry to her bird, who shot back a bunch of images at her.

"Well, that's very interesting," Quinn mused as they walked toward the culinary branch. Her mind raced.

"What's interesting?" Malakai asked when Quinn didn't offer up anything.

"They encouraged Aradie to come with me, as if they didn't want her in the room. That makes me think they're talking about things they don't want me to overhear." She couldn't shake the fact that she was certain she was missing something. Chalk it up to one of those gut feelings.

"You know, you could always ask Lynx to listen in if you really needed to know everything."

Quinn grimaced. "That's not gonna work. The Library would know he was there. They're connected. As much as I love the cat, he is very much the Library's manifestation."

Malakai frowned. "Any idea what they might be talking about?"

Quinn shrugged. "Not to sound too self-involved and vain, but it's probably me."

He watched her for several steps before nodding with a grin. "Yeah, I'd be willing to bet it's about you, too. Or, you know, about you, the Library's potential destruction, maybe the bomb sitting in one of the pillars down there and how to rectify it. Not to mention the constant sabotage attacks on the Library. But definitely, there will be talk of you."

Quinn laughed. She knew he was right. Even more so than she'd been. Quinn was certain that at least some of the discussion would be about her. But what else weren't they telling her? And why couldn't she be there to discuss it?

She was starving and the kitchen felt so far away. Time to give them the benefit of the doubt for a few hours. But if they didn't tell her before she started training the next day, well, she'd just plain ask. After all, the logical side of her said that they could also be doing sibling catch-up stuff.

"I need food," she said and clomped the last few steps into the culinary branch.

Somehow, stepping inside the area always let Quinn relax. She wasn't sure if it was the barrage of smells that assaulted her senses or the way the space reminded her of her grandmother, who always baked and cooked and allowed Quinn to sit on the island while she did. They were some of the best memories Quinn had. Cozy, with good food on a Sunday afternoon. Making the most of her week, preparing her for the next one. A part of her felt pained. She'd never really known her family. She guessed she'd known as much as she needed to. They were good to her and they'd been killed because of her.

"Are you okay?" Malakai's voice was soothing and soft.

Quinn shrugged, looking around for Cook. They were on the far side, so she stood and waited working the kinks out of her neck. She had the time to spare.

"I'm okay," she answered belatedly, "just thinking about how so many people have already died to get me here."

"No offense, Quinn, but you *do* know it's not just about you, right?" Malakai's tone was harder than expected. "If the experiment had been someone else, then it would have been them. It's always been about preserving the Library, about preserving the filtration method that keeps chaos from going on a rampage and devouring everybody and the universe"

"Yeah," Quinn said, slightly shocked at his bluntness and yet grateful for it. "Guess it's not just me, it's more about the universe. I like that much better."

"Good," he said.

Cook arrived. They frowned, looking her up and down. "Hmm, you need comfort food. How about a nice risotto? Would that hit the spot?"

Quinn brightened. She hadn't had a risotto in a while. "Yes," she said.

"Mushroom?" they asked.

Quinn nodded.

"Chicken today?"

"No, just mushroom will do."

"Excellent, sit down and I'll have it right with you."

Maybe Cook wasn't Quinn's grandmother, but the sensation and the feeling of relaxation and calm held an almost eerie similarity. Quinn decided her favorite branch was the culinary branch, because it just felt home.

51

UNIMPRESSED

Despite the best laid plans, the next day didn't dawn quite as Quinn expected. Instead of waking in the morning to have breakfast and then confront her relatives about what they weren't telling her, an owl woke Quinn.

However, the owl wasn't Aradie, who seemed to be in the process of waking up at a ridiculously slow pace. The night owl blinked at her in complete and utter confusion.

It was that tiny, pale owl who'd had all those nasty images implanted in its head to mislead their investigation when they'd been trying to piece together the Library events through the observations of others. Despite at least being hundreds of years old, the owl had a certain juvenile charm.

Funny, she'd really thought the owl stayed with Harish, which suddenly made Quinn sit up as if hit by lightning.

"Harish?" she blurted out. The little owl practically squeaked.

Suddenly, information in the form of images bombarded Quinn's mind, and she nodded. "I've got this, I think." Her brain sorted through all the pictures of Harish's room, Harish's screens, Harish with a decidedly manic-leaning smile on his face. It spurred her on. She threw herself out of bed, washed up and dressed in no time. She shouted to Aradie, "Come on, go get Mal. We're heading to Harish's office."

And before the bird could even respond, Quinn took off down the stairs, landing softly by cushioning herself with a condensed gust of wind. A part of her wondered why she didn't just jump off the landing every day. It easily saved twenty seconds. She didn't stop to look at anybody else. She didn't stop to assess the Library or the check-in desk. Instead, she ran straight for Harish's office and burst in.

The door was open when she got there with Harish inside, pacing. His office had changed. The center console was more compact now and had floating holographic images all around it, turning pictures that she didn't recognize or understand on a consistent basis. Along the walls hung HUD images. They appeared to be running a whole plethora of equations she couldn't fathom for the life of her. It looked like futuristic computer images against the dark stone walls, sort of like she'd seen in movies before back on Earth. A pale blue glow suffused the entire room, giving Harish an almost fanatical glow.

She'd been in there several seconds when Aradie landed on her shoulder and the low hoot she greeted Quinn with made Harish turn around and focus on her. "Librarian," he said, and she'd never heard such a joyous tone from him.

"Your owl fetched me," she said cautiously. He seemed to be happy and not maniacal. At least the sense of his magic felt like that.

"Oh, fantastic," he said, his eyes bright and smile wide. "I've figured it out. Now, these magical signatures you brought me were really challenging. Their consistency was off, though, as if somebody had tried to overlay them, make them disappear, combine them, even. Or perhaps combined them hoping to obscure any singular thread. Now, I'm terribly sorry this took me so long, but you have to understand that unravelling different magical essences and signatures from each other takes time."

Quinn blinked. She'd never heard him speak this much. In fact, she was certain this was the most he'd ever spoken to her combined. He didn't seem to notice her startlement. He carried on and the way he gestured, the way he spoke, it was captivating. His eyes lit up, his magic scrolled through all the diagrams as he spoke, showing her what he meant.

"As you see here, I had to separate out the different strands. They had intertwined them with such complexity . . . but there is one thing I believe is also in human science, I believe, on your planet, you have blood. I mean, we all have blood or the equivalent, but . . . anyway, it can be mostly washed away by certain chemicals. Magic doesn't do the same thing." And even as Harish spoke, the magical threads he was showing her that looked similar to DNA strands, but were obviously different, spiraled around, demonstrating to Quinn how they joined together to form a total entity.

Quinn frowned at them and Harish continued, positively aglow. "Now, magical traces are even more finicky than your blood. They require delicate handling, and you can never truly hide a signature. There are no chemicals that can wash them clear, even though that is not always foolproof, but I digress. As I was saying, if somebody knows what they're doing and I know what I'm doing, they can't hide behind the traces, you see." He laughed as if he'd made a joke.

Blindsided.

That's what it felt like seeing this person appear completely other than what she was used to.

In fact, she began to wonder if he'd maybe taken some medicine or perhaps he was just completely sleep deprived. There were massive shadows under his eyes, but he continued. "So you see, the essence you extracted from the tree ended up being the key to it all, even though that was mightily difficult to separate. You have to understand that there were hundreds of years of magical signatures, traces of people dead and gone."

Quinn listened, enraptured.

"But not all of those traces were completely inactive despite how much effort was put into making them appear so." His energy levels seemed to spike. He was getting more and more worked up, and Quinn had no idea how to calm him down. She wasn't about to start experimenting on the scientist that helped them research pretty much everything.

That's when she felt an overwhelming serenity settle around her. A calmness. A split second before Siliqua walked into the room with Malakai and Milaro in tow. Harish paused his explanation and the smile that overcame his face, though tired, was brilliant.

"I told you to wait until I'd retrieved the others," Siliqua admonished him, her tone slightly exasperated but filled with a sense of love as she looked at her husband. She turned to Quinn. "He's a little worked up. Loves a good puzzle, you know. And this one you gave him? This one's kept him up at night. He's probably been babbling to you."

Quinn shook her head. "No, not really. Maybe a little fast and but overall, mostly coherent." She gestured around at the walls and the diagrams. "I must admit, the pictures helped. I didn't really have much trouble following along."

Siliqua laughed. "Excellent. I'm glad they've done their job. Although I dare say you didn't require the images in order to understand." Siliqua walked a couple of steps forward and turned to her husband. "Sit down, love, and rest. I've got this. Don't worry."

Harish's face practically glowed with relief. When he sat, his robes almost swallowed him. Quinn could practically feel the waves of fatigue rushing over him. She glanced at Siliqua, who shook her head almost imperceptibly. Well, maybe she didn't need to worry about him. That didn't mean she wouldn't.

But Siliqua turned around to them and clapped her hands. "Sorry, I didn't anticipate you arriving so fast, Quinn."

Quinn grinned. "I need to know who and what we're facing and figured this was the best way to get an answer."

"Obviously," Siliqua said. "I mean, otherwise, you wouldn't have had those other vials. Correct?"

"No, we wouldn't have. Do you know what happened that caused them to step in?" Quinn knew Siliqua knew that "them" in this case meant the Chroniclers.

Siliqua shook her head. "I don't even have an inkling."

Quinn knew she had to dive deeper into the journals. They already contained information on Korradine's species and how they navigated, getting her specifically the role of Librarian. It was still something she didn't completely understand. Quinn also didn't add that she really was dying to know who set them up. Who'd done this? That way she'd know precisely who to target. A bit of a personal vendetta wouldn't hurt anyone she cared about . . .

Malakai slipped his hand into hers and squeezed as if he could read her mind. He probably could. He could probably at least read her facial expressions and knew her well enough by now to understand that she was thinking brooding thoughts. She squeezed back and didn't let go of his hand. It was a comfort.

"Anyway," Siliqua said, "where were we?"

"Oh," Quinn piped up. "He was explaining the complexity of magical signatures as how they can like never be completely removed, only mostly overwritten. Also that he's been unravelling them."

Siliqua raised an eyebrow. "That's a very good summation. It's exactly what happened. They really tried to cover these signatures up. It wasn't just a passage of time, although that contributed to some of it in regard to the . . . what did you call it, death tree?"

Quinn chuckled this time. Even though in hindsight, it wasn't funny, just all of it was overwhelmingly nervous. "Yeah, death tree. Good nickname."

Siliqua cringed. "Anyway, they tried to cover up several of the signatures. Korradine's, Adrito's, and even Kajaro's signatures were layered over the top, but along with the severely degraded signatures you brought with you, there were also those in the little jars that the Chroniclers gave to you. Those were crystal clear at least by comparison to the others. So much that I . . . we've retested them multiple times. Did he tell you about the key?"

Quinn shook her head. "He mentioned it but didn't elaborate."

"Hmm," Siliqua said. "There are several signatures in the vials given to you by Carafax, and we have your sample, and everybody else's who works here. We have Malakai's, Milaro's . . . everybody's. So we could differentiate and make sure we weren't crossing our wires, since so many people went over the tree area after the fact. But when we unraveled the tree's, those signatures contained in the vials were hiding under so many layers yet clearer and less muddled than the ones that appeared to be there the longest. The other two that we confirmed were Ardenil."

Malakai gasped.

"I'm sorry, Mal. I wish it wasn't her as well." Siliqua said soflty.

He shrugged. "It's not like I know her. It's not like she knows me. It's just that she's related to me and automatically makes me feel guilty."

Siliqua chuckled. "That's the curse of family sometimes. Anyway, also Karella."

Quinn paused and held up a hand. "Wait a second. Karella? The mother we rescued from the Balisor incident? The one whose daughter the mamoria coopted? Are you sure?"

"We've gone over it numerous times. I went to ask for samples personally. I hoped to triple check and then figure out a way to approach them. But her and her daughter disappeared from the Library. The doctors didn't release them." Siliqua seemed unimpressed.

Quinn sighed. "I have to admit, I wasn't expecting that.

"I know you . . . you're a little close with them."

"Not exactly. I mean, we saved them, or at least I thought we'd saved them." Quinn mulled it over in her mind. Maybe she'd only seen what she wanted to see. "Karella is one hell of an actress."

5 2

PERSONALLY

KARELLA WAS A NAME THAT QUINN HADN'T THOUGHT ABOUT RECENTLY. Not since they'd returned from the disastrous visit to the Balisors, retrieved the book that helped open the alchemical division from her, and healed her daughter, who had surprisingly still been alive. She'd not exchanged more than a couple of conversations with the woman, who'd seemed so distraught when her husband died. She'd seemed so genuine. Quinn had even double-checked Dr. Miles's records.

So how had she fooled Quinn so totally?

Quinn hadn't expected any of these results to be related to Karella. Ardenil, sure, they'd already had several suspicious things happen because of Ardenil. But adding both to the board now, since Ardenil wasn't apparently as missing as they thought. She leaned forward, slowly bashing her head against the wall next to her board, as she looked at it out of the corner of her eye.

"Murder board" wasn't entirely accurate. But it'd probably end up killing her through frustration in the end.

A light pop in the room drew Quinn's attention. She looked around to her right, curiosity piqued.

"That's very odd," Lynx muttered more to himself from her left-hand side.

Quinn eyed him curiously. She hadn't felt his essence morph into form beside her like she usually did. Quinn was close enough that she could see the runic bands in his hair swirling quickly. She wondered what information he was processing.

"Sorry," he said, sounding a little sheepish, "I didn't mean to startle you. I just heard."

Quinn sighed. "Are you going to share what you find odd with me, or are you just going to stand there and stare at the board and make me try to guess?"

He cocked his head to one side and pointed at the board. "Kajaro is gone, dead, whatever. Drav's still out there, but we aren't even sure if Kajaro was fully on Drav's side or not. Remember? It's like Kajaro was playing things from different angles, multiple possibilities, and all of them with the caveat that in the end he would win."

Quinn nodded. "That's generally why people make plans, right? And he was sort of a bad guy."

"Obviously not in his eyes. He also didn't win," Lynx mused.

Quinn raised an eyebrow this time. "Look at you, getting all philosophical."

"Yes," Lynx said, "I'm starting to feel much more myself, almost like my very own entity."

"That'd be nice, wouldn't it," Quinn said, watching him closely, "to be your very own entity? Not just a manifestation? Is that something that can happen?"

Lynx watched her for several seconds. "Well, of course it's something I'd want."

"But whether or not it's possible." She pushed a little more.

"I'm not sure yet. I'd have to investigate."

The way he said it gave Quinn pause, as if it was something he wanted so badly and yet couldn't be certain he'd ever get. And yet? Something about him tugged at her senses. Not in a bad way, just a different one.

"Anyway," Lynx was saying, "I felt like he was his own double agent. At least if Sarila is anything to go by."

Quinn frowned. "We're missing elements here."

"Yes"—he pointed to Kajaro's name—"and then here as well." He indicated where Karella's name appeared. "What is the binding event? What connects Karella to Sarila apart from the fact that Karella was in the Balisor camp when the toxin entered the root system?"

Quinn shrugged hopelessly. "I have no idea."

"Neither do I," Lynx said. "But we should probably find out what that was supposed to accomplish in the first place and why Karella felt the need to hide from us, if she wasn't out to fully destroy the Library."

"I guess if she was involved in that," Quinn said, "she wouldn't want us to know because killing thousands upon thousands of the Balisor clan wasn't a good way to approach us? I mean, that's a very bad thing."

"You can say evil, Quinn," Lynx said. "We need to know why they were on the same side."

Quinn groaned. "You're not helping. The board is complex enough as it is. Why can't it just—" She glared at the board as if she was willing it to give her the right answers so she didn't have to work them out herself. She stopped lamenting, took a few deep breaths, and turned to face Lynx. "So where have you been since we got back?"

A bit of static flickered through Lynx's eyes so fast Quinn thought she might have imagined it. "I've been . . . calibrating," he answered, finally turning to face Quinn full on. "My memories are almost fully restored." He hesitated, as if he wasn't entirely sure how to phrase what he wanted to tell her. "I'm still working on and through some discrepancies, but I think I might have answers to several more of Korradine's plans."

Quinn studied him for a minute. "Including Ashiron, right? Because let's face it, that one is a little more imminent than anything else."

Lynx hesitated before he answered. "Some of it. The synchronization between the pillar and the Library is still unusually high for one that is partially displaced. I do know that Korradine and I had many conversations that I'd completely and utterly forgotten. Retrieval is a slow process. And Siliqua now has to split her time between myself,

Milaro's kingdom, and whatever Harish is currently working on. Which is only fair. I can't monopolize her completely."

Quinn watched him closely, as if that way maybe she could figure out why the back of her brain itched every time he spoke. "Any ideas on how we can solve the Ashiron situation?"

Lynx shrugged. "I have some theories on how we can fix it."

Frustration welled up in Quinn. She knew why they couldn't. Sort of. But she didn't necessarily agree that they couldn't try. She knew the answer before the words even came out of her mouth. "Can't we just replace the pillar?"

"We've already been over this Quinn. We can't just replace the pillar without causing extreme instability to the Library. To its structure as a whole. If it were that easy, I'd have initiated it already. As soon as I have all these greyer areas cleared up, I promise that we'll get around to fixing Ashiron, okay?" There was a pleading note in his tone and eyes. As if he just needed her to trust him for a little while longer.

Quinn really hoped it didn't come back to bite her. "Well, just keep in mind, we've only got like eighty plus days until it explodes and we all die."

"No pressure," he mumbled, looking back at the board. "I know we're on a timer."

Quinn knew unequivocally that Lynx was keeping something from her. This, coupled with her uncles and aunt also withholding information, made her feel as though she was back in her first couple of weeks in the Library. She took a deep breath to center herself. "Is there something you're keeping from me again? Something that I need to know to do my job?" She tried hard to keep her voice steady, to separate emotion from analytical processing.

Lynx's eyes swirled, bleeding out into the sclera. His runes activated in a frenzy of movement. If she hadn't been paying such close attention to his facial expressions, she would have been lost in those hypnotic circles. He hesitated, started to speak, stopped, and then began again.

"Not like you're thinking," he said finally, looking nervously from side to side and biting his bottom lip in a very human way. His gaze avoided hers momentarily before he sighed. "It's not bad. I can't tell you what it is right now because I haven't verified it yet. I'm not certain. But when I can, you're the first person I'll tell."

He held her gaze for several seconds, his eyes still flickering. And then he popped out of her sight.

Quinn blinked. He was just gone. He hadn't even said he'd be back later. That was no way to end a conversation. She sighed.

Not only did she have a once again sulking and silent Library, but also a secretive manifestation.

"Nice bit of avoidance there, Lynx," she said to the empty room. She stared at the spot where he'd stood, deep in thought. Had he discovered something else about his memories? Or someone else's? Or the Library's? Was there a piece of information she hadn't considered that would make him act this way?

Lynx hadn't seemed angry or frustrated at her at least. She could feel the headache pounding again. But she wasn't so out of it that she failed to notice Malakai approaching.

"What are you looking at?" he asked, tilting his head as he took in the murder board and its new additions.

"Oh, that. I'm just trying to figure out where what fits, and what we still need to do, and who we still need to find, and who is involved in what," she said, covering her eyes with her hands. "And now Lynx is just acting really weird."

Aradie chose that moment to coo and land on her shoulder. Images flashed in front of Quinn's eyes.

"I guess Aradie also thinks he's acting oddly," she said. Aradie brushed her mind with a series of other images.

"That's concerning," Malakai said.

Quinn frowned. "I think he's figuring some things out. He might be evolving, maybe."

Malakai gave her a quizzical look. "Can a manifestation evolve?"

She sighed. "I don't know. Eight months ago, if you'd have asked me if magic was real, I would have laughed in your face. Now, isn't anything possible with magic? That's what your grandfather always says."

Malakai frowned. "Perhaps." He didn't sound very convinced. "What else is on your mind?"

"You mean other than the pillar of doom underneath us that's going to blow us all up and kill the universe? Nothing much has changed since the last time you asked." All the words on the murder board bled together in her vision. She rubbed at her eyes. "It's not all that bad. I know they're working on a solution, and they're close."

"I got that impression from Lynx, too."

"I'd prefer it to already be solved. It's like a dark cloud hanging over me that I can't seem to get rid of."

"You take things so personally, Quinn."

She glared at him. "How am I not supposed to take things personally? They tried to wipe out every single potential Librarian with a compatible signature in the universe. They've tried to kill me multiple times. Even succeeded in killing my makeshift family. They've got a bomb in the Library that they have to know is there and works as a failsafe to implode the Library when their plan fails, which it has. It's very difficult not to take this personally."

"I see your point."

"And now," Quinn said, "I want to sit here in front of my damn murder board, and figure out exactly what we need to do next."

"Really? Why don't we study the memories with my grandfather? Failing that, study the journals Carafax gave us?"

Quinn took a step back. Her frustration at the lack of progress wasn't helping her decision making. She turned and looked at him. "Yeah, let's take a look at the journals."

At least . . . until she could get a hold of Milaro to discuss the damned visions.

53

NOT ENTIRELY SURE

QUINN GRABBED THE JOURNAL FROM HER DESK, HOLDING IT GENTLY IN her hands before plopping back down on the couch. The soft leather of the journal felt as if it'd been worn by ages of care and love. It *felt* like magic. Even sitting down on the couch with Mal to share it, Quinn couldn't quite shake the feeling something was wrong.

Again.

She was missing something and hated that feeling.

Malakai nudged her with his elbow. "Okay, what thought is trying to give you wrinkles?"

She blinked at him and raised an eyebrow, not quite understanding. He laughed. "Right here," he said, and reached out to poke the middle of her forehead where her brow had furrowed. "It's making you scowl fiercely."

Quinn blinked at him. "I'm just—"

But that was just it. How did she explain what she was just, and how she was just? It didn't even make sense in her own head. Like somebody had reached in and was stirring all the ingredients together, so there was no clear picture of any individual item.

She sighed. "Lynx felt decidedly off when he was in here earlier. He's almost back to his old self."

Malakai paused, the journals forgotten across their laps. "Well, they have them all restored now, though, right? The memories? Isn't that the whole reason Harish, Siliqua, and Cadre were holed up in that room for ages?"

Quinn grimaced. "That's just it. Lynx is still having problems recovering some of them. They both are. It doesn't seem quite as straightforward as they originally thought, I guess."

Mal pouted. "But that was months ago."

"Exactly," Quinn said and threw her hands up in the air in exasperation. "That's just it. This makes no sense. I don't see how Harish, Siliqua, and Cadre could have been so off with the estimation of the memory retrieval."

She sighed again and sat back, pulling her ponytail up behind her and wiggling some strands loose with her other hand.

"So much seems inconsistent," he mused softly.

"That's exactly it," Quinn agreed. "I keep feeling like I've missed something obvious or big or that should have smacked me in the face and screamed 'It's me!'"

He nudged her. "We also didn't think a Librarian and her entire species would try to plot the end of the Library, did we? But now that happened."

Quinn glared at him and despite that, he continued. "And when you think of it, none of us ever thought that the Librarian strain would be under attack where hundreds of potential Librarians got killed to destroy the Library? Stop the system working? The motivations make no sense to me. What I do know is that where we are right now is a direct result of nobody knowing that this could happen in the first place. It's not new, and it's not just you, and you're not alone."

Quinn let out another very put-upon sigh. Mal's irrefutable logic stung a bit. Concern still ate at her, but he had a point. She groaned, tugged over the journal, and began leafing through the pages with an overdramatic sigh. "Fine, let's assume your logic has some good reasoning behind it and let's look at it from that point of view."

"I'm listening," Mal said.

"The first thing they did was have Korradine begin to sabotage the Library in different ways. Making sure important dimensional information got into hands it shouldn't have. Considering we're in a pocket dimension, I'd say that's pretty important."

Mal nodded, sticking with her so far.

"Then, Korradine began to wipe any evidence of her doings out of the memory of both Lynx, the Library, and anybody else they came across in pursuit of pure evil."

"It wasn't just her," Malakai said. "It was also my great-aunt, right?"

Quinn nodded slowly. "And maybe Karella. I'm sure there's plenty more. At least from the few memories and pieces of information we've been able to put together," she admitted.

He laughed. "No, it was. I know. And then tried to turn herself into a bomb to destroy the Library, right?"

"That does seem what a bomb in the filtration chamber would mean."

"And then Lynx saved the day, knocked himself out, and lost that memory. Yet he still managed to evacuate, and then shift the Library into emergency mode in order to preserve what he could. That's right, right?"

Mal laughed. "These memories are still being a pain. At least partially, having the Library and Lynx still unable to recall everything that happened, even though those pathways should still be there, if what Cadre explained makes any sense."

"Well, the memories apparently still exist. They're just fragmented so badly that retrieval has been difficult. And, as we've experienced," Quinn went on, "Harish is ridiculously good at all this crap, so I assumed we'll eventually find them all.

"I think so," Mal said.

"But I'm so confused as to why they're still missing them."

"I don't know. I guess that's what we must figure out."

"Yeah." She slumped in her seat, feeling absolutely defeated, which was when Dottie trotted into the room.

"Librarian, just the person I wanted to see."

The bench's bright and cheery voice was such a distinct juxtaposition to Quinn's current mood. She raised an eyebrow. Sometimes Dottie's exuberance grated on Quinn's nerves. But it'd be like kicking a puppy to comment on it.

"And what can I do for you?" She hoped she didn't come off as impatient, ungrateful, or hell, even remotely offensive, but she had a horrible gut feeling they were running out of time, in some ways, more than others. Every little interruption seemed to add more to her plate.

The itch in the back of her mind needed to be scratched, yet she'd overlooked or forgotten something what she could scratch it with. Dottie didn't deserve for Quinn to take a mood out on her even though the bench didn't seem to notice the Librarian was in a mood.

"I just wanted to let you know we only need another few books for the crafting branch, and several more for the bardic one. That's all we need in order to open those branches." Dottie seemed just so full of life, zest, and enthusiasm. Quinn wished she could maybe just siphon some off and bottle it to take a swig from whenever she felt completely defeated.

"Oh," Dottie said, interrupting Quinn's melancholy train of thoughts. "I did want to double-check, though. How you were coming along with that whole, you know, power boost for the Library thing?"

Quinn's eyes narrowed. Dottie's perkiness grated when all Quinn could see were obstacles. One of which was in the filtration chamber, powering the Library. Quinn felt close to panic lately every time the chamber came up even adjacently.

She was wallowing again.

"Wait," she said as she remembered they'd still needed like fifteen books for the bardic section earlier and like seven or nine or something for the crafting one. "That was really fast," Quinn said to Dottie.

"Well, of course it was." Dottie practically preened.

Quinn watched the bench through her magic, trying to find the subtle inflections and color as Dottie answered. There had to be answers somewhere, after all. Dottie would have beamed if she'd had a face with which to smile, and the bright colors of her aura reinforced precisely that.

The bench just barreled on. "We might need your help to get a couple of the books. I think it's two of the crafting books. They're being held in the Hirish Highlands again, and I mean, you *have* been there before."

Quinn frowned. "Is that the place with the time dilation?"

Dottie nodded enthusiastically.

Quinn groaned.

"Oh, not that place," Malakai said. "I hate time dilation. My stomach is in knots for days after a trip there."

Quinn nodded solemnly. "I know. It was my least favorite place, too. But if they've got some of the crafting books, do they have any of the bardic ones as well that we could knock out?"

Dottie shook herself. "Nope, just the crafting ones. The Walry are a lot more physically inclined. I'd prefer the crafting ones in the next day or two."

Quinn gathered herself up and flashed Dottie a smile. "Well, we'll put that on our list." She turned to Malakai, hoping he'd help her confirm what they needed to do since her head felt a bit goopy. "I don't think your grandfather is ready for me yet. I suppose we could head to the Highlands as soon as possible. We can open a door right out into the village now, right?"

Malakai tried to hide a grimace as he nodded agreement. "At least that makes the trip so much easier than running across that damned wasteland and winding our way down the cliff face."

Quinn chuckled. "So a whole chunk of time has passed there, right?"

"Yes, I believe it has."

"I don't suppose you want to come with me, do you?"

"I'd like to see you stop me. Who else is going to make sure you don't embarrass yourself, Librarian?" Malakai gave her a wink.

She raised an eyebrow and turned her attention back to Dottie. "Guess that means we'll go grab the books."

"Oh, that's fantastic," Dottie said. "That means you and Malakai will retrieve those two crafting books. Thank you for offering to deal with them, Librarian. That's so much appreciated."

Quinn's breath hitched. She was glad that it wasn't Jasper's home world. Because that was one place she couldn't handle going back to just yet. Mal, as if he could read her mind, squeezed her hand and she leaned into his shoulder, pulling some strength from him that she suddenly felt lacking in herself.

"Well, visiting the Hirish Highlands is easy enough to do." Mal sat up straight. "Can I get the locations, Dottie, to plan out the trip?"

Quinn wasn't sure if she imagined it, but for just a split second as Mal asked that question, a flicker of something showed in Dottie's aura. Just a fraction of a second, though, so maybe she just blinked oddly and glitched what she saw. It'd been confusing and dark. Like a brief splinter in her vision. Then again, she was tired.

Dottie began to say something else but was interrupted with a brightly cool, "Dottie, where did you go?" as Betty, the supervisor, came to the door and popped her tiny sprite head in.

"Oh, my apologies, Librarian. You do know how eager she gets. I just gave her an updated number of the books that we need to retrieve, and her first thought was to come to you and let you know. We would have let you know anyway, as you know, but I also realized you're extremely busy and thus not always available to talk. Dottie, you really should leave the Librarian in peace."

If Dottie could have expressed it, Quinn was sure she'd have scowled at Betty. Quinn wasn't sure whether to be entertained, amused, or concerned by that.

"Very well, I'll leave the list with you, Librarian, and I shall go back to the front desk." With that, Dottie trotted out of the room.

Quinn got a message through her HUD.

Betty watched the bench go. "I'm so very sorry about that, Librarian. Dottie has been a bit sporadic lately." And then the sprite was gone as well.

Quinn watched them both leave thoughtfully.

"Penny for your thoughts?" Mal said.

"Just . . . Dottie can't leave the Library, can she?" Quinn spoke out the thought slowly still watching where the bench had departed. Then she turned to Mal. "Do you have any idea why?"

He shook his head. "Nope. I think it has something to do with her species and her role with the Library since its inception."

Quinn nodded slowly. Maybe it was time she looked into that.

54

DEAR LIBRARIAN

QUINN GROANED. IT WAS PROBABLY THE LAST PLACE SHE'D EVER WANTED to return to. Thoughts of Dottie, the bomb, and putting the Library back to rights aside, the Dinetian hometown was the last place she wanted to visit. Maybe she just needed to learn how to manipulate time herself, and then a place where time was distorted wouldn't bother her so much.

"I really despise time dilation aspects of anything," Quinn said as she checked her supplies over prior to leaving. Aradie hooted irritably.

Malakai chuckled from next to her as he checked his own equipment, fingering the string on his bow with a thoughtful expression on his face. "Is it really the time dilation aspects you hate, or is it just the Hirish Highlands and the Dinetian town that you dislike so strongly?" He raised an eyebrow at her with a knowing smirk.

Quinn glared at him. "Look, that whole being thrown in jail wasn't fun. The place itself is beautiful. That cliffside village that overlooks the ocean. Just breathtaking. Pity the Walry aren't the nicest."

"On the bright side," Malakai said, "at least this time we don't have to stop a megalomaniacal snake man from trying to take over the world inside of seventy-two hours. So really, maybe you were just apprehensive last time."

Quinn shook her head. "I agree to a bright side. At least our seventy-two-hour timeline is gone. At least we've still got a couple of months to save the universe meltdown this time." She sighed, tried to pull her ponytail tighter. They were about as ready as they'd get.

"Exactly. This time we have a couple of months. Are you all right there?" Malakai asked.

"Just peachy." Quinn grimaced and rolled her shoulders, trying to work out some of the tension in them.

"Do you have the book names?" Malakai asked.

Quinn nodded. *"Crafting as an Avenue to Energy Management* and *Bar Hillel's Guide to Whittling with Magic."*

"Those sound dreadfully dull," Malakai said.

Quinn shrugged and raised an eyebrow. "Maybe, but you should remember, especially when it comes to whittling, some of these books probably provided a base to work on things like that bow you're so in love with."

Mal groaned, flicked the string once more, made a couple of adjustments, and popped it over his back. Where it shimmered into invisibility. She'd always thought he kept it in storage, but perhaps it simply camouflaged itself. That was a small thing to notice after so long together. Maybe she was just unobservant.

He didn't comment. "Are you at least ready to go?"

"I guess I am. Aradie, you hold down the fort here." The bird literally glided to her perch, turned herself around, and pointedly placed her back to Quinn. "I'm sorry, I don't think they'll appreciate a night owl coming with us. They're an extremely skittish species."

"Not to mention they like throwing people in jail," Mal added.

Quinn wasn't entirely sure what to expect when she opened the door into the Dinetian town hall, the place they'd exited from last time. It seemed so long ago now when it was barely seven months.

Weekends seemed to be a thing of her past.

They did, in fact, exit straight into the Dinetian town hall, and Quinn admitted to being surprised. She knew the moment they set through the door, time in the Library effectively moved faster. But what she didn't expect was for Tillip, the newer leader of the walrus-resembling species, the Walry, to be standing there and waiting for them along with the guard Marron who'd truly seemed to hate them last time.

The two of them stood there expectantly, watching her as if they'd known exactly when she'd step through. Who would have told them she was coming? How did they know? Paranoia about where the next potential attack on the Librarian would happen was starting to eat at her.

Malakai seemed surprised too. He reached for his weapon immediately, his face a stony mask. But Tillip stepped forward, his hands held up in a placating gesture in front of his very walrus-like face.

"Thank you, thank you for coming," Tillip said, lowering his hands together where his fingers intertwined nervously.

Quinn eyed him. "You were expecting us?"

Tillip shrugged. "The overdue notice was quite adamant that the book would be retrieved if we didn't bring it in. I wasn't entirely certain it would be you, but I hoped it would be since you'd been here before."

Quinn waited for more of an explanation.

Tillip laughed nervously, his eyes darting to and fro as if he was expecting somebody to burst into the little town hall at any point in time. "I didn't realize my father had other books, you see. I kept hearing this faint dinging, sort of like a little bell. I only dug around in the chests in my attic a few weeks ago actually, which is when I found that he did have other books we should have probably returned along with the one we returned months ago. Or for you . . . maybe years? Anyway I realized it sooner if I'd had the heart to go through his things."

He paused as if waiting for Quinn or Malakai to ask him questions. When they didn't, he knotted his fingers again and continued, "Well, when I went to pick the books up out of the chest to return to you, this fell out and I just . . . I wasn't entirely sure what to do with it."

In his hand, he clutched an envelope, which he held out toward Quinn. In filigree, beautiful handwriting was one word: Librarian.

Quinn blinked at the envelope he held out to her. She reached as if to take it, but Malakai gently stopped her hand, pulling it back to her side.

"Check if it's okay first," he said. "You know, just in case."

He didn't state the bleeding obvious. That they didn't want to risk it being a trap of some sort which could potentially deprive the Library of another Librarian.

Quinn raised an eyebrow as if asking how exactly he intended to check if it was okay. Tillip looked confused and then realization hit the Walry and he stammered, "No, no, I'd never."

Malakai raised an eyebrow. "Really? You'd never? Last time you had us thrown in jail."

Tillip cringed. "That's different. I didn't mean for that to happen. You were foreigners and you were trespassing in our village. We had no idea who you were and as far as we knew the Library was completely defunct and incapable of producing a Librarian. But I *am* sorry for that," he said lamely at the end of it.

Mal shrugged, waved his hand toward the envelope which caused a ring of light around it to appear and spark blue. It made Tillip drop the letter. Malakai caught it deftly and then handed it to Quinn.

"It's safe," he said. "There's no magical intentions, or insidious magical traps, or poisons or other detrimental substances on it as far as I can tell."

Quinn raised an eyebrow at him. "Since when can you do that?"

He shrugged. "Since always. It's one of my security affinity elements, I guess."

Yet another piece of information for Quinn to file away. Every time she thought she had his measure, she learned a new thing about Mal. She took the envelope cautiously and studied it.

Tillip rushed to elaborate. "I mean, it wasn't deliberate that we didn't return these books, and I suppose if we had returned them on time or with the other book in a timely manner, then you would have already had this letter. But it hasn't been long here, I really hope you understand that."

Quinn nodded slowly, still a little hesitant to open the thing.

"It's only that"—he paused; Tillip acted like he wanted to say something he wasn't sure would be welcome—"I felt like for some reason, you should receive this letter as privately as possible. Or I wouldn't have kept it here. I wouldn't have refused to return the books. I truly hoped you'd come."

He motioned for Quinn to sit down.

"I thought you'd appreciate privacy, so we've had the town hall cleared for the last few days."

Quinn looked at him quizzically. "Privacy?" she asked, although she did refuse to sit down. "You're worried I wouldn't have privacy?"

He gave her an unreadable look and then paused. "Well, you do live and work within the Library, right? I apologize for overstepping. We'll leave you to it," he said suddenly.

Quinn was curious, and called out, "Wait. What do you mean? I live with and work with the Library and therefore have no privacy?"

"Oh, I didn't say you have no privacy. I just said . . . well, the Library is sort of everywhere around you there, isn't it?"

Quinn nodded slowly and Tillip inclined his head politely. "If you need anything, Marron will be right outside the doors here. I really . . . I'm sorry again."

Tillip backed away, the door closed, and Quinn studied the carvings on it, almost lost in thought for a second.

Mal looked at Quinn. "Was that batshit crazy or is it just me?"

"No," Quinn said, still trying to process that a dead village leader had written a Librarian-specific letter to one of them. "No, it wasn't just you."

She wasn't sure how to react to this. But she did want to read it. Still refusing to sit, she decided to open it very carefully, just in case Malakai's proved incorrect.

The pages didn't feel too old or brittle, so it had probably been written right before he died.

Librarian, it began, *I can only hope that they found you. You are their one hope. I tell you this as an erstwhile friend of a Librarian. There are things I cannot say or write on pain of death right now. But as the latter is close anyway, I must at least try. So, please heed these words of warning, as well as I might give them. When all around you is frustrating and nothing quite adds up, the answer could be closer than you realize and nothing like you thought. Pay attention to your instincts once you have honed them. Remember, not all foes are enemies, and not all friends are allies. Be careful, watch your back, and know who to trust.*

Quinn frowned. She reread the letter again.

"Cryptic much?" Malakai said, having read it over her shoulder.

Quinn shook her head very slowly. "Well, it is . . . it's sort of advice. He's not really telling me much, is he?"

"No," Malakai said thoughtfully, "and yet."

Quinn couldn't help but draw the parallels between this letter and what Carafax had told her. Was she missing something about who to trust? Was there something she hadn't seen or realized? She sighed deeply. There were probably ten thousand things she hadn't realized.

Maybe this was the universe's way of trying to tell her something. She really wished it would just spell it out.

"This really doesn't help."

"Are you sure?" Malakai asked.

"What do you mean, am I sure if it doesn't help?"

"I mean, it's telling you that not everything around you is as it seems. Which must mean we're overlooking something in the Library. Something important."

Quinn sighed. "When isn't something important lately?"

"Exactly," Malakai said. "Now, let's get home before too many days have passed."

Quinn chuckled. "Well, we've probably just lost the rest of the day."

"Oh, good," Malakai said. "I could really go another round of sleep."

5 5

PAYMENT PLAN

Quinn's head pounded like a bass drum. The rhythm banged out behind her eyes. She rubbed at her temples, staring at the murder board while Mal fetched them a late snack.

His wish for sleep went unanswered. They hadn't been gone long enough.

Idly, Quinn wondered if she had any affinities that could help her just skip sleep. It didn't seem so.

Quinn sighed and turned her thoughts away from procrastination and back to the matters at hand.

Since the Library came from organic origins, she had to wonder how it coped now with no sleep now it was an all-powerful-pocket-dimension-portal wielding Library. Quinn was a wreck after one all-nighter. She couldn't fathom an eternity of them. Or did it have respites and she hadn't noticed?

Pulling her mind back from the tangent, she looked down at her hands where they still clutched Dinal's letter.

She read it again.

Librarian,

I can only hope that they found you. You are their one hope. I tell you this as an erstwhile friend of a Librarian. There are things I cannot say or write on pain of death right now. But as the latter is close anyway, I must at least try. So, please heed these words of warning, as well as I might give them. When all around you is frustrating and nothing quite adds up, the answer could be closer than you realize and nothing like you thought. Pay attention to your instincts once you have honed them. Remember, not all foes are enemies, and not all friends are allies. Be careful, watch your back, and know who to trust.

It hadn't changed.

It still drove her absolutely up the wall. She rubbed her hands over her face after putting the letter down, when a whiff of something absolutely delectable reached her nostrils.

"Hey." Malakai sat a small tub of soup on the table in front of her, followed by a fresh piece of bread with butter. It smelled heavenly. He nudged her to move over. "Cook said they felt like your current mood matched goulash. They said to remind you not to inhale it, savor it instead."

Quinn looked up at him quizzically. "What's that supposed to mean?"

Mal shrugged. "No clue. Cryptic seems to follow you around, Quinn."

She smiled but didn't think it translated into her expression. Shaking her head, she wished she'd insisted on sleep. The time dilation always did a number on her, apparently. She sighed and dug in, wincing as she moved to get more comfortable.

"Are you sore?" Mal asked, concern tinging his voice.

She nodded.

"Can I help?"

She looked up at him and shrugged. "Sure, if you think you can."

He moved behind the couch, put his hands on her shoulders, and began working out the knots. Quinn breathed deeply, and before long, a sense of relaxation overtook her. Her shoulder tension lessened as Malakai worked, and Quinn devoured her food slowly. It tasted divine. She wasn't entirely sure what meats or ingredients Cook used, but it definitely mimicked the Hungarian goulash she'd loved so much back home.

Which reminded her she needed to be more consistent about checking her phone. She hadn't replied to anyone for a few days. She looked around for it.

"What are you trying to find?" Mal asked.

"Just my phone."

"It's over on your desk. Do you need it?"

"I'd like it."

He chuckled as he walked away to get it.

Even though he was back a few seconds later, Quinn felt the absence of the heat from his hands. Shivers ran down her back, and suddenly she felt cold. She took the phone in one hand while she ate with the other. The bread was already gone.

She frowned at the phone, scrolling through her messages. "Hmm. One from my stepbrother and one from Hallie."

"She seems to send you messages regularly," Mal said.

"Yeah, she does. Just check-ins. She keeps asking to have coffee. I keep telling her I'm out of town."

"Technically," Malakai said, "that's not a lie."

Quinn laughed.

"You tell the truth."

"Do you know who else tells the truth?"

Mal shook his head.

"They were right, you know."

He chuckled. "About?"

Quinn gestured vaguely. "Cook. About all of it. Especially dinner. They're always right about dinner. Attuned to my moods."

She knew she couldn't keep procrastinating. Despite wanting to stay right where she was, she shrugged off Malakai's massage, slurped up the last of her goulash, put her phone down, and pulled up the pillar controls through her HUD. She took a deep breath.

"Two more branches are about to open up, you know," she said. "We'll need more power."

Mal waited for her while Quinn worked through the information. His presence always lent her a sense of calm. Eight pillars down, two to go, and that Ashiron was one of them made her palms sweat.

"Are we really any closer to a solution about Ashiron?" she muttered, half hoping Mal had an answer to that and half talking to herself.

Mal frowned. "I know they're working on it?" He didn't exactly answer the question.

Quinn laughed, absently paying attention to the HUD as it informed her the system needed twenty-four hours to calibrate the new pillar activation. She knew it'd say that. It's how it instigated every new pillar activation.

She idly wondered if the system got nervous or worried. If it knew they needed to activate Ashiron shortly.

Quinn turned around to Mal. "The system is a digital representation of what it takes to run and utilize the magic encased by the Library, right? Do you think the system personally feels anything? Or is the Library the system?"

He looked thoughtful as he munched on his bread. "Technically, I think the system came from the Library, but is separate from it. You should probably talk to the Library about that."

She considered that, even though the Library had been in weird moods lately, but something bugged at her. "But isn't Lynx technically also the system?"

"Sort of, maybe?" Mal didn't seem to want to guess at answers. "Isn't Lynx more the Library?"

Quinn barely resisted the urge to put her head down in her hands. Maybe she should be asking Milaro these questions. "Either way," she said, "the crafting branch can open tomorrow once the pillar boots up."

Mal watched her carefully. "That's a good thing, Quinn."

She laughed again, but this time, even to her own ears, it sounded hollow and empty. She suddenly felt bereft, lost.

"Is it really?" she asked.

Malakai watched her, seeming to form his words carefully. "You're asking that a lot lately," he said.

She watched him for a few seconds. "For good reasons." She gestured around them and out into the Library. "Is this good? If we don't figure out that damned pillar soon, none of what we've done will matter. We won't reach or exceed peak capacity if the soul bomb takes us and the universe out once chaos gets free. Nothing will survive in the end. I don't care what those Sölem people keep saying about the strongest surviving."

She sat down heavily, her head back in her hands, unsure of when she'd even stood up to begin with. Everything around her felt so heavy. What did it matter that she'd killed people now? What did it matter that friends she'd grown close to had died, that they'd been betrayed, when everything was about to implode anyway?

She'd barely stopped since she came to this Library. She'd done everything she could, whenever she was asked. Sure, she questioned things and refused to go in blind. But the whole point was that in the end, she'd done what needed to be done.

And they were back at square one anyway. All because of that damn soul bomb.

The couch sank a bit under Malakai's weight as he sat down next to her. She didn't even want to look at him. She didn't want to look at anything.

A few seconds later, he pulled her into a side hug. It was warm, and he smelled oddly like cedar and pine. with a faint undertone of leather and wax. She leaned into that hug, feeling so many levels of exhaustion wash away as she did.

She wished she could pass the buck right now, give somebody else the responsibility to do what needed to be done. But she couldn't.

Quinn let out a huge sigh. Malakai might have been chuckling. At least his chest felt like he was.

"Does it feel any better to get that out?" he asked softly.

She nodded, knowing he'd feel it. Neither of them spoke for a moment, but when Mal did, his voice was gentle. "You can't think of it that way, Quinn. How about you look at everything that's happened in the last seven months, okay? Everything we've done, everything you've learned and accomplished, all the places you've been, all the people you've helped out, all the information found. Think about it. Seven months, that's it."

Quinn processed that. He had a point. She got sucked into the Library, discovered magic wasn't only real, but she could wield it. In fact, she wielded all the affinities. She'd even created one.

Not only that, but most solar systems and regions had magical planets. And Earth was simply one planet that didn't. She'd met so many species.

They'd stopped imminent universe meltdowns. Plural! She'd discovered more about her family. About who they were, where she'd come from, and how they'd truly died. Her horizons were so much broader than they'd been only seven months ago.

Malakai watched the expressions flit across her face, looking down at her at an awkward angle. He'd probably have a crick in his neck later. Quinn glanced up at him and leaned against his shoulder again. He smiled. She could feel it against the top of her head.

"You're usually so good at staying upbeat," he said to her. "So how about I help lift you up until you can regain some of that positivity again?"

Quinn chuckled. More of her tension disappeared. "Sure, but what will I owe you after that?"

Mal laughed. "Oh, I'm sure we can work out a payment plan."

Quinn, feeling lighter than she had only moments ago, thought that, yeah, they'd be able to work that out.

5 6

PLAN OF ACTION

THE SHEER SENSE OF CALM, OR EVEN JUST THE RELIEF OF GETTING things off her chest, suddenly gave Quinn ideas and a plan.

First up, she had to find Milaro. She had to learn those brain-melting mind attacks. Immolating was fine and all, but not all locations handle flames well. Case in point: they were in a Library. Not to mention the nature of the attack probably avoided most enemy shields, which made it ideal for her own arsenal.

In one day, the pillar would be ready. She'd be busy opening the branch then. Since she had time now, she sent a message through to Milaro about her visions. She had to understand why she could project herself into other people's mind spaces.

Before their last foray into Halschius, she'd thought her shields were solid, but now she knew they needed to be stronger. Quinn had learned a lot on that trip, including that mind attacks weren't restricted to just witnessing someone's dreams.

"Are you okay?" Malakai asked.

That's when she realized she was still leaning into him on the couch.

"Yeah," she said, surprised at how safe it felt to sit close to somebody. Malakai's presence just made it a bonus. "I'm just tired."

"Maybe it'd help if you actually slept for once," he teased her.

"Well, it's not like I'm out there having heaps of fun instead of sleeping," she retorted.

He laughed. "Well, if you *were* out there having fun instead of sleeping, maybe it would be more acceptable."

She raised an eyebrow and chuckled. "Maybe it would. I'm going to bed." She stood and stretched.

"Makes two of us," Malakai said before copying her actions.

Quinn thought for a moment that he'd perhaps been slightly suggestive. She wasn't always sure how to interpret his playful flirting. To be honest, she had too much to do to see if he reciprocated her growing feelings. Once they had everything where it needed to be, she could worry about it.

Before she left the room while he was still picking up after them, she stopped at the door jamb and turned to face him. "Hey, Malakai."

"Yeah?" He looked up at her.

"Thank you. I really needed this."

He smiled. "I know," he said. "And you're welcome."

Quinn turned around, with Aradie flying slowly next to her and headed up to her room. Warm, fuzzy feelings embraced her, and she fell into bed after changing quickly and doing a very brief nighttime routine. Just before she let herself sleep, she got an affirmative reply from Milaro. He'd be there first thing in the Library day. Smiling, she was asleep before her head hit the pillow.

Of course, regardless of how badly she needed or wanted to sleep, it appeared those specific nights were a magnet for denying her just that.

All she knew when she opened her eyes was that she wasn't asleep, and wherever she wasn't asleep, it wasn't her bed.

She heard Aradie as an echo outside her mind if she concentrated carefully. The soft hiss of her breath was barely audible. But that could only mean that she'd been sucked into someone else's dream or mind.

Although this didn't feel the way other dream encounters had, she was a bit confused. Her main concern centered around the fact that

Kajaro had died. She'd always thought her dream abilities came from his influence. Apparently not.

Maybe her Areiltháhnish genetic components had something to do with it? Mind-related skills seemed pretty close to dreams. Maybe encountering Kajaro triggered some of her latent abilities.

If her senses worked correctly, she appeared to be suspended against the sky. Floating there like a ghost in the firmament.

It was mostly dark around her, yet she could see an estate as she looked out below her. Deep green lawns with evergreen trees that were all strictly shaped into that traditional conical Christmas tree design that decorations were made out of. Strange blood-red and black flowers she didn't recognize sprouted all around the ground. They bordered the house, buildings, and patios, lending a slightly macabre air to the whole affair.

Quinn drifted closer, pulled ever so subtly by a tugging she felt in her gut. She knew she had to be careful. Extending her senses, she felt that the beckoning seemed neutral. It let her know she needed to do, hear, or see something.

Drifting closer to the conical trees, she realized they formed a copse which surrounded a gazebo. The small building blended in with the trees in the dim light. It was a pretty hexagonal structure, where the pieces let up to a roof peak with a filigree weathervane at the top. She hoped the tugging she'd felt hadn't led her into a trap.

She also got flashbacks to the tree in the middle of that nightmare copse and wondered what these bad guys had against copses of trees.

The pretty gazebo made her wish she could circumnavigate the entire estate and figure out who lived here, what they wanted, and what they did. Curiosity tugged at her, yet the pull toward the gazebo was stronger. Almost as if the universe was saying, *Hey, Librarian, over here. This is what you need to pay attention to.* So she headed there, since her gut feelings rarely steered her wrong.

Once close enough, she could see into the gazebo and realized a few people had gathered there. More accurately, a small group of traitorous dragon bastards and accomplices. They all had humanoid forms.

Quinn first recognized Dravishk. She'd know him anywhere, especially after the fight that sent Escadril, the Salosier, to his death and caused Ikeshal's the satyr's injuries. And then there was the final sibling. Quinn never got a chance to see her in detail in the fight where Jasper died. She had to push down at her anger and remember she needed to observe. Dronar gesticulated wildly about her, obviously irritated at something, as she spoke to her brother.

The Serpensiril who'd conversed with Kajaro in Quinn's very first mind walking experience was also present. As well as a vaguely recognizable Sedimentite. The dark stone of his body warped the reflection the moonlight that crept in from the opening closest to him.

Their mouths moved, but she couldn't hear what they said. There was a static overlay, as if they'd put up protection so that nobody could eavesdrop on their conversation.

Another tug in the back of her head. Maybe the universe had its own collective consciousness of some sort and didn't want to be destroyed by the reemergence of chaos magic if the Library did go down. Perhaps that's why it felt as if the universe guided her.

Quinn followed that instinct and closed her eyes briefly, focusing on the sound below. It was sort of like twisting the dials on an old-fashioned wireless radio to adjust the reception. A few times the cracking got louder. But once she had the specific concentration in place, she finally homed in on the right frequency. One person at a time.

Quinn couldn't just sit there with her eyes closed, she had to actively concentrate on the individual.

Once the words finally became clear, she caught Dronar in the middle of what she was saying, "What do you mean you don't know what went wrong? This was supposed to be a straightforward element for us to get Drukala out of the way and to gain permanent access into the Library at its control point."

Dravishk simply shrugged. "I don't know what you want me to tell you."

"I want you to explain what it is that went wrong so we can make it go right," Dronar said.

Dravishk seemed a lot more relaxed than Quinn expected, considering his plan appeared to be falling down around his ears. She had to be missing something. He leaned back and crossed his arms. She noticed his morph included a tail, which swished irritably. If dragons were anything like cats, which she thought they probably were, that was a sign of annoyance.

"That's exactly it, Dro. We had everything in place. The trap should have triggered once we got that damned tracking location from that Alyenarvor. Except it didn't, did it?" The glare he leveled at his sister was surprisingly mild.

Quinn barely stopped herself from growling out loud. That's why they killed Jasper? She wasn't impressed. It took effort to push those thoughts aside. Grudgingly, she returned her attention to the conversation with renewed determination. If she didn't solve this, Jasper had died for nothing.

The Serpensiril looked like he was about to interject with something. However, Dro beat him to it. "You did create the opening, right? I mean, I know it's been a long time, but you didn't just plan to create one and forget?"

Drav seemed slightly irritated by his sister. "Of course I did! But even with the coordinates, it didn't trigger. Something broke or went wrong during the installation process. It should have allowed us entry. I'm still trying to . . ." He shrugged. It seemed his go-to action when he didn't know what to say or do or care enough to talk about it at that moment.

Dronar didn't appreciate it. "So there's no physical entry for us. You lost the physical entry."

"I created the path to physical entry," he said, snapping at her. "Though I can still feel its existence faintly, I cannot access it."

Dro narrowed her eyes. "What do you mean you can still feel it? Keeping it rather close to your chest, eh?"

Dravishk leveled a glare at her. "You just want a taste of revenge."

She seemed confused for a second before scowling in response.

He shrugged again and grimaced.

She laughed without a hint of mirth and rolled her shoulders as if she hated being in human form and felt too big for her skin. "I feel so restricted," she said. "We've taken enough time. What's your plan B?"

Drav leaned forward and put his hand under his chin, watching her. "You miss the influxes of power when chaos devoured worlds, don't you?"

"Of course I do. So do you. So does anybody who knows what that sort of power feels like."

He nodded slowly. "Yes, yes, we do miss it, don't we?"

A shiver ran down Quinn's spine, and she adjusted herself, knowing that she wasn't going to like what else was coming.

57

RUBBER BAND

QUINN WATCHED THE SCENE UNFOLD IN FRONT OF HER WITH BATED breath. Her fingers itched for popcorn to watch the drama with. However, this wasn't entertainment. No matter what she tried to do, everything pointed to it getting worse before the situation got resolved.

The silence lasted for several seconds before the Sedimentite spoke up. "I hate to interrupt this sibling heart-to-heart, but we still have troops on standby. They cost money, they cost resources, and nobody likes be on standby for this long, especially not when being held in constant combat-ready mode. Not good for morale, you know."

Quinn's heart skipped a beat. She understood their opponents would be violent. After all, humans had violent potential, especially when it came to territorial complications. It shouldn't surprise her that the same existed in every other corner of the universe. Still, sieging a Library and potentially massacring patrons? Who thought books were that dangerous?

That wasn't it, though, was it? It didn't necessarily have anything to do with the books, but the massive filtration chamber contained within the Library's dimension shift instead. Killing the books and the people was just a sad coincidence. The Library didn't have the defenses to combat something like that. They didn't have any secretly sequestered army in a room somewhere. Other than their security, they had no defenses Quinn knew of.

Almost as if it'd heard her thoughts, the Serpensiril spoke up. "No, you know it has too many fail-safes. There's no way for your troops to get in with the way the Library's security system is set up."

Quinn leaned in to pay closer attention as Dronar laughed. "My darling paranoid sibling has always judged on pure intentions," she said. "The only being alive who's fooled it even for a tiny bit is my brother here. Drev has only got better over time at identifying motives."

Drav scowled. "That's why I set up an alternate entry," he said.

"Which isn't working," the sedimentite interrupted.

"I know it's not working, Daskin. There's no need to state the bleeding obvious." Drav snapped out the words at the Sedimentite, his eyes flashing in anger. "Keep yourself to the council and its business and attend a meeting. See if you can't distract Milaro in a better way than this. It's what you were supposed to do anyway, and you haven't succeeded. We can't have his nose poking into everything."

Drav and Daskin glared at each other across the small table in the middle of the gazebo. The glaring match lasted for so long, Quinn expected to wake up. Finally, Daskin looked away, giving the victory to Dravishk.

The Sedimentite's voice held contained anger when he finally spoke. "I will bring up trade disputes at the next meeting and attempt to do my best as a distraction." He practically spat out the last words.

"Haven't you already screwed up your trade deals with Milaro's worlds?" Dronar asked in a very bored tone.

"They are not irreparable," Daskin said, sounding slightly affronted. "It was a deliberate move to shake up some of the council members at the time."

"Sure it was," Dronar said.

"Stop needling him," Dravishk snapped at his sister.

Quinn wondered if he was always that snappy or if it was just because things weren't quite going the way he'd expected it to and thus caused the snappiness. If this was indicative of his usual personality, then he was a bit of an ass. Quinn couldn't really see the Library and its brother getting on all that well.

"Anyway," Drav said, turning back to the Sedimentite, "provided you attend a meeting for once, you can go shake it up however you want. The more Milaro has on his plate, the less likely he is to notice the things we're doing."

"You think?" Daskin deadpanned.

"I also know. I've known the man for millennia. Keep him occupied. His dream sense, his ability to locate minds and figure out what they're doing, to intrude upon our thoughts from a distance. It's unparalleled, and we would do well to guard our thoughts."

Quinn had to suppress a chuckle. She wasn't entirely sure how this specific magic she was using worked. She couldn't read Dravishk's thoughts right now, but she could definitely hear the words he was saying. Whatever magical attribute allowed her to do this, she was grateful for it. Just more questions for Milaro. She maneuvered herself slightly to have a better view and to hear better.

Drav turned his attention back to his sister. "The shutdown only occurred because we forgot to factor the manifestation into things."

A strange flicker of doubt? Maybe? Passed through Dronar's eyes. But then she laughed again. It sounded rather jovial in a strange and cold sort of way. "How could you forget that?"

"I didn't realize he was that level of separated from her." Dravishk sounded suitably chastised. After interrupting his sister, Dravishk took another deep breath and continued on. "I assumed and understood that he was simply an extension of Drevicia and thus just another part of her, which meant that when Korradine took memories from the main Library section, it was supposed to affect Lynx as well and vice versa. Apparently, I had my wires crossed and did not realize she'd simply done double the work in removing those memories. It's not irreparable. It's just inconvenient. Kor did a fantastic job, working with what she had."

Dronar watched her brother and nodded, her face suddenly very solemn. "I'm so sorry. I shouldn't have hibernated for so long. I was just exhausted." She didn't sound exhausted. Her voice held a sadness that seemed in direct juxtaposition to her brother's.

Arguing with his sister seemed to trigger Dravishk's typical habitual shrug. "It is what it is," he said. "Once I figure out why the connection refuses to establish itself, despite having laid the backdoor myself and having the essence of the Library's coordinates, well, then we proceed to bring the universe back to what it's supposed to be."

Dro watched her brother closely, then nodded once, her solemn expression still present. "That sounds like a plan."

The sibilant words rang in Quinn's ears as the Serpensiril spoke slowly and carefully. "But my liege grows weary of your inaction, of your dropped promises."

"I haven't dropped a promise," Drav said, his eyes firing up.

"Not yet," the Serpensiril drawled.

Dravishk raised an eyebrow and his tail swished back and forth in agitation, reminding Quinn yet again of an angry cat. His dark eyes glittered with such a hint of anger that the Serpensiril backed up a couple of steps.

Dravishk obviously decided intimidation was the best action. He must have measured an easy eight feet tall, well-built, with broad shoulders. His form was less compact than when they'd fought with him, but somehow more powerful. He stalked forward. They weren't just steps, they were deliberately planted, carefully chosen for impact. He moved toward the Serpensiril as if the snake man was prey. Then he smiled such a wide, toothy grin that no one could ever mistake him for human. He seemed like the nightmare Cheshire cat in that Alice video game Quinn saw years ago. It sent a row of shivers down her spine as she watched the way he towered over the Serpensiril.

"Boshan, my dear, dear collaborator, have you already forgotten how shaky our alliance became in light of the Tenejo incident that you orchestrated? In the light of Kajaro's unfortunate demise."

The latter sent shivers down Quinn's spine. She'd known it was him. Just knew it.

Boshan shook his head and seemed like he wanted to back up further, through the wall and trees behind him, if necessary.

Drav held up his hand to not be interrupted. "Not to mention we didn't manage to take out any of the opposing parties in full. Just Escadril and that tracker. We couldn't even rid ourselves of the pesky Librarian that came out of left field."

Boshan made to speak, but it appeared that Dravishk didn't want that to happen. He held up his hand, effectively silencing the Serpensiril's words with a slight flick of his fingers as if he'd cast a spell.

"Yes, yes, I know you're about to tell me that you failed doubly, considering Sarila is the one that ended Escadril instead of us. She killed her own husband. That took a lot of guts. I'm not entirely sure where her loyalties lie, but that was one favor she did us before her untimely demise. I claim that kill for us."

He paused for a second, but it seemed Boshan had learned his lesson. His lips didn't even quiver.

"So no," Dravishk continued, "we won't make it into the Library of my dear sibling through any door that opens until such a time as the shields are dropped to allow hostile beings to enter."

Quinn remembered they'd reinforced the shields. They'd made sure the Library's wards and protections held, including adjusting the acceptance of patrons into the Library based on a scan given by the Library as the door was activated. Not once they crossed the threshold. As soon as they touched the door that would transport them in the scan was a fraction of a second. Should it detect any hostility toward the Library at all in that person's demeanor or aura, they'd be transported to a holding entryway until such a time that security golems or other combatants could get to them. She couldn't believe that'd slipped her mind.

Quinn wondered if it was possible for the Library to produce army golems. That was an idea if they needed physical defense.

The group below watched Dravishk silently. As if they knew better than to argue or perhaps even provoke him. Especially in a mood like this. He was like a coiled snake ready to strike at any moment if somebody displeased him, which it appeared every single person employed by the Library had already done.

Finally, he sighed deeply and looked up at everybody with that same languid, wide, toothy grin. "Yes, yes," he said as he stepped back to his seat and made himself comfortable once more on the bench. "Don't worry, just amass your troops while we move to plan C and I will take care of our . . . entry fees."

He chuckled at his own joke.

Quinn had no idea what it meant.

"Plan C?" Dronar asked cautiously, her voice automatically reflecting submission.

Glee flashed through Dravishk's eyes. "Why, taking the Library by force instead? That is our plan C."

Quinn's world froze. By force? Surely they couldn't get through the gaps that easily. She was about to leave when she heard Daskin clear his throat.

"Do we need to plan logistics?"

"No," Dravishk said, laughing self-deprecatingly. "No, you just do your thing, and I'll take care of the rest. I will contact you with the next meeting time."

Quinn was glad she'd stayed, because everything seemed worse than she'd imagined. Having a heads up could prove invaluable once they'd vetted her vision. Drav was already working on a plan of attack. She allowed herself to rubber band back to her bed, tiredness completely gone, with plenty of room for panic to set in.

For a moment, she forced herself to do breathing exercises, calming her whirling mind into some semblance of working. She sat up, even though she knew it was too early for Milaro, and headed down to rearrange her murder board.

5 8

PERSPECTIVE

Quinn was still working on her murder board a couple of hours later when Milaro walked in armed with pastry and something that smelled suspiciously like coffee. She didn't stop what she was doing, nor did she really acknowledge the fact that he'd arrived, but she knew he knew she was there. If she thought about it anymore, she was probably going to confuse herself.

"Morning," he said in that super gentle, grandfatherly tone he often spoke to her in.

"Here?" Quinn replied, eyes never leaving the board as she squinted at it.

Milaro shrugged. "Well, it's morning somewhere, isn't it?"

Quinn laughed. She needed that. The stress of the night was getting to her.

"So," he said, sidling up to her, "how is my favorite student?"

"Don't you mean only student?" she retorted.

"Not true. I have my grandson, too, technically." He laughed.

Even without looking at him, Quinn knew Milaro was studying her. He seemed concerned from what she could tell about the leakage of aura surrounding him.

"Is something troubling you?" he asked.

She shrugged, not entirely sure how to approach the subject, but she figured just going for it would work. Sort of. "I had a dream, or more accurately, perhaps a mind walk or something?"

Milaro sighed, reached over and placed some food down on her desk, and then took a step over to hand her another bag of what appeared to be cinnamon-sugar doughnuts and a coffee. All without saying a word. Apparently, Cook and Milaro were in cahoots to bring her exactly what she'd been craving.

She refused to even pretend she was angry about it.

Then, Milaro moved back a couple of steps and scanned the murder board, taking it in. She heard a soft intake of breath from him and looked over to see him frowning.

"Yeah, it's not so great, is it?" she asked him.

He shook his head, but she could see he was deep in thought. Maybe he could see something she couldn't.

"So," he said, as if he was running over all of it in his mind and trying to make sense of it, "we have two factions that occasionally overlap, a. malfunctioning back door, a Sedimentite distraction for me, and a potential military assault if they gain entrance. Am I reading this right?"

Quinn nodded. "That about sums it up, I think."

"Have you checked permissions?" He asked.

"First thing I did when I woke up was go over all of the permissions for every single role in the Library and even some we haven't created yet. The Library, Lynx, myself. We're the only ones who can order any changes until this is all over. I even took the doctors and Misha's creation abilities and security permissions away from them so as to, you know, avoid any potential infiltration or somebody deciding they could build an army out of the golems by forcing their awareness into Misha's head again because that would be so much fun."

Milaro stepped forward, pointing to a note next to Lynx's name. "Can you explain this to me?" he asked.

Quinn squinted and sighed. "Well, they mentioned not having understood his connection to the Library fully while they were talking. It was like they'd underestimated the manifestation, from what I could understand. They didn't realize quite how connected the Library and its manifestation were and yet didn't realize just how separate they are as entities. I think. To be fair, I'm still a little hazy on all the details of what it means to be a manifestation."

"Have you spoken to him about it yet?"

"Well, of course I have. He's the first one I spoke to this morning. He's already looking into ideas he has. We had a strange conversation a few days ago, and I think he's trying to make sure no potential double agent overhears what he's trying to accomplish."

Milaro pursed his lips and then asked. "What about the Library? What does it say?"

"Well, it's not been in the best mood of late. We've had a couple of strained squabbles as if it's attempting to take its mood out on me. I'm not sure. Maybe it's tired. I know I'd be tired if I was the Library."

"I don't think it works like that," Milaro said.

"Anyway, I know the Library is doubling down on the wards and the lockout method we've got in place."

Milaro nodded again, a thoughtful look entering his eyes and then he turned to face her completely. "So," he said, "tell me in light of all of this, what is it that you need from me?"

Quinn thought over his words for a few seconds and she sighed because the truth was she wasn't entirely certain which direction to take this in. "I need to double-check my mental shields are tight enough so I can know this isn't planted information. Do you understand? Like the bomb. Like the tip-off we got that was a trap."

"Oh, but that wasn't an infiltration into your mind. It was information dropped for you that time. Like breadcrumbs for you to follow." He tried to comfort her.

But she didn't need comfort, she needed not to endanger people by walking into a stupid trap. "Exactly. We can't afford that to happen again."

"True enough, I suppose."

"It's very true, and I don't want to lose anyone like we did the last time we walked into a trap. Tell me, is Ikeshal even healed enough to be of assistance to Uncle Hal anymore?"

Milaro looked away for a second, giving her the answer. "He still commands a legion . . ."

"Yeah, I'm sure he's ecstatic about that."

He sighed and his gaze softened momentarily, but Quinn continued, "I need our defenses to be impenetrable. I also need you to explain this thought-walking thing to me, because I thought it was dream-based, like I was visiting people in their dreams or their subconscious minds as they slept."

Milaro shook his head. "No, that's not exactly right, but because the process happens when *you* sleep, that's why they called it that."

"Well, that's misleading," she said. "I need to understand how to direct this type of power so it benefits us as a whole."

"I agree."

"Then teach me how to do it," Quinn said and then continued, "and I want to know that brain-melt spell that you used and to walk you through everything I saw last night, because there's so much about it, so many nuances that I probably missed and you might just understand it a lot better than I did. In the moment, I don't think I gleaned as much from it as I should have."

Milaro smiled. "Looks like we have a lot cut out for us then."

"Yeah, and we only have until this afternoon to do it," Quinn said, "because then I have to open a new branch of the Library."

"Oh," Milaro said and turned all business-like. "What do you want us to tackle first?"

Quinn thought about it for a few seconds. Maybe it was better to go through the visions first, but there was something niggling in the back of her mind. She realized that even though she was almost certain her defenses were perfect, there was something telling her to check them. It was the logical thing to put first.

"Shielding," she said. "I think that's my best bet right now. If we're working on Library security, it'll mean nothing if the Librarian's security key, as in me, has broken security of her own."

"Logical perspective," Milaro said and nodded.

Reinforcing and double-checking her shielding didn't take as long as she'd expected it would. But at least she left the session feeling better about her own protections. Milaro threw everything at her, testing every corner, every brick, every single nook and cranny that he could. She'd let nothing through. After which they'd spent time rebuilding her walls to make them even more impenetrable.

Then Milaro surprised her by offering to teach her brain drain before they did anything else.

"That's a catchy name," she said.

"Well," Milaro said self-deprecatingly, "I thought so. Seemed to make sense since that's exactly what it does."

"Does it just literally heat up their brain and melt it out of their ears and nose and mouth and stuff?"

"No." Milaro laughed. "That's not right at all. It's a very complex ability, and since we don't actually have a target to practice on, this will only be theory and prep work so you understand the methodologies behind activating the spell."

"Okay," Quinn said, throwing herself onto one of the couches. She was tired and sick of staring at the murder board while they did everything else. "Now tell me the theory."

She looked up at him expectantly.

Milaro smiled and acquiesced. "Brain drain stems from an attempt to drain or read the thoughts of your target from a distance."

"Wait, so it wasn't initially an offensive spell?" she asked.

"Exactly. Brain drain's combative properties, I would call them, stems from an overzealousness on my part during a battle where I was attempting to read the other general's thoughts and pull out the information he knew from a distance."

"And you accidentally boiled his brain?"

"In a way," Milaro said, sort of cagily.

"Come on. Tell me. I need to know the downsides too."

"It's not so much a downside. You need to understand, Quinn, that everything like . . ."

"Like?" Quinn said. "Are you, like, mocking me?" She cocked her head to one side and waited.

"No, I . . ." He stammered slightly.

"Have you been hanging around me too much, Milaro?"

He flashed her a brief scowl and then laughed. "I guess I have. Let me start again. Once the information has been withdrawn from the brain, it is highly susceptible to any other actions. If you continue to pull, it overextends the, I guess, synapses and the brainwaves and it pushes too far, overloading it and basically overheats and melts the brain, turning it to mush."

"That's fascinating," Quinn said, ideas already whirling in her brain.

Milaro eyed her for a second. "Well, thank you. Even though its conception was unintentional, I think you need to be aware that something beneficial is always capable of being reversed. If I can heal you, I also know how to do the reverse. Do you understand?"

She nodded vigorously. "So because you know the way the blood runs through the body as a healer, you'd also know how to deprive the body of said blood or oxygen or wow, even the electronic pulses, right?"

"Precisely. That's how healers can kill. Generally, they're the sort of people who take an oath not to do any harm to anyone or any living thing and yet there are dark healers who don't abide by that. Thus, if I were to give you a warming charm when you're cold, technically, I also know how to push it far enough that it could cause serious damage and or kill you depending on how hot I allow that temperature to rise."

"Ah. Then I think I have a grasp on the concept. Basically, you accidentally overextended the ability and turned the brain to mush, thus creating brain drain's offensive capacity." Quinn was proud of being able to distill it down to a simpler form of explanation.

"It is very effective when I'm actually looking for death as the result."

"Okay."

"I wouldn't recommend you using it as a commonplace attack," Milaro cautioned.

Quinn held up her hands. "I don't plan on using it as any type of attack unless I need to. I just want to be able to if I have to."

"Good," Milaro said. "You've always got to remember many things are a matter of perspective."

Quinn nodded, her mind racing at the possibilities of the ability, and they moved on to the next thing.

"Now, shall we endeavor to look into your memory of last night's encounter?" Milaro asked.

"Yes," she breathed out, steadying herself.

"And after that," he said, "we should really study Kajaro's pertinent memories."

"Sounds like so much fun." She could practically feel the sarcasm dripping down her chin.

Milaro chuckled. "Again, Quinn, it's just matter of perspective."

Well, she couldn't argue with that.

59

TIME TO PROCESS

Going back through all of Quinn's recollections of the thought-walking from earlier was tough. It took a lot of energy and focus on her part, which exhausted her brain. But Milaro seemed to pull up aspects of her memory Quinn didn't even recall from her initial observations. Small actions like hand and finger movements, the way somebody's eyes quirked or nose scrunched, slight expressions of disdain, quick looks of derision that flashed through people's eyes. He examined literally everything multiple times.

She felt like she was sitting in the back seat of a car, watching someone else drive.

It was interesting to see what reactions and actions she'd picked up unconsciously without concentrating on them at all, as well as the interactions between all the attendees who'd been there. Their respect for Dravishk didn't appear to be as genuine as she'd first thought. However, it seemed that their fear of him was. Pauses and rewinding sequences occurred frequently so Milaro could pull out specific things Drav said.

Then again, she guessed if a person took a photograph they were focused on one subject, but it was possible for the background information in that photo to potentially change the whole dynamic.

403

"Why do you keep doing that?" she asked, pulling her focus back with effort. "That's the third time you've gone over that line."

"I know," he said. "Deeper interpretations, Quinn. Intonations and references that perhaps mean more than what was just said."

Quinn got it, but her brain felt tired. She shook her head and let him carry on. When Milaro was finally done, they sat down while he organized his thoughts and Quinn was at a bit of a loss. Her head felt like it was stuffed with cotton wool that had been watered and seeded and was about sprout alfalfa. She stared at the now-cold coffee clutched in her hands while she brought her breathing back in line. Slowly breathing in, slowly breathing out with a slight second-long hold in the middle.

She let herself sigh deeply, shrugged her shoulders around a little to move them because she'd been stuck in the same position for at least an hour. She was ready to drop. Then, still mournfully gazing at her cold coffee, she dipped a finger in the liquid, allowed a very small amount of heat to trickle through it, gauging the temperature and the ferocity of it, making sure it was a calm and minuscule amount as she heated her coffee back up. She grinned as it reached the perfect temperature.

Fire abilities. Not just for rampant death.

"Quinn," Milaro said as if he'd been trying to get her attention for a while. He probably had been as she'd been concentrating on making sure she didn't boil her coffee over into her lap.

"Sorry, my thoughts are all a bit whirly right now," she said.

"That's perfectly fine," Milaro said. "I apologize. That was more invasive and tiring than I expected."

She nodded, sipping at her perfect coffee, giving him her full attention.

"There were some telling bits in what Drav said. I want to calm your fears, even though I know what he said sounded terrifying."

"The interaction wasn't fabricated?" Quinn asked, wishing he hadn't paused waiting on her.

"It's a genuine interaction, Quinn. They weren't aware of your presence in the slightest. That whole transparent floating thing you did probably helped."

Quinn shrugged because she had nothing to do with that. "I didn't do it deliberately. It's just how I appeared when I, I guess, woke up there?"

"Oh." Milaro looked confused, and then shook his head and smiled. "The wonders of our new Librarian. Anyway, there were a couple of things they said that do concern me, however."

"The council?" she asked quickly.

He waved that away as if it was completely unimportant. "Not really. I haven't trusted that man for a while. There might even be ways to misdirect him, actually. Maybe even misdirect them as a whole." He seemed contemplative as he tapped his chin and thought. "I'll dwell on that later. There were a couple of lines that show me the backdoor isn't actually a physical one, such as the type you found embedded in the shielding. That must be something else. I do need to go over the words and over the inflections to double-check the meanings."

"Which lines are those?" she asked.

He pulled up one and projected the image of Drav speaking it. "*I created the path to physical entry.* See here how he's not quite looking at his sister or anybody else. There's no eye contact and while he's completely still, it's too much. It's as if he's trying not to be read. You'd think with so many years to perfect it; he'd be better at lying. But that's where the distinction is. It's not a lie, but it is also not entirely the truth."

Quinn couldn't quite see it, but she did realize that the way he phrased it was odd, considering the question at hand. "Do you think he's just splitting hairs?"

Milaro frowned. "Likely, although I am unsure why."

One of the lies occurred to Quinn too, then. "*That's why I set up an alternate entry*, right? That's one of them as well."

"Exactly." Milaro looked delighted. "You're such a fast learner. You've got to look for the way people phrase things. When they're challenged, when something goes against them, they're often on the back foot and it's then, especially then, that they tend to expound their lies just that little too much. Anyway." He looked delighted. "I'll continue working on this, but I've also organized, or perhaps ordered, is a more accurate term, Kajaro's mess of memories."

Quinn perked up at that. "Do you need mine? Can you take them now? They sometimes flash in just the weirdest moments."

He raised an eyebrow. "How so?"

"Well, I don't know. Walking around the Library, sometimes when I see a book at a specific angle in a certain place."

"Oh," Milaro said, "They're acting like flashbacks even though they aren't your own."

"Pretty much," agreed Quinn.

"I thought you concealed them behind their own shielding." He frowned at her.

"I did, but . . . for some reason they won't stay compartmentalized."

"If that's the case," Milaro said, "I shall remove them from you now. I do have another backup."

"We don't need them anymore?"

"I believe I have the same memories as you, but we funneled them to you as well, just in case something corrupted my collection of them. However, I think I'll extract yours into a holding device." He fumbled around in his storage and pulled out a glowing crystal orb. It wasn't quite round and smooth like a crystal ball. It was rough on the surface and was slightly off being a perfect sphere.

"They'll all fit in there?" Quinn asked.

"Yes, this side should hold enough for me to transport the memories and compare them to the others. I just didn't have one of these with us when he was dying."

She gave the almost orb one final look and nodded. "I'm fine with that. Are we going to go through them?"

"Just the one directly pertinent to our current situation for now. The other memories are for things we'll address after we put out our little fires."

Quinn nodded, nervous about Milaro diving into her head again. She always was when someone used mind magic on her, even when

Nishpa healed her. Of course, considering her introduction to mind magic had come in the form of a mind bomb Kajaro placed in her head when he first met her, it didn't seem like such a surprise to her that anybody diving into her mind made her nervous. She actually trembled; she could see her hands shaking.

Aradie swooped down from her perch and landed on Quinn's shoulder. She snuffled into Quinn's hair, her soft feathers brushing against her shoulders, and the sheer comfort of it allowed Quinn to breathe normally and nod as she looked up at Milaro. He watched her expectantly. Mind magic was so potent and the mind so fragile. Half the Library problems stemmed from memory tampering. So even though it was Milaro doing it, and she did trust him, she really did, but Quinn still found it difficult to relax.

"Quinn?" Milaro asked, pulling her attention again.

"Sorry."

"You should really stop saying sorry," he said. She chuckled. "Anyway, would you prefer to keep the memories?" Milaro asked gently.

Quinn felt so embarrassed that she should show such vulnerability in front of anyone, even if it was just Milaro. She sighed and shook her head.

"Okay, I'll take that as a no," he said. "How about instead of me diving in and retrieving them, you gather them and push them to the edge of your awareness so I can grab them from there? Does that sound better?"

Quinn nodded very slowly.

"It allows me to obtain them without actually fully entering your mind, Quinn."

"That sounds reasonable." Relief flooded her as she realized that this wouldn't be as dangerous—accidentally or deliberately—as she'd originally anticipated.

It was surprisingly easy to pass Kajaro's memories through to Milaro to take care of. They weren't too attached to her, given that they weren't hers to begin with, and she really wasn't overly interested in diving into them, considering what she'd seen in Tenejo's memory way back when the Serpensiril youth attempted to destroy the Library himself.

A measure of immense pressure released in her mind as Milaro took those memories. Like using a cleansing wipe to clean her brain. She sighed with relief, feeling light and more like a cloud than drenched cotton wool.

"Thanks." She smiled.

"Now," he said, clapping his hands and practically scaring the crap out of Quinn, "let us discuss."

"Oh," Quinn said, and Milaro began by projecting one of Kajaro's thoughts and memories to the wall. She sat there watching it play as if it was an old-fashioned eight-millimeter film, with the way it sort of stuttered onto the wall. It contained images of Kajaro and Tenejo with multiple engagements, cementing the connection they'd had.

The younger Tenejo seemed to worship Kajaro, and the older Serpensiril took complete and utter advantage of that. Quinn looked away. She'd seen enough of that in her encounters with Tenejo and the other Serpensiril who'd accompanied him. She didn't want to relive it.

But then there was one of Kajaro and Sarila, and Quinn couldn't pull her eyes away from it. They spoke very quietly about taking over the Library until Sarila snapped at him. *"If we maintain the filtration, you have direct access to the chaotic elements as they filter through the Library. You can simply extract the chaotic energy you need for your experimentation and your . . . hunger,* "she said the last word with distaste. *"If that's what you want to do, you don't need to destroy the rest of the universe in the process."*

Kajaro leaned back and looked at the woman. *"Very well. I can certainly understand the advantage of being the most powerful one in the universe. I could keep all of that to myself."*

"Yes, you could," Sarila said. *"As long as you can help us."*

Quinn got a glimpse of his thoughts, that he didn't see how this wasn't just a win-win situation, because either way, one of his sides would win, and thus he'd end up with the power.

Next set of memories showed a meeting with Karella *and* Sarila, putting together the Balisor plot as a means to gain access to the Library, as at least an assistant, and then they'd put their plan into action.

"There's a lot to unpack in there," Quinn said, as Milaro began putting his things together.

"True. And I'm afraid it's less help than I'd hoped," he said, and then changed the subject. "And now you should eat to replenish your energy, and then I believe you have to get ready for an opening."

"Oh," Quinn groaned. Opening a new branch should cheer everyone up, and perhaps even pull the Library out of its funk. She pushed herself to her feet, but Milaro held out a hand.

"Ah, wait, I forgot this." He handed her over a scroll of parchment. "The list of the books that are missing from the restricted section. I do believe, after a lot of comparisons and observations, we finally nailed down which ones were removed."

Quinn blinked at it, suddenly eager to read it. "Thanks!"

"Might not want to thank me yet. There's probably a lot of legwork in those." He smiled at her. "Now I must visit Harish, Siliqua, and Cadre. Have a very happy opening."

6 0

BOOK NAMES

QUINN CLUTCHED THE LIST OF BOOK NAMES IN HER HAND AND LOOKED down at them. The names flickered up at her, as if dashing in and out of her vision, like they didn't want to be seen, least of all by her. But after several minutes, she finally managed to read through the list.

It contained a few books that Milaro had mentioned previously, but the others were new names to her. She knew all about *Seveshall Lineage of Mind Healing and How to Break It, The Ashelan Mind Capitulation Device,* and *Chmilenko's Guide to Dimensional Complacency.* Or at least she knew all about their existence, if not their precise content.

Considering the names had been wiped from its memory, there was no reason for the system to register books that, according to it weren't in its catalogue. That's why they remained on the written list of missing books.

Idly, she wondered exactly how Milaro, Malakai, Harish, and everybody else who'd helped find the books had managed to figure out precisely which ones were missing. She knew they'd been watching hours upon hours of owl memories, but surely they hadn't had to do all of it in such a mind-numbing way? She'd ask one of them

She was starting to think it'd always be this hectic.

Quinn went through the rest of the names:

Lhose's Myriad Dimensional Weaves and Unbindings

Oswald's Journeys Beyond Dimensional Restrictions

Trial and Errors of Karei's Pocket Dimensional Deconstructions,

Rimmel's Majesty of Dimensional Dissolution

The Stovalian Method: Untouchable & Undetectable Process of Mind Resetting

Doug's Mind Control and Twisting the Narrative

Ameye's Mental Drain and Memory Replacement

Mind as an Escape from Forced Reality

Clarke's Reality Manipulations and Perception Insertions

Collins's Lives, Memories, and True Subjectivity

Shock's Twists on Microaggressions and Their Removal

Merame's Studies of Mind Containment Without Mental Deterioration

Quinn sat there and blinked at the titles for several seconds. Some of them were so vastly specific it was a little shocking. She frowned at their highly pointed titles, a sick feeling of nausea seeping through her very being. They were so focused, based exactly around the type of information necessary to bring the Library out of synchronization, to pull it apart dimensional brick by dimensional brick, that she found their existence to be highly suspect in the first place.

Add to that the focus on mind and memory manipulation, and it made the missing books even more foreboding. Not that she'd ever thought they'd be innocent. For the Library to have specifically forgotten about these very books . . . the sheer magnitude of manipulation astounded Quinn. If it wasn't Korradine, it had to be somebody else close to the Library who'd allowed these books to go missing.

Such deliberate sabotage shouldn't have come as a shock to her, but she'd still wanted to believe in the inherent goodness of beings. This list disabused her of that notion.

It didn't matter that they only had a couple more pillars to reactivate.

Because whoever had these books—and she was almost willing to bet they went by Sölem—aimed to destroy the Library in a very permanent manner. That is, if they could get that specific affinity-based magic to work for them.

She sighed and ran a hand through her ponytail. Because all cosmicisodracus possessed all affinities, she knew at least two of their opponents were true threats. She only hoped their opponents didn't have backup she and her allies hadn't considered.

Quinn picked herself up from the couch and took steps toward her murder board, absently leafing through the handwritten list and basic descriptions of the books Milaro gave her. Not that she needed the basic descriptions, because the titles were completely self-explanatory.

But it did help her understand several of them. The mind-based ones boiled down to how to adjust, wipe, alter, hide memories, and make it so the recipient was none the wiser. And then there were the basic guidelines on how to dismantle dimensions. Some of them, specifically the Stovalian method—how would anyone detect mind tampering?

Just like Lynx and the Library hadn't had a clue.

She stopped her mind from going down rabbit holes. It was best to focus on the positives. From what she could tell from the descriptions, most of the dimension-based books dealt with unraveling dimensions as a theory only. Nobody had successfully achieved these potential outcomes.

It gave her a weird sense of hope. Sort of.

What they had to do was find out where the books on this list were located. She tapped her chin in thought, getting ready to sketch the information out on the board in the portion she'd left open just for that event. It'd help her visualize it better. Maybe there was a pattern, she mused out loud. But then she flicked through all her notes again.

Tracking the books wouldn't work. Which was both frustrating and disheartening. They'd had their best people on this. Milaro. Harish. Siliqua. And Quinn believed Cadre had even looked into it at one point. Which meant all the information they had to go on was here, and it wasn't enough.

Something about the list worried Quinn. It was as if they should know where those books were. Specifically. It was almost as if she'd seen them before. But she shook her head. Probably just her mind playing tricks. That niggling little sensation in the back of her head that she was forgetting something pertinent.

Her frustration boiled up. "Son of a . . ."

But a notification popped up right in her view before she had a chance to yell at the board.

New pillar successfully activated.

Next pillar available for activation in 24 hours.

Caution: Only one of two remaining pillars is functionally available.

Ashiron is offline and cannot be activated until repaired.

The Academy cannot be activated before Ashiron is online.

Quinn stood staring at the notification. They couldn't complete the Library restoration until that damned pillar was fixed.

"Damn it!" She'd known this, of course, but had somehow managed to completely and utterly ignore it. Aradie alighted softly on her shoulder and nuzzled at her ear. The soft feathers around the harsh beak provided comfort.

Immediately, Quinn felt a slight weight lift off her. The owl seemed to know the best times to offer support. Aradie had a way of helping her relax and refocus on the things that were most important. She wondered how much of those books Aradie knew about.

"I guess you know all about the books, hey, girl?" Aradie nodded, still pushing into her neck. "This is pretty bad, isn't it?"

Aradie nodded again, but then there was a hesitation and a shrug that vibrated through the owl's body.

"What, you don't think it's that bad?"

Aradie leaned around and looked Quinn directly in the eye from a couple of inches away. It was an oddly disconcerting experience for Quinn. She liked the attempt at communication and tried her best to decipher it.

"Oh, are you saying . . ." Images flashed in front of Quinn's eyes of the books, all in a pile in the restricted section, behind barred doors and massive locks and then of them disappearing with cloaked figures taking them. "Yeah, I think that's the idea."

Aradie cooed, flashing more images of Dravishk, Dronar, and the taking back of books.

Quinn ruffled Aradie's feathers. "Exactly. We'll get them back and keep them safe. Shouldn't we destroy them?"

Aradie actually managed to raise an owl eyebrow.

Quinn laughed. "Okay, okay, we don't destroy books, we just keep them under lock and key in a much more secure fashion." Something about that statement resonated in the back of Quinn's mind, but she couldn't tell quite why. "Well, then, I guess we should head to the crafting branch now?"

Aradie cooed in response and lifted off Quinn's shoulder to fly around her head and urge her in the direction of the new branch.

In no time at all, Quinn stood in front of the beginner crafting area. A buzz persisted around the area, as if it was on fire, alive. Quinn glanced around, taking it all in.

There were a lot of people hanging around. She could feel this nervous energy suffusing the entire area, excitement on the tip of everybody's tongues. Not only were there a few dozen patrons, but there was also Betty, Dottie, Geneva, Eric, Milaro, and, of course, Malakai.

He strolled up to her and nudged her slightly with his shoulder. "Are you ready for this?" he asked playfully.

She rolled her eyes in response.

"Wow, you're that excited, huh?"

Quinn shook her head. "No, not like that. It's more of a worry about Ashiron. We can't fully restore the Library until, well, until we open the academy. And without Ashiron, we can't hope to open the academy, and thus, we can't fully restore the Library."

"Ah." Malakai frowned. "I think what you're saying is . . . putting the cart before the horse?" He pulled a face as if he was seriously concentrating.

"Yes, I think that's it," Quinn said, looking at him skeptically. "How do you know that saying?"

"I've been reading some light Earth novels."

"Earth, light novels?"

"Well, yes, those too, but not-too-serious novels is what I meant. As in light in subject."

Quinn smiled and made a note to ask how and where he'd gotten the idea for those. But she guessed it was a wide universe.

He nudged her again, but this time softly. "Don't worry, Quinn. We'll figure this out. I have faith in you and the Library."

"I'll be counting on that." She nodded absently, turning her attention back to Dottie and Betty, who were practically dragging her forward to stand on the threshold of the crafting section.

"Librarian," Dottie said, her over exuberance in evidence once again. "We did it. We really did it."

"You don't need to talk her ear off," Betty said. "Let the girl concentrate and put the Library to rights so we can move one more step closer to having the whole thing restored. Now, I gave Aradie a new batch of sprite dust earlier."

Aradie came to settle on Quinn's shoulder once more and cooed in her ear. Quinn saw another flutter of different images flash before her mind. They were pictures of Aradie flying over the filtration chamber and allowing the sprite dust to settle over everything in a thin, briefly sparkling layer. Quinn watched and realized that Aradie took special care not to go anywhere near Ashiron.

"Thanks for doing that," she told Aradie. The owl leaned against Quinn's head, effectively giving an owl hug.

Betty watched, her eyes bright. "It was well received, then. It'll make sure the mana we're churning through is at its peak capacity and functionality. Any shadows banished and all that. I can't wait for this. I wasn't here for the first few openings. This should be fantastic." She clapped her tiny sprite hands, and if she hadn't already been hovering like a hummingbird, Quinn was certain she'd be jumping up and down.

Quinn couldn't help but smile. Betty and Dottie together were just like this rush of fresh air. She was grateful to the bench and her assistant supervisor. After all, Quinn had been so very busy with everything to do with the Balisors, with Jasper's death, with retrieving books and organizing alliances. She just hadn't had time to go and check on *every* book that needed collecting.

This had saved her so much time and worry.

She patted Dottie and smiled at Betty and then scritched Aradie's neck. "Well," she said, "looks like this is as good a time as any." And she pulled up the crafting branch's information.

Crafting Branch Opening Requirements Met
730/730 books retrieved
Energy level required: High Medium
Mana required: 8,675
Energy requirement: 9,234
Patronage level required: Generous
Non-restrictive, all borrowing privileges established.
Calibrating . . .
Calculating . . .
Patronage level met.
Mana requirement met.
Energy requirement met.
Librarian strength required: 12.
Assessing . . .
Calibrating . . .
Accepted . . .
Librarian strength met.
All requirements pending fusion.
Combat branch extending.
397/397 Ingredients sourced.
438/438 Materials allocated.
783/783 Tools gained.
Assessing.
Calibrating.
Crafting branch established.
All requirements met for Crafting Branch to be opened.
Do you wish to proceed?
Yes, No, Place Process on Hold?

Quinn smiled and chose *Yes*.

It was always amazing to watch the way the Library morphed, extended, and pushed out within its own dimension, molding the walls and floors as it needed, sprouting bookcases, revealing workstations.

It was absolutely captivating as the branch established itself.

61

CRAFTING BRANCH

Crafting branch officially opened.

Beginner books verified, relegated to main branch Library.

Analyzing intermediate, advanced, master, legendary, and beyond content.

All crafting subjects accounting for.

Processing current tome complement.

Processing.

Processing.

Error.

Missing the following number of books.

Crafting Branch books missing: 7,685

Would you like a categorical breakdown?

Yes, or No?

And just like that, without any sort of hitch whatsoever, without any weird mana-eating eels, strange bookworm creatures, or reactive training dummies—the newly reinvigorated crafting branch of the Library of Everywhere opened.

No strange phenomena whatsoever.

Quinn found herself still waiting, though, as if something would jump out at the last minute.

She tried to ignore the statistics in front of her eyes and groaned at the significant number of overdue books that needed recovering. 7,685 books. That was not what she wanted to see, especially not beeping in her face. She wasn't about to look at an update of books needing retrieval, either. She had enough to do.

That was for future Quinn to worry about. And for her to delegate to her supervisors.

She finally chose *No*, because the categorical breakdown would likely just give her a headache. She could worry about that once the Library was fully established.

Quinn spent several moments just staring at the amazing feat in front of her.

While she'd been in the Library for a good chunk of time now, magic still held wonder for her. Slowly, she stepped toward the newly opened advanced crafting section, stood on the threshold, and smiled. All around the entrance were rows and rows of ingredients. Things used for dyes, curing, and the like. They were placed at even intervals across from the entrance, the whole width of the branch. Some were held in magical stasis and others simply stored in jars or holding pouches.

Materials and other tools beyond the ingredients lined shelving on tidy display. The center held many crafting stations and machines. Some of those she recognized like weaving machines, forges, anvils, leather tanning stations, leather stretching racks, and tools. The latter filled bookshelves too, bookshelves of tools. Maybe they were just shelves of tools. Quinn wasn't entirely sure if there was a technical term for it.

And then, along the walls were rows and rows of books. Each subject was arranged as close to the machines that went to it as possible. Quinn found herself squinting to try to discern the order.

She couldn't even guesstimate at the number of tomes in this branch. She could see the gaps where the missing books belonged. It made her feel a bit better about the listed missing overdue books because sometimes she wondered if the system wasn't just trying make more work for her.

She allowed herself a rare few moments to relax just as she took in everything. Pure joy radiated through the air of the Library in that moment.

Malakai smiled at her from where he stood. "I thought you'd forgotten how to relax, let alone smile."

Quinn shook her head. "Nah, I haven't forgotten. I've just found, well, I guess it's been difficult to find the time or the inclination. I feel . . . everything feels . . ." She held out her hands as she shrugged, but her voice faded, and she wasn't entirely sure she should say what she was thinking out loud or even if she should say what she was thinking at all. It just made everything more real.

"You know you're allowed to feel things, right?" Malakai asked, his voice very soft.

"Yeah." She sighed. " But not all feelings are healthy for myself or for others to experience me having, if that makes sense."

"It makes perfect sense," he said. "And it's true, but bottling up your feelings or your worries, it's even worse, Quinn."

She raised an eyebrow at him but didn't say anything else.

He continued, "We've already got one bomb down in the filtration chambers that we have to diffuse. We don't need to be watching you for implosion too."

Quinn laughed in surprise. "Oh, fantastic. Is that what I am? You've got me. I'll make sure I don't put us in any more danger with my mildly overwhelmed, panic-induced wallowing."

He smiled at her. "Good, see that you don't."

Quinn laughed again, this time a freer sound, but she didn't mind. She felt lighter, despite having been called a bomb in a strange, oddly roundabout way. Because it was as if she'd been relieved of some of the burden, with the reminder that she wasn't actually alone in all of this. An overwhelming sense of gratitude spread over her as she realized Malakai always looked out for her. Just now, it was in a much different way than it had begun. He wasn't teaching her to fight anymore or defend herself. He was just there. A constant, comforting presence.

"Thank you," she said sincerely.

"No problem," he said. "I'll gladly tell you when you're being silly."

Then he grabbed her hand and pulled her into the actual crafting area, guiding her toward all the different areas and allowed her to lose herself in the wonder of the devices. She wandered into the middle of it and looked around, mainly concerned with the patrons.

There were a lot of them. While she knew they had miles to go, she also realized how much closer they were to opening. Minuscule though it was, she grabbed onto the hope that brought her.

Thank you.

The Library's voice was in and out of her head in the space it took her to breathe. Quinn almost worried she'd imagined it. She really hoped the Library lifted out of its funk sooner rather than later. When it shut her out, Quinn found it easy to assume the worst.

The new crafting section in the Library continued to fill up. So many patrons wandered into it. Quinn thought she might have lost some time somewhere.

"This is remarkable," Malakai supplied, raising an eyebrow at her as he, too, viewed the crowd flowing into the space.

"Sort of," she said. "I mean, I wasn't expecting it to be this popular."

"Keep in mind, Quinn," he said, "that while the Library wasn't around, many projects had to be put on hold. Many tomes weren't accessible, specific magic for certain things wouldn't have been available."

"Wouldn't have been available?" she asked, quirking an eyebrow.

"You know what I mean. I mean that people who possessed specific types of skill sets may not have been readily available to assist people in the way that Library books often are. If you're of a level and you want to learn a new skill, be it anything, you can often create said skill yourself. But when it comes to crafting, there are only so many ways that metal will bend or that twine will fray. There are specific instances where magic needs to infuse every single hammer blow on an axe. Without the Library, many crafters were at a disadvantage. Dottie has been telling everybody that the crafting branch was near completion. I'm certain many of these people have been waiting centuries for this moment."

"Oh," she said, looking at everyone else in the branch right then through a different perspective. "I didn't think of it like that."

"Of course you didn't. Why would you?"

"I guess I just . . . the others didn't have people flock in this way."

"No," he said, "Many family have healing tomes to pass on. Specific recipes and castings that rely on familial magic. It's a generational thing. Cooking is another one of those, driven mainly through familial bonds. Of course, there are certain things that can only be obtained through the Library's knowledge but genuinely they're not dependent on it. Combat as well, familial training, and guild training are other options. But when it comes to crafting, the sheer amount of knowledge housed in the Library is a culmination of many species, even extinct ones, who've had amazing armor-reinforcing capabilities, so"—he gestured widely—"this is what you get."

Quinn nodded and looked around at the new branch with a new appreciation.

"I think I get it," she said as she continued to observe. There were apparently silencing spells in place, because one of the anvils was already being used, yet no sound reached her, no matter how they walked through the Library.

It was quite inspiring.

She checked her notifications, and it seemed that her interlude was over. The next pillar needed to be activated to enable both the bardic and horticulture expansions, which would happen next. While the academy had to wait for Ashiron to be done, she needed the other branches online as soon as possible.

Just as she was about to speak to Malakai, another notification popped up.

Crafting branch golems required.

Specific crafting golems ready for production.

Process halted, awaiting Librarian orders.

Completion activation required.

Librarian code engaged.

Of course, Quinn allowed it to do that. What would a crafting branch be without information assistance like the combat wing had?

With that out of her way, she turned her attention back to her other notifications. She closed her eyes and activated the ninth and final pillar before Ashiron. She could feel the shift of power in her mind. It was like a shock ran through to her core. The chamber thrummed underneath her, as if proving it was dangerous, powerful, and only one step away from being fully capable.

And it gave her another twenty-four hours wait time.

Less than three months, and they were either going to sink or swim. Hopefully, she'd really prefer it if they could fly. Ideally, they needed Ashiron up and running as soon as possible so the filtration chamber could begin acclimating to the level of power running through it.

She just hoped this recent lull in action wasn't tempting fate.

"What are you doing?"

Quinn jumped at Lynx's sudden appearance, took a breath, and answered. "I'm opening a branch. I would have thought that was obvious."

He raised an eyebrow, seemingly nonplussed that he'd probably shortened her lifespan with that fright. "I meant with the system."

"Bringing the final, non-Ashiron pillar online," she said shortly.

"Oh." He looked out over the branch, a thoughtful look on his face. "Would you have time to talk for a . . ."

That's as far as he got, because a booming and very unexpected voice talked over everyone.

"Ah, Quinn, just the Librarian I wanted to see," Uncle Hal boomed, his smile genuine. "It is good to be here again."

62

OBLIVIOUS

QUINN HADN'T EXPECTED UNCLE HAL TO TURN UP FOR THE OPENING. But she hadn't seen Uncle Hal for more than a quick stop in quite some time, not since just after the betrayal on Halschius.

Lynx took a step back and nodded at Hal. Quinn eyed him quizzically, but the Library manifestation shook his head and shrugged before dissipating completely, as if he was saying, *It's okay, I'll catch you later.* Still, seeing Uncle Hal appear also gave her a rush of happiness. He'd been so busy lately with his whole thing on Halschius that she'd missed him.

"It's good to see you again," she said, and Quinn found she truly meant it.

"Of course," he said, a big grin on his satyr face. "I've missed you, little egg." His voice and tone were filled with his usual fondness.

She rolled her eyes. She really hated that nickname, but at least now she understood it. Her mind calmed. Regardless of everything else she had on her plate, Uncle Hal always made her feel safe. And right then, with all the surrounding uncertainty, Quinn found unexpected solace in his presence. Which was, considering his visage, quite unusual. An eight-foot-tall satyr, complete with the horns, the blood-like coloring, and the dark, foreboding aura didn't exactly scream safety. But for her, it felt different.

"Do you have time for a chat?" he asked, his voice sincere, curious.

Quinn nodded, looking back over the newly opened crafting branch. Everything seemed well in hand. She looked over at Malakai, who only stood a couple of feet away. He was already watching her. He crossed his arms and smiled good-naturedly.

"You know I'll take care of it. If we need you, I'll come and find you."

Quinn smiled. "Thanks."

"Don't forget to eat," he admonished her, as if she'd already forgotten to do so.

"I won't forget to eat," Quinn said, and turned to leave. Aradie, however, wasn't yet done, and hooted in Malakai's direction.

"Exactly, old bird. You see to it that she's fed," he said with a solemn nod in the owl's direction.

Quinn scowled at the both of them, but not with any ferocity. She knew they cared. Maybe she couldn't fully relax right now, but at least she could chatter, have a snack, and revel in this sense of security.

She motioned for Hal to follow her, and they headed down to her office, per usual. As soon as they reached the door, Aradie flew off, probably obeying Malakai's order. Quinn *was* hungry, and so her companion likely sensed the incoming hangriness.

The owl sent back brief flashes of food and drink, confirming for Quinn that Aradie was indeed headed to get her something to eat.

Quinn motioned for Uncle Hal to enter the office before her and then followed him in. She let herself drop onto the couch, her head falling against the pillows on the back of it, with an audible sigh.

"Is it that bad?" he asked.

Quinn shrugged. "It's a bit exhausting."

"Just today?" he spoke softly.

"No, not even really today." Quinn had to think about it for a second. "It's more of a constant, never-ending exhaustion. Like, I never get to take a break. And to be honest, it's quite a lot. But it's okay, because I know that eventually I'll get to rest. Right?" She looked at him.

"Yes, when this is all over, you'll have time to rest," he said. It sounded like he was placating her.

She raised an eyebrow at him. "Do you really think it'll ever be over?"

Hal let out a low, rueful chuckle. "Why do you ask, little egg?"

She waved her hands around in general, indicating the vast universe. "This. I didn't think reopening a Library would take so much energy, effort, or take so long."

Uncle Hal laughed. "Well, it was gone for almost five hundred years, so the odds are that it will probably take more than seven months to right everything, don't you think?"

Quinn cringed. He made a lot of sense. And at some level, she'd known that. It didn't mean she had to like it.

"Well, that kind of makes sense," she admitted. "I probably should have looked at it like that."

Uncle Hal chuckled this time and flashed her a smile. "Again, you're a little egg, and I know you hate that name, but it's true. Technically, you should probably still be incubating. There are some of us who are here, willing and able to help and guide you as much as you'll allow us to."

"Yeah, I know," she said with a deep sigh. She knew he was right. "But what with all the leaks and betrayals, I find myself somewhat skeptical about everything and everyone. All of this, all around us . . ." She pinched the bridge of her nose and took in a deep breath, settling herself back down.

Hal and Milaro. Malakai. Geneva, Eric. Dottie. Well, probably Dottie. She really had to ask somebody about why Dottie wasn't allowed to leave the Library. Maybe even Harish and Siliqua. They were all people that Quinn did trust, and yet, she found herself hesitant to trust so much.

After all, she was the only person who wouldn't let her down.

Uncle Hal's voice was gentle when he spoke. "That's no way to exist, little egg," he said sadly. "All that turmoil inside isn't healthy."

"I know." She wasn't sure what else to say. She would have thought he'd read her mind if it wasn't for the fact that she knew she wore her emotions in her expression.

Uncle Hal smiled at her, reaching down to briefly take one of her hands and give it a reassuring squeeze. "Don't fret. There are always solutions, and we'll work hard to find them."

"I know," she said again, feeling like she sounded extremely repetitive. She looked up at him. "Now, why are you here?"

"Am I that unwelcome?" Uncle Hal said, but she could tell he was kidding. He finally relented. "We should probably talk about that."

"Not that I don't enjoy your company," she qualified.

"Well," he said, as if feeling out exactly what to say. "The whole nine lives thing. I promised you that I'd tell you about it. And I've only just had a break long enough to do so."

"Exactly what about it? You removed it from Kajaro, correct?" Quinn asked, wondering exactly what she'd missed.

"Yes, and it's in relation to exactly what we found out with regard to how Kajaro obtained the nine lives skill that I wanted to talk to you about."

Quinn sat up. At the same time, Aradie brought in food and dropped it on the table. Quinn leaned forward, grabbed a sandwich and then rested back where Aradie alighted on her shoulder.

"Thanks," she muttered to the bird, biting into a sandwich and finally turning her full attention back on Hal. "Are you going to elaborate, or?"

"I thought you were eating."

"I am eating. I can listen and eat at the same time. Shocking, I know," she said drolly.

He sighed and stood up to pace. The carpet swallowed the sound of his hooves in the process. "Ardenil," he finally said.

"Oh! Yes, we haven't got around to visiting her." Quinn hated realizing she'd essentially dropped a ball. She was curious. They had already determined they needed to speak to her. "What about her?"

"She provided Kajaro with the magic for the ability graft."

"What, she gave them to him?" Quinn asked incredulously.

"No, an ancient ritual to acquire a creature's innate ability. Not a pretty one, either. Once she gave it to him, she was left in stasis in Kajaro's basement." He said the last word as if it left a bad taste in his mouth.

"Torture chamber," Quinn asked.

He hesitated before answering. "Yes, I think that would be a less diplomatic way to say it."

"You don't need to be diplomatic with me."

"No, Quinn, I'm trying to be diplomatic with myself. I dislike torture chambers, despite the type of reputation my kind has. Anyway, we retrieved her. She's in our facility but she's in a bad way."

It looked like he was about to say something else, but wasn't sure how he should phrase it.

So Quinn asked. "Why is she there? Why was she with Kajaro? I'm missing something."

"As far as we can tell, she was held for a very long time. I have to glean from her mind instead of asking her questions and getting answers because her mind is slightly jumbled right now."

"And you have no idea how long she was held?"

"I'd be willing to bet it's probably been a century or four."

"And she was held prisoner there? She wasn't there of her own will?"

"Believe me, Quinn," Hal said seriously. "If you'd seen the condition we found her in, you'd understand that nobody, not even the most masochistic person in existence, would choose that."

Quinn felt a shiver go up her spine.

"Anyway," Hal carried on, clapping his hands, waking himself up from whatever dark visions he'd conjured for himself. "In our investigation so far, it appears that Ardenil has always been a supporter of chaotic magic. Not to destroy the universe, however, more to, shall we say, leech harnessed chaotic power and distribute it to specific people who might benefit her in some way. An agenda, if you will."

Quinn ran it through her head. "She didn't want to destroy the universe. She just wanted the energy for herself and her allies so she could be more powerful."

"Pretty much. However," Hal continued, "if what I've read from the memories is true, she appeared to want her power through taking over the Library."

"Of course!" Quinn said suddenly understanding. "Chaotic magic is filtered here and distributed throughout the universe so everybody can use it. If they had control of the Library, it'd be much easier for her to simply leech off the top of that chaotic energy, correct?"

"Excellent, little egg. You understand." He sounded relieved.

"Now explain the nine lives secret?" Quinn pushed for more answers.

Hal laughed. "You are a tenacious little egg. Ardenil knew of a way to extract the nine lives ability from the Chezishila cat, the original creature with the nine lives. From what I understand, she figured out a way to implant it into another living being. We believe Kajaro took the knowledge and held onto her for the last several hundred years so that nobody else could get their hands on it, which is why everyone thought she'd disappeared."

Quinn mulled that over. She disliked Kajaro more and more and was quite glad he was dead. Not saying Ardenil was a saint, but still . . . "Why wouldn't we have known he'd imprisoned her immediately from his memories?"

Hal sighed. "While I'm fairly sure we got most of his memories, because Milaro yanked a lot of them, he might have withheld some, or else he could have been too close to death. That can really screw with memory retention."

Quinn nodded. "Maybe he withheld them like out of spite because you took away his nine lives?"

"He only had about six of them left."

"Hal, don't be pedantic."

The satyr laughed his deeply resonant laugh. "Yes, yes, you're right. Probably because we took away his respawns."

"How did they figure out the nine lives thing?" Quinn asked.

"I don't yet have a handle on it. The extraction technique appears difficult and painful for the subject. I still need to dive into Ardenil's mind a little more, since she devised the process," he said, and changed the subject. "And then there's Sölem. I believe we're closing in on a location."

"Oh, good." Quinn sighed with relief.

Hal fidgeted slightly. "I don't have the time right now to go into more detail. Suffice it to say that as soon as I have a location, you will have it too. As it is, I need more time to sort out the whole betrayal thing back at home. But I'll come back shortly and visit."

Right as Quinn was about to respond, Lynx popped into the office. "So do you have time now?" he asked, oblivious to the fact he might have been intruding.

6 3

____

AS SOON AS POSSIBLE

"Ah, Manifestation," Hal said, his voice filled with warmth. He didn't appear put out by the interruption at all. "How nice to see you again."

Lynx turned around and blinked at him but didn't say anything.

Hal continued, "What brings you here?"

Lynx cocked his head to one side. "I needed to speak to the Librarian."

Hal raised an eyebrow. "I imagine you get to speak to her fairly frequently."

"I do," Lynx admitted, "I was about to speak to her about certain important matters when you arrived. I understood that concerns would likely take precedence over mine as the King of Halschius, so I stepped away for a while."

"Ah," Hal said, a smile playing on his lips. "That makes more sense. I appreciate the consideration, Lynx."

Lynx nodded and turned to Quinn. "There's a slight problem with a book for the bardic branch. I was about to speak to you about it when Hal arrived. But if you're not done yet, I can leave and go away again until you are."

"No, not necessary at all," Hal assured him. "I was actually just about to take my leave." He turned to Quinn and said, "Good luck with the next branch, little egg."

Quinn nodded and turned to see Lynx's runic bands were swirling. There was something off about the way he was acting, yet Quinn couldn't understand it, even from observing the interactions. The manifestation seemed disinclined to speak with Hal still there.

Hal's eyes narrowed ever so briefly, as if he'd noticed something strange as well. Only he didn't bring it up at all. Instead, he turned back to Quinn and gave a half-mocking bow before grinning.

"Little egg, I take my leave. The others will watch over you."

Quinn laughed. "You always have to be so melodramatic, don't you?"

"Of course! I'm a satyr, I'm theatrical."

Quinn raised an eyebrow and then nodded. "Yes, you are dramatic."

He laughed and clutched his chest. "Oh, you wound me, little egg."

"Yes, yes, completely deliberately," Quinn said.

She pushed down the minor melancholy that she felt at Hal's departure. There never seemed to be enough time. When Uncle Hal came to visit, she always wished he could stay longer. Give her that tiny bit more of a safety net. Not that she didn't think that others could protect her here, especially Aradie. She was quite certain the night owl hadn't shown her everything yet. And yet, Hal, just by his very presence, not even through actions, made her feel cared for.

"I'll be here," she said to the satyr. "You get your stuff sorted."

"That's the plan," he said. And Quinn rolled her eyes as he reached out and ruffled the hair on top of her head. Again. She sighed.

As he left, he called over his shoulder. "I will endeavor to do everything possible to help solve this universe-world thing for you. We will do our best to keep you safe." And then he was gone.

Quinn felt oddly emotional. Perhaps she was just too tired. She'd been doing so much. The days just ran into each other and she lost complete and utter track of them. Despite having sleep and knowing that she'd slept, it didn't feel like she'd had any actual rest recently at all.

"Okay, Lynx," she said, "what's up?"

Lynx had been off for a few days now. Even when he'd talked to her a few days ago, she could sense something was on his mind.

Maybe something magical was affecting him. She didn't feel comfortable enough with magic yet to try and discern what it might be. And she had a deep down gut feeling that whatever he wanted to say, was something she wouldn't like. She sighed, and Lynx moved closer.

"Are you all right, Quinn?" he asked, the concern genuine, just like she was used to seeing.

She looked up at him, watching as the purple in his sclera swirled around his eyes, like a whirlpool, tugging everything into its vicinity. His runes still hadn't stopped swirling, either. Which made her wonder just what he was afraid of, because this? This wasn't normal Lynx behavior. She should have spoken to him a day or two ago, after she'd first realized something was off, and now she felt like the worst Librarian ever.

"Can you tell me what's up?" she asked, putting as much genuine curiosity into the statement as she could.

Lynx stood there for several seconds, just watching her, as if he was trying to figure out if anyone was eavesdropping. He started to speak several times, but stopped himself and then finally sighed. He looked at Quinn, almost like he was trying to look through her, to find out what she thought about everything.

"Are *you* okay, Lynx?" she asked, starting to worry for real.

He blinked rapidly, as if he'd almost forgotten she was there.

"I'm okay," he said, and she got the distinct impression that wasn't the truth. His hesitancy to speak with her worried her.

"Good, so what's up?" she asked.

"We need to retrieve the last book for the bardic expansion."

Quinn raised an eyebrow, peering at him intensely. "Is this one of those 'we need the Librarian to get the book back' sort of things because the people who have it are keeping it and being stubborn and annoying and refusing to give it back?"

He smiled faintly, chuckling ever so softly. "Something like that," he said.

Quinn frowned, slightly confused by his response. Something prevented her from saying so out loud. There was a part of her worried he might scamper off if she asked too suddenly. She watched him, trying to figure it out. Lynx didn't waver; he simply stood there and waited for her answer. She watched each small flicker of his eyes, each swirl of his runic bonds, and she knew with a startling clarity that Lynx was afraid.

What could scare an almost-immortal Library manifestation? If he needed to speak to her outside of the Library . . . all of a sudden, Tillip's words, the chieftain from the Hirish Highlands, came back to her. He'd mentioned that she lived in the Library and thus had no privacy. Because there were always people in the Library, and the Library itself was always there and listening.

She'd understood what he said at the time. but she'd never thought about how it would feel for Lynx, who was an actual part of the Library. It softened her a little, because she suddenly felt very sorry for her friend. Perhaps it was too easy for people to spy on them in here. Maybe that's where his caution came from.

And she realized that this was all conjecture in her head, all suppositions on her behalf. If it was the case, though, then getting out of the Library to communicate made sense. She smiled, hoping she'd at least figured out some of the problem. In any case, her thoughts made some sort of logical progression.

"Where do we have to go to get this book?"

Lynx smiled, and she could swear she saw some relief in his expression. "We need to head to the Furionas fae homeworld. That's where the book is," Lynx said, a tone of eagerness in his words.

Just as Quinn was about to ask, he shook his head. She frowned. She'd wanted to push him further but she could practically feel the conflicting thoughts in his mind. His smile finally widened when he realized she wasn't going to speak any further.

"Should we go with just us?" Quinn asked.

"No," Lynx said, smiling and obviously glad that she hadn't pushed the why question. "We should bring Malakai, Aradie, and probably Eric with us." He glanced around the room, as if trying to see if anyone was hiding. Maybe he was growing paranoid in his vast age.

"When should we go?" Quinn asked.

"As soon as possible," Lynx said. "Since the pillar is ready tomorrow?"

"Yes, it will be ready tomorrow," Quinn reaffirmed.

"We should definitely get the next branch up and running as soon as we can. And then we only have two more left to go." He sounded dedicated, determined even.

"Yeah," Quinn said. He'd never been this excited about opening branches before. But whatever it was, he was afraid of, Quinn didn't want to give it a chance to get a hold of his paranoia. And so she continued. "Excellent. You just tell me where to go and when to be there and I'll be there."

"Great. I'll go and round the others up." And then he was gone. Winked out of existence, or at least out of her office, anyway.

Aradie hooted with an underlying tone of irritation. Quinn scritched her owl absently. "Yeah, I know."

Another coo, this time mildly amused.

"You know I never leave you when I don't have to," Quinn muttered.

A few more coos punctuated by a hoot.

Quinn chuckled. "Silly bird."

Aradie nipped her finger playfully.

Quinn trusted Lynx. She only hoped that this wasn't some sort of trap.

6 4

BETTER OPTION

QUINN KNEW HER SLEEP SCHEDULE WAS A DISASTER. SHE DIDN'T SEEM to get sleepy, only tired. Once everything was over, she vowed to sleep sixteen hours a day for a week. She got herself ready, gathering a few things into her storage ring, and then she waited until everybody else traipsed in.

She was only mildly surprised to see that Nishpa was coming with them. As the Furionas fae entered the room, Quinn raised an eyebrow.

"Nishpa!" Quinn smiled, happy to see the mind healer. She'd missed her while she'd been healing.

"It's good to see you, Quinn," Nishpa said, a soft smile on her face. "Lynx asked for a guide to the Royal Library, and I figured I may as well visit my brother while I show you it."

"Are you sure you're well enough to travel?" Quinn asked, slightly concerned. Nishpa still hadn't regained that golden glow she'd always had. She still had a pale undertone.

But Nishpa nodded. "I'm well enough to travel for now, and perhaps I'll stay in the capital for some time. I haven't decided yet if I'll come back with you or stay there for a few days."

"Okay." Quinn nodded, genuinely happy to see her friend again.

436

She looked at the others expectantly. Lynx's eyes sparkled a brighter shade of purple, as if he held barely contained excitement. Eric had his arms crossed in typical grump pose. She wondered if grump was an innate imp skill. One where they could hover in the air with their wings beating rapidly, while they crossed their arms and managed to look completely and utterly inconvenienced no matter what the occasion. She had to admit she was quite fond of Eric, of everybody in this room, if she was honest. She nodded at Eric, and he smirked at her.

Malakai stood in the corner with a backpack slung over one shoulder. She wondered why he insisted on taking backpacks with him when she knew he had access to dimensional storage. But then she smelled the telltale sign of cinnamon doughnuts, and she realized he probably had a reason for not placing them in dimensional storage.

Aradie sat on her shoulder, as usual, preening herself.

Malakai gave her a smile. "Can't get rid of me."

"We were taking you anyway, you know," Quinn said.

He mock pouted. "I know, sounds better when I tell you I'm coming and will accept no argument."

She laughed, some of her tension easing. "I guess we're going, then?"

Lynx nodded and smiled at everybody. Nervous anxiety sparked in his aura. He twisted the knob on the door and opened it, taking them through to the Furionas fae capital.

Quinn hadn't been there before. It was all she could do not to gape at everything. It reminded her of the Ishiposa Isle, part of the Esposian fae homeworld.

This capital was situated on a floating island too, surrounded above and below by other islands. They reminded Quinn, yet again, of one of her favorite video games, where you got to sky surf from island to island, had a gliding suit and a glider. She'd sunk many hours into that franchise.

She shook her head though; there was no time to think about that right now. Maybe she could get Malakai to adapt her handheld console, if she could get back to Earth again sometime. She shook her head and refocused on the site before her.

The islands were the only thing the Furionas appeared to have in common with the Esposians on Ishiposa, because the architecture was beautiful and breathtaking in a regal way, though warmer and less imposing. Maybe it was the fact that no one was trying to kill the survivors of a horrific attack, or to sic a giant golem on them by sacrificing most of the city like Adrito had.

The palace reminded Quinn of Neuschwanstein Castle in Germany, back on earth. It didn't have a surrounding forest, but it did have lovely cobblestones and beautiful little Tudor-like buildings everywhere. The building itself rose out of the center of the island, regal and majestic. Tall trees lined the sides of the sweeping, pristinely marbled staircase that wound up toward the entrance. It made her truly wonder how all of this built this on an island. The growing trees, the plants. She realized they looked like pieces of land just hefted out of the earth and set to float in the sky.

She guessed magic allowed a lot of handwaving.

Quinn did notice Lynx was still quiet and hadn't spoken yet. Along with that, he also seemed much at ease than he had been recently in the Library. She waited for him to speak to her. So she'd give him a little bit more time and then she was just going to ask him.

"Everything here's so flammable," Eric said.

Nishpa snorted a laugh. It sounded very unlike her. "It's all warded, Eric. There are magical protections as far as the eye can see. And some places it can't."

Eric just smirked at her. "Anything's flammable if you try hard enough," he said.

For a second Quinn wondered if it was entirely safe to have the imp working in a building full of books.

Keeping Lynx in the back of her mind and the snarky chat between Nishpa and Eric on her periphery, Quinn studied every single building as they walked leisurely through the city center. The rest of the city matched the castle. It was like something taken from one of those Christmas village displays that ran around the top of people's cupboards. Tiny Tudor shop fronts littered the roadside with beautifully quaint shop displays. Cakes in some, clothes in others.

One of the displays they walked past appeared to be a toy shop. The toys appeared to be playing on their own. Things she would never have seen on Earth. Magic made everything automatically more fun. She wouldn't say better, though, because magic sometimes seemed to complicate everything.

If she looked down the cobbled streets toward the outside of the island, she could spy townhouses around the perimeter. All perfectly in line with the style of the city and yet somehow still individual. None of that *Stepford Wives* stuff here. From different window placements to stained glass and ostentatious curtains. The wooden beam placements were all in subtly different patterns. She didn't think even one of the ones she'd seen was the same. And then the color combinations. Some were as vibrant as the city, others were plain black and brown or black and white. She felt like she'd walked into a technicolor fantasy dream.

It didn't help that most of the inhabitants of the city were all Furionas fae. Every single one of the Furionas were between two and three feet tall. All hovering around and flitting about with vibrant wings in a plethora of colors. From blues and greens to purples and pinks, yellows and oranges and even some fall colors like maroon and browns. She did notice there weren't that many reds. She'd gotten used to that color combination because of the red and gold colors of both Geneva and Nishpa. She wondered why that was.

"It's like a rainbow here," Quinn murmured to her companions.

"It is a bit," Nishpa said, pride in her voice. She looked around hovering next to Quinn. "Do you like it? Do you want to go into any of the shops?"

Quinn noticed the shops weren't necessarily made only for Furionas fae. Instead, they were completely human-sized. She guessed that made sense because the capital would be visited by other species than just the Furionas fae. They had to have shops everybody could frequent.

"I don't think we've really got time for that right now. Once the

Library is completely up and functioning and we've sorted all that other crap out, I'd love to take you up on the offer to go shopping. I haven't been shopping in, like, seven months."

Nishpa chuckled. "Very well, I'll hold you to that."

"See that you do," Quinn said. "Why are there so few red Furionas?"

Nishpa chuckled at that. "Red is the color of royalty. That's why you don't see many out in the street. The royal family is quite well interspersed through the city and the rest of the islands. But as it's the middle of the day here, they're all probably in the palace working and governing and whatnot."

Quinn managed to prevent herself from raising her eyebrow too high. She wasn't entirely sure how much she believed any politicians did anything worthwhile, but she kept that to herself.

"Anyway," Nishpa said, "I hope you like the city."

"As long as you can promise me that nobody will set an island-destroying golem on me, I think I like it quite fine," Quinn quipped.

Nishpa cringed. "I don't think my brother will do that. He'd probably like to meet you, though, if you can drop by after the Library."

Quinn nodded. She couldn't very well be rude and just come to the Royal Library and nick off. "If there's time, I'd love to."

Eric grumbled under his breath. "Blood ties are magic. It's so stupid the royal family does that."

"What are you grumbling about?" Quinn asked.

"Blood ties. That's why the royal color is red." He sounded irritated. But then again, when didn't he?

"Blood ties," Nishpa said. "Not blood magic. There's a big difference."

"What do you mean, blood ties?" Quinn asked.

"There's a ceremony which ties you into governance, I guess, where it requires that you put the good of the Furionas fae as a species, as a whole, before any personal wants."

Quinn blinked. "Really? And what do the blood ties do?"

"If you don't live up to them, you are cast out from the royal lineage."

"Wow," Quinn said. "I think I like that."

"Oh yes, you don't just marry into the royal family to be rich and wear pretty dresses." She paused and then chuckled. "Of course, those are some nice perks."

Quinn raised an eyebrow. And Eric started in on Nishpa again.

So Quinn turned her attention to Lynx, noticing that there were quite a few imps interspersed amongst all the people in the city as well. It was strange to see what she'd known as fairies and devil creatures traveling the streets amicably chatting to one another.

She nudged Lynx as they made their way through to the palace. It was such a bustling city. "Are you going to tell me why you wanted to get out of the Library so desperately?" She lowered her voice.

He hesitated, his gaze darting around.

"Lynx, you can talk to me," she said.

"That's just it," Lynx said, his voice a hushed whisper. "I can only talk to you. No. No, that's not what I meant to say. Once we're in the Royal Library . . . I can say more."

"And that's where the book is?" Quinn asked.

"Yes, it's in the Royal Library. I need you to retrieve it because when the Library didn't open, they simply filed that book in with their books."

"Couldn't we have just had it sent over?"

"Yes, we could have just had it sent over," Lynx responded. "I thought this would be a better option."

"Because you want to talk, don't you?" Quinn asked.

"Yes. Of course I do. But in the Library, everyone is always listening, and here we can avoid that." He looked around as if worried. "You'll need to be the one to speak to their librarian and ask for the book back anyway. It'll go much smoother with you in person. While we're looking for it, I can tell you about my memories."

"Have you got them all back?" Quinn asked.

"That's just it. Sort of, mostly. And the most recent restoration? Has me a little worried about the state of the Library."

Well, that didn't sound good.

65

MANIFESTATION

There were times, when Quinn first came to the Library, that she didn't quite trust or even understand Lynx. Now, if she was being honest with herself, he was acting even more suspicious than he had back then. If she hadn't known better, she'd think he was leading her into an ambush.

Then again, what did she know about cosmic Library manifestations? She'd just have to trust him enough to know that he believed whatever he was doing would be for the good of the Library.

Keeping him in her peripheral vision, she turned to the others and began to ask a barrage of questions. Most of them directed at Nishpa, but surprisingly, not all of them were answered by her.

"How old is this city?" Quinn asked, looking around. It felt timeless in the way it appeared, but also the architecture, even though it resembled the Tudor styles of Europe, didn't feel dated.

Nishpa chuckled. "Eons. I wasn't alive when the city was built. My ancestors helped found it. The current emperor is my brother."

Which sparked curiosity for Quinn. "He's contracted for life to the position through this blood binding?"

"Yes, he was born into responsibility. He could have opted to marry out of the line and refuse the oath. We all can. You can't force a duty on a person who doesn't want it or might abuse it. The magic won't let that happen. He chose to take on a ruler's mantle when he came of age and began to assist our father. While we don't have to take the oath, once you do take the blood bond, then you are obligated to put the will and good of the Furionas fae before yourself."

Quinn thought it was fascinating, and an idea struck her. "Wait . . . is it the same for the Esposians?"

Nishpa's expression darkened. "I'd always assumed so. If it is, then I'm unsure as to how Adrito broke his bonds."

"Glad to see your brother isn't like that." Quinn opted for a light tone.

Luckily, Nishpa laughed. "I think my brother's been ruling for close to five hundred years now. Just before the Library went into hiatus, I believe. And he loves taking care of his people. Which is why I help in the Library."

Quinn mulled that information over for a bit. She was still a little confused. "But not all Furionas are like this."

"No, not all of them," Malakai interjected. "The Treaty of Friesbein. That's the city." He added the last with a wink, obviously teasing.

Quinn glared at him, even if she was a bit grateful for the reminder of the city's name.

"Anyway," he carried on, "there's a Treaty of Friesbein and the greater alliance of the universe that allows all people to reside here now."

"And that includes Halschius?" Quinn asked hesitantly.

"Yes," Malakai said.

"Of course it includes us. The fae are our cousins," Eric snapped. "Mostly, anyway. Why is it so hard to believe that we'd be welcome here?"

Quinn gave him an apologetic smile. "Sorry, still some of my old-world belief systems floating around in my head."

"Well, don't let them float," Eric said. "We're not inherently evil, you know, nor are we inherently mischievous. We just like a bit of fun."

"And leveraging fines?" Quinn asked.

"Yes," Eric said proudly. "And leveraging fines, which may I add, I am exceptionally talented at."

Finally, after what felt like ten thousand steps through the town, up the massive staircase, and to the palace direct, they entered through the rightmost door, bypassing guards who realized Nishpa was with them.

"For public access," it said above the door they used. Inside, there was a waiting line leading to a counter, where two slightly frazzled public servants leafed through inquiries. The room was opulent, yet not in a way that screamed wealth or tried to show off how rich such a palace would have to be.

Instead, there were tasteful paintings that lined the check-in area walls, obviously depicting moments in the city's history. The walls themselves were warm colored with a soft beige undertone. Comfortable, enduring furniture was scattered throughout the room, instead of the more ornate and mostly priceless furniture she'd seen in European castle tour documentaries. Those looked like they cost too much to sit on, just in case it broke. But in here, she was certain she could just flop down on one of the couches, and it would envelop her like a warm hug.

Instead of having to check in, Nishpa simply led them all past the desk, waving at one of the ladies who tended it, and headed up another flight of stairs. If Quinn didn't have to see another flight of stairs in her lifetime, she'd be . . . and that's when she remembered she could have been hovering the whole damn time. Still, at least her legs got a workout.

Quinn had to remember to be fair, because since seeing the Library of Everywhere—which was majestic, imposing, and stuck in its own pocket dimension—her view of many of the things she'd loved had changed. One of those things was libraries.

The Friesbein Library put in a valiant effort to look amazing. It had beautiful, soft-colored wooden pillars that rose up, supporting its two levels. The upper level, just like in her Library, was more like a balcony with a beautiful wrought-iron railing that went all around it, and bookshelves behind it lined the walls while some desks and chairs decorated the rest of the landings.

Furionas fae darted around the area, picking out books, gathering with friends. A slight murmur of discourse was audible throughout the entire area. It really was beautiful, and yet, completely underwhelming. Which felt sad in a way, because she'd always loved libraries before, and now she'd sort of been spoiled forever, especially when her own Library could conform to whatever she wanted it to do.

Once in the library, Lynx finally spoke up. "Quinn and I will hunt down that book," he said, his tone making it clear that he didn't want anybody else to come with them. "I know Eric wanted to visit friends, and I thought Malakai might like to check out the array of healing books in here. It's well known for those."

Malakai perked up and nodded, turned around, and walked toward a set of shelves.

Nishpa smiled. "I'll harass my brother and see if he wants to insist on you meeting him."

Quinn asked, "Is he always busy?"

"Usually, but he can probably make time for his little sister." And with that, she fluttered away.

Eric grumbled. "I do have a cousin who works here. Haven't seen him for ages." And the grumpy imp was gone.

Aradie, however, remained on Quinn's shoulder, glaring defiantly at Lynx, whose shoulders finally slumped. "Fine, but this stays between us."

Aradie sort of chortled. Lynx glared at her. "You will bind on an oath, that if you speak to others without my express permission to share the information, you will speak no more."

Aradie's slight laughter stopped, and the bird held Lynx's gaze for several seconds before the owl finally nodded her dark head solemnly. Quinn felt something tingle through her mind and down her spine at the acceptance of what appeared to be a binding oath. It was as if something within the system, the universe, or however that worked, had recognized the words Aradie agreed to. And from all appearances, took it quite seriously.

Lynx, continued on in his completely infuriating refusal to say anything, and led them through the Library. Aradie brushed Quinn's ear as if to say, "What the?" Quinn shrugged, starting to get a bit worried about the manifestation now her irritation had fallen by the wayside.

He picked a book off a shelf and walked to the very back corner of the Library where nobody was around and motioned for everybody to sit down. He put the book down on the table before he sat down. "So we don't forget what we came here for in the first place."

And then a shield sprang into being around them. It felt like he'd just cast noise-cancelling headphones on all three of them.

Quinn resisted the urge to drum her fingertips on the desk and waited. Lynx grimaced. "There, no one should be able to penetrate that shield."

Quinn raised an eyebrow. "You didn't need me to come and get this book at all, did you?" She tapped it, noticing that it was literally a generic book on flutes for beginners.

Lynx shook his head. "No, I didn't really, but it really will be easier for you to get it out of this library. You can just talk to your counterpart here. This seemed like the most plausible reason that you and others would believe in, for us to leave the Library."

Quinn frowned, not liking the implications. "Well, we're here now, so are you going to tell me what has you so worried? Why you've been acting so weird lately?"

Lynx sighed. The runes in his hair stuttered through several cycles, and his eyes glowed slightly. He fidgeted, flipped through the book, closed it again, and finally looked up and made eye contact with Quinn, obviously coming to a decision. "You know when you're told you are one thing and you believe it, but then things keep happening so much that you end up questioning it?"

Quinn shook her head, but then really thought about it and sort of shrug-nodded. "I guess, sort of. It took me a while to catch on to this whole Librarian thing and believe it and then the dragon thing, so I guess I do understand. Can't you just say what's bothering you?"

Lynx looked like he really wanted to and then finally he spoke. "My most recent recollection of memories sparked a line of thought I hadn't expected."

Quinn wisely remained silent, hoping he'd get it all out this time.

"The more I reunited with my memories, the more I realized how much overall damage I'd received. The thing is, it's not even the type of damage I expected."

There was a natural pause in his speaking, so Quinn asked, "What do you mean?"

It still looked like Lynx was struggling to find the words he wanted to use to explain whatever was on his mind.

His behavior worried Quinn. "Look, if it's too hard to let me know . . ."

"I've got to do this," Lynx said. "You have to know."

Quinn nodded, wanting to understand, to help. But the cryptic chafed her nerves, even though she waited patiently.

"The thing is," he said, "I distinctly have these memories of coming into being after the Library tried dozens and dozens of manifestations. Eighty-two others. And I know that I can be incorporeal or solid in the Library, depending on how much power I pull from it. I'm aware of my manifestation status. But when you arrived, and for five hundred years before that, I was positive that the only way for me to do anything was to be attached to the Library because I was a part of the Library."

So many things started running around screaming in Quinn's mind, but she soldiered on listening to her friend.

"Except now I've had these memories retrieved that I know are me. They clicked. And I remember that I'm Lynx. I'm actually my own person."

She'd already thought that Lynx was extremely individual, so the revelation didn't click right for her. "I don't think I'm understanding the significance here. You've always been you."

"Yes, I've always been me. But I always believed, or I thought I always believed that I was me in direct relation with the Library. That without the Library, I could not and did not exist."

Quinn wrapped her head around that. To be honest, she'd assumed the same thing. "Are you telling me that's not the case?"

"Yes, I'm telling you that I am of the Library, but I'm my own entity. I don't—I don't have to stay with the Library if I don't want to. I'm not saying I don't want to, but I'm saying that I don't just think Korradine was the only one digging around in my head and pulling memories. She had all the reasons to alienate me. If I'd left, that was one less security check. So someone else had to have been involved."

6 6

POSSIBILITIES

QUINN WATCHED LYNX, TRYING TO DIGEST HIS WORDS. HE FIDGETED, his gaze constantly alert for any type of potential danger. It was as if he expected someone to attack them at any moment. She worried about him, was genuinely concerned, and could feel his mild panic through their intricate connection.

"How do you think this happened?" she asked, trying to be careful about how she phrased it so as not to offend him. She, personally, didn't like any of the potential culprits.

"I don't know," he said, "but I do know, at least . . . I know now that something also tampered with the Library itself."

Quinn cocked her head to one side and raised an eyebrow as if to say, *Yeah, we know the Library was tampered with because it was shut for almost five hundred years and we're still picking up the pieces and it might all blow apart at the end, anyway.*

He shook his head as if he'd read her thoughts. "No, I mean the Library itself, the Library as a being, not as a depository of books. There's something wrong."

Shivers ran down Quinn's spine with a chill that she couldn't place. She thought over recent events: Tillip's words about how she was never alone in the Library and her thoughts weren't necessarily

449

her own, about Dravishk's confidence when he was speaking to his little group of end-of-the-world planners, and the Library's recent moods. Pieces began clicking together and sudden worry ran through Quinn, because even if they clicked together, the picture wasn't whole and she didn't know what she was looking at. And she wasn't sure what it could see.

It must have showed on her face because Lynx reacted quickly. "No, it can't see us through the system. That's not how it works. The system belongs to the universe now. Don't worry. It's just that I'm not entirely sure what to do."

Quinn looked at him quizzically. "You're saying there's something else wrong with the Library other than everything we've been trying to fix up till now?"

"Yes, there are protocols and my position, I guess, as a manifestation, gives me separate autonomy. It always had. I just didn't remember. I didn't realize until my last memory recovery."

Quinn perked up at that. "So you can be completely separate from the Library and general system?"

"Yes," Lynx answered, "but also like you, I am hooked into and thus an integral part of the Library system. It gives us both a deeper connection which can only be severed voluntarily, like when a Librarian decides to retire, or through death."

"Death doesn't exactly sound voluntary . . ." Quinn said. She didn't relish the idea of more Serpensiril or strange Salosiers coming to try to kill her. She'd already had enough of that.

"Don't worry. We'd be extremely difficult to kill, both you and I. Well, especially me, because I can be incorporeal."

"Do you think I can do that?" Quinn asked, curious.

"It's worth experimenting with," Lynx said, "but wait, we can't digress. We don't have the time."

He was right, she knew that. But Quinn couldn't help all the ideas that ran through her mind. She shook her head to try to focus again. "We're separate entities but are an integral part of the Library system. Without us, it wouldn't work, would it?"

"Exactly. Not properly anyway." He leaned forward, eagerness shining in his eyes. "We both synchronize. It's part of what gives us that deeper connection. As much as I've recalled, though, my memories are still spotty. There are still things I know I'm missing."

"Damn," Quinn said. It was a lot to take in that something *else* was wrong with the system. Although the Library really had been acting out of character lately. A sudden thought struck her. "What about Dottie? She's mentioned once or twice that she can't leave the Library. Is it a deal or an agreement?"

Lynx nodded. "Dottie is supposed to help ground the Library. Her own longevity is tied to it."

"Oh, can superellex futora die?"

"Of course they can die. They get old and brittle and crack and die, just like any furniture. Usually."

Quinn still couldn't quite wrap her head around that, but she'd take his word for it. "So, if the Library dies, Dottie dies."

"Well, right now, if the Library dies, everybody dies."

"Pedantic, but a good point anyway."

He sighed and looked like he was trying to figure out how to explain it better. "It's more that Dottie's there to provide equilibrium for the Library, to keep both the Library and the Librarian on an even keel, so to speak."

Quinn took that in and thought over it. Dottie did always calm her. She always felt in a much better mood when the little bench wandered in with her bright and cheery Librarian greeting. She could see what Lynx was saying. "Do you remember anything else?" she asked him.

"There are still so many holes in my memory, but they're all closer and closer to the shutdown. I remember that when I imprisoned Korradine's soul, or what was left of it, that the Library wasn't impressed. But I put that down to being worried about the shutdown."

"Is the Library against us?" Quinn asked. Tremors ran through her at the thought.

"I don't believe so," Lynx said, "at least not consciously. But something feels wrong. We must halt its memory restorations if we can until we understand what's happening."

"As soon as possible, then," Quinn said. She knew he wasn't lying, and Aradie's images confirmed her conclusion. The owl was sending her brief images that showed she agreed with Lynx's assessment.

Quinn sighed. She didn't understand why it had to be so difficult. She turned to Aradie, a question in her eyes. "Why did none of the owls know about this?"

Aradie actually spoke to them both to answer it instead of flinging images. "Non-corporeal behavior isn't something we can pick up on unless I'm sitting here on your shoulder."

Quinn nodded and scritched the owl's neck before turning back to Lynx. "Well, do you think we should talk to it?"

"Yes." Lynx seemed relieved. "But give me some time to figure other things out, including how best to approach this. Maybe . . . maybe I've just been worrying for nothing."

Quinn didn't think that for a second, but she didn't offer up her thoughts yet. Too many pieces suddenly fit for it to be coincidence.

He continued, unaware of her thoughts. "The Library has been worried for hundreds of years about the shutdown potentially affecting everyone. I don't want to come off accusatory, but can't you feel it through your connection?"

Quinn closed her eyes and frowned. "I think I need to be in the Library to feel it."

"Oh, sorry," Lynx said, his eyes blinking rapidly. "That was the whole point of bringing you out here, so that it couldn't reach."

"Not to be completely dense, but what exactly do we suspect here?" She needed to hear him say it, because the assumption was killing her.

Lynx blinked at her. "I'm still figuring out all the details. But I do know that more than one individual interfered with my memories. Not only did I forget Korradine's, but I also forgot that while a part of the Library, I'm my own entity. That is a huge thing to forget. Who or what would that have benefited? Who, or what, could have gained enough access to do that? It required a fundamental loss of self. Korradine might have been powerful and cunning, but I don't see how she would have cared about me being me."

Quinn had to admit, he had a point. She wanted to know as well. He spoke up again. "I wanted to know if you'd noticed anything."

She thought it over. "The Library has been kind of grumpy lately. A bit snappy, quite impatient, not as forthcoming. Almost disappointed in itself, I think."

Lynx snorted thoughtfully. "Maybe it's having unexpected memories restored too, just like me. Maybe it didn't remember any of this either."

"But why wouldn't it talk to us?" Quinn asked. "I don't understand why it's keeping things to itself. Does it think it's alone?"

Lynx shrugged. "I have no idea. I've been around it for longer than anyone except its siblings, and I can't answer that."

"Okay then," she said. "Let's gather whatever we can. And as soon as Bardic is open, we'll talk to the Library."

Lynx grinned. "That's right. That's why we're here. Sorry, I'm running a thousand algorithms at once and I just . . . anyway, let's do this."

Quinn glanced at the lighting outside and realized they'd been there a lot longer than she thought. She was certain this island at least didn't have any problem with time dilation, but it really seemed as if they'd been there a while. Especially when Nishpa came to find them with the other two in tow. Eric appeared irritated, but then the imp often seemed irritated. And Mal frowned, his eyes filled with concern. She could almost hear him asking her to *Tell me all about it.*

But instead he asked, "Did you get what you were after?"

Quinn tapped the book. "Yeah, we just got lost in discussion." She hoped concern no longer adorned her face and pushed herself to her feet, gripping the book. As they walked toward the counter, she struck up a conversation with Nishpa. "Did you enjoy the catch up with your brother?"

"Yes and no. In order to speak to him, I had to sit through some audiences, which is never fun." She pulled a funny face.

Quinn chuckled.

"Don't laugh, it's so dull. The good thing is he's far too busy and made me promise to bring you with some warning next time."

"Excellent. I'll gladly come and visit when, you know, I actually have time."

This time, Nishpa laughed. "Well, I also visited a few friends who live nearby. I think I might stay a few days in the city, calm down a bit, but I'll be right here if you need me. Milaro knows how to reach me, so does Geneva, and you could just send me a message too. I'll take you to a door now that's best to reach the Library with."

Quinn glanced at the book in her hands and wondered why it hadn't started walking back to the Library by itself. She got the distinct feeling it had just been content being among other books. She placed the book on the counter, and the librarian there looked up at her, a strange recognition passing through her features.

"Librarian?" she asked, her voice a hushed whisper, which, ironically, was quite loud in the Library.

"That's me," Quinn said.

"Oh, what can I do for you? You're here to get a book?"

Quinn grimaced. "Actually, I'm here to reclaim a book that was shelved in your library."

"What? We have a Library book here?" She seemed horrified.

Quinn had to chuckle, because yes, they had like thousands of library books here, but not necessarily from *the* Library. But she didn't laugh and was extremely proud of her restraint. "Apparently," she said, "you do. But as long as you're okay with it, I'll just take it back now."

"I'm so sorry. If I'd have known about this, I'd have had it returned to you."

Quinn showed her the stamping on the spine, and the librarian turned even a brighter red. "This is . . ."

"Don't worry about it. It seems it likes the books in your library as well."

"Oh, excellent. Is there anything else I can help you with?"

"No, thank you."

They left, following Nishpa to a doorway that took them right into Quinn's office. She was so relieved to step through back to home, in her comfortable, quiet office. Eric hovered and scowled. "You didn't really need me to come, did you?"

"No, but I like your company when we travel. And besides, what if something bad had happened? You would have been there to protect me."

He hiked a thumb and pointed it towards Malakai. "That's what he's here for. Anyway, next time, at least bring me some witty repartee along with it. I need to report to Hal." And he zipped out of the room.

Aradie alighted to her perch, while Lynx waved once and disappeared on the spot. Malakai, however, crossed his arms and frowned at her. "How about you tell me what all this was about? You didn't need me to come. I didn't need to bring food."

"It's sort of complicated," she said, and held her hand out for a now-cold donut. "But I should have an answer I can give you soon."

He raised an eyebrow as he handed her food. "Should I be worried?"

Quinn sort of shook her head. "I'm not sure if any of us should be worried. It could simply just be a mood swing."

At that, his eyebrows raised even further. And she was about to explain a little more when there was a knock on the door, followed by Harish, Siliqua, and Cadre bursting in.

"Librarian, I think we have a way to fix Ashiron," Siliqua said.

67

CACOPHONY

Quinn's first response to the statement was sheer relief. It rushed through her, sending adrenaline racing along her veins. Then she took a breath, took stock of the situation, and calmed herself down. It required real effort not to just jump up into a celebration dance.

"How exactly do you mean you think you've figured out how to restore Ashiron?" she asked, carefully, just in case she'd misunderstood.

"Exactly that!" Siliqua's eyes were full of exhausted fervor. But she held herself tall and straight. Quinn could read from her body language and aura that this was real. They weren't just basing it on supposition.

Then Cadre stepped into the room too. Quinn took a second to look him over. He still had that distinct gecko-like countenance at four feet tall. It was always a little disconcerting to look at him, but his grin took up most of his face and she knew they'd hit gold.

"I didn't realize you were here, Cadre," she said to him. She was racing through all the probabilities but stopped, calmed herself again, and pulled herself back. She held her hands up. "You need to explain this. You can't just come in and make that statement and not say anything else."

Cadre grinned before launching into an explanation. "You see, we need to remove the soul bomb and its enclosure without exploding the universe."

"Yes," Quinn said. "That would, of course, be ideal." She'd never been a fan of people stating the bleeding obvious, though she knew she did it sometimes too.

"Of course, of course," Cadre said. "While I do need access to the actual pillar first to just triple-check that our theory will work, I am hopeful. There are certain calculations I must perform within its vicinity, so I haven't got the ultimate calculations yet, but I am quite certain that once we're down there and have the calculations inputted, we can move forward without causing the Library any instability."

Quinn narrowed her eyes. It sounded way too good to be true and still didn't actually answer the question. "How sure is 'you're quite certain'?" she asked.

He looked like he was calculating it in his head. "Oh, about ninety-six-point-seven percent certain," he answered.

Quinn cringed a bit at that, although that meant he was only three-point-three percent uncertain, which sounded relatively small, if not acceptable. "What do I need to do to bring that closer to a hundred percent, and what do you need from me to get to the end of it?"

"Yes!" Cadre exclaimed excitedly. "Exactly." He actually clapped his hands. "I'll need the readings from the actual pillar."

"I know you've said that already. I'm guessing I'll also need to activate it and instigate whatever this is." Quinn was proud of her patience.

Siliqua put a hand on Cadre's shoulder and stepped in front of him. "You've gone off on a tangent, Cadre."

The wood elf turned toward her. "Both you and Lynx will need to perform the shifting ritual."

"Shifting ritual?" Quinn asked. She'd been wary of rituals, especially since Jasper never gotten around to teaching her more about them. It was only one of the many things she missed about her friend.

"Ah, yes," Siliqua confirmed. "We had to devise it ourselves because there's no precedence for this, and that's why it's taken so long. It's involved so many calculations and projections." She paused and looked at Quinn. "Sorry, there's just so much involved in this it's hard not to want to share it all."

Quinn smiled. "It *is* a huge accomplishment."

"Thank you." Siliqua paused and then continued. "I realize you're busy, Librarian, but we wanted to let you know as soon as we could."

Quinn was certain they needed to get this shifting done sooner than later, even though the timer ticking down still gave them, what, two and a half months and some change? That didn't fill her with confidence. There'd been so many hiccups. Wasting time or taking too much of it just felt like a fool's errand. She couldn't quite put her finger on why though. It was just that same old gut feeling that had already served her so well so many times. And, like usual, she went with it.

"When will you be ready to perform this ritual?" she asked.

It was best to get the details out of the way before getting ahead of themselves, anyway. Quinn had to understand if this was a viable theory.

Cadre's smile practically split his face. "Very soon. There are some calculations I want to go over again just to make sure they work, but once I've done that, we do need to venture down to the actual pillar and obtain two specific measurements. Though they'll fluctuate and we have to time things with the utmost precision . . ." He paused and Quinn dove in.

"You'll have to measure it while I'm down there just before we do the ritual?"

"Exactly. The measurements we need will fluctuate due to the nature of the soul bomb and its dimensional shift. One hour will differ from another. Actually, a ten-minute window is probably the best we can hope for. Using the same calculations from one day to the next could potentially be catastrophic."

Quinn took a breath and counted to three, instilling patience in her, and asked again. "When do you think we can do the ritual?"

"Probably tomorrow evening," Cadre said, and that's when Milaro walked in to join them all.

His presence was, as always, calming, sort of like Dottie, but without the genuine cuteness factor. It helped ease the tension in the room, as well as her head.

He chuckled. "You're always so enthusiastic, Cadre, but we won't be ready until after the bardic branch opens. Let Quinn grab some sleep, open the branch, and then we should be able to venture down." He spoke kindly and looked in good health for the first time in ages.

As much as Milaro had brought some calm to the room, and Malakai was doing his best not to pout at the interruption, Quinn had to let him down.

"I think the sleep has to wait. I'm quite certain we're super close to being able to open the branch," she said. She squinted as she glanced at her notifications, realizing the pillar had just come online. "Branch first. Sleep next. Ashiron third. And then the universe!"

She grinned and Milaro laughed. Everybody else chuckled.

"That's the spirit. Shall we make our way up, then?" Her mentor held out an arm and Quinn followed him up to the bardic beginner's section, her step lighter than it had been in a very long time. If they could get Ashiron back online, then she could breathe for a bit. It didn't solve everything. It didn't automatically return the books. It didn't automatically open the branches, and it certainly didn't get rid of the threat that still faced the Library. But it did help.

Drukala and Drivok fell into line with them.

"Hello," Quinn said to her aunt and uncle, suspicious about their sudden appearance. "I don't have time to train right now. I have to open a branch."

"Oh, we know, little niece," Drukala said, ruffling Quinn's hair.

She scowled at her aunt. "And?" she asked, pulling away and closer to Milaro as if he'd shelter her from them.

"And we want to watch. I haven't seen any of these branches opened before. Back when we made the Library, it was just the one big room to start with. Now it's sort of majestic." Drukala sounded oddly nostalgic.

"There's nothing 'sort of' about it," Drivok said. His eyes shone.

The little procession made its way to the section and up the stairs. They needed to open this branch, which only left horticulture and the academy. Quinn felt giddy that they were getting close to something that had stumped them for so long.

Without the threat of accidentally blowing up the Library—and with it the universe—her stress levels might even diminish.

People had already begun to linger around the area. There were a couple of dozen onlookers all excitedly chatting, including some kids with wide eyes that clutched instruments standing next to their parents. She frowned. What if this turned out like the medical and alchemical branch had and ended up getting danger-ous? Those kids and hell, those people, they could all be injured badly.

Dottie trotted up excitedly to her. Quinn could practically feel it radiating off her. It was a very pleasant experience. A sudden influx of serotonin that she so desperately needed. Now she understood a little bit more about Dottie's role in the whole Library. She couldn't help but appreciate the bench even more. Plus, she was perceptive.

"Why, Librarian, you look less happy and more concerned than I thought you would," she said. She sounded disappointed, but not in Quinn, just in the fact that Quinn had to feel upset about something. Quinn tried a weak smile at her despite the serotonin influx into her brain. She was still a little stressed.

"To be honest," Quinn said and glanced at the kids not too far away from her, "I'm a little worried about the safety of opening a branch with this many spectators. I should have thought about it with the crafting one and we're just lucky that everything went off without a hitch."

"That makes perfect sense," Dottie said. "You just leave this to me. I've got this."

And she trotted off.

Quinn watched open-mouthed as a little bench made very short work of the group of people, asking them to please step back beyond the crafting railing and if they really wanted to watch, they had to observe from that distance until the branch had been declared safe for patrons.

"Oh, that was easy," Quinn said.

Milaro chuckled.

Malakai nudged her. "Are you up for this?"

"I'm awake, right?"

He laughed. "I think you are. I think we'd know if you weren't."

She looked at him quizzically. "You're being enigmatic."

"It's working? Fantastic. Eric's tips are paying off."

"I'm fine, Mal. I just . . . I've got a lot on my mind."

"I know, and for some of that, you owe me an explanation."

"True, but let's get this stuff done first." She sighed.

"Okay, but I'll hold you to that."

She nodded and checked over the statistics for the Library.

Bardic Musical Branch Opening Requirements Met

897/897 books retrieved

282/282 instruments retrieved

Energy level required: High Medium

Mana required: 9,211

Energy requirement: 9,875

Patronage level required: Generous

Non-restrictive, all borrowing privileges established.

Calibrating . . .

Calculating . . .

Patronage level met.

Mana requirement met.

Energy requirement met.

Librarian strength required: 12.

Assessing . . .

Calibrating . . .

Accepted . . .

Librarian strength met.

All requirements pending fusion.

Combat branch extending.

282/282 instruments sourced.

Reminder: Duplicate instruments required after opening.
Assessing.
Calibrating.
Bardic Musical branch established.
All requirements met for Bardic Musical Branch to be opened.
Do you wish to proceed?
Yes, No, Place Process on Hold?

This branch was an easy one. Instruments were all there. Everything was clear. She set it to activation, standing back enough to let the magic of the Library do its work. It was wonderful to watch this. Books swirled around. The whole upper section pushed out, creating almost like an amphitheater design in the center of it.

Massive shelves lined the interior of the outer walls of the whole structure and then the cases filled with so many instruments that Quinn couldn't even count. Things like lutes and guitars and mandolins through to ukuleles and zithers and she was quite certain she saw several harps, too. Not even just violins and cellos and violas, but other ones she didn't recognize that obviously needed more than two hands, some more than three hands, even.

Woodwind instruments adorned other shelves. Ones that she was used to like flutes and clarinets and saxophones, but others that looked like an oboe for three mouths and bagpipes for several heads.

The way the building lengthened and twisted into the appropriate shapes me her giddy with excitement for the simple fact that magic existed. It was the amphitheater that really caught her attention. The way it angled toward the back. She was quite certain with the way the domed ceiling was set that the acoustics had to be amazing. She wondered if there was a magical barrier set up so as not to disturb other patrons.

Before she could think any further, a massive cacophony of horns sounded, blaring like an alarm.

Quinn groaned.

At least it wasn't an eel.

6 8

ODDLY SILENT

QUINN KNEW SHE SHOULD HAVE KNOWN BETTER, AND SHE SWORE SHE did. Still, being lulled into a false sense of security was such an easy trap to fall into. Honestly, she shouldn't have expected a second branch opening to go off without a hitch, especially not making it two in a row.

The note of the horn blaring rose very slightly, just a fraction, and what began as a half-funny cacophony was sure to develop into ear bleeding pain if they couldn't find it and shut it down. Except Quinn wasn't entirely sure where to start. She looked around, glancing at everybody who stood with her, staring in auditory pain at the Library's new branch.

Lynx popped into being right next to her. "The main Library won't be affected. The protective shielding is already active. But we need to keep everybody out of the branch expansion and the beginners' section. The alarm extends into those."

"Fantastic," Quinn said. "More ground to cover."

"You sound irritated."

"I feel like my eardrums are about to rupture." She sighed and took a second to glance at the manifestation. He seemed, somehow, more solid, almost more vibrant. Despite all the confusion surrounding his memories, she was quite certain the restoration had been good for him.

"Okay," she said, "I'm over my pity party. What do I need to do?"

He shrugged. "I don't know, find the source of the horn?"

"Isn't that something you can, like, pinpoint as the manifestation?"

He took a step back and raised an eyebrow. "Isn't that something you can look into as a fully fledged Librarian?"

"Shut up," she said, but laughed.

She needed that. It took away some of the tension and allowed her to look at things objectively. Several seconds had passed by now, and all she knew was that they couldn't afford for it to keep going. She nodded at him, and they set about looking for the source of the noise.

The whole bunch of them, Quinn, Geneva, Malakai, Milaro, Betty, Drukala, Drivok, and Lynx all made themselves busy, darting into different areas of the Library's newly opened branch in order to find the damned noise. It echoed in such a way that it seemed to come from nowhere and everywhere all at once.

Dottie, meanwhile, took control of the patrons, effectively ushering them back and away from the beginners' section, out into the crafting beginners' section, effectively preventing them from entering the newly formed, slightly malfunctioning branch.

Naturally, it wasn't easy to locate the damned horn. Quinn saw a few others checking through the instrument storage cabinets in the center area. The dragons worked through the amphitheater, looking behind and underneath seats and on lecterns. She'd leave that to them.

Personally, Quinn discounted the instruments. Her instincts told her it wouldn't be somewhere obvious, because why, oh why, would the universe make anything easier for them, or more specifically, for her, when it could make it as difficult as possible?

Just once, she would like it if things would go off without a hitch. A small voice in the back of her head that she knew belonged to her mentioned that the crafting branch had gone off marvelously.

She had a traitorous brain.

"Okay, maybe I'd like two things to go off without a hitch," she mumbled under her breath as she approached the horn section of the books. Nobody else had visited it yet, so using her own rather unique brand of logic, she stood in front of the horn section and decided to simply go book by book. Starting from the top.

Considering the section was directly adjacent to the glass cabinets which held brass instruments, the section wasn't difficult to locate.

She began moving the books around, pulling them out, double-checking each book wasn't attached to a secret panel, or that it wasn't attached to a hollow book that had a tiny horn in it blaring out the noise. She wouldn't put it past magic for a blaring horn this loud to be minuscule.

She finished with the second shelf, which was up quite high on the ladder she rolled along the shelves. The alarm note went up another notch. She sighed, trying to figure out if she could block the sound somehow. Given the constant crescendo of the sound, she knew she didn't have time to formulate that sort of spell or ability. It'd take time for her to figure out the magic, and it was better spent trying to reason out where the damn horn was and stop it.

She methodically yanked out book after book, flipped them open, and put them back in place. Yanked out, flipped open, replaced. They were dusty, and for the first few she managed to cough herself silly, until she pulled her hoodie up and closed it above her nose so that she could at least stop pushing dust into her face.

She worked through the shelves while the note went another two notches higher. She could already see Betty covering her ears as she, too, flitted about trying to find the sound. Perhaps it affected smaller creatures worse? Or maybe sprites specifically?

Finally, Quinn managed to make it down to the last shelf. She didn't like her chances. She'd probably have to go through another one of the bookshelves, although some people had seen what she was doing, and had followed her lead. Sadly, there were hundreds of different instruments, and thus hundreds of different book shelves.

She didn't like their odds.

Resigned, she settled herself down on the floor, pushing the ladder away, and began pulling the books on the bottom shelf out too. Remove. Open. Replace.

Franticness rose in her as she approached the end of the shelf and realized there was still no horn. The note went up yet again, and Quinn's head started to pound.

When she got to the last book and pulled at it, it didn't come free. There was definite resistance, as if it was attached to something. Nothing moved, no hidden door opened, and so Quinn leveraged herself onto the floor on her stomach and looked for the problem. She blinked and did a double take, not quite understanding what she saw.

Of all the things she'd expected or even anticipated, what stood in front of her right now was not one of them. A tiny sprite-like creature looked up at her, its mouth wide, emitting a sound. Somehow, it wasn't louder now that she was closer to it. Its eyes were almost comically large for its tiny round head. Its little body reminded her of a Funko Pop in its proportions. Tiny clothes, teensy shoes, and it was silver in coloring with a strange pearly sheen to it. It had tufts of magenta hair sticking out of its little head, almost like one of those old troll dolls' hair. Not the rest of it, just the hair.

And it still held tightly to the book she'd attempted to pull out, as if it had been running the length of the bookshelves the whole time, trying to outpace her and hoping she'd give up. The poor little thing must have been terrified. Its tiny face, full of panic.

"Excuse me," she said softly, somehow certain it could hear her and somehow just as positive that it wasn't about to bite her finger off. "I'm the new Librarian, and we've just reopened this branch, pulling it back into the right dimension. Could you stop the noise, please? It's hurting our ears just a bit."

The creature blinked up at her, nodded once, and finally, it closed its mouth. The sound cut off immediately, the silence practically more deafening than the horn had been. Everybody gasped, whether it was with relief or perhaps pain now their ears were used to the sound. Quinn wasn't quite sure, but she couldn't help the relief that flooded through her.

"Hi," she said and inspected the little thing.

Name: E

Species: Key

Library inhabitants loyal and attached to the Library.
Place and the universe: Bardic Collegium.

"Ah, hello little E Key," she said softly.

It chuckled, but the sound reverberated in her head. She didn't get surprised by much these days.

"How are you?" she asked it. It cocked its massive head to one side and smiled up at her. Images of many other little creatures just like it, with slight variations in hair and skin tone, flashed through her mind. She felt an overwhelming sense of fear emanating from them, in the weird sort of stasis that they fell into.

Likely from when Lynx plunged the Library into hiatus.

When the re-emergence began, E was tasked with scaring off any foes that might be around. They had no way of knowing the Librarian had returned to restore the Library, nor what happened initially. Sounding the alarm and then recognizing the Librarian with a rush of relief were the last couple of images that fluttered through her mind.

"Ah," she said to it. "Thank you for letting me know. You're safe now. Everything will be fine." She really tried to believe in her words herself. She had so many questions for the little creature. "Do you want to come and meet the others?"

It nodded quickly and then leapt out of the bookcase. Her shoulder barely registered its—his?—weight, and he held onto her hair, wrapping it around his little arm. Lynx, Malakai, and Milaro appeared at her side almost immediately.

"Oh," Milaro said, as she stood up, dusting herself off. "You found a key. Hello, little E, it's good to see you again."

The tiny creature chittered in Quinn's mind, and she knew that somehow the others around them heard it in theirs, too.

Lynx poked her. "I promise it'll get easier than this to run the Library."

Quinn smiled at her friend. "I really hope you're right. I had a thought." She pulled away ever so slightly from Milaro and Malakai, who were chattering about the keys. Little E stayed on her shoulder as she focused her attention back to Lynx.

"What is it?" he asked.

"About our discussion. I thought it might be pertinent for you to take Carafax's journals and compare any notes."

His eyes widened. "That is an excellent research opportunity. I think I'll take you up on that. Where are they?"

"They're in my office, in my desk. You should have access to it and them." She double-checked herself, sure she'd allowed Lynx access to most of her things.

Lynx nodded, his face already thoughtful, and Quinn smiled to herself. She'd had the thought after they'd returned from retrieving the last book. It seemed that the chroniclers never spoke in direct language. Never spoke plainly when they could hint at them and guide you vaguely in the right direction. Carafax had told her to read them carefully. Maybe Lynx would pick up something Quinn and Malakai had missed.

It wasn't until she was left to her own devices as Lynx went away and E sat peacefully on her shoulder that a thought in the back of her mind really bugged Quinn. The Library had been oddly silent throughout the whole branch opening.

Not even a thank you this time.

69

—————

FUTURE SELF

QUINN SHOOK HERSELF OUT OF HER THOUGHTS ABOUT THE LIBRARY. Surely, it was dealing with its own crap. Add to that the fact that it had to perform all the functions of a library all the time, and surely it was simply exhausted. She could make excuses, right?

To distract herself, Quinn pulled up the Library statistics specifically for the bardic branch, now it had opened.

Bardic Musical Branch officially opened.

Beginner books verified, relegated to main branch Library.

Analyzing intermediate, advanced, master, legendary, and beyond content.

All Bardic Musical subjects accounted for.

All Bardic Musical instruments accounted for.

Processing current tome complement.

Processing.

Processing.

Error.

Missing the following number of books.

Bardic Musical Branch books missing: 8,254

Would you like a categorical breakdown?

Yes, or No?

She cringed at the stats. So many books were overdue. It had just escalated so much with all the rest of the branches open. She always thought eighteen thousand wasn't really a lot of books. She'd never realized quite how grateful she'd be for such a low number initially. The total of books climbed as the restoration of the Library progressed, and it felt absolutely staggering.

She guessed it should have been expected for a Library of Everywhere.

Betty fluttered over to her, a smile beaming on her beautiful sprite face. "Oh, it's a key!" she exclaimed at Quinn's little buddy on her shoulder.

Quinn resisted the urge to roll her eyes at everybody, stating the bleeding obvious. Yes, E was a key. And E was too cute to be annoyed at everyone's reactions. Plus, his name rhymed. E the key. She could say that ten times fast.

She shook her head. "He just got worried when the branch was brought out of its dimensional stasis."

Tiny barks echoed through the Library, getting closer. All of a sudden, there were three little dog ears nipping at Quinn's heels. Their triangular, dog-ear-shaped bodies bounced as if they were trying to get to the key. E, for his part, stood on Quinn's shoulder, shaking a fist at them.

Betty raised an eyebrow and smiled again. "Ah, they are reunited. I hope they don't give E extra anxiety. The keys are still readjusting," the sprite said, all businesslike. "I think we have an excellent candidate for the bardic branch supervisor," she said, changing the subject as she focused her gaze on the Librarian.

Quinn did a double take. "Oh, that's excellent?" she half asked, unsure of exactly how to respond. Then again, she *had* delegated supervision of all the Library staff over to Betty.

The sprite motioned over to somebody, beckoning them with a slight wave of her tiny hand. A human with very slightly pointy ears, closer to Quinn's height, moved over. She had brown, ringlet-y hair that went way past her shoulders and bright, inquisitive blue eyes. A wry smile graced her face as Quinn inspected her.

Name: Sarah James
Species: half-elf
Ally to the Library.

Quinn raised an eyebrow at the species descriptor. It had never listed elf as a species before. Was it poking fun at her? She'd delve into that later, along with the other seventeen thousand things that she had to make time for once they'd solved the problems of the Library.

"Nice to meet you, Librarian," Sarah said. "I was the supervisor here before the Library closed down. Luckily, I had that day off."

"Just call me Quinn." Sarah's words made Quinn wonder exactly what might have happened to patrons or employees when Lynx activated the dimensional shift. Another things for later. Her list for future Quinn kept growing, and she didn't think she'd like her past self-much in the future.

Sarah cocked her head to one side. "Can do. That's a simple request."

Quinn nodded. It wasn't that the title felt uncomfortable. It was just so heavy.

"Excellent," Betty piped up. "I'm so glad you'll get along well. I'll vouch for Sarah. She's marvelous. Always a favorite among the patrons."

"Great." Quinn liked the ease of the transfer and the fact that Sarah was also side-eyeing Betty. It made Quinn feel like she'd found a kindred spirit. E took that moment to jump from her shoulder to Sarah's, chittering mentally with notes of excitement.

Quinn didn't expect to miss the little key. He'd only been there for a little while, but she'd sort of grown used to the way he'd twined his arm around her hair.

Maybe when she'd finished the plethora of things she had to do, she'd come back and get to know all the keys that lived in the branch. She was willing to bet there were more than just the standard keys in the earthen music staves.

Quinn clapped her hands together, trying to push herself into action. "Now we just have to get the branch all set up, so it's no longer messy."

She turned and looked around, noticing that Dottie had let patrons in once the horn stopped. They all picked up books, chattering with each other, inspecting instruments and display cases. Most of them seemed to know each other, and quite a few appeared to know Sarah, or at least appeared to remember her.

Quinn took a moment to observe the Library's newest branch again. She sighed, quite content for just a moment. This sense of peace was what she worked for. It's what they did everything, all of this crap, for. And she loved it.

The smell of books.

The beautiful sea of knowledge in their shelves.

It was amazing.

As much as she'd loved being able to devour series on an electronic device and just download them constantly, one after another without having to pause between them, it wasn't healthy for her. She often spent so many nights reading, because why not if she could just grab the next book in the series.

Even so, she'd always missed the smell and feel of physical books.

She was sort of glad that nowadays, when she absorbed books every night before she went to sleep, she had to do a bit of reading along with it, just to cement it for herself. She technically didn't have to, but she liked to understand it sooner than later.

One day soon, hopefully she'd just be able to enjoy the books and get a chance to love her Library.

Milaro appeared next to her, but she didn't start as much anymore.

"Peaceful, isn't it?" he observed, not looking at her, but simply looking out over the newly opened branch.

Children ran around in the amphitheater, chasing one another. Quinn didn't think it was supposed to be used for that but looked like they were having so much fun. They'd definitely have to step in once there were instruments in place. It wouldn't do to have them getting broken. But for now, maybe they could revel in a bit of joy.

She simply nodded, still drinking in the tranquility.

"It's deceptive," he added, and she nodded again.

But after a second of thought, she looked up at him and smiled. "For now it is."

His eyes crinkled at the corners with amusement. "Well, that's what we're working toward."

Quinn didn't answer, but Milaro was obviously aware of how she felt. They stood there for several moments, just absorbing the atmosphere.

Malakai approached. He nudged her. He'd gotten into a habit of doing that, and she found that she didn't mind. "You're just watching the rest of us work, aren't you?" he asked playfully.

"Yep, I'm the boss"—she grinned at him—"so you do as I say and not as I do."

He laughed. "I like that saying. That's excellent."

She didn't bother to tell him it was very well known on Earth and not her own.

"You know you have a lot of work to do tomorrow, right?" he asked a little more directly.

"Yeah." She sighed out the word. It was the only answer she could give. The pillar and all the expectations that went with it.

A cold sensation ran through her blood. What if she was down there and they applied the calculations, and she shifted the pillar and it didn't work? Was she potentially consigning the entire universe to its doom by trying to fix it and not giving it the next two months of research?

Maybe they could just limp along for those couple of months until they were a hundred and twenty percent certain that it *would* work, instead of like—what was it—ninety-seven-point-three? And had Harish, Siliqua, and Cadre really managed to calculate the right way to fix the pillar? After all, they hadn't actually been down to the filtration chamber, they hadn't seen the pillar, nor did they understand how the soul actually was imprisoned. All they'd done was talk to Lynx and experience his memories and taken it from there.

She found herself getting worked up and took a very deep breath. But it didn't stop the fact that she was worried. Her brain ran around in circles.

Milaro said something, but she was so deep in the spiral inside her own mind that she didn't notice it at first. It wasn't until Malakai squeezed her hand and brought her back to herself that she realized she'd probably zoned out for several minutes.

"I'm sorry," she said, looking at her mentor. "I got caught up in my head there for a bit."

He looked down at her and offered her a very winning smile. "Cadre knows what he's doing, Quinn. He does things like this for multiple worlds, many species. It's his specialty. He fixes inter-species, interplanetary, and now interdimensional problems."

"But can you be sure?" Quinn knew she sounded plaintive, but her concern for the potential repercussions was painful.

"Nobody can ever be a hundred percent sure, Quinn. There is always, even if it's ever so tiny, a margin for error. His calculations are second to no one else in the universe, and he is a perfectionist, so he will do his utmost to get as close to a hundred percent certainty as he can. That's something you don't need to worry about."

She nodded. Slowly. "I just . . ."

Malakai squeezed her hand again, and she stopped. Milaro continued. "Don't just anything. By the time he's ready, it will be as close to guarantee as anyone in the universe can make, Quinn. Do you understand that? We're not risking an entire universe on a whim. Don't worry about that aspect of it."

She nodded her head slowly, this time slightly more hopeful. "Okay, I can see it from that viewpoint. It makes sense. Thank you."

Milaro continued gently. "I personally think you should go to bed and *actually* get some decent sleep in for once. If you're having trouble going to sleep, speak to Cook. He'll have something to help you. It should provide help getting to sleep."

Quinn felt another sensation that marked the Library as home rush through her. The fact that so many of the people she'd met and come to rely on did their utmost to make her feel welcome, safe, and cared for went a long way to making her feel exactly that. It drove home how fiercely she intended to fight to keep this home. And if that meant as long as they had the best chance possible, she would shift the damn pillar and bring the Library back to full functionality.

"Okay," she said, "I'm going to bed."

Malakai squeezed her hand once more and let it go. Yet another thing her future self had to sort out.

"Thanks, Milaro," she said to her mentor and then turned around to walk to bed. She refused to look back as she made her way downstairs, past the kitchen where she picked up a warm milk-looking type of drink without a word from Cook, who had read her mind again.

On the way to her room, she stopped quickly by her office where Lynx sat at the desk, perusing the journal, just to check on him and make sure he'd understood. Their eyes locked, and he nodded once.

"I'm going to get some sleep, Lynx."

He smiled. "About damn time."

And she left with a smile on her face and wondering just when he'd started using such human phrases. She made her way upstairs, hovering lightly. The more she slept, the faster they'd get to fix that damn pillar.

70

MOCK ASTONISHMENT

IF ONLY QUINN'S WILL TO SLEEP TRANSLATED IMMEDIATELY INTO action. Instead, she lay for a while, just staring up at the admittedly very entertaining ceiling.

It still showed images from all around the Library with wooden people walking around as if it was a stop motion movie. They picked up books, talked to each other, and huddled in the sitting areas over books. Golems ferried Carty and others around as they retrieved and shelved books. Assistants wandered around, answering questions that patrons gave them, checking books in and out.

It was oddly soothing to watch the amazing carved ceiling. Magic had a way of making so many things possible.

Aradie looked down at her from her perch at the head of the bed. The owl, for once, just seemed calm and quite relaxed. There was no judgment in her gaze, no side-eyeing, and no expectations of her to understand images she'd spammed into Quinn's mind.

Quinn took the peaceful moments to run over everything in her mind and practice some breathing exercises.

More branches were open than not. They'd zapped them into existence and set them to fully functional. They were finally getting the pillars sorted, and they'd discovered what it was Kajaro did in order to get nine lives. That he had technically held Ardenil prisoner for so long regardless of her own actions made Quinn queasy.

She was itching to get her hands on the information Hal was gathering about Sölem. Not to mention, she finally had the list of the missing restricted books. Listing everything in her mind had the same effect as counting sheep, and she fell asleep.

When she woke, it was with a feeling of restlessness she hadn't experienced in a long time. A sensation of having recovered during sleep. She instinctively knew everyone had let her sleep in and couldn't help the slight shiver of trepidation that washed over her.

Something sat at the back of her mind, on the tip of her tongue, that just wouldn't come to her.

Frustrated, but aware that she didn't have the time to just sit and wrack her brains until she figured out what was bugging her, she stretched her arms up and dragged herself out of bed. Aradie's absence was unexpected and quite unwelcome. She'd grown so used to the owl being a constant companion.

Showered, hair brushed, dressed, and marginally alive, Quinn headed downstairs. She paused on the landing at the top of the spiral staircase to look out over the vast main floor of the Library. The check-in desk had grown again. Which was a good thing because there seemed to be a need for multiple check-in and borrowing lines as far as she could see. Several people bustled about behind the desk, working under Betty's guidance. Quinn watched as the little sprite flitted around, checking and double-checking on all of her employees.

Around them and beyond, at the chairs and couches, desks and alcoves, people gathered. The discussion areas all appeared to be full, although she had no doubt if someone needed more, the Library would oblige.

Patrons wandered around, half the time getting in the golems' way. However, the golems didn't appear to mind. They'd had so much growth that the patrons looked like a sea of people from upstairs. She wasn't sure why, but a surge of warmth entered her. If she discounted everything else going on, she actually felt quite proud.

The Library thrived.

If she concentrated, she could hear and sense all the opening and closing doors, allowing for patrons to enter the library and leave. Surges of magic chipping ineffectually away at their malachite stone storage. And even though the library seemed full, it wasn't anywhere near capacity.

An underlying thrum ran through the Library, almost like a purr, as if it was happy and content. Such a contrast to how the Library's personality had been lately—sulky and quite quiet. Perhaps it had to do with trepidation at the upcoming reactivation of Ashiron. It could only go two ways, bad, or everybody survived. She supposed that could cause grumpiness.

Quinn frowned and headed toward the kitchen, her contemplative mood gone. Now she found herself worried about the actual Library. When she entered the culinary division, Cook didn't even speak up but instead handed her a doughnut for one hand and a coffee for the other. She smiled, took a swig, and then a bite. The cinnamon and dough melted on her tongue, as it was just the right warmth. An absolutely perfect reminder of how much she loved the Library.

When she was done, Cook finally looked up. Their eyes narrowed, and they leaned back against the counter, watching her. "You have much on your mind." And now Cook's eyes were practically slits as they narrowed further, which was comical given the mostly flat golem face they had. "Be careful," they continued. "You are not looking at everything you need to from the best angles."

Quinn blinked. "What do you mean?" she asked.

"I mean exactly that. You need to be careful what angle you look at things from. Sometimes, I believe you get stuck in your own head."

She raised an eyebrow. "That's very astute of you."

Cook managed a small smile. "It is rather. Anyway, you should list things out to organize your course of action. It will help you focus and make it easier on yourself."

"Well, I already make lists. I just . . ." She motioned widely with her hands, floundering slightly.

Cook smiled. "You get bogged down in them. You allow them to govern what it is you are thinking. I ask you to focus on one thing at a time when you make a list. Stop making things more difficult than they have to be."

Quinn narrowed her eyes. Cook was always so observant. "How do you—"

Cook shrugged. "Your aura is quite splintered today. You are trying to concentrate on too many things at once."

"Could you always read this about me?" Quinn asked.

Cook moved their head from side to side as if to say "not exactly."

"Aura perception allows me to interpret perfect meals for anyone who might need one. It allows me to base what I make given the general atmosphere in the Library on any given day. And more specifically for you and for other supervisors who are extremely important to the operations of the Library, it enables me to further tailor your dining experience. I can also use that ability for other things."

"Like these chats?" Quinn asked with a smile, feeling more light-hearted than she had before.

They chuckled. "Yes. Technically. Like these chats. I am not sure what it is that leads you to me, but I am proud that you choose to come to me when you are uncertain about things."

"Thank you," she said.

"Food probably helps with the feeling of comfort."

Quinn laughed. "Yes. I think it does."

Cook's mouth stretched into a smile, or at least what passed for one on their golem face. "Anyway, I will have some goulash sent to your office as soon as it's ready. I believe you have many things to do today."

She smiled, feeling cared for. "Thank you."

"No thanks," Cook said. "I just need you to promise me you will talk and reason things out with those close to you who are in a position to help you with your quandary."

Quinn nodded and felt very somber. "Is there something I should know?" she asked.

Cook shook their head. "No, I cannot see the future as much . . . as I get inklings of what needs to happen. I simply sense those around me. And I am especially attuned to you, Librarian. Thus, I feel caution is advised in this moment, and so this is what I do."

"Okay," Quinn said, mulling the words over. It meant there was something she should be paying attention to. "Thank you. I sometimes don't know what I'd do without you."

"And I you, Librarian," Cook said. "After all, none of us would be here if you hadn't found us."

And they turned away, focusing back on their cooking. Quinn walked to her office, still sipping her coffee, slightly perplexed, but determined to take Cook's advice. When she got there, her office was empty for once.

She turned around in it, realized the couches were still there and the conference table was still gone. Not even Aradie was on her perch. Disappointment flooded her. She wished her owl was there to talk to. She'd missed her this morning when she woke up.

Instead, Quinn plopped herself down in her huge comfy chair and pulled up the list of restricted books. It had been gnawing at the back of her mind, and she couldn't put her finger on it. They were familiar in a way that they shouldn't be, except for the last few. She'd never heard of *Lohse's Myriad of Dimensional Weaves and Unbindings*, had she?

She definitely hadn't memorized them. *Oswald's Journey Beyond Dimensional Restrictions*? They all sounded like foreboding and should-not-be-out-of-the-Library type of books. But still, maybe it was just that she had known about the *Seveshall Lineage* book and the *Ashelan Mind Capitulation Device* and *Chmilenko's Guide to Dimensional Complacency*. That had to be it. She knew a few, so her mind inserted a vague notion that she should know the rest.

Malakai wandered in and she put the list down. Even writing it out by hand hadn't jogged her memory. He came in, rested a thigh against her desk and leaned toward her. "I had a strange feeling you might need to talk. But I'm not sure why."

"I just needed to reason through some things," she said.

"Like what?"

"I swear I know these names," she said, indicating the list. "The books. Maybe it's all in my head. But I feel like I've seen these names before. That I should be able to place where."

"Yes, they're all missing restricted books," Malakai said. A fond smile on his face.

She tossed him a half-hearted glare. "I know that. But I can't help thinking I've seen them before."

"Well, that can hold until we've fixed the pillar, right?" he asked.

"Oh, yeah." She frowned. "It has nothing to do with that."

Malakai shrugged. "Well, probably not, right?"

"Exactly," Harish said as he swept into her room with Siliqua, Cadre and Milaro hot on his heels. "Librarian," he went on. "I believe we are about ready to get this underway. Are you excited?"

"What, to finally have a pillar that isn't going to explode and take the entire universe with it?" she asked in mock astonishment.

Milaro chuckled. "Yes. Are you ready?"

"No time like the present," she said, hoping they weren't the universe's famous last words.

71

HERE GOES NOTHING

ASHIRON HAD BEEN A THORN IN HER SIDE FOR SO LONG THAT QUINN had to pinch herself to make sure she wasn't dreaming. She settled herself down and focused her attention on the people with her. Once they fixed the pillar, she could turn her focus to other things. If they didn't fix it . . . well, it really didn't matter then, did it?

It made sense in a macabre sort of way.

"Well," she said, "what do we do to fix it?"

Cadre's entire countenance lit up before he launched into his spiel, and Quinn found herself completely mesmerized by the Migalexutal. The slightly elongated fingers with the pads that looked like they could suction to anything. The tones to his skin that reminded her of the natural colors of a gecko. He *was* like a little gecko in short human size.

"Well," he said, "we finished the calculations. We've been able to project a favorable outcome with those figures despite not visiting the chambers yet."

Quinn frowned. She'd known this, but it still set her on edge.

Milaro spoke up. "I know you're brimming with questions, so just ask. Everything will go smoother if we're all on the same page."

Relief flooded Quinn and even though she knew they didn't just expect her to follow along, it was always nice to have confirmation. She mulled over several questions in her mind at once. "What precisely is it we *are* doing?"

Cadre looked like all his Christmases had come at once. Siliqua and Harish watched, smiling fondly as if he were their little brother.

"Well," Cadre began, "the problem as we see it. After examining Milaro, Lynx, and your experience with the soul bomb, as you've so aptly named it . . ."

Quinn figured her perspective came from Milaro, since they'd been linked when they'd extended the longevity of the imprisonment.

Meanwhile, Cadre continued, ". . . the soul bomb is currently located in a dimensional time fissure."

"Wait!" Quinn stopped him, stumbling over the last. "What do you mean time fissure?" Her mind raced. Wasn't time magic virtually impossible?

Cadre blinked at the interruption. He seemed off-kilter, not used to having his trains of thought derailed. Siliqua stepped in, taking over for a moment.

"Time magic is difficult to control and has far too much destructive potential. We don't mess with time because of all the ramifications and the way futures can be just maligned and extinguished. However, stasis spells are all based on a variant of time magic manipulated to a minuscule amount. The fissure he speaks of is just another way of saying a moment of frozen time."

"Which itself is a misnomer," Harish interjected eagerly. "Time can't be frozen. It simply moves at such an infinitesimal rate that it appears to have stopped."

Quinn looked at all three of them and then glanced at Milaro, who gave her a very subtle head nod.

"So," Quinn reasoned out, slowly running everything through her brain to make sure she'd understood what they were saying all while trying not to panic, "the soul bomb, after its initial sealing and even after we resealed it, has actually been moving this entire time. Since Lynx initially set it up?"

"Yes," Siliqua said.

"So even when we were resealing it, it was still moving. It's still live, not frozen." Quinn realized she was repeating herself but figured the shock of the revelation warranted double- and triple-checking that she'd understood things correctly.

"Yes." Cadre nodded, delight flooding his features that she'd grasped this much. "Precisely. Hence, I must finish the calculations as close as possible to the time you initiate the ritual to phase the pillar, to free it of its burden with as little side effects or ill results as we can manage."

Quinn raised an eyebrow. "Side effects or ill results?" That didn't sound appealing at all.

Milaro put a hand on her shoulder briefly. "We'll explain that as soon as everything else is sorted."

"Okay," she said, motioning for Cadre to continue.

"If we don't do it this way, we run a huge risk of the bomb actually going off while we initiate the transfer."

"Transfer?" Quinn asked, even though it made a heap of sense. Why hadn't she thought the solution would include extracting it? She'd assumed they'd figure out a remote way to trigger a contained version.

Are you hearing this? Quinn asked, sending the thought to the Library. But as usual, over the last while, indeed, since her training with the siblings, there wasn't even a flicker of response.

"Of course you understand," Cadre was saying.

Quinn held up a hand to stop him from speaking. "Wait, I'm sorry. I missed a bit of that in all my inner turmoil."

Milaro snorted under his breath while Cadre smiled and repeated himself. "Quite all right, Librarian. Transfer. We cannot risk attempting a contained detonation within the Library and thus must remove the bomb completely. Of course, you understand that to do this, it means we must remove the entire containment field carefully and quickly, lest too much time lapse between the calculations and the ritual causing us to lose the balance." He watched her expectantly, almost as if looking for praise.

She nodded slowly, taking in the information and making sure she could visualize what he meant. "Okay, so we calculate the differentials, initiate a transfer protocol, and how do we move it?"

Harish piped up. "Well, that's where I come in," he said. "Siliqua and I devised a portable temporal stasis device. Although, it is quite large. It can only withstand certain amounts of stress on its joints and thus calculations must precisely coincide with the current state of the mana bomb. We have zero-point-four-five percent margin of error."

"Oh," Quinn said, "is that all?"

"It sounds a lot scarier than it is," Siliqua said. "We've run so many numbers on this, Quinn. We've designed the container to be capable of containing anything with temporal displacement. Within reason, this should give us a good several minutes to get everything organized and destroy it."

Quinn admitted to being impressed even if five to nine minutes didn't feel like nearly enough time. "Where is this portable stasis device?"

"In Harish's lab," Siliqua said. "We'll pick it up on our way down."

"Excellent. It's quite large, then I take it?"

"Yes."

Quinn sensed the wood elf hesitating. "What aren't you telling me?"

"Ideally, we'd like to bring other people with us to help reinforce the barrier we erect around you."

"Come again?" she said. "What barrier?"

"Well . . ." Lynx popped into view, with a perfectly timed interruption of Siliqua's incoming explanation.

"You're late," Quinn said.

"It's okay. I catch up quickly," Lynx said.

There was something more vibrant about him since he'd learned he wasn't technically confined to the Library. They really needed to have a few more discussions about that whole thing, anyway.

"Catching you up quickly," Milaro said, as Malakai joined them as well, followed by Geneva and Eric. Quinn glanced around as Milaro began to speak. "We have a device that can help us rid the Library of the soul bomb in the pillar. We require your aid to help Quinn transfer it while the rest of us erect a magical ritual barrier around you and the pillar."

Lynx raised an eyebrow at Quinn, turned into a much tinier version of his Lynx cat self, and promptly jumped up to sit on Quinn's lap. She looked down at him and automatically scratched behind his ears. He purred and then spoke, which was odd coming from a tiny, miniature Lynx.

"Displacing it without taking the Library with it?"

"Yes." Cadre leaned forward, close to the cat's ear, as if he was telling it a secret. "It's a temporal stasis portable device to adjust for the temporal shifts in the stasis chamber."

Lynx let out a tiny purr and nodded his head. He then jumped up to stand on the desk and morphed back into himself so that he was sitting with his legs dangling over the side.

"Don't sit on my desk, Lynx," Quinn said, slightly amused, and suddenly feeling less stressed.

"I know," he said, "but you feel better now, don't you?"

Malakai snorted in a perfect mimicry of his grandfather.

"Do we have your consent to do this?" Milaro asked the group gathered there.

Geneva paled slightly. "Wouldn't my aunt be better at this? She's far stronger than I."

"Wrong type of magic, Geneva," Milaro said, understanding in his voice. "If you can't do it . . ."

"Oh no, I *can* do it," Geneva said. "I'm perfectly capable, I just . . . I don't want us to be lacking power because of me."

Milaro smiled at her. "You won't be lacking power."

Eric grunted. "Of course I'll do it. I never lack power."

Milaro gave him a smile of gratitude. "Thank you for standing in for Hal, since he can't make it."

"I guess," Quinn said, taking a deep breath, "I guess we make our way down."

"As good a time as any," Siliqua said.

Quinn stood up. She could feel her hands shaking ever so slightly, nerves shooting through her. As everybody began to file out, Malakai lingered back with her.

"You're nervous, aren't you?"

"Gee, you think so? I drop this ball and the universe implodes. No pressure whatsoever." Her voice barely shook, and she felt sweat beading her forehead, but she wasn't nervous at all. She wondered how difficult it might be to eye roll at herself.

"To be fair . . . even without you knowing about all this magic and stuff, the universe was going to implode. When you think about it, you've just given it seven months longer."

"That's not helping."

"Isn't it?" Malakai asked.

"Fine, it helps a little. Let's go catch up. They're getting the device."

It was a somber troop that headed to the elevator.

"I haven't ridden down in this yet," Milaro said. "I remember when you made it. I just haven't had time. A very nice ask of the Library, Quinn."

"Yeah, it works," she said. Still concerned that the Library hadn't reached out to her about the Ashiron situation. She raised an eyebrow at Lynx. "Have you heard from it?" she asked.

He shook his head. "Curiouser and curiouser" was turning into "really bloody concerneder." A word which she'd just created.

The elevator landed down at the bottom, and they all exited. Harish and Milaro bore the burden of what looked like a rather large, mostly square cube. Sometimes the edges rippled, which, Quinn guessed, was probably what allowed it to adapt to different temporal calculations or something. Maybe. She really had no idea.

They waited on the shore of the mana lake until everyone triggered their hovering or flying abilities and then made their way over to Ashiron.

"Here goes nothing," she said under her breath. And Lynx purred.

7 2

PREDATORY

LYNX AND QUINN STOOD AS CLOSE TO THE MIDDLE OF THE MASSIVE pillar as they could get. The gravity of the situation thrummed through Quinn from the close proximity to the soul-bomb. She could feel its shift bubble wavering.

This was it. She breathed in some of the surrounding power, emanating from the waves of mana, from the way her friends and mentors gathered around them. The power sang to her, pure energy and mana overflowing from the lake and glancing through her system, welcoming her.

Under the direction of Cadre, the others began to encircle the pillar. They stood on strange platforms conjured by Cadre, spaced what seemed evenly apart from what Quinn could see so far. She could tell Cadre's intentions were to form a complete circle around her, Lynx, and the pillar.

Despite Lynx leaning close to speak to her, she could barely hear him over the sound of the other pillars filtration and the lapping of the mana lake against the supports. She concentrated hard, focusing solely on what he said.

"The journals are confusing, but I think I'm starting to understand why we were given them."

"Care to enlighten me?" she whispered.

Lynx smiled, glancing around, as if to make sure that no one could overhear him. But everyone else was being directed by Cadre. "Suffice it to say, the Chronicler's mysterious reputation is warranted. It's taken me ages to draw the parallels. If we can sort this pillar out, then we only have the saboteurs to worry about, and far less pressure."

Quinn nodded her understanding, even though she wanted the information so she could distract herself from her brain trying to convince her there was impending doom. Her gut twisted, and she had to hope it was nerves. At least it didn't present like a gut feeling. Maybe she should have eaten more earlier. She sighed. The wait only gave her more time to worry. "Do you understand what we're doing here?"

Lynx shrugged. "Sort of. Cadre is the most intelligent individual I've ever met. His knowledge of dimensional theory and practice is second to none. Except maybe Drav."

"Speak of the devil," Quinn murmured, ignoring Lynx's quizzical look.

Cadre approached, his mouth spread wide in a huge smile. Glee practically radiated off him as he used levitation to place the containment cube down in front of them. "I will stand behind you to your left, Quinn, and Milaro will be on your right, should we need to step in for any reason."

He poked several areas on the cube, and Quinn heard beeps emanate from it. Soft, like tiny bells ringing.

"What can I do to help?" Quinn's nerves jumped all over the place. She was sure her hands were shaking, so she crossed her arms in an effort to stop them.

Cadre's smile softened. "As soon as we are all in place and prepared to begin, I will input the calculations. Milaro and I will guide you through the process. Essentially, I need to reconfigure the cube to match the containment field, mere seconds before you begin the transfer. Once I've done that, you'll be able to initiate the transfer itself."

Quinn took a deep breath, willing herself not to panic. "That's the dangerous part, right?"

Cadre blinked, his eyes closing briefly in that fascinating lizard like way. "Well, more dangerous anyway. Just standing here is dangerous enough as is. After all, the soul bomb is contained only several feet from us at this moment."

It sounded like he was trying to soothe her, but Quinn just gulped.

Milaro spoke from just behind her. "We know you're capable of pulling this off, Quinn."

She was glad someone thought she could do it. Because she'd have to pull on that belief to kickstart herself.

Milaro rested his hand briefly on her shoulder, in that way which always managed to help her release tension. In that same brief touch, he managed to lend courage, reassurance, and strength. It always helped calm her, let her remember all her strengths, and to breathe. To do what she was good at.

"Thanks," she said.

He chuckled. "We've linked before. This is no different. I'll help both you and Lynx through this whole process. We're all here for you."

Quinn knew what he wasn't saying. That if it didn't work, even their greatest attempt at a shield wouldn't help the Library or the universe. But she appreciated the confidence he tried to lend her anyway. Glancing to her right, she saw Malakai sending her a reassuring grin. When they came out of this whole mess, she was going to sit his flirty butt down and talk to him.

Siliqua piped up from her place next to Cadre, and Quinn knew the others were at intervals around the other side of the pillar. "Okay, we're almost ready here. Are you prepared?"

Quinn felt Milaro brush her mind, and she nodded. "Ready as I can be."

And then there was a flash in the cube, and it immediately connected to her mind. She could practically feel the countdown ticking away in the corner. It reminded her of those stupid timed standardized tests she'd had to take through school and immediately set her on edge.

Milaro guided her mind and Lynx's awareness gently toward the sealed soul bomb. It was where they'd left it, but when she tried to recall its previous exact position, she knew it had moved slightly. The realization filled her with a strange sort of existential dread.

The dimensional shift tugged on her mind, swirling in great globs of mist as it sought to pull her with it. But this time she was prepared, and not as lost as she'd been in their initial foray months ago. The bomb felt different, as if it knew its time was approaching and rebelled against it.

The surrounding barrier hummed, its magical resonance leaking through to her, bolstering her strength while at the same time solidifying the surroundings.

Time slowed.

The ticking clock continued in slow motion.

Can you hear that?

Quinn listened intently, able to discern the mild buzzing in her mind. It tingled there, as if waiting for her, ready to zap anything that tried to harm her, that came too close to doing so. *I hear it.*

That's our signal. When that buzzing speeds up, it means time is running out. Do you understand? If that happens, we must carefully withdraw and allow them to reset the calculations.

Sure, she said, forcing her mind to focus and put away all fear she might have felt. *No pressure.*

Milaro's chuckle resonated throughout her mind. *None at all.*

His typical humor helped ground her, and she clenched her teeth, ready to do this. They'd been right, though. It wasn't that difficult a thing to do once she began to trust herself.

She felt Milaro's guidance reaching through to her, helping her wrap what seemed like psychic bands around the bomb, shrinking its dimensional shift. She felt like the work was taking all the time in the world. As if they were bound to run out. But she breathed, calmed herself, and continued with the aid of Lynx's power.

We're doing well. You're doing great.

The words helped. She focused on the bands that held the initial containment, shrinking them slowly, moving them carefully until they fully encased the bomb. At the edges of her perception, she could feel sweat running down her back. Lynx's power next to her was hot and fed right into her own energy pools, allowing her own power to feel full and strong.

Lynx's energy bolstered her own, lending her confidence, and allowed her to take Milaro's guidance calmly.

I think it's ready? She wasn't entirely sure it was, but it felt secure.

I agree. Do you think you and Lynx can manage this? Milaro asked gently, but Quinn knew why. Milaro needed to bolster the protections while they transferred the soul bomb. Now came the real challenge.

She nodded and realized he couldn't see it. *Ready.*

Milaro gave her one mental squeeze and then his direct presence in her mind was gone.

Just us now. Lynx's voice held encouragement and a hint of excitement.

Quinn understood, even if she couldn't exactly sympathize. *Just us.*

It was easier to blend her power with Lynx than she'd anticipated. Their power merged seamlessly, and they began to remove the bomb, slowly bringing it to rest within the cube. It wasn't as easy as it sounded. There were constant accommodations for the swell of the vibrations against the pillar base, for the thrum of the magic all around them, for its tangibility.

When they finally dropped it in the chamber, there was a low rumble as it settled. It lasted a few seconds too long, and Quinn was almost certain the thing was about to explode and take them all with it.

But then it calmed.

And it was done.

She squeezed her eyes shut as Cadre and Siliqua dove on the containment unit, sealing, resealing, double checking the containment values.

Milaro and Malakai had moved to maintain the shields around the pillar. Just in case.

"You can open your eyes," Lynx whispered.

Quinn peeled one open and glanced at him skeptically. Then both . . . she watched the others fuss around it.

"What do we do now?" she asked when Cadre finally stepped back from it.

Cadre smiled. "We located a nice black hole for its new home. Now that it's not in a pillar . . . we can transport it with numerous precautions."

She heaved a sigh of relief and turned to see Malakai, who'd been given the all clear, to let the barrier drop. He grinned at her as he undid his part of the ritual, and Quinn heaved a sigh of relief. "Well, that's one thing off our plate."

She didn't add that it had been so much easier than she expected. After all, that was just something one didn't say out loud.

"Quinn, fly up!" came a sudden call. Cadre's voice was panicked.

She turned around, expecting the containment field to be failing, but they'd already moved it, and from what she could tell in that split second, it was fine.

What wasn't fine was the strange sludge like mist that rose up from the floor. It reminded her of the muck that used to sit over the mana lake. The remnants of chaos magic. It hit her foot before she could move.

And everything went black.

Quinn came to, sitting in a chair.

A comfortable chair.

Which felt very odd considering she'd just been down in the filtration chamber.

The entire room was black. But it wasn't. Instead, there were stars everywhere. Maybe it had exploded and she'd survived and was floating in a void.

The faint smell of pinecones lingered around her. A familiar scent. She felt like she should know where she was.

The sky began to brighten for her, and the room slowly revealed itself. At least she hadn't blown up the Library.

That's when she saw the stack of books lined up along the table. From *Lohse's Myriad Dimensional Weaves & Unbindings*, through to *Chmilenko's Guide to Dimensional Complacency.*

The whole. Damn. List.

She knew she'd seen them before, but she'd been so focused on training while here she hadn't processed it.

The cosmicisodracus vault, where Drevicia kept all the remnants of her species history, everything others would need to know to understand the Library's weaknesses.

Standing quietly, Quinn was surprised she wasn't locked in place somehow and stepped gingerly across the room to look at the books. *Ameye's Mental Drain, The Ashelan Mind Capitulation Device* . . . All there, not missing, and not damaged.

None of it made sense. She knew she was missing a major piece. Just like she didn't know why she'd been transported here. She couldn't feel the Library, couldn't feel any of the others from where she was. A cold shiver stole down her spine.

"So good of you to come, Librarian."

Quinn started at the sound. While somewhat familiar, Quinn couldn't quite identify the voice. There was no warmth in it. No recognition. Slowly, she turned to face it.

Scaled and blue, the humanoid dragon was such a deep ocean blue whose scales rippled across the surface like water lapping at the edges of a beach. Almost translucent, it had the clearest blue eyes, several shades lighter than its body. And it was there. Tangible. Not a projection. Not a shadow.

Real.

Quinn pushed down on the fear.

She knew who this was. Instinctively. There were qualities of her own inherent in this creature. Things she'd inherited. The only thing was, she didn't know why.

Without a shadow of a doubt, she knew this was Drevicia. Not the Library extension, but the true cosmicisodracus version.

"Drevicia . . ." she stated, inclining her head.

The dragon smiled, showing rows of sharp teeth. "Ah. Excellent. Not as dense as I'd feared."

Quinn wasn't sure what to make of it. But before she could say anything, a glint entered the dragon's eye.

"Let's see what they've poisoned you with." Drevicia's grin was predatory, and Quinn had but a moment to feel pressure trying to crush her soul before she started screaming.

EPILOGUE

MILARO BLINKED.

One second Quinn had been standing directly in front of him, and the next second, she was gone.

"What just happened?" Malakai asked.

But no one answered, all of them gathering around the thrumming cube containing the damned death device, searching for Quinn.

Lynx frowned. "No alarms are triggered, not even silently."

"Could she have warped?" Milaro murmured his question, only half paying attention as he spread out his senses to try to locate her. He couldn't sense her presence anywhere. Not that he had the reach she did within the Library, but still . . . he should be able to sense something of her if she was still there.

"No." Lynx sounded completely confident in his answer, even if the following words held nothing but frustration. "She's just not here. I . . ."

Malakai moved to face the manifestation. "You mean she's not in the Library?"

Lynx frowned and slowly shook his head. "I mean, I can't tell where she is. The link we have is just . . . vacant."

His eyes began to flicker and his runes sped up in their twisting patterns.

Milaro watched the others, replaying the scene in his own mind, making sure he had every single frame of the memory intact. He examined it and frowned.

Cadre cleared his throat. "As concerning as the Librarian's sudden absence is, we should remove the cube and dispose of it. I didn't create the cube as the permanent solution. And once we find her, it would be nice for her to have somewhere to return to."

Milaro nodded, trying not to let his exasperation show. "Understandable. Can I leave it to you three to get rid of it?"

Harish nodded and Siliqua responded. "Of course you can."

The three of them moved away, while Eric and Geneva settled around Lynx and Malakai, concern on all their faces.

"You can't feel her at all then, Lynx?" Eric asked, oddly solemn for once.

He shook his head. "No."

"Damn it." Milaro pinched the bridge of his nose as he looked around the chamber. Ashiron was finally freed of its burden. But it needed restoration and repair as soon as possible. He knew golems could take care of it. But they needed their Librarian.

"What is it?" Malakai sounded slightly scared, and Milaro wanted nothing more than to comfort his grandson, but that had to wait while they figured out what to do.

"It's not a good sign if Lynx can't sense her," Geneva spoke softly, her golden skin pale.

"Explain." Malakai's tone shifted, impatience evident.

Geneva looked like she wanted nothing more in the world than to sink through the ground.

Milaro sighed and stepped in. "If Lynx can't sense her, that means anyone tracking the Library status will see a blank."

"But she's not severed," Lynx sounded highly confused. "Just not present. Not there. I can't decipher it."

Milaro grimaced and continued. "Which means, as far as Sölem and anyone else wishing harm on the Library is concerned, we just got a whole lot more vulnerable."

As if waiting for the perfect time, the Library alarms began to blare.

———

Preorder Book 6 Now!

Can't Wait? Pop over to Patreon!

ABOUT THE AUTHOR

Born in Australia, K.T. Hanna met her husband in a computer game, moved to the U.S.A. and went into culture shock. Bonus? Not as many creatures specifically designed to kill you.
KT creates science-fiction, fantasy, and LitRPG, with a dash of horror for fun! She is a member of the SFWA and NINC. Her hobbies include gaming, reading, and lake time!
No, she doesn't sleep. She is entirely powered by caffeine, Chipotle, and sarcasm.

Find her on her website: kthanna.com
Join her in all the places, including Discord!

ALSO BY K.T. HANNA

Library System Reset

Somnia Online

System Apocalypse Australia

The Domino Project

Last Chance Trilogy

KT Hanna's Author Page

ACKNOWLEDGMENTS

I have a lot of people to thank. Even those who don't contribute directly through the writing craft keep me going and help me write my best stories.

Love of my life, Trevor, and my little Kam. It's his fault I found the genre, and their fault I never give up on writing.

I wouldn't be here without the following friends (and I know I've probably forgotten to mention someone:

SSODA

Crown

Eric Ugland

Quinton Shyn

Andrea Parseneau

M Evan MacGregor

Daniel Schinhofen

Michael Chatfield

Luke Chmilenko

Tao

Jami

Geneva

Jez

Ririn

DE Sherman

Ino

Honor

J.M.

Jenn & Jay

<u>And of course my family:</u>
Mumskin & Papilie, Tracey, Jett, & Robbie
<u>The entire Coteh server</u>
<u>My Legion Family</u>

<u>And every one of my Patrons.</u>
Faelor
Ma & Pa
Foxies
Quinton
Matt D
Warren
Kristen
Joshua
Renn
Irene
ChaosOmega98
Table Top
Kevin
Pyro4224
Cybernetic Angel
Colin
Naomi
Ron
Bjbrewster
June
Samuel
Felix
Rando
Ginna
Anthony
Michelle
Ethra
Kristiana & Michael
Sandra

Wes
Maria
David Z
Lida
Azull
David J
McMelon
Marsh
Amy
Vanessa
Marcemellow
Gordon
Robert
Miriam
Timothy
Michael S
John
Not to mention my FB Group/Page, and people in my discord.
Thank you
You all help me maintain a level of sanity.

LITRPG & PROGRESSION FANTASY

Do you love LitRPG?
Do you want to find more of it?

These are amazing places to do just that!
FaceBook:
LitRPG Books
LitRPG Legion
GamelitRPG Society

Reddit:
LitRPG

Adjacent genres like Progression Fantasy/Cultivation:
Reddit: Progression Fantasy
Facebook: Cultivation Novels

MORE LITRPG

Love LitRPG?

To learn more about LitRPG, talk to authors including myself, and just have an awesome time, please join the LitRPG Group!